Writers at War

Writers at War addresses the most immediate representations of the First World War in the prose of Ford Madox Ford, May Sinclair, Siegfried Sassoon and Mary Borden; it interrogates the various ways in which these writers contended with conveying their war experience from the temporal and spatial proximity of the warzone and investigates the multifarious impact of the war on the (re)development of their aesthetics. It also interrogates to what extent these texts aligned with or challenged existing social, cultural, philosophical and aesthetic norms.

While this book is concerned with literary technique, the rich existing scholarship on questions of gender, trauma and cultural studies on World War I literature serves as a foundation. This book does not oppose these perspectives but offers a complementary approach based on close critical reading. The distinctiveness of this study stems from its focus on the question of representation and form and on the specific role of the war in the four authors' literary careers. This is the first scholarly work concerned exclusively with theorising prose written from the immediacy of the war.

This book is intended for academics, researchers, PhD candidates, postgraduates and anyone interested in war literature.

Isabelle Brasme is Senior Lecturer in British Literature at the Université de Nîmes, France, and Researcher at Université Paul-Valéry Montpellier 3, France. She has published books on Ford Madox Ford, a collaborative volume on war writing and essays on Ford Madox Ford, May Sinclair, modernism and war writing. She is the Review Editor for the *Cahiers Victoriens et Édouardiens*.

Among the Victorians and Modernists
Edited by Dennis Denisoff

This series publishes monographs and essay collections on literature, art, and culture in the context of the diverse aesthetic, political, social, technological, and scientific innovations that arose among the Victorians and Modernists. Viable topics include, but are not limited to, artistic and cultural debates and movements; influential figures and communities; and agitations and developments regarding subjects such as animals, commodification, decadence, degeneracy, democracy, desire, ecology, gender, nationalism, the paranormal, performance, public art, sex, socialism, spiritualities, transnationalism, and the urban. Studies that address continuities between the Victorians and Modernists are welcome. Work on recent responses to the periods such as Neo-Victorian novels, graphic novels, and film will also be considered.

Strange Gods
Love and Idolatry in the Victorian Novel
Timothy L. Carens

Re-Reading the Age of Innovation
Victorians, Moderns, and Literary Newness, 1830–1950
Edited by Louise Kane

Critical Essays on Arthur Morrison and the East End
Edited by Diana Maltz

Writers at War
Exploring the Prose of Ford Madox Ford, May Sinclair, Siegfried Sassoon and Mary Borden
Isabelle Brasme

Hotel Modernisms
Edited by Anna Despotopoulou, Vassiliki Kolocotroni and Efterpi Mitsi

For more information about this series, please visit: https://www.routledge.com/Among-the-Victorians-and-Modernists/book-series/ASHSER4035

Writers at War
Exploring the Prose of Ford Madox Ford, May Sinclair, Siegfried Sassoon and Mary Borden

Isabelle Brasme

NEW YORK AND LONDON

First published 2023
by Routledge
605 Third Avenue, New York, NY 10158

and by Routledge
4 Park Square, Milton Park, Abingdon, Oxon, OX14 4RN

Routledge is an imprint of the Taylor & Francis Group, an informa business

© 2023 Isabelle Brasme

The right of Isabelle Brasme to be identified as author of this work has been asserted in accordance with sections 77 and 78 of the Copyright, Designs and Patents Act 1988.

All rights reserved. No part of this book may be reprinted or reproduced or utilised in any form or by any electronic, mechanical, or other means, now known or hereafter invented, including photocopying and recording, or in any information storage or retrieval system, without permission in writing from the publishers.

Trademark notice: Product or corporate names may be trademarks or registered trademarks, and are used only for identification and explanation without intent to infringe.

ISBN: 978-1-032-21966-0 (hbk)
ISBN: 978-1-032-21993-6 (pbk)
ISBN: 978-1-003-27081-2 (ebk)

DOI: 10.4324/9781003270812

Typeset in Bembo
by SPi Technologies India Pvt Ltd (Straive)

In memory of my father, fervent humanist
To Flora and Olivier, passionate readers
And to Sébastien, always

Contents

List of Figures   ix
Acknowledgements   x

Introduction   1

1 Ford Madox Ford's Unrelatable Narrative of War   16
Introduction 16
The Elusive 'Muse of War' 20
Writing as Ethical Imperative 29
From Ethical Injunction to Aesthetic Reinvention 38
Conclusion: Towards Parade's End 48

**2 'The Fantastic Dislocation of War':
May Sinclair's Aporetic War Chronicle**   55
Introduction 55
A War Journal? 59
'The High Comedy of Disaster': Sinclair's Carnivalesque
   Narrative 66
From Representational Crisis to an Alternative Mimesis 79
Conclusion 90

**3 Writing Oneself at War: Siegfried Sassoon's
War Diaries**   96
Introduction 96
The Generic Fluidity of Sassoon's War Diaries 100
Writing a Myth of Oneself 115
An Instance of Intensely Layered Writing: Recounting the Attack on
   Fontaine-lès-Croisilles (11–17 April 1917) 121
Conclusion 125

4 **From the 'Bleeding Edge' of War:
   The Singular Voice of Mary Borden** 130
   Introduction 130
   Writing in Defiance of the Conventional Nurse Figure 134
   A Liminal Geography of Care 142
   Writing Alienation 154
   Conclusion: Modernism and Mimesis 161

Epilogue 169

Index 170

Figures

2.1 Page 10 of May Sinclair's manuscript for *A Journal of Impressions*. May Sinclair papers, Ms. Coll. 184, Kislak Center for Special Collections, Rare Books and Manuscripts, University of Pennsylvania   82

2.2 Page 3 of May Sinclair's typescript for *A Journal of Impressions*. May Sinclair papers, Ms. Coll. 184, Kislak Center for Special Collections, Rare Books and Manuscripts, University of Pennsylvania   83

Acknowledgements

The completion of this volume would not have been possible without the generous spirit of the Republic of Letters.

My deepest thanks go to Christine Reynier for her unflinching encouragement and advice over the many years leading up to this volume, as well as for her attentive and constructive reading of the chapters in this book. Christine has been an inspiration as a researcher ever since I arrived in Montpellier in 2009.

I am grateful to Catherine Bernard for the conversation that we had as this project was in its budding stages during the ESSE Conference in Brno, Czech Republic, in 2018. Catherine was my PhD supervisor in the late 2000s; her incandescent writing has never ceased to stimulate my research.

My warm thanks extend to my colleagues in my research centre, the Études Montpelliéraines du Monde Anglophone (EMMA), for their kindness and encouragement, as well as for thoughtful and stimulating exchanges, and particularly to Jean-Michel Ganteau and Sandrine Sorlin for their constant and friendly support. I cannot omit the PhD candidates with whom I have shared many a studious—and cheerful—day in EMMA's common research room: Marie Bertrand, Camille Chane, Yahya Daldoul, Théo Maligeay, Katia Marcellin, Carine Nibakure and Constance Pompié. Special thanks to Katia Marcellin, my research pal, whose work on metalepsis has been quite thought-provoking.

Bénédicte Coste has also offered constant encouragement and priceless advice. She steered me towards Dennis Denisoff, the editor of the Among the Victorians and Modernists Series in which this volume is published. Dennis was himself tremendously helpful in reading my publishing proposal and in making very useful suggestions. My sincere thanks go to them both.

My gratitude also goes to Sylvain Belluc, Jean-Louis Brunel and Hélène Hory, my colleagues at the Université de Nîmes, for their support and for lightening my administrative duties in the months preceding the submission of this manuscript.

I am grateful to the Ford Madox Ford Society and to the May Sinclair Society for providing spaces of friendly and lively intellectual exchange. Max Saunders kindly sent me the initial French version of Ford's 'Pon… ti… pri… ith'; Rebecca Bowler generously shared all her scanned material of the manuscript and typescript of Sinclair's *A Journal of Impressions*; Christine Battersby offered invaluable insight on Sinclair's links with Nietzsche and Schopenhauer in several email exchanges.

Special thanks to Leslie de Bont and Florence Marie, with whom working on Sinclair has been a delight over the past few years. Leslie has also kindly read my chapter devoted to Sinclair and provided deeply insightful comments.

Thanks to the EMMA research centre for covering the permission fees that were necessary to quote from Siegfried Sassoon's diaries.

Thanks to the Kislak Center for Special Collections, Rare Books and Manuscripts, University of Pennsylvania, for graciously scanning and sending pages from Sinclair's manuscript and typescript of *A Journal of Impressions*.

Lastly, I am more grateful than I could express to my family for allowing me to complete this volume even as our life was complicated by the pandemic. Thank you for your patience, your unfailing support and for filling every day with joy.

Introduction

When the First World War broke out, each of the four authors considered in this book had been engaging in activities that reflect their involvement in the effervescence of artistic London. On 15 July 1914, May Sinclair was present at the dinner that launched Wyndham Lewis's *Blast!* (Boll 106). In late July, Ford Madox Ford was at a country party hosted by none other than Mary Borden; among the guests were E. M. Forster and Wyndham Lewis (Saunders 1996a, 466). Siegfried Sassoon, though far less assured a figure in literary London before the war, attended the *première* of the *Ballets russes* in early July 1914 and, fascinated, returned night after night over the next few weeks (Wilson 101–2). Although their success and authority on the London intellectual scene varied in 1914, participating in contemporary literary and artistic movements was equally central to their lives, and they identified first and foremost as authors. Borden, Sinclair, Ford and Sassoon also all happened to be first-hand witnesses of the First World War on the Western Front; and each of them strove to convey their experience as they were living through it, using an outlet that was fundamental to their self-construction both as individuals and professionals: literary writing.

This book addresses the most immediate representations of the First World War in the prose of Ford Madox Ford, May Sinclair, Siegfried Sassoon and Mary Borden; it interrogates the various ways in which these four writers contended with conveying their war experience from the temporal and spatial proximity of the warzone and investigates the multifarious impact of the war on the (re) development of their aesthetics. It also interrogates to what extent these texts aligned with or challenged existing social, cultural, philosophical and aesthetic norms.

World War One has been a favoured topic in the literary prose and poetry of the past hundred years, not only by contemporaries of the war but also by more recent authors. In *The Great War and Modern Memory*, first published in 1975, Paul Fussell was already noting that 'a striking phenomenon of the last 25 years is this obsession with the images and myths of the Great War among novelists and poets too young to have experienced it directly' (Fussell 321). This phenomenon has certainly not abated half a century later; and it has attracted a corresponding volume of critical work. This monograph aims however to focus

DOI: 10.4324/9781003270812-1

on accounts and narratives that were written by direct witnesses of the war, within the timeframe of World War One. Most scholarship on the Anglo-American literature written from the Western Front of the First World War has focused on poetry, with a particular emphasis on the war poets. Academic work on the prose that was written about the direct experience of the First World War has centred heavily on novels written a decade or more after the war itself: Ford's *Parade's End* tetralogy (1924–1928), Erich Maria Remarque's *All Quiet on the West Front* (1929), Ernest Hemingway's *A Farewell to Arms* (1929), Robert Graves's *Goodbye to All That* (1929) and Siegfried Sassoon's *Memoirs of an Infantry Officer* (1930). Judging from this timeline, it may appear that a decade was needed for these authors to come to terms with the trauma of the Great War in a manner that would allow them to produce a literary narrative. This may explain why the prose written by authors who had an immediate experience of the war has been the object of little attention. When taking a closer look at the prose written from the immediacy or the close proximity of the warzone, however, we discover that far from failing to articulate their experience in a prose form, authors did so through highly individual and often innovative styles.

Each of the four writers considered in this book had a markedly different role in the war. Borden served as a nurse in the evacuation hospital that she set up and managed; Ford was an officer in charge of transport; Sassoon took direct part in combat; Sinclair was briefly secretary and reporter for the Munro Ambulance corps in Belgium. As a result, their experience varied significantly. Each resorted to distinct modes of writing to attempt to render their specific experience. The prose considered in this volume is therefore diverse. It comprises essays and letters that Ford Madox Ford mostly wrote while he was in service (1915–18); May Sinclair's *A Journal of Impressions in Belgium* (published in 1915), written during and briefly after the 19 days that she spent in Belgium during the siege and fall of Antwerp (25 September–13 October 1914); Siegfried Sassoon's war diaries, written between 1915 and 1918; and the segments from Mary Borden's *The Forbidden Zone* (1929) that she wrote during her time as a war nurse (1915–18). Besides the variety of these four sets of texts, each of the texts or collections analysed here is in itself strikingly heterogeneous. The most obvious instance is Ford's war prose, as it includes writings that were not originally designed to be published as a whole; Borden's collection is an assemblage of fragments, or 'sketches', in Borden's own terms; Sassoon's diary entries display strong variations, from the blankest factual statement to lyrical surges; Sinclair's entries likewise travel through a staggering variety of tones and content.

Scholarship on Sassoon's writing has mostly focused on his poetry or his after-war work (Moeyes 1997, Hemmings 2008). Biographies do rely on his war diaries (Egremont 2005, Wilson 2014) but do not consider them from a literary standpoint. Moyes's monograph, which aims at examining all the literary output written by Sassoon, excludes his war diaries as non-literary. Likewise, critical work on Ford Madox Ford has been mostly concerned with his Edwardian and pre-war work, especially *The Good Soldier*, which was completed before he reached the front, and with *Parade's End*. Apart from Max Saunders's rich introduction to his edition of Ford's *War Prose*, the nonfictional prose that Ford wrote from the front has not yet been the object of much research (for an in-depth survey of criticism on Ford's war writing, see Frayn 179–92). That being said, some of the criticism on other aspects of Ford's writing is productive when put in the perspective of his war prose, such as Laura Colombino's study on visuality (2008), Andrew Frayn's work on disenchantment (2014) or the two excellent volumes on *Parade's End* edited by Ashley Chantler and Rob Hawkes, particularly *War and the Mind: Ford Madox Ford, Parade's End, and Psychology* (2014).

Although women's writing of the First World War was disregarded for decades in favour of male combatant writing, recent historical and literary research has been paying closer attention to the contribution of women—particularly of nurses—to the war effort, and to the vast range of textual production that was generated as a result. To date, most research on women's experience of the First World War either has focused on questions of gender, often from the perspective of cultural studies (Gilbert 1983; Higonnet and Higonnet 1987; Gilbert and Gubar 1989; Tylee 1990; Higonnet 1993; Gallagher 1998; Geiger 2015; Grayzel and Proctor 2017) or has examined women's writing from a psychological standpoint and addressed questions of trauma and resilience (Higonnet 2002; Hallett 2009; Acton and Potter 2012, 2015; Fell and Hallett 2013). All these works have brought invaluable insight into female war writing; yet much consideration remains to be given to the specific form in which female witnesses of the war wrote of their experience. Carol Acton and Jane Potter acknowledge the limitations of a consideration of war writing from the only angle of trauma:

> The complexities, ambiguities and contradictions in these writings at once affirm the reality of the experience as traumatic and contest the idea that such experience is inevitably dominated and silenced by trauma.
> (Acton and Potter 2015, 51)

This is a fertile remark, as it not only sustains the relevance of alternative readings from the psychological perspective but also suggests that a witnessing voice can nevertheless rise out of the unbearable and the unspeakable. Likewise, Acton offers elsewhere an enlightening analysis of the shift in the representation of the soldier and of nursing in terms of gender (Acton 2013, 123–38). I argue that this shift in gender representation occurs within a larger frame where the very matter of representation is questioned at its core. Traditional narrative technique is made obsolete by the unprecedented experience of the war. Beyond the issue of finding the right words, the 'refiguration' (Ricœur) of war and its actors into a narrative with actants is attempted, yet often abandoned by writers who were direct witnesses of the mass destruction of the First World War. Nevertheless, the four writers I address each negotiated in a very specific manner this representational crisis, and did not automatically turn to innovative techniques. Furthermore, most of the studies aforementioned have, in a useful and quite necessary manner, aimed at documenting and acknowledging the tremendous amount of texts written by female witnesses of the war; yet because they tend to address a large number of authors, they often cannot offer a detailed scrutiny of the aesthetic choices made by these writers.

The governing principle of this study is close textual analysis, and the issues of representation and mimesis underpin the volume as a whole. The inability to represent the experience of the First World War has been addressed in countless studies, starting with Fussell's *The Great War and Modern Memory* and, in its wake, Hynes's *A War Imagined*, in which Hynes delineates the creation of a 'Myth' that functions as a screen, distancing the reality of the war even further from the recipients of the texts produced. In 1915, Henry James lamented his sense of the impotence of language in the context of the First World War:

> The war has used up words; they have weakened, they have deteriorated like motor car tires; they have, like millions of other things, been more overstrained and knocked about and voided of the happy semblance during the last six months than in all the long ages before, and we are now confronted with a depreciation of all our terms.
>
> (James 362, qtd in Gallagher 15)

The experience of the First World War generated a double isolation in its witnesses: it was utterly disconnected from one's past and familiar experience, and it was felt as incommunicable to others. It was literally *unrelatable*, both in terms of its being told and represented, or *related*, and of the impossibility for others to fully connect to, or *relate* with, such an unfathomable experience. As a result, representational aporia is inseparable from the ontological impasse met by the subject in contact with the war. Such an aporia is faced unflinchingly and addressed openly in the texts here studied, particularly by Ford, Borden and Sinclair. Making the failures of representation manifest is an integral part in their project of signalling the subject's disarray in the face of war, and of recreating in the reader an impression of this breakdown.

My choice of authors originates in my aspiration to offer an approach that goes beyond gender divides, and that draws connections between combatant and non-combatant experiences and representations of the war. Another reason for this choice is the fact that these authors were influenced both by 19th-century writing and modernist innovation, and navigated these various influences differently when it came to rendering their experience of the war. This study, therefore, contests the notion that the First World War automatically precipitated a literary divide between traditional and modernist modes of writing. While some specific techniques typically associated with modernism are apprehended, such as vorticism, futurism, cubism and, more importantly, literary impressionism, as well as the ironisation of traditional tropes such as the pastoral mode, these coexist with stylistic traits that endure from the 19th century. Mark Larabee has already underscored the limitations of Fussell's and Hynes's analysis of war writing in terms of a binary opposition between traditional and modernist techniques, and of their favouring modernist techniques as more relevant to the changed conditions of experience. Larabee warns us of the distorting effect of such a dichotomy:

> [T]hese analyses risk reducing the artistic response to the wartime landscape to a binary of old and new in both literature and the visual arts: discredited romanticism and privileged modernism.
>
> (Larabee 94)

Far from enacting a break from tradition typically associated with modernist writing, the authors associate avant-garde and earlier influences as they attempt to formulate an updated mimesis that may account for the extreme and radically unfamiliar experience of the war. Although modernist modes of representation can be considered as anti-mimetic, and thus as obstructing the witnessing duty felt by writers at war, they are often used in these texts to generate an updated mimesis. The aim of this study is therefore not to determine to what extent each text is, or is not, modernist, but to altogether discard the constraints of the modernist 'canon' and of modernist categorisation, often retrospective and artificial, in order to examine the individuality of each style as these authors came to terms with their war experience and with the impact of such experience on their aesthetics.

In terms of enunciative framework, the prose analysed in this book can be organised along a more or less stable gradient of distantiation. This flexible gradient can be correlated to the generic fluidity that is common to them all, though the reasons for this fluidity differ. Sassoon's diary, written *in medias res*, was composed in closest spatial and temporal proximity to the events, although the chapter devoted to Sassoon will delineate the complex ways in which Sassoon's journal writing shifts through the genres of diary, autobiography, memoir and self-eulogy. Despite its title, Sinclair's text has a much less reliable identity than Sassoon's as a 'journal' since the text constantly signals its flaws as an accurate record and highlights its increasing temporal distance from the events narrated. Ford's essays and letters were written at varying degrees of proximity to the front; although some were directly written from the Somme or Ypres, the form of the essay implies a degree of critical distance; this nevertheless begs to be nuanced in the case of Ford, as his writing always bears a strong autobiographical element. The flexible format of the essay also allows Ford to adopt a multiplicity of tones and devices. The enunciative frame of Borden's hospital sketches is the most disconcerting, as the persona, constantly hovering between the first and the third person—sometimes even the second—and between intra- and extra-diegesis, is unstable and can never be safely or wholly identified as a projection of Borden. All these texts thus evade stable generic classification: this is one of the instances in which they resist normative war writing and its corresponding conventional and consensual content.

The diversity of the texts here studied explains the variety of the critical outlooks that are conjured up in the book. Nonetheless, some paradigms do recur in all or most of the texts. Common to all four authors is a nexus of irresolvable tensions inherent in the war experience and its representation. The most evident is the opposition between the compulsion to write a testimony of the war and the feeling of expressive powerlessness. This is associated with a scopic paradox: all four texts reveal a tension between an intense visuality that translates into minute descriptions of the warscape and scopic issues that have been explored in a number of studies (Fussell 2013, Das 2005, Virilio 2009, Gallagher 1998, Larabee 2011, to name but a few). On the one hand, the immense scale of the First World War exceeded the cognitive capacities of the human brain; on the other, trench warfare implied that the soldier could only see a fraction of the scene, as underscored by Fussell, among many others:

> To be in the trenches was to experience an unreal, unforgettable enclosure and constraint, as well as a sense of being unoriented and lost. One saw two things only: the walls of an unlocalized, undifferentiated earth and the sky above.
>
> (Fussell 54)

For women writers, this limitation of the gaze intrinsic to the trench experience was replaced by an exclusion from the warzone, which remained tantalisingly close yet inaccessible. Conversely, for both men and women witnesses, sounds were omnipresent—unbearably so for those closest to the line (see Das 79–84). The soundscape of war pervades all four sets of texts at varying degrees, depending on the proximity to the line. However, sounds can be equally confusing: Sinclair cannot differentiate between the noise of artillery and the barking of dogs; Ford mistakes thunder for a bombardment. Sassoon favours the depiction of pastoral sounds to those of war, though his descriptions of noise as he is under fire are of striking poetic force, whereas Borden rejects the sounds of civilian life over those of the warzone, which now feel more familiar to the war nurse.

Scopic constraints are paired with the sense that unavoidable screens persist between the retina and the scene of war: these can be ideological or aesthetic. The inescapable filter of culture is especially highlighted: for these men and women of letters, the war is always apprehended through the prism of their rich literary and artistic knowledge. This cultural lens undermines any hope of an adherence between reality and testimony; rather than being lamented, it is often embraced by the authors as offering a potential—albeit skewed—entryway into the apprehension and representation of the war experience. More largely, the unavoidable bias inseparable from individual perception is conveyed by all four authors through an insistence on the gaze through which the scenes of war are perceived. The plethoric lexical field of sight in all four sets of texts points to the stance from which the description emanates. These texts do not simply record war scenes, but rather the authors' or their personas' singular and necessarily limited perspectives on them. This is particularly manifest in Borden's sketches, where the gaze is often framed by windows. Through the insistence on the observer of the scenes described, war is openly depicted as a spectacle. Virilio opens *War and Cinema* on the indissociable link between war and representation—and therefore, on the indispensable presence of spectators to validate the war: 'War can never break free from the magical spectacle because its very purpose is to *produce* that spectacle […]. There is no war, then, without representation' (Virilio 7–8).

The scopic paradox is paired with the authors' common fascination for the geography of war. Each of the texts under scrutiny shares a pervasive concern for geography and topography, and for the limitations thereof induced by the war experience. The writers' constant attention to geographical precision is undermined by the failure of traditional, positivist topographical tools in the context of the First World War. This often translates into an ironical map-like rendering of the landscape that ends up being relentlessly sabotaged. Mark Larabee's study on this topic has provided analyses that prove relevant and fertile for all four authors considered here.

Another tension concerns the simultaneous exhilaration of going through momentous events and the overwhelming sense of the horror that is unfolding. All authors express intense happiness at some point or other; Borden does so perhaps less openly in *The Forbidden Zone*, but her elation transpires in the letters she wrote to her lover, Captain Edward Louis Spears: 'What fun it is to be in love in the very centre of the whirlpool of the world as you and I are—you're there, at the heart of the struggle & I'm with you' (21 September 1917, qtd in Conway 81). Edith Wharton, who also visited the front, captured this paradox in the following statement: 'It is one of the most detestable things about war that everything connected with it, except the death and ruin that result, is such a heightening of life, so visually stimulating and absorbing' (Wharton 146). All four authors relish the increased sensory perception triggered by the sense of precarious living; this often translates into a celebration of the splendour of the countryside of Northern France and Belgium, either lying just a few kilometres away from landscapes ravaged by the war or itself on the verge of devastation.

The war prose considered in this book also enacts antithetical temporal dynamics. The texts reveal authors who are concurrently caught in the temporality of the war experience and that of its recording. This tension either goes forwards, from the present of the event to its upcoming record, or backwards, from narrating to narrated time. Even as they are going through the war experience, the authors anticipate their upcoming writing and the way in which this experience will shape them, prospectively considering this present as a future perfect. At other times, the narrator intervenes from beyond the time of the event to comment on her past self, which also creates a dissociation between the past and the present selves, perhaps best encapsulated in Borden's phrase 'that woman, myself' (Borden 151). Such metaleptic[1] intrusions generate a multilayered account, where different temporalities coexist and intersect, and enrich these texts with both a cubist and a palimpsestic quality. The opposite prospective and retrospective dynamics of these texts evoke Walter Benjamin's Angel of History, whose gaze is fixed on the past yet who is 'propelled' towards 'the future to which his back is turned' (Benjamin 249).

Each of the sets of texts examined in this book develops a phenomenology of the war experience that is individual to its author. By phenomenology, I mean each author's effort at capturing the essence of their sensorial and cultural experience on or near the warzone. In turn, these texts generate a phenomenology for the reader, along Merleau-Ponty's definition of the phenomenological experience of art:

> When he paints, the painter manifests and shows how the world becomes under and through his eyes, for the painter paints both the world and his world. While putting himself totally into what he paints, the painter is the servant of what is in front of him.[2]
>
> (Merleau-Ponty 617)

Santanu Das's study of the haptic experience of the First World War has been fundamental in the reflection process that has led to the present volume and in my attention to the phenomenology of the war that surfaces in the texts analysed here. His redirection of the focus on war literature towards what Sassoon called 'sensuous frontline experience' (qtd in Das 5) has supplied an enlightening perspective on First World War literature. Das has also explored the testimonial power inherent in the war memoir, in whatever form it may be written:

> Writing a journal, testament or memoir becomes a ritual in owning experience as much to oneself [...] as to the rest of the world: it is the record of a subjectivity whose trauma and effacement are simultaneously inherent in the act of bearing witness to another's wound, and ignored by a less than empathetic world.
>
> (Das 226)

Das relates this to Shoshana Felman and Dori Laub's work on witnessing, in which witnessing enacts a transformation of the subject into an 'apprentice[...] in *history* through an apprenticeship in witnessing' (Felman and Laub 109–10).

The paradigm of witnessing introduces the larger question of the ethical dimension of this war prose. This dimension was manifold: not only did it differ from writer to writer, but it varied over time within their writing. Nevertheless, some common traits can be noted. The ethical purpose inherent in the urge to witness through writing is double: it aims at making the wounded and the dead persist on the page, and at making us feel if only a modicum of the experience of the war. Felman and Laub define the witness as a 'bridge': 'Joining events to language, the narrator as eye-witness is the testimonial *bridge* which, mediating between narrative and history, guarantees their correspondence and adherence to each other' (Felman and Laub 101). Another fundamental aspect through which these texts are endowed with an ethical dimension is their negotiation of alterity and vulnerability. This second aspect is where the texts most markedly differ. Sassoon's and Sinclair's texts are more self-centred, a predictable consequence of their format as journals: they develop a growing interest in and opening to alterity that is usually not very intricate. Ford's and Borden's pieces, by contrast, reveal a constant and central attention to the radical alterity and vulnerability of the wounded or the dying; Ford also includes civilians in his consideration and develops a complex ethics of singularity that goes against the established collective morality of war propaganda. Borden's relationship to the other is perhaps the most profound, as it confronts and resists the shift from subject to abject that takes place in the dying soldier, and as she carries over his dignity as subject in her own voice. Ford's and Borden's pieces maintain an ethical resistance to the totalising vision imposed by propaganda, focusing instead on the individual experience of the narrating witness, but also refusing to erase the singularity of the wounded soldier—and sometimes, as in Ford's case, the civilian—who is witnessed. As will be analysed in the chapters devoted to these two authors, this ethical pull played no small part in prompting them both to experiment with their representation of the war. This confirms the drawbacks of a narrow definition of 'modernist' writing as 'autonomous', as Stephen Ross has demonstrated in much of his critical work:

> I contend that there is a direct correlation between formal experimentation, critique as a fundamental dissatisfaction with the status quo, and an ethical impulse to improve upon the status quo.
>
> (Ross 2013, 55)

Each chapter addresses one of the four writers considered in the volume, although connections between them are drawn throughout the book. The first chapter examines Ford's nonfictional writing during the First World War; it investigates the reasons for Ford's representational aporia while in active service, yet nuances this aesthetic draught. Among the texts studied are 'A Day of Battle', 'Just People', 'Epilogue', 'Pon... ti... pri... ith', essays for literary magazines and letters. This chapter focuses on two main questions: the evolution of Ford's principles and practice of literary impressionism on the one hand, and the ethical dimension of Ford's representation of the war—or more precisely, of the people at war—on the other. It surveys the multifarious tensions within Ford's war prose and brings to light their paradoxical fertility and long-lasting consequences on his post-war writing. Ford's initial literary response to the war is marked with a variety of scopic, narratological and psychological predicaments that seem to defeat his writing endeavours. The ethical pull intrinsic in Ford's writing led him however to persevere and build an alternative ethos to the totalising morality enforced by war propaganda. Grappling with the (quasi) impossibility of relating the war to non-combatants led Ford to update his impressionist mode of representation; this development ultimately strengthened the validity of his aesthetic principles as Ford enriched his impressionist technique with an ethical dimension. The works of Levinas, Adorno and Butler are used to elucidate this aspect. Out of this ethical shift emerges a reinvestment of Ford's principles of literary impressionism. Against the grain of what was to be labelled as 'high modernism', and against the notion of the autonomy of modernist aesthetics, Ford's updating of his technique as he experienced the war stemmed directly from his impulse to write for the sake of humanity. Ethics and aesthetics are indissoluble in his representation of the war, in a manner that was only to be confirmed in *Parade's End*.

The second chapter examines the textual detail of May Sinclair's *A Journal of Impressions* (1915), which has been the object of significantly less consideration than Sinclair's other works. It explores the manner in which Sinclair's writing allowed her to confront and navigate her awkward position during her very brief yet, to her, momentous time as secretary and reporter for an ambulance corps in invaded Belgium. This close reading reveals a profoundly complex and uncomfortably ambivalent text, blatantly unconvincing as a war diary, overtly failing and even sabotaging itself as a reportage of war. Yet irony, humour and the carnivalesque mode surface as an improbable overtone that in turn subverts the journal's negativity and interrogates conventions of war writing. Despite the deep unconventionality of her account, Sinclair captures the unofficial 'high comedy of disaster' (159) that the war could occasion at times, while rendering in an oblique manner devoid of pathos the sense of chaos, trauma and horror that it caused. The concept of liminality is also examined as a useful paradigm to appraise Sinclair's stance as she is forever kept at the periphery of events. This chapter demonstrates that despite the generally accepted view of Sinclair's status on the avant-garde scene as marginal and fragile, her *Journal of Impressions* succeeds not as a war journal, but as a fascinating and sophisticated exercise in literary impressionism and modernist experimentation.

Sassoon's journals have been the object of little to no critical attention and have not yet been examined as a work of literature. The third chapter assesses Sassoon's war diaries as a genre and literary object. Lejeune's work on the diary as distinct from autobiography is used to delineate the generic singularity of Sassoon's war journal, which circumvents the traditional divide between diary writing, autobiography and memoir. Besides the wish to record and bear witness, Sassoon in his journal enacts a construction of himself as a myth. This invites questions as to the immediacy of representation in his war diaries. Additionally, Sassoon's war journal can be identified as a writing workshop, a repository of literary experiments for his future work. It is a well-known fact that Sassoon's war diaries paved the way for the *Sherston Memoirs* and his later memoirs. The crucial role that the diaries played in the genesis of his war poetry is however much less notorious, and is examined here. Finally, this chapter explores the way in which Sassoon's variety of styles can be organised along a gradient of expressivity, where the blankest phrasing is paradoxically the most expressive of the reality of war. The abundance of self-portrayal and the richness of the descriptions of landscape and soundscape surrounding combat do not suppress the representational impasse when faced with the shock and horror of direct fighting, bombing and being wounded. Yet it allows for the introduction of affect and gives the reader the closest possible glimpse of what it was to live—and to constantly expect to die—at the front.

The final chapter examines the singularity of Borden's *The Forbidden Zone* and the interconnections between the form of Borden's 'memoir by fragment' (Saunders 2009, 181) and her ideological and ethical stance. This chapter contends that the strategies she adopts in her writing, disorienting and often strikingly innovative, directly derive from her wish to dissociate herself from the traditional and consensual figures of the nurse as a whole, and of the nurse writer in particular. The attributes of the conventional nurse figure are systematically debunked, and the nurse persona, most often handled from an outside perspective, can never wholly be identified as Borden. Writing of herself from an external stance is one of Borden's strategies to write outside of the conventions of war nurses' writing. This also bears consequences on the genre of her war 'memoir': Borden's text is the least autobiographical of the four sets of texts studied in this volume. This resistance to traditional self-expression has a far-reaching aesthetic impact on the text, as Borden emancipates herself from chronology and a stable narrative voice. Borden establishes a phenomenology of the war through an emphasis on visuality that demonstrates the nurse's scopic power, as well as on sounds and on geography, through the generation of an ironical cartography. The chapter delineates the manifold significance of the 'Forbidden Zone' as a liminal space, sitting 'on the bleeding edge of war'; as a 'non-place'; and as a 'zone of uninhabitability': the space of the abject. The expressive force of *The Forbidden Zone* resides in 'the rest that can never be written' ('Preface', n.p.), which can only be approached peripherally. Developing around absence, Borden's prose displays an unstable narrative voice and a paradoxical sophistication; it navigates between mimetic representation and innovative techniques that cause these fragments, like their author, to evade categorisation. Borden's resistance to convention bears a profoundly ethical significance. The nurse-patient relationship is revisited, with the aim of delineating the articulation between an ethics of care and vulnerability on the one hand and Borden's aesthetic choices on the other. The representation of the nurse, of the wounded and dying, and of the relationship between the two in *The Forbidden Zone* can be related to Irving Goh's theorisation of the *reject*; it expresses a constructive force of resistance to the outside gaze that considers the wounded and their carer as abject.

The position of Ford's Sinclair's, Borden's and Sassoon's war writing within their literary career varied enormously. Sassoon's diaries served as an inexhaustible reservoir from which he continued to draw for the rest of his career. Ford's war essays allowed him to update and refine his impressionist principles and techniques, both theoretically and through practice, and to find a renewed impetus that led him to *No Enemy* and *Parade's End*. Sinclair's *A Journal of Impressions* was also a writing laboratory where she experimented with tropes and techniques that she instilled into her later novels; she was and remains however far more celebrated for her novels than for the *Journal*. Conversely, while Borden's novels are today largely forgotten (although Hutchison has investigated the influence of her war writing on her later prose [2016]), *The Forbidden Zone* endures as an object of criticism that often recurs in war literature studies. Beyond the manifold tensions that intersect in this war prose, the ultimate paradox is that while centring on representational aporia, it led to an increase in expressiveness and literary inspiration in the ensuing years.

A Note

I was born in Béthune and spent my early years in Auchel, just a few kilometres from Bourecq and Lillers (incidentally, we lived Rue du 11 Novembre); my parents taught for a while at the high school in Armentières. I grew up in Lille and frequently visited my grandparents in the countryside between Boulogne-sur-Mer and Hazebrouck, and in the mining country of La Bassée. These names will be familiar to anyone reading accounts of the First World War by its most direct participants—soldiers, officers, nurses, ambulance drivers, reporters. As a result, every occurrence of place names in the prose written from the warzone contributes to making the scenes forcibly vivid to my mind.

Besides the grave sites and memorials that abound everywhere in this part of France, both wars bore material traces on the environment that still make them present to its inhabitants and visitors. In the 1980s and 1990s, my siblings and I often played in the vast crater left by a shell during the Second World War, in the field just behind my grandparents' farm. This crater, though less pronounced, remains visible to this day: the imprint of the violence of the two World Wars over the landscape and its inhabitants endures. In Didi-Huberman's words,

> Everywhere footprints precede or follow us. Many escape us, many disappear, sometimes before our very eyes. [...] Others have long since disappeared, but something tells us that they remain, buried, locatable by some archaeological diversion of desire or method.[3]
>
> (Didi-Huberman 11)

I believe that at the core of the four sets of texts scrutinised in this volume lies the urge on the part of each writer to leave an imprint of what they witnessed onto our minds, to create a zone of contact between their experience and ours. This book proposes to carry out an archaeological process that may bring to light the way in which these texts aimed at leaving this imprint; I hope it may in turn modestly contribute to highlighting and perpetuating the trace that they left in the world.

About Primary References

Because many of the texts here studied are now out of print, or have been republished incompletely, I have opted to use editions that are the most widely available as the main references. In each chapter, when no reference is given before a page number, the text used is the main primary source for this chapter, as specified in the introduction to each chapter.

Notes

1 The question of metalepsis has been brought to my attention by Katia Marcellin, whose PhD thesis investigates the poetics of metalepsis in contemporary British fiction.

2 My translation. Original text: 'En peignant, le peintre manifeste et montre comment le monde devient sous et par ses yeux, car le peintre peint à la fois le monde et son monde. Tout en se mettant totalement dans ce qu'il peint, le peintre est le serviteur de ce qui est en face à lui'.
3 My translation. Original text: 'Partout des empreintes nous précèdent ou bien nous suivent. Beaucoup nous échappent, beaucoup disparaissent, quelquefois sous nos yeux mêmes. […] D'autres ont disparu depuis longtemps, mais quelque chose nous dit qu'elles demeurent, enfouies, repérables par quelque détour archéologique du désir ou de la méthode'.

Bibliography

Primary Sources

Borden, Mary. *The Forbidden Zone*. London: Heinemann, 1929, https://archive.org/details/forbiddenzone00bord/.
Ford, Ford Madox. *War Prose*. Edited by Max Saunders. Manchester: Carcanet, 1999.
James, Henry, and Preston Lockwood. 'An Interview on the War with Henry James'. *The New York Times Current History of the European War* 2, no. 2 (1915): 358–62.
Sassoon, Siegfried. *Diaries, 1915–1918*, edited by Rupert Hart-Davis. London: Faber and Faber, 1983.
Sinclair, May. *A Journal of Impressions in Belgium*. New York: Macmillan, 1915, https://archive.org/details/journalofimpress00sinciala/; https://gutenberg.org/ebooks/31332.
Wharton, Edith. *Fighting France: From Dunkerque to Belfort*. London: Macmillan, 1915.

Secondary Sources

Acton, Carol. 'Negotiating Injury and Masculinity in First World War Nurses' Writing'. In *First World War Nursing: New Perspectives*. Edited by Alison Fell and Christine Hallett, 123–38. London: Routledge, 2013.
Acton, Carol, and Jane Potter. '"These frightful sights would work havoc with one's brain": Subjective Experience, Trauma, and Resilience in First World War Writings by Medical Personnel'. *Literature and Medicine* 30, no. 1 (Spring 2012): 61–85.
———. *Working in a World of Hurt: Trauma and Resilience in the Narratives of Medical Personnel in Warzones*. Manchester University Press: Manchester, 2015.
Adorno, Theodor W. *Problems of Moral Philosophy*. Stanford: Stanford University Press, 2001.
Bakhtin, Mikhail. *Problems of Dostoevsky's Poetics*. Translated by Caryl Emerson, and Wayne C. Booth. Minneapolis: University of Minnesota Press, 1984.
Benjamin, Walter. *The Arcades Project*. Translated by Howard Eiland and Kevin McLaughlin. Cambridge, Massachusetts: Belknap Press, 1999.
Blanchot, Maurice. *L'Écriture du désastre*. Paris: Gallimard, 1980.
Boll, Theophilus. *Miss May Sinclair*. Rutherford, NJ: Fairleigh Dickinson University Press, 1973.
Butler, Judith. *Giving an Account of Oneself*. New York: Fordham University Press, 2005.
Chantler, Ashley, and Rob Hawkes, eds. *War and the Mind: Ford Madox Ford, Parade's End, and Psychology*. Edinburgh: Edinburgh University Press, 2014.
Colombino, Laura. *Ford Madox Ford: Vision, Visuality and Writing*. Bern: Peter Lang, 2008.
Conway, Jane. *Mary Borden: A Woman of Two Wars*. London: Munday Books, 2010.

Das, Santanu. *Touch and Intimacy in First World War Literature*. Cambridge: Cambridge University Press, 2005.
Didi-Huberman, Georges. *La Ressemblance Par Contact*. Paris: Les Éditions de Minuit, 2008.
Egremont, Max. *Siegfried Sassoon: A Biography*. London: Picador, 2005.
Fell, Alison, and Christine Hallett, eds. *First World War Nursing: New Perspectives*. London: Routledge, 2013.
Felman, Shoshana, and Dori Laub. *Testimony: Crises of Witnessing in Literature, Psychoanalysis, and History*. London: Routledge, 1991.
Frayn, Andrew. *Writing Disenchantment: British First World War Prose, 1914–30*. Manchester: Manchester University Press, 2014.
———. 'Ford and the First World War'. In *The Routledge Research Companion to Ford Madox Ford*. Edited by Sara Haslam, Laura Colombino, and Seamus O'Malley, 179–92. London: Routledge, 2019.
Fussell, Paul. *The Great War and Modern Memory*. Oxford: Oxford University Press, 2013. First published 1975.
Gallagher, Jean. *The World Wars through the Female Gaze*. Carbondale: Southern Illinois University Press, 1998.
Geiger, Maria. 'No Trench Required: Validating the Voices of Female Poets of WWI'. *War, Literature and The Arts* 27 (2015): 1–13.
Gilbert, Sandra. 'Soldier's Heart: Literary Men, Literary Women, and the Great War'. *Signs* 8, no. 3 (1983): 422–50.
Gilbert, Sandra, and Susan Gubar, *No Man's Land: The War of Words*. New Haven: Yale University Press, 1989.
Goh, Irving. *The Reject: Community, Politics, and Religion After the Subject*. New York: Fordham University Press, 2014.
Grayzel, Susan R., and Tammy Proctor, eds. *Gender and the Great War*. Oxford: Oxford University Press, 2017.
Hallett, Christine E., *Containing Trauma: Nursing Work in the First World War*. Manchester: Manchester University Press, 2009.
———. '"Emotional Nursing": Involvement, Engagement, and Detachment in the Writings of First World War Nurses and VADs'. In *First World War Nursing: New Perspectives*. Edited by Alison Fell, and Christine Hallett, 87–102. New York: Routledge, 2013.
Haslam, Sara, Laura Colombino, and Seamus O'Malley, eds. *The Routledge Research Companion to Ford Madox Ford*. London: Routledge, 2019.
Hemmings, Robert. '"The Blameless Physician": Narrative and Pain, Sassoon and Rivers'. *Literature and Medicine* 24, no. 1 (2005): 109–26.
———. 'Landscape as Palimpsest: Wordsworthian Topography in the War Writings of Blunden and Sassoon'. *Papers on Language and Literature* 43, no. 3 (2007): 264–90.
———. *Modern Nostalgia: Siegfried Sassoon, Trauma and the Second World War*. Edinburgh: Edinburgh University Press, 2008.
Higonnet, Margaret. 'Not so Quiet in No-Woman's-Land'. In *Gendering War Talk*. Edited by Miriam Cooke and Angela Woollacott, 205–26. Princeton: Princeton University Press, 1993.
———. 'Authenticity and Art in Trauma Narratives of World War I'. *Modernism/Modernity* 9, no. 1 (2002): 91–107.
Higonnet, Margaret, and Patrice Higonnet. 'The Double Helix'. In *Behind the Lines: Gender and the Two World Wars*. Edited by Margaret Higonnet, Jane Jenson, Sonya Michel, and Margaret Collins Weitz, 31–48. New Haven: Yale University Press, 1987.

Hutchison, Hazel. *The War That Used Up Words: American Writers and the First World War.* New York: Yale University Press, 2015.

———. 'Very Chicago: Mary Borden and the Art of Fiction'. *Midwestern Miscellany: Journal of the Society for the Study of Midwestern Literature* (2016), https://aura.abdn.ac.uk/handle/2164/6174.

Larabee, Mark Douglas. *Front Lines of Modernism Remapping the Great War in British Fiction.* New York: Palgrave Macmillan, 2011.

Lejeune, Philippe. 'Le journal comme "antifiction"'. *Poétique* 149, no. 1 (2007): 3–14.

———. *On Diary.* Translated and Edited by Jeremy Popkin, and Julie Rak. Honolulu: University of Hawai'i Press, 2009.

Levinas, Emmanuel. *Ethics and Infinity: Conversations with Philippe Nemo.* Translated by Richard A. Cohen. Pittsburgh: Duquesne UP, 1985.

———. *Totality and Infinity: An Essay on Exteriority.* Translated by Alphonso Lingis. Dordrecht: Kluwer Academic, 1991.

———. *Alterity & Transcendence.* Translated by Michael B. Smith. New York: Columbia University Press, 1999.

Marcellin, Katia. 'Faire le vide: performativité de la métalepse et expression du trauma dans 6 romans britanniques contemporains'. PhD Diss. Université Montpellier 3 - Paul Valéry, 2022.

Merleau-Ponty, 'Phénoménologie', In *Dictionnaire des concepts philosophiques.* Edited by Michel Blay, 617. Paris: Larousse, 2013.

Moeyes, Paul. *Siegfried Sassoon, Scorched Glory: A Critical Study.* New York: St. Martin's Press, 1997.

Paterson, Adrian, and Christine Reynier. 'Introduction: "We Are Also Hospital". Modernist Non-fictional Narratives of War and Peace (1914–1950)'. *E-rea* 17, no. 2 (2020). http://journals.openedition.org/erea/9452; https://doi.org/10.4000/erea.9452.

Ricœur, Paul. *Temps Et Récit.* Paris: Édition du Seuil, 1983.

Ross, Stephen, ed. *Modernism and Theory: A Critical Debate.* London and New York: Routledge, 2009.

———. 'Modernist Ethics, Critique, and Utopia'. In *Ethics of Alterity, Confrontation and Responsibility in 19th- to 21st-Century British Literature.* Edited by Jean-Michel Ganteau and Christine Reynier, 49–63. Montpellier: Presses universitaires de la Méditerranée, 2013.

Saunders, Max. *Ford Madox Ford: A Dual Life. Volume 1: The World before the War.* Oxford: Oxford University Press, 1996a.

———. *Ford Madox Ford: A Dual Life. Volume 2: The After-War World.* Oxford: Oxford University Press, 1996b.

———. 'War Literature, Bearing Witness, and the Problem of Sacralization: Trauma and Desire in the Writing of Mary Borden and Others'. In *Memories and Representations of War: The Case of World War I and World War II.* Edited by Elena Lamberti, and Vita Fortunati, 177–92. Amsterdam: Brill, 2009.

Scarry, Elaine. *The Body in Pain.* Oxford: Oxford University Press, 1985.

Tylee, Claire. *The Great War and Women's Consciousness: Images of Militarism and Womanhood in Women's Writings 1914–64.* Iowa City: University of Iowa Press, 1990.

Virilio, Paul. *War and Cinema: The Logistics of Perception.* Translated by Patrick Camiller. London: Verso, 2009. First published 1989. Original French version 1984.

Wilson, Jean Moorcroft. *Siegfried Sassoon.* New York: Duckworth, 2014.

1 Ford Madox Ford's Unrelatable Narrative of War

Introduction

Writing to Joseph Conrad from the midst of the Somme offensive, at a short distance from the front line, Ford Madox Ford mused on his urge to record the war:

> I wonder if it is just vanity that in these cataclysmic moments makes one desire to *record*. I hope it is, rather, the annalist's wish to help the historian— or, in a humble sort of way, my desire to help you, cher maître!—if you ever wanted to do anything in '*this line*'.
>
> (Ludwig 75)

The antithetical pull that Ford expresses between the egotism of the novelist and the ethical duty of witnessing encapsulates the many paradoxes that were inherent in his experience of the war. Ford's war writings furthermore demonstrate a constant tension between his sense of a duty to bear testimony to the war and that of numb speechlessness in the face of indescribable horror. These tensions are hardly surprising on the part of an author who saw himself as '*homo duplex*', 'subject to the agonies of the duplex personality' (qtd in Saunders 1996b, 463).[1] Ford's duality took on a new significance during the First World War, which resonated in his war writing as well as much of his post-war writing.

When the First World War broke out, Ford Madox Ford was an active and established member of the London literary scene, as a poet, novelist and essayist, as well as an editor of literary magazines and patron of promising young authors of the British literary avant-garde. He was completing the novel he remains best known for today, *The Good Soldier*, which was published in 1915. The war is absent from the novel's main subject and plotline, and indeed, most of the narrative was written before the war started. In the novel's dedicatory letter, Ford himself termed it 'the best book of mine of a pre-war period' (Ford 1915a, 3). Nevertheless, the title, the background against which the novel came out, as well as the fourth of August date that recurs like a fateful knell through the narration and matches that of the United Kingdom's declaration of war on Germany, all attest to the implicit yet pervasive weight of the war on the text. Furthermore,

DOI: 10.4324/9781003270812-2

with its stark comment on the depravity of society and its staggering deconstruction of temporality and of the narratorial instance, *The Good Soldier* can be construed as a diagnosis of the dysfunction of Western civilisation in the early twentieth century, and as a strikingly clairvoyant exercise in some of the ways in which literature would be profoundly transformed in the decades following the war. Ford's second most celebrated work, his *Parade's End* tetralogy (1924–1928), revolves explicitly around the First World War and its impact on the civilisation inherited from the 18th century. This extensive saga has been saluted time and again as one of the most important contributions to First World War literature: Malcolm Bradbury regarded it as 'the most important and complex British novel to deal with the overwhelming subject of the Great War' (Bradbury xii); Samuel Hynes likewise considered *Parade's End* to be 'the greatest war novel ever written by an Englishman' (Hynes 1986, 140) and granted it a prominent place within his momentous *A War Imagined*, although he also acknowledged the impact of the tetralogy not just as a war novel but as 'something more comprehensive—a novel of twentieth-century historical change' (Hynes 1990, 430).

Judging from these novels, which remain Ford's two most acclaimed works and were written at either end of the war, one may be tempted to infer that the war came to be integrated seamlessly within Ford's fiction. However, when examining Ford's war writing at closer range, a sharp dividing line emerges, that coincides with the moment when Ford enrolled in the British Army in 1915, and even more particularly when he reached the Western Front in the summer of 1916 and was no longer a spectator from afar, but became a direct witness of the unprecedented mass killing that was taking place on the front. The confident and assertive tone of his pre-enlistment writing, notably palpable in his first essay on impressionism published in *Poetry and Drama* in June 1914, gave way to questions on the role and relevance of literature and to a sense of inadequacy as a writer; and as was the case with the vast majority of the other authors who were in active service, a decade elapsed before Ford succeeded in rendering his war experience in a novelistic form, through *Parade's End*. As soon as the war broke out, Ford discerned that it would mark a watershed in the way the world could be apprehended and represented. He kept this view for the rest of his life, writing in 1931, 'The world before the war is one thing and must be written about in one manner; the afterwar world is quite another and calls for quite different treatment' (Letter to T. R. Smith, 27 July 1931, quoted as epigraph to the second volume of Max Saunders's *Ford Madox Ford: A Dual Life*). Ford also said of the year 1914 that it was 'cut in half' (*WP* 211). This sharp divide also applies to Ford's literary career and personal life, which were profoundly disrupted and transformed by the war.

Britain declaring war on Germany had a particular resonance for this man who was English on the maternal side and German on the paternal side, and whose birth name was Ford Hermann Hueffer (he only adopted the Ford Madox Ford penname in 1919); for this cosmopolitan artist who was passionate about bridging the gap between English, French and German cultures, yet who was also deeply patriotic. Ford had an unusual perspective on the conflict: his dual origins led him at first to distance himself from the Anglo-German antagonism that was then being fuelled, but he soon became fully involved in the war effort, first contributing to British propaganda and later enlisting in the British Army. Hynes outlined this complexity in *A War Imagined* (Hynes 1990, 71–2). Overt patriotism became all the more necessary as Ford was suspected of spying for the enemy due to his paternal origins; this may have been one of the reasons why he started writing articles for the British War Propaganda Bureau, which was headed by his friend Charles Masterman. These were collected in 1915 into two books: *Between Saint Dennis and Saint George* and *When Blood Is Their Argument*. Ford's propaganda is, unsurprisingly for anyone familiar with his work, deeply singular and unconventional; it has been examined on a number of occasions, as delineated by Andrew Frayn (2019, 182). The present chapter does not centre on the political and patriotic dimension of Ford's war writing, but on the views on literature that he shared in his essays during the war. At a much deeper level than propaganda, Ford sensed very early on, and with striking prescience, the far-reaching impact that the war would have on Western civilisation, on humanity and, as an inevitable corollary, on literature and the arts.

In the summer of 1915, Ford enrolled in the British Army, despite his age—he was then 42—and his fragile physical and psychological health. After training in Britain for a year, Ford was sent to France in July 1916 and contributed to organising the transport of the 9th Battalion of the Welch Regiment in the Bataille of the Somme. Being in charge of first-line transport, he was stationed just behind the front line, and as a result under daily bombardment. In late July, he was caught in an explosion, wounded and shell-shocked, with a 36-hour memory loss. His battalion was then stationed at Ypres. In September 1916, Ford was diagnosed with shell-shock when collapsing on leave in Paris, as he related in a letter to Masterman (Ludwig 76), but decided to go back to his battalion; in the few days following this episode, he wrote 'A Day of Battle' from the front, a pair of essays that features prominently in this chapter. In December, Ford had a respiratory illness that he ascribed to breathing in gas, and although he expected several times to be sent back to France during the whole of 1917 and right until the Armistice, he spent the rest of the war on military duty in Britain.[2]

Ford intuited that enlisting would have critical consequences on his activity as a writer. In a letter to his publisher John Lane, he correlated enlisting with renouncing literature: 'I have had to give up literature and offer myself up for service to George Five' (Ludwig 61). As the primary aim of this letter was to claim money that he was owed for the publication of *The Good Soldier*, and as Ford often applied the principle of 'impressionist' truths to his own life, one is allowed to doubt whether this was meant definitely; it does nonetheless intimate that Ford felt his joining the war effort might jeopardise his *métier*. In a letter to Charles Masterman a fortnight later, he stated, 'Literature seems to have died out of a world that is mostly interesting from its contours' (Ludwig 61). Saunders does note that even before enlisting, 'he was making repeated farewells to literature' (Saunders 1996a, 465) during the early months of the war, quoting among other instances the second instalment of the essay 'On Impressionism', published in December 1914, where Ford declares, '[F]or my part I am determined to drop creative writing for good' (Ford 1914b, 326). Despite such a bleak outlook, Ford never stopped writing when he served on the Western Front: he wrote the preface to Violet Hunt's novel *Their Lives* (1916c); several poems that remain among his most celebrated and republished; countless letters, some of which include fertile reflections on literature and the arts; and many essays. Despite this literary production, Ford hardly wrote any fiction while he was in France and Belgium: the short story 'Pink Flannel' was the only one presumably written behind the line, 'in a tent on Kemmel Hill' (Saunders in *War Prose* 140), and it is quite minor when contrasted with the vastness and scope of Ford's pre- and post-war fictional work. The source for Ford's prolixity as an author of fiction seems to have dried up momentarily in contact with the war. This inability to write fiction must have felt alarming to an author who identified primarily as a novelist. The main purpose of the present study is to investigate the reasons for Ford's narrative silence while in active service, as well as to nuance this aesthetic draught.

War Prose, a collection put together by Max Saunders for Carcanet Press (1999), is the major textual resource for this chapter, especially as Saunders's selection privileges texts written after Ford joined the army, 'to give a more coherent concentration on the effects and after-effects of first-hand experience of military life and military conflict' (*WP* 3).[3] Saunders's selection is complemented by the letters Ford wrote while in service that are included in the *Letters* edited by Richard Ludwig, and the *Correspondence of Ford Madox Ford and Stella Bowen* edited by Sondra Stang and Karen Cochran. In the present chapter, the essays that Ford wrote between the beginning of the First World War and his enlisting are briefly considered before moving on to his writing whilst in service. The texts under consideration include Ford's essays for various periodicals, prefaces and some of his letters, all written from the Western Front. Such diversity in Ford's prose allows us to grasp the eclecticism of Ford's war writing, but also the cross-influences from one genre to another. As Saunders argues,

> [T]he distinction between autobiography, fiction and criticism is rarely an easy or useful one in Ford's writing, and the parallels to be found here often bring out how the fiction draws upon autobiography, how the reminiscences are fictionalised, and how Ford's critical intelligence is constantly at work in all genres.
>
> (*WP* 12)

The autobiographical vein, which is at the core of Sassoon's diaries, is here but one of the multiple elements of Ford's war prose. Ford's heterogeneous war writing speaks of a mind experiencing the simultaneousness of detachment and emotion; egotism and ethical investment; immense interest and *ennui*; intense happiness and fear; numbness and sharpness; representational helplessness and aesthetic experimentation. This chapter surveys these multifarious tensions and brings to light their paradoxical fertility and their long-lasting consequences on

Ford's post-war writing. Ford's initial literary response to the war is marked with a variety of predicaments—scopic, narratological, as well as psychological—that seem to defeat his writing endeavours. Ford however persevered in his efforts, out of his sense of 'mission' as a man of letters. The ethical pull intrinsic in Ford's war writing led him to build an alternative ethos to the totalising morality enforced by war propaganda. Out of this ethical shift emerges a reinvention and a reinvestment of Ford's principles of literary impressionism that had crucial consequences on the rest of Ford's literary career. The aesthetic and ethical dilemmas that Ford faced during the war and articulated in his war writing had indeed countless reverberations over his post-war texts.

The Elusive 'Muse of War'

Ford's Scopic Predicament: From Far-Sightedness to Near-Sightedness

The outbreak of the war certainly occasioned no dearth of writing on the part of Ford: besides his extensive propaganda work, he published a weekly series entitled 'Literary Portraits' in *Outlook*. The magazine's strapline, 'The Outlook: In Politics, Life, Letters, and the Arts', foregrounded the periodical's interweaving of arts and politics. In this spirit, Ford used his 'Literary Portraits' not only as a place to reflect on literature but as a platform to express his views on the world, often establishing connections between both aspects. As early as August 1914, he contemplated the future of literature, the psychological consequences of mass combat and the future of humanity at a time when technological progress was used towards the systematic destruction of human beings, against the Enlightenment ideal of a humanity bent on learning in order to continually improve itself and its condition.

Despite this prolific nonfictional prose output, it appears that the First World War caused a rift in Ford's creative process. His Literary Portrait entitled 'The Muse of War', published in *Outlook* on 12 September 1914, revealed him as feeling 'absolutely and helplessly unable—to write a poem about the present war' (*WP* 209), confessing to 'sheer impotence' when it came to writing literary pieces in relation to the war. The reasons he ascribes to his 'blank sheet' (*WP* 209) syndrome stand in complete adequacy with Ford's aesthetics principles as exposed before the war, but they also allow us to understand the fundamental crisis that these principles met with during the war, and the turning point enacted by the conflict in Ford's representational mode. Ford's sense of inadequacy is of a scopic nature: he is too far from the theatre of war to see, and make us see, anything:

> It is, I think, because of the hazy remoteness of the war-grounds; the impossibility of visualising anything, because of a total incapacity to believe any single thing that I read in the daily papers. [...] [T]he roots of poetry draw their nourishment from seeing and from beliefs. Here I see nothing... [...] This present war is just a cloud—a hideous and relieved pall of doom.

> [...] That is how I see poetry about war or about anything else. I want something to stir my emotions and something sharply visual to symbolise them. I want a gesture, a tone of the voice, a turn of the eye. I don't think I could make a poem out of fine words like avenging slaughtered saints or unsheathing freedom's sword. I cannot see things in that way.
>
> (*WP* 209–10)

Teeming with visual terms, the whole article expounds Ford's principles of literary impressionism in a manner that brings to mind the articles he published in *Poetry and Drama* in June and December 1914; but these principles are here rephrased and reconsidered so as to address the war context. When he developed his theory of literary impressionism before the war, in the wake of pictorial impressionism, and in collaboration with Conrad and his famous doctrine of the 'make you see', Ford posited visuality at the centre of literary creation. Ford's aesthetic mode is thus logically challenged by his distance from the scenes he is asked, and wishes, to depict: he is unable to see the war and, therefore, to 'make [us] see' it.

Since Ford's reason for not being able to write about the war is his distance from the action, one may be led to infer that this predicament was lifted once he arrived on the Western Front; yet Ford's inability to see due to distance was replaced with an opposite incapacity to encompass the whole scene of the war owing to excessive closeness. This issue is addressed in 'Arms and the Mind', one of the most arresting essays that Ford wrote while in active service. The first in a pair grouped under the heading 'A Day of Battle', 'Arms and the Mind' was written on the Ypres Salient in the fall of 1916 and engages in Ford's recent experience of the Somme. Commenting on 'A Day of Battle' in *A War Imagined*, Samuel Hynes argues that Ford's 'imaginative vacuum' (Hynes 1990, 106) was due in part to the immeasurable vastness that was specific to the First World War:

> The war was too vast to be understood. Parts of it, like the territory that he saw from his hilltop, might be *described*—the places named, the numbers of men estimated—but the war itself could not be *imagined*. For to imagine it would be to discover its significance; and as Hueffer looked down at it, 'it all seemed to signify nothing'.
>
> (Hynes 1990, 106)

In 'Arms and the Mind', Ford articulates a perceptual issue that was shared by many on the front, and that is also prevalent in Sassoon's and Borden's texts: the fact that the scale of the war exceeded the cognitive capacities of a single mind. The immensity of the Battle of the Somme is brought forward:

> The push was on.
> And it came into my head to think that here was the most amazing fact of history. For in the territory beneath the eye, or just hidden by folds in

> the ground, there must have been—on the two sides—a million men, moving one against the other [...]. It was an extraordinary feeling to have in a wide landscape.
> But there it stopped.
>
> (*WP* 38)

Ford opposes what his intellect knows factually of the vastness of the offensive, described earlier, and what little he can actually see, using a polyptoton on 'limit':

> Even work that, on the face of it is individualistic is too controlled to be anything other than delimited. If you are patrol officer your limits are laid down: if you are Battalion Intelligence Officer up on an Observation Point, the class of object that is laid down for your observation is strictly limited in range. And, within the prescribed limits there is so much to which one must pay attention that other sights, sounds and speculations are very much dimmed. And of course, if you are actually firing a rifle your range of observation is still more limited.
>
> (*WP* 38)

This scopic dilemma is encapsulated in a sentence that can be found in another piece of Ford's war prose, 'Epilogue': '*One is always too close or too remote*' (emphasis Ford's, *WP* 59). The topic of the epistemological and phenomenological limitations of the war for its most direct actors has been addressed by scholarship: delving on the 'troglodyte world' of the trenches, Fussell thus highlights the disorientation of the soldiers, who 'experience[d] an unreal, unforgettable enclosure and restraint, as well as a sense of being unoriented and lost' (Fussell 51); he remarks that the most familiar sight for any soldier was in fact the sky, seen from the bottom of the trenches. In his study on the haptic dimension of the war, Santanu Das has also delved into the limitations of the sense of sight in the war, emphasising instead the importance of touch in the writing produced by first-hand actors and witnesses of the war. Mark Larabee has devoted a monograph to the spatial representation of the First World War by British writers. His first chapter, concerned with authors who went to the front, examines with acumen the epistemological and subsequent representational challenges caused by the scale of the war. Larabee investigates the collapse of the map as 'the infallible product of positivist inquiry' (Larabee 15), arguing that 'the Great War was the locus of spaces that disrupted and frustrated a given logic of visual comprehension and depiction' (21). In 'War and the Mind', Ford thus reflects on the 'division of the mind' between factual topographical knowledge and cognitive apprehension of the space actually experienced. The lines that Ford as a transport officer is tasked with drawing onto the maps do not match his experience of the space of war:

[T]hose lines which represented Brigade and Divisional boundaries, new trenches, the enemy's new lines, MG emplacements and so on, represented nothing visual at all to my intelligence.

(*WP* 43)

Most significantly, Ford formulates this discrepancy in terms of block and fragmentation: 'No: the mind connected nothing from the maps' (*WP* 43). The map is of course a metaphor for the text, and this inability to connect the dots brings forward the consequences of the fragmented experience of war over narrative writing.

A Narratorial Impasse

Because the war can only be envisioned through fragments, and not as a whole, Ford senses he cannot render his experience through a narrative form, which would attempt to vectorise the war in some way or other and imply a causality between events. Hynes has already related the disconnectedness of the war experience to the impossibility of writing narratives:

> A writer might experience the war, but he could not verbalize it in a way that would make his experience seem real to a reader who had not been there. And he could not put his experience into a narrative form—a story with causal connections, direction, and a resolving ending—because that would give it the significance it did not possess, or did not reveal. For Hueffer, in 1916, writing a war novel seemed an impossible task.
>
> (Hynes 1990, 106)

In 'A Day of Battle', the shock of the war is only approached through fragments, and peripherally, with a process of defamiliarisation of the extreme violence of constant bombing. Space is circumscribed to the combatant's duties; even the targeted enemy, seen through the restricted frame of the rifle's sight, is fragmented to the point of losing humanity: 'the dark, smallish, potlike object upon whose "six o'clock" you must align both bar and loophole has none of the aspects of a man's head. It is just a pot' (*WP* 39). The traditional ingredients for fiction: landscape, characters and causality, have thus all vanished. Rob Hawkes wonders,

> How [...] does this newly heightened sense of instability affect Ford's already profoundly destabilising narrative practices? How, in other words, does Ford address the problem of imposing narrative shape on to a war which specifically damaged the foundations of narrative?
>
> (Hawkes 2012, 102)

This may contribute to explaining why Ford wrote so little fiction during the war. Only 'Pink Flannel' is known to have been written from active duty; *True*

Love and a G.C.M, Ford's first attempted novel after the war, was left unfinished. While Saunders does argue that it bears some 'imaginative completeness' (*WP* 13), he also contends that Ford was then at an impressionist impasse:

> Ford finds the war has left his impressionism in an impasse: the sheer vividness of his memories, combined with the sense of powerful repressions, disturbs his sense of identity and its coherence.
>
> (*WP* 78)

Ford was acutely aware of this predicament. This deadlock is also central to *No Enemy*, which was mostly written in 1919 but published in 1929. This hybrid, half nonfictional and half fictional work, delineates Ford's difficulty in finding a proper literary form to represent the war. The Envoi of *No Enemy*, written in French, is particularly salient:

> Je vous présente ces considérations en forme de lettre, mon cher… j'aurais voulu plutôt écrire un essai, soigné, balancé, bien pensant. Mais il m'est impossible de ciseler de la prose ces jours-ci. « Que voulez-vous, »—comme disent nos Tommies,—« c'est la guerre ! » J'ai passé vingt-cinq ans à chercher des cadences, à chasser des assonances, avec une rage acharnée, comme celle du bon père Flaubert. Mais aujourd'hui je n'écris que des lettres,— longues, diffuses, banales.[4]
>
> (Ford 2002, 149)

In 'Just People', Ford ascribes the reasons for this impasse to a representational issue, opposing reality and fiction: he declares that his direct experience of the war, which has been so much more momentous than any reality he has known so far, has rendered all attempt at fiction futile because it would inevitably fail to approach the intensity of reality as experienced on the front:

> I wonder if such other writers as actually served in the front lines during the War have been affected like myself. For I find nowadays […] almost all invented, thought out and worked up stories, by myself, or even those of great masters almost uninteresting. As if the life had gone out of them! […]
> I find my mind mostly dormant in the matter of inventions and my thoughts turning inwards to the recollection of real happenings in which Destiny seems to have played tricks on human beings who were just people, inscrutably and with a rather aimless finger.
>
> ('Just People', undated, *WP* 262)

Ford here establishes a correlation between the inability to write fiction after the war and his involvement in the reality of the war: as if emotional detachment were necessary in fiction writing, yet unattainable while he is still reeling from his time in service. 'Just People' reveals that there is an ethical dimension to Ford's predicament as a novelist: the trauma caused by his witnessing the deaths and suffering of so many 'human beings who were just people' prohibits any attempt at writing fiction, as it would be unavoidably paler and more trivial. Yet this very same ethical pull, as we will understand later, is what allows him to resolve the representational aporia caused by the war.

Although he never stopped writing, Ford felt an acute inability to write what he considered a truly literary prose at the contact of the war. Besides the visual challenges just examined, a number of other issues contribute to this struggle.

The Impediment of Overwork

A cause that may appear as trite, yet was in fact quite substantial, for Ford's difficulties in writing at the front, was the sheer lack of time due to intense and unceasing activity, of which Ford complained often in his letters. This situation persisted—and judging from his letters, seems to have even increased—when Ford was stationed in Britain in 1917 and 1918. While in Yorkshire in October 1917, Ford thus wrote to Lucy Masterman that he didn't have much time to devote to publishing his poems:

> I am so hard-worked here that I hardly have any time to consider these matters. I spend all day wrestling with the wild beast of Ephesus & just tumble into bed, worn out, at night.
>
> (Ludwig 85)

Likewise, in August 1918, at the beginning of his correspondence with Stella Bowen, he laments,

> You write such nice letters—& I only send back scraps. That, I suppose, is because I can't as a rule write till nearly the end of the day when I am pretty tired.
>
> (Ford and Bowen 6)

However, even as Ford's days become considerably less busy when he is sent to a hospital due to his gassed lungs, and then to the Riviera to convalesce, he identifies another cause for his lack of writing, and finally openly acknowledges that one of the main reasons for his inability to write was shell-shock. He confesses as much to Charles Masterman in January 1917:

> I think I shall be sent to Menton pretty soon & I shd. Be fairly contented if I didn't chafe at the inactivity. But of course I couldn't very well be active— even at writing proclamations because all day I am as stupid as an owl & all night I lie awake & perceive the ward full of Huns of forbidding aspect— except when they give me a sleeping draft.
>
> I am in short rather ill still & sometimes doubt my own sanity—indeed, quite frequently I do. I suppose that, really, the Somme was a pretty severe ordeal, though I wasn't conscious of it at the time.
>
> (Ludwig 82)

Even though Ford here explicitly recognises the tribute his psyche paid to the war, he was already aware of the consequences of trauma on writing when he was in the Somme and on the Ypres Salient.

Trauma as a Hindrance to Impressionist Writing

'Arms and the Mind' deals ostensibly with the psychological aspect of the war experience, but it is manifest from the first few lines that, for someone who also identifies first and foremost as an author, the effects of mass fighting on the psyche are inseparable from the effects on his writing. The essay reads like an *ars poetica* in reverse, describing as it does the way in which the very foundations of Fordian writing are undermined by the traumatic experience of the front. When examining *Parade's End*, Karolyn Steffens highlights the fact that literary impressionism was challenged by the war not merely from an epistemological point of view, but also in its representation of the historical response to the trauma of the First World War. She identifies the trenches as a

> 'historical site[…] of violence pressuring the Impressionist to respond to lived experiences in addition to epistemological challenges', and contends that 'Ford revises his previous Impressionist aesthetic when representing the historical trauma of the Great War'.
>
> (Steffens 38)

This argument is even more valid when considering the essays that Ford wrote while in active service. In 'Arms and the Mind', Ford starts by reminding us of his pre-war ability to conjure up highly visual tableaux, using Conrad's famous phrase: 'I could make you see the court of Henry VIII; the underground at Gower Street; palaces in Cuba; the coronation—anything I had seen, and still better, anything I hadn't seen' (*WP* 36–7). In the same vein as Ford's earlier critical work on literary impressionism, as well as of his early war prose expressing the struggle of writing about the war before he reached the front line, the lexical field of sight prevails throughout the essay and is inseparable from that of writing. The struggle to articulate the visuality of the war is expressed in terms of psychological resistance:

> But, as for putting them—into words! No: the mind stops dead; and something in the brain stops and shuts down. [...] As far as I am concerned an invisible barrier in my brain seems to lie between the profession of Arms and the mind that puts things into words. And I ask myself: why? And I ask myself: why?
>
> (*WP* 37)

This 'barrier' may bring to mind Blanchot's reflections on disaster: 'Disaster is separate—that which is most separate' (Blanchot 7, my translation). Alan Munton identifies this passage as a self-diagnosis of war neurosis:

> Brain, mind, words, repetitive self-questioning: the incipient breakup is clear [...]. The block on writing is [...] a real mental event. [...] This closed-down mind exists, for Ford, in a landscape, and for him [...] it is the Observation Post, or OP, that is the point of entry through which the troubled Subject enters the landscape.
>
> (Munton 113–4)

Madness becomes invested with a mythical and metaphysical dimension when Ford implicitly quotes *Macbeth* further on: 'it all seemed to signify nothing' (*WP* 40). The use of punctuation, always so singular and expressive in Ford's prose and poetry, is particularly eloquent in this text: the initial strong question or exclamation marks, which imply a powerful presence of the writer, are gradually replaced with suspension dots that become increasingly pervasive—sometimes as many as six in a row—as well as with dashes, which express the 'stopping dead' of the brain. Ford's text thus appears visually perforated, strafed, and threatened with silence: 'It is a feeling of an anger ... an anger... a deep anger! It shakes you like a force that is beyond all other forces in the world: unimaginable, irresistible ....' (*WP* 41). The suspension dots enact the hollowing out of discourse which results from the loss of articulate consciousness within the subject. The subject appears to escape from the text in an attempt to preserve his integrity: meaning evades the text and seems to be taking refuge in the unspoken.

This threat of silence, however, stands in stark contrast with the extremely detailed description of the factual minutiae of war, through a plethora of military titles and acronyms, numbers, location names or technical military terms. On the one hand, this excess of precision can be analysed as a strategy to repress trauma. Focusing on smaller elements pertaining to fighting or to army life is a means of putting shock at bay through the apprehension of fragmented and therefore more manageable elements of the war. On the other hand, the use of military acronyms and highly technical words in the text endows the description with a degree of abstruseness for the common reader: the excess of detail thus voids its purpose and generates an opposite effect of vagueness. We find here an illustration of Ford's impressionist theory, which opposes factual dryness with a deeper, more authentic truth. In Ford's fictional and nonfictional work alike, truth lies in impressions: conversely, the most factual report will prove the least effective in rendering life.

'*What Is the Good of Writing About Literature*' During the War?

At a more fundamental level, the war threatened the passionate and long-lasting relationship between Ford and literature, as it caused a profound self-questioning on his part as to the relevance of literature, and consequently of his role as a writer. As Saunders notes in his introduction to *War Prose*, 'Even before he saw active service, he realised that the war presented a new kind of challenge to literature, and to his own form of literary impressionism in particular' (*WP* 2). On the 8th of August, only 4 days after Britain declared war on Germany, Ford pondered:

> What is the good of writing about literature—the 'edler Beruf', the noble calling? There will not be a soul that will want to read about literature for years and years. We go out. We writers go out. And when the world again has leisure to think about letters the whole world will have changed. It will have changed in morality, in manners, in all human relationships, in all views of life, possibly even in language, certainly in its estimates of literature. What then is the good of it all? I don't know.
>
> (*WP* 207)

This issue took on added significance when Ford experienced the front. In a letter to Charles Masterman on 25 October 1916, Ford ascribed his writing difficulties to a lack of purpose:

> No: I am not doing any writing; to write one must have some purpose in life—& I simply haven't any. You see one has phases of misfortune that get too heavy for one as one gradually loses resiliency.
>
> (Ludwig 77)

Ford also revisited the consequences of the war on his relationship to literature in later works. In his novelistic autobiography published in 1934, *It Was The Nightingale*, he asserts that to anyone who had experienced the line, the pre-war and the post-war worlds were opposed along an axis of order and chaos:

> It had been revealed to you that beneath Ordered Life itself was stretched, the merest film with, beneath it, the abysses of Chaos. One had come from the frail shelters of the Line to a world that was more frail than any canvas hut.
>
> (Ford 2007, 49, qtd in *WP* 263)

And indeed, evoking his life in 1919, he declares rather nonchalantly: 'literature seemed to be done for as far as I was concerned' (Ford 2007, 107); in a later chapter, and on a more poignant note, he muses that his renunciation to literature can be dated from 'February 1916', as he was going back to the line despite his very poor health:

> It was then, I think, that I had really taken my farewell of literature. Under the shrouded lamps of the railway bookstall at Hazebrouck I had seen one of my own books. That had filled me with intense melancholy—with overpowering sadness. ... [...] In that ghostly station it was as if the silver cord had snapped.
>
> (Ford 1934, 173–4)

However, this fateful hour is immediately contrasted in Ford's narrative with the rekindling of inspiration that led him to start *Parade's End* in late 1922:

> But I was no sooner installed on those Riviera heights [...] than at once, to invert the words of M. Herriot, this English poet, no longer so very young, threw away the sword and grasped the goose quill. ... I wrote the first words of an immense novel. ...
>
> (Ford 1934, 174)

Although elusive and tentative due to the many reasons exposed here, inspiration never forsook Ford entirely during his time in service. His letters in particular, ripe with a flowing and vivid prose often interspersed with colourful French idioms—much to the glee of the present writer—, reveal the constancy of his attachment to writing in general and to his literary career in particular. He was quite gratified when his French translation of *Between St Dennis and St George* was met with critical acclaim in France, and exulted in a letter to Lucy Masterman in August 1916: 'according to the publisher, the book ought to make me famous in France' (Ludwig 70). He was also very keen on having poems published in English magazines, thus confiding to Imagist poet F. S. Flint: 'I somehow pine to publish a vol. of poems before the war ends or I am killed' (Ludwig 83), in a manner that eerily echoes Sassoon's thoughts on the publication of *The Old Huntsman*: 'No sign of my book yet. I do want to see it before I get killed' (Sassoon 1983, 148). After much exertion, Ford did succeed in having his collection *On Heaven and Poems Written on Active Service* published in April 1918, while he was still in service. To Joseph Conrad, he confessed his hopes to be remembered as a writer:

> I daresay eulogia of the French Press which continues to blaze and coruscate about my gifts has remonté my morale.[5] It *is* gratifying, you know, to feel that even if one dies among the rats in these drains one won't be—if only for nine days—just like the other rats.
>
> (Ludwig 72)

This is again remarkably akin to Sassoon's constant concern for his posterity as a poet, were he to die at the front; although this trait appears far less recurrently in Ford's war writing than in Sassoon's. Indeed, Ford's main reason for his persistence in writing despite the many obstacles just delineated was not his concern for posterity; it was rather, an ongoing ethical concern, which to his mind was fundamental to what he termed his '*métier*' as a writer.

Writing as Ethical Imperative

The Mission to 'Express Emotion'

In contrast with this feeling of helplessness, or even uselessness, as a writer, Ford formulated as early as August 1914 what he considered was a writer's 'job' or even 'mission' in the face of the war:

> I think that our job in life—the job of us intellectuals at this moment—is to extract, for the sake of humanity and of the humaner letters, all the poetry that is to be got out of war. I, at any rate, have no other mission at this moment.
>
> (*WP* 209)

This sense of the writer's mission grew more precise as the war went on: in 'From China to Peru', published in *Outlook* on 19 June 1915, Ford ascribes the causes of the war to a failure of communication among humanity and affirms that the paramount mission of literature is not beauty, but the power of affect:

> Man is to mankind a wolf—*homo homini lupus*—largely because the means of communication between man and man are very limited. I daresay that if words direct enough could have been found, the fiend who sanctioned the use of poisonous gases in the present war could have been so touched to the heart that he would never have signed that order, calamitous, since it marks a definite retrogression in civilisation such as had not yet happened in the Christian era. Beauty is a very valuable thing; perhaps it is the most valuable thing in life; but the power to express emotion so that it shall communicate itself intact and exactly is almost more valuable.
>
> (Qtd in *WP*, epigraph, n. p.)

This ideal of the poet as endowed with the mission of expressing and communicating emotion to the rest of humankind is redolent of Wordsworth's definition of the role of the poet, such as he described it in his preface to the 1802 edition of *Lyrical Ballads*:

> What is a Poet? [...] He is a man speaking to men: a man, it is true, endued with more lively sensibility, more enthusiasm and tenderness, who has a greater knowledge of human nature, and a more comprehensive soul, than are supposed to be common among mankind.
>
> (Wordsworth and Coleridge 2013, 103)

In August 1914, Ford 'prophesied' there would be a 'Neo-Romantic movement' after the war (*WP* 208), which corroborates this possible connection. The ethical dimension of literary creation pervades Ford's writing during and after the war, and far exceeds—and indeed, counterbalances—his task as propagandist, as it encompasses a feeling of duty to humanity as a whole. The testimonial purpose of Ford's war writing is twofold: it is on the one hand to recreate a vivid memory of and pay tribute to its victims, and on the other to convey its horror to its survivors in such a way that no one would want to reiterate such a large-scale conflict: to 'end war as possibilities' (*WP* 197). This dual aim persists in Ford's later writing about the war, particularly in *Parade's End*, as stated in the dedicatory letter for *No More Parades*, which contains the phrase quoted above, and in *A Man Could Stand Up*—:

> [I]n [this book], I have been trying to say to as much of humanity as I can reach, and, in particular to such members of the public as, because of age or for other reasons did not experience the shocks and anxieties of the late struggle:
>> This is what the late war was like: this is how modern fighting of the organised, scientific type affects the mind. If, for reasons of gain or, as is still more likely out of dislike for collective types other than your own, you choose to permit your rulers to embark on another war, this—or something very accentuated along similar lines—is what you will have to put up with!
>
> I hope, in fact, that this series of books, for what it is worth, may make war seem undesirable.
>
> (*WP* 200)

Ethical Numbness

However, and just as the very act of writing is a struggle, as analysed earlier, such a purpose was fraught with its own challenges. 'Arms and the Mind' is thus not only concerned with a representational struggle but expresses an ethical aporia, as Ford confesses to being unable to see and remember 'lamentably wounded men':

> The preoccupations of my mission absolutely numbed my powers of observation. [...] It is, in fact, the sense of responsibility that is really numbing: your 'job' is so infinitely more important than any other human necessity, or the considerations of humanity, pity, or compassion. With your backsight and foresight aligned on that dark object like a pot you are incapable of remembering that that pot shelters hopes, fears, aspirations or has significance for wives, children, father and mother ..... It is just the 'falling plate' that you bring down on the range. [...]
>
> It is all just matter—all humanity, just matter; one with the trees, the shells by the roadside, the limbered wagons, the howitzers and the few upstanding housewalls. On the face of it I am a man who has taken a keen interest in the aspects of humanity—in the turn of an eyelash, an expression of joy, a gesture of despair. [...]
>
> But, stepping out of Max Redoubt into the Bécourt Road, that day, I came right into the middle of ten or a dozen lamentably wounded men, waiting by a loop of the tramline, I suppose for a trolley to take them to a CCS. I remember the fact: but of the aspects of these men—nothing! Or so very little. [...] [T]hey are as dim in my memory as forgotten trees.
>
> (*WP* 39–40)

The chilling 'it is all just matter—all humanity, just matter' is contrasted with Ford's deep interest in humanity in much of his writing before coming to the front. He wrote in the same vein to Joseph Conrad on 6 September 1916, 'I saw two men and three mules (the first time I saw a casualty) killed by one shell.

These things gave me no *emotion* at all—they seemed *obvious*; rather as it wd. be' (Ludwig 73–4). Trauma certainly plays a part in Ford's emotional numbness here described, but Ford's incapacity to perceive the target as a man's head can also be related to Levinas's reflection on the impossibility to see faces in battle. In *Ethics and Infinity*, to Philippe Nemo's remark that 'war stories tell us in fact that it is difficult to kill someone who looks straight at you', Levinas replies, '[T]he relation to the face is straightaway ethical. The face is what one cannot kill, or at least it is that whose *meaning* consists in saying: "thou shalt not kill"' (Levinas 1985, 86, 87). Yet Ford's candidness in describing his struggle to consider the humanity of soldiers may be interpreted as a paradoxical act of ethical resistance to conventional and collective morality. Ford's helpless account comes in stark contrast with the sentimental and even at times saccharine representations of soldiers at war in posters or in the propagandist fiction and poetry that were flourishing in those years. Theodor Adorno's reluctance to a collective ethos that has been voided of its initial values may help understand the act of resistance inherent in Ford's ostensibly callous account of his lack of emotion:

> [N]othing is more degenerate than the kind of ethics or morality that survives in the shape of collective ideas even after the World Spirit has ceased to inhabit them—to use the Hegelian expression as a kind of shorthand. Once the state of human consciousness and the state of social forces of production have abandoned these collective ideas, these ideas acquire repressive and violent qualities.
>
> (Adorno 17)

Here, Ford's depiction of the maimed bodies and corpses as 'matter' defuses the recuperation of the bodies by ideology and political authorities in the context of war, as analysed by Elaine Scarry:

> War [...] has within it a large element of the symbolic and is ultimately [...] based on a simple and startling blend of the real and the fictional. In each, the incontestable reality of the body—the body in pain, the body maimed, the body dead and hard to dispose of—is separated from its source and conferred on an ideology or issue or instance of political authority impatient of, or deserted by, benign sources of substantiation.
>
> (Scarry 62)

In 'Arms and the Mind', Ford refuses this derealisation of the wounded or killed body at war and its subsequent conversion into a symbol. In Ford's war representation, bodies remain irreducibly 'matter' and do not become mere signifiers within a larger ideological discourse.

Furthermore, Ford's blunt acknowledgement and overt examination of the mind's numbness, as horror becomes habitual, can in fact be considered as initiating an alternative *ethos* from that of collective morality. Ford's ethics is deeply individual—not just because it is singular to him, but above all because it seeks to retrieve the individual out of the collective. Ford's focus on individuals singled out from the 'millions of men' is epitomised by the final vision on which 'Arms and the Mind' concludes, of 'a darkness out of which shine—like swiftly obscured fragments of pallid moons—white faces of the little, dark, raven-voiced, Evanses, and Lewises, and Joneses and Thomases..... Our dead!' (*WP* 42). Besides the visual emergence of singular soldiers from the mass of men and the chaos of war, naming here consecrates the soldiers as individuals who are each personally remembered. Sinclair has a similar intent when naming the ambulance drivers in the last few lines of her article 'Chauffeurs at the Front': 'After all, you cannot "write about the chauffeurs". You can only say: "this and this is what they did, Tom and Bert, Ascot and Newlands—and Smith, and hundreds more"' (Sinclair 1914, 296). In both cases, Ford and Sinclair strive to save from oblivion figures whose actions and loss are least likely to be commemorated: Welsh soldiers, whose sacrifice was largely downplayed, as Ford illustrates at the end of 'War and the Mind' (*WP* 47–8), and ambulance drivers, whose role was far less celebrated than that of other fighters or carers. Both categories tended to be invisible from the collective gaze, and as such, were doubly vulnerable: to death and to oblivion.

Towards an Ethics of Singularity

The shift to an ethics of vulnerability that seeks to bring individuals to the foreground is particularly palpable in 'Epilogue', which remained unpublished until Saunders included it in *War Prose*. Saunders tells us it was composed 'after February 17, and before 7 January 1919' (*WP* 52). The essay starts in a generic mode: the main pronoun for the initial descriptive chapter is the indefinite 'one', displacing the experience from that of Ford to one that may be undergone by any soldier. The pronoun then shifts to 'I' in the next paragraph, recentring the episode onto Ford's specific experience. The end of the paragraph depicts another shift, this time to the third person; this shift is initiated by Ford seeing 'the gleam of a forehead' and identifying it—with a true novelist's sensitivity—as that of a woman sewing:

> In a dark window I perceived the gleam of a forehead. A woman was sewing there in the dusk—for there is a certain angle that women's foreheads have when they sew by the window in the dusk. No man ever attains to that angle ......
>
> (*WP* 53)

This opening prefigures the general movement of 'Epilogue'. In contrast with the first section of the piece, where Ford is given conflicting but worrying information that 60 men from his battalion may have been killed when their company was shelled in transport, Ford devotes several pages of the second section to a chronicle of his hostess, Rosalie Martin, who is mending his shirt's cuffs: he details her life and losses in the war, complete with names, dates and places. This precise account of a singular civilian's life thus overlays Ford's continued worry about his men. Besides the impressionist quality of this dual account, which will be addressed more directly later in this chapter, this superimposition of the individual over the general is an ethical gesture. Ford here transcribes this chronicle from Rosalie's speech, as shown by the sentence 'so at least she said in a sudden burst of speech that came from her when she had nearly finished sewing the second cuff on my shirt' (*WP* 59). Ford's focus on her head, bent over her sewing, moves to her speech along a logic described by Levinas in *Ethics and Infinity*: 'Face and discourse are tied. The face speaks. It speaks, it is in this that it renders possible and begins all discourse' (Levinas 1985, 87). Significantly, when Rosalie's voice is rendered in direct speech to conclude her account, she resorts to the 'one' pronoun—most probably a transcription on the part of Ford of '*on*' in Rosalie's French, which has the same generic scope:

> One gives oneself so much trouble to bring men children into the world, and one gives so much trouble in order to keep them alive and in the straight road. And the days go on and the years go on and the fields are there and the troops come marching, over them. And one's male children are gone ....
>
> (*WP* 59)

Ford's account of Rosalie's singular experience thus leads to a more universal consideration of the fate of mothers and their 'male children'. The paradox here is that it is when Rosalie is granted direct speech—when we are given to hear her singular voice—that this shift from the singular to the universal is enacted. This interplay between the generic and the particular is then addressed in explicit terms in the rest of 'Epilogue', where Ford develops his own reaction and reflection to the episode. This is where Ford redefines the scopic issue of the war experience, examined earlier, in ethical terms:

> We *don't know how many men have been killed* .... One is always too close or too remote. On the Somme in July 1916, or under Vimy Ridge in February 1917 one saw, on the one hand, such an infinite number of our own male dead, or, on the other, such an infinite number of dead—and frequently mouldering—Huns, that it seemed as if the future of the World must be settled. [...]
>
> At any rate, when you see the dead lie in heaps, in thousands, half buried, intact, reposeful as if they had fallen asleep, contorted as if they were still in agony, the heaps of men following the lines of hillocks, of shell holes, like so much rubbish spread before an incinerator in the quarter of a town where refuse is disposed of ..... Well, you think of Armageddon, and on any hill of that Line, as I have seen it [...]. And the War seems of infinite importance.
>
> (*WP* 59–60)

The problem that arises from the scopic limitations of the war is here presented first and foremost as ethical: it precludes an apprehension of the dead as human. Due to their 'infinite number', the dead are reified as lying in 'heaps' and assimilated to 'rubbish', in an echo to the startling sentence, 'it is all just matter—all humanity, just matter' at the heart of 'Arms and the Mind' (*WP* 39). Ford links this ethical failure to the process of generalisation, musing: 'And the considerations and the generalisings rise up in the mind ......' (*WP* 60). Yet he also depicts a resistance to such generalisation and subsequent indiscrimination of the dead: 'But, mostly', he tells us, 'the tired brain refuses to generalise' (*WP* 61). The choice of verb, 'refuse', is significant, as it implies a moral choice. To him, generalising and theorising on the war is cognitively impossible as well as ethically unacceptable:

> But, in any case, I can't theorize—and it's a marvel to me that anybody can. Yet they are doing it—all over the shop. I don't dislike or despise the theorists, Heaven help me. But I don't see upon what hill they can stand in order to get their bird's eye views. Of course there are remote persons who stand aloof from humanity—but if you stand aloof from humanity how can you know about us poor people?
>
> (*WP* 62–3)

Ford's severe consideration of those in power, unwilling to consider the citizens as individuals and making callous decisions as a result, is widespread in his writing; it extends much beyond the war, to *Parade's End* as well as his nonfictional essays. 'Preparedness', an article published in the *New York Herald Tribune Books* in 1927, thus disparages the totalising perspective of the rulers:

> Normally we do not count—we, the decent quiet subjects or citizens of great empires. We are in the hands of politicians over whom we have no influence, they being unable or disinclined to know what we are thinking.
>
> (*WP* 70)

The rest of 'Epilogue' expands upon his resistance to distant theorisation and opposes it to his sensitivity to individual suffering. Quite significantly, in his conclusion, Ford resorts to a sustained metaphor of the face to defend singularity over generalisation:

> But, indeed, one couldn't ever really theorise worth twopence. Just as every human face differs, if just by the hair's breadth turn of a nostril, from every other human face, so every human life differs from every other human life if only by a little dimple on the stream of it. And the hair's breadth turn of the nostril—the hair's breadth dimple on the stream of life when they come in contact with the lives of others just make all the difference—all the huge difference in the fates of men and women.

'Epilogue' is thus beautifully consistent, ending with a celebration of the face that has been put in practice beforehand through the description of Rosalie. Today's reader cannot help but relate this metaphor to the Levinassian identification of the face as the site of irreducible individuality and vulnerability from which the responsibility to the other arises. When evoking Rosalie, Ford mentions her bent forehead as she mends his cuffs—a part of the face that he has identified earlier in the essay as infinitely particular: 'In a dark window I perceived the gleam of a forehead' (*WP* 53). Ford's acute attention to Rosalie's 'head bent over her sewing, silent and engrossed' (*WP* 57) and his avowal that Rosalie's 'is the woman's figure that has struck [his] imagination most since the 4th August 1914' (*WP* 59) prefigure Levinas's reflections on the ethical act inherent in looking at the other as radically other. Rosalie Martin endured in Ford's writing as Rosalie Prudent in *No Enemy*; the one passage in direct speech that Ford transcribed from Rosalie's words in 'Epilogue' finds a clear resonance in *No Enemy*, also in direct speech:

> And I ask you, M. *l'officier*, for what purpose is it that one brings men children into the world if this is to be the end? […] It is difficult to keep them alive so that they reach men's estate. And then it is difficult to keep them in the paths of virtue. And then they are gone.
>
> (Ford 1929, 130)

The whole narration of this episode in *No Enemy* (Ford 1929, 114–30) bears many direct echoes to 'Epilogue', written while Ford was in active service. Besides Levinas's well-known reflections on the face, Ford's focus on the individuality of human beings, as opposed to the totalising perspective of European leaders, heralds Levinas's theories in 'Totality and Totalisation':

> We recognize a whole when a multiplicity of objects—or, in a homogeneous continuum, a multiplicity of points or elements—form a unity, or come, without remainder, under a sole act of thought.
>
> (Levinas 1999, 39)

Totalisation is achieved when the singularity of the components is erased within the whole. In the case of human beings, totalisation amounts to denying the singularity of individuals. Levinas describes totalisation in visual terms that match Ford's attempts in 'Arms and the Mind':

> The intellectual act rises from perception, in which everything is shown within the limits of the 'visible', i.e. already as a part, to thought properly so called. This latter is […] one that is panoramic and limited and conditioned by an encompassing whole.
>
> (Levinas 1999, 40)

Yet Levinas alerts us to the limits of such a perspective:

> But does the intellectual act not rise up in the void in this way? Do not such totalizations and totalities limit themselves to the pure form of the thinkable—to an absolutely indeterminate *something*, more devoid of content than the most general genera? Do they not belong to pure logic, moving between an *analysis* that distinguishes, in any whole, parts that it conditions, parts further divisible, either infinitely so, or down to the level of elements arbitrarily posited as absolutely simple, and a *synthesis* taking each whole as a part of a vaster whole that conditions it, thus going either to infinity, or, arbitrarily, to an absolute whole? [...] This is a Kantian problem: Does not the idea of absolute totality reduce to a pure concatenation of notions without any hold on reality?
>
> (Levinas 1999, 40–1)

Levinas here opposes the pure intellect to actual, embodied experience. His reflections on totality allow us to consider anew Ford's expression of the mind's struggle to gain a totalising view of the war in the essays he wrote during and immediately after his experience of Ypres and the Somme. It also sheds a new light on Ford's opposing the 'reality' of the war in 'Just People' to whatever fiction he might attempt, which would inevitably enact a metonymical process (see Lodge 2015) that would lead to 'generalising'. This struggle goes far beyond the expression—and lament—of perceptual and cognitive limitations: it is in fact an active gesture of ethical resistance to totalisation. If we go back to Adorno's resistance to a collective ethos, Judith Butler's analysis is illuminating when applied to Ford's considerations. Adorno, she tells us,

> worr[ies] that the collective ethos is invariably a conservative one, which postulates a false unity that attempts to suppress the difficulty and discontinuity existing within any contemporary ethos. It is not that there was once a unity that subsequently has come apart, only that there was once an idealization, indeed, a nationalism, that is no longer credible, and ought not to be. As a result, Adorno cautions against the recourse to ethics as a certain kind of repression and violence.
>
> (Butler 4)

As an alternative to the collective ethos that was vigorously forced upon the population during the war, and in spite of his own contribution to British propaganda, Ford proposes an ethics that considers the singular. 'Epilogue' thus pits Ford's acute sensitivity to the particularity of Rosalie's life against a disembodied representation of the war that would be satisfyingly whole. This vastly unread essay is an essential piece within Ford's war writing, as it helps crystallise and bring to the fore the ethical pull inherent in all of Ford's war writing during and after his time at the Somme and in Belgium.

This ethical injunction is one of the major paradigms of *Parade's End*, as I have argued in 'Towards an Ethics of Singularity: The Shattered Mirror of Identity in Ford Madox Ford's *Parade's End*' (Brasme 2013). In *No More Parades*, Tietjens thus realises that his responsibility towards his men also entails the preservation of their singularity:

> Men. Not just populations. Men you worried over there. Each man a man with a backbone, knees, breeches, braces, a rifle, a home, passions, fornications, drunks, pals, some scheme of the universe, corns, inherited diseases, a greengrocer's business, a milk walk, a paper stall, brats, a slut of a wife... The Men: the Other Ranks!
>
> (Ford 2011c, 16)

The capitalised 'Men' and 'Other Ranks' take on connotations of an ethical nature. The technique that allows Ford to write about the 'human beings who were just people' is literary impressionism, thanks to which he renders people in their radical alterity through manifold dabs of the brush. Along what one might argue is a typically Fordian paradox, the ethical injunction that causes the move in Ford's writing from the immensity of the 'untold millions' (*WP* 70) to an ethics of the individual is precisely what allows him to resolve the representational aporia that he felt when confronted with the war. It is his effort to make the individuality of soldiers—and sometimes civilians, as with Rosalie—emerge that paves the way for his reinvestment of literary impressionism.

From Ethical Injunction to Aesthetic Reinvention

An Anamorphic Mode of Representation

Ford's sense of an ethical injunction may explain why he remained resolutely bent on exploring and refining literary impressionism while he was in service, despite his sense that writing was impossible. In 'War and the Mind', the second essay from the pair that composes 'A Day of Battle', Ford muses over a German sniper who has fired at him. This description of the sniper undergoes a transformation that is simultaneously and inseparably ethical and aesthetic:

> Curiously enough that sniper—if it was a sniper—is the most present in my mind of all the thousands of bluegrey beasts that, in one capacity or another, one saw out there .... And yet I, naturally, never saw him. I *do* see him. He has a black moustache, a jovial but intent expression: he lies beside a bit of ruined wall, one dark eye cocked against his telescopic sight, the other closed. And through the circle of the sight he sees me riding slowly over the down: a small, unknown figure of a man upon a sleepy roan mare. And his finger is just curling tenderly round the trigger. He is a Bavarian. And so he lies, and so he will continue to lie, in my mind, for ever.
>
> (*WP* 46)

Saunders comments on this scene:

> What is remarkable in this piece, written soon after the event and long before he had fully recovered, is its novelistic combination of detachment from himself and sympathetic imagination of his enemy's point of view.
>
> (Saunders 1996b, 26)

Here the shift is prompted by the change in the referent of the first-person pronoun: in 'I [...] never saw him', the pronoun points to Ford the soldier and belongs to the temporality of the scene. In the next sentence, 'I *do* see him', it means Ford the writer and belongs to the time of writing. The parataxis between the two sentences makes this shift all the more salient. The description moves from a factual evocation where the mind is once again aware of the vast number of enemies encountered and of the dehumanising and indiscriminating effect of this number, to a masterful exercise in Fordian impressionism. Here the poet's ability to imagine—and indeed feel, and make *us* feel—the other's individuality and precise sensorial experience, has deep ethical consequences. The description is anamorphic: the sniper's radical alterity—he is the enemy and has just attempted to kill Ford—gives way to a profoundly human description. It is Ford's very technique of literary impressionism—in particular the doubling of vision—that allows him to resolve the ethical conundrum of the representation of the war. The ethical injunction generated by Ford's experience of the war is thus not simply to write, but to make use of the techniques of literary impressionism. Against the grain of the canonical—and today largely questioned in the wake of the new modernist studies—definition of 'high modernism' as autonomous, Ford's modernism gained in depth and scope precisely because his experience of the war prompted him to become aware of and solidify his ethical commitment as a writer. Arguing that modernism 'was a fundamentally ethical set of projects', Stephen Ross declares,

> I contend that there is a direct correlation between formal experimentation, critique as a fundamental dissatisfaction with the status quo, and an ethical impulse to improve upon the status quo.
>
> (Ross 2013, 55)

Despite its claiming an apparent failure to express the impressions of the war, 'A Day of Battle' thus hinges on a crucial paradox. Although it posits that the psychological void caused by the trauma of war is responsible in turn for a representational vacuum, there is no denying that the text does ultimately manage to render an impression of the war, culminating in the conclusion of 'Arms and the Mind' through a quintessentially Fordian vignette, both highly visual and musical:

> Yes, I have just one War Picture in my mind: it is a hurrying black cloud, like the dark cloud of the Hun schrapnel. It sweeps down at any moment: over Mametz Wood: over the Veryd Range; over the grey level of the

> North Sew: over the parade ground, in the sunlight, with the band, and the goat shining like silver and the RSM shouting: 'Right Markers! Stead a......ye!' A darkness out of which shine—like swiftly obscured fragments of pallid moons—white faces of the little, dark, raven-voiced, Evanses, and Lewises, and Joneses and Thomases..... Our dead!
>
> (*WP* 42)

This fragment bears a strong poetic and impressionist intensity; in addition, the simultaneity of the dark murkiness associated with the German bombing and of the sparkle associated with the British Army finds a striking echo in the narration of *No More Parades*, particularly in the last few pages that emphasise the contrast between the general sense of 'darkness' and of a 'cloud' sitting over the British Army throughout the volume, and the 'shining', 'polished', 'varnished' cook-houses (Ford 1925, 247–8), handled by 'white tubular beings' (247) and inspected by General Campion who is repeatedly described as 'shining' (220, 247, 248). Even more strikingly, this 'cloud' was already present in Ford's aforementioned 'Literary Portrait' from 12 September 1914, when he considered he didn't have a clear enough view of the war to be able to write about it in literary terms: '[T]his present war is just a cloud—a hideous and unrelieved pall of doom' (*WP* 209). The cloud certainly seems to have acquired some substance through the direct experience of war, but this echo, bringing together an essay from early wartime, a piece written from the front and the post-war *No More Parades*, may invite us to reconsider the sense that Ford had of a sharp dividing line between his writing before, and his writing during or after his time at the front. Hynes also quotes Ford in 1934, as he defines his aim in *Parade's End* in a manner strikingly akin to the final picture of 'Arms and the Mind':

> The work that at that time—and now—I wanted to see done was something on an immense scale, a little cloudy in immediate attack, but with the salient points and the final impression extraordinarily clear. I wanted the Novelist in fact to appear in his really proud position as historian of his own time. Proust being dead I could see no one who was doing that ...
>
> (Ford 1934, 180, qtd in Hynes 1990, 431)

Both texts evoke a nebulous vision of enormous proportions, constellated with a few bright details. This confirms that the representational mode that was to become Ford's after the war was already germinating at the front. Of course, in another quintessentially Fordian paradox, the very spark of this renewed narrative form emerges out of the murky, uncertain outlines of a cloud. In Saunders's words, 'A Day of Battle [...] is a deeply paradoxical piece, vividly recreating the predicament of someone who feels he can no longer create vivid representations' (*WP* 15). Through a contradictory *mise en abyme*, Ford writes an entire piece on his inability to *write* on the psychology of war. The reflexive and metatextual quality of these two essays positions them at the core of modernism's concern with its own process of creation. This reflexiveness also matches the shift from military mapping to individual consciousness that Larabee posits as inherently modernist when the focus moves 'from the intentions of the creators of space to the consciousnesses of the observers of it':

> Consequent literary techniques of visualization then amount to acts of resistance against both this logic and its breakdown, ultimately recasting mapping as an opportunity for carrying out artistic strategies of compensation and transcendence in the face of the experience of battle.
>
> (Larabee 21)

Despite Ford's often being considered a marginal modernist, partly due to his being seen as one of '*les vieux*', partly due to his highly individual aesthetics, this pair of essays thus unmistakably partakes of modernist self-consciousness.

Developing Auditory Impressionism

An aspect in which Ford enriched his pre-war theories on literary impressionism was his new interest in sounds. In a few letters to Conrad and Lucy Masterman, and as a logical consequence of the inability to 'see', Ford explores the aesthetic potential of developing literary impressionism from the perspective of sounds. In early September 1916, he thus writes to Conrad,

> I have just had a curious opportunity with regard to sound wh. I hasten to communicate to you.
>
> This aftn then, we have a *very* big artillery strafe on [...]. I did not notice that it was raining and suddenly and automatically I got under the table on the way to my tin hat. [...] Well I was under the table and frightened out of my life—so indeed was the other man with me. There was shelling just overhead—apparently thousands of shells bursting for miles around and overhead. [...]
>
> It was of course thunder. It completely extinguished the sound of the heavy art[iller]y, and even the how[itzer] about 50 yds. away was inaudible during the actual peals and sounded like *stage thunder* in the intervals. [...]
>
> I thought this might interest you as a constatation of some exactness.
>
> (Ludwig 71)

This episode may also bring to mind Sinclair's confusion of the barking of dogs and the firing of machine guns analysed in the next chapter: the experience of misperception was undeniably felt as an exciting aesthetic occasion for writers inclined towards literary impressionism. The use of words such as 'opportunity' and 'interest' reveals that despite the terror of bombing—and despite his claiming, as noted earlier, that literature was over for him—Ford never ceased to be captivated by writing. Saunders identifies this letter as expressive of Ford's awareness of the potential fertility of the war experience for literary impressionism: 'It is these paradoxes of subliminal consciousness and surprised perception that fascinate him' (*WP* 5). This is confirmed by the concluding line of the letter: 'An R. F. A. man has just come along & explained that the "rain has put the kybosh on the strafe"—so there, my dear, you have the mot juste' (Ludwig 72).

The second letter that Ford sent Conrad in September 1916 goes further in his development of an aural form of impressionism that may come to enrich the predominantly visual character of this literary movement as it was developed before the war.

> I will continue, 'for yr information and necessary action, please,' my notes upon sounds.
>
> In woody country heavy artillery makes *most* noise, because of the echoes—and most prolonged in a *diluted* way.
>
> On marshland—like the Romney Marsh—the *sound* seems alarmingly close: I have seldom heard the *Hun* artillery in the middle of a strafe except on marshy land. The *sound*, not the diluted sound, is also at its longest in the air. [...]
>
> On dry down land the sound is much *sharper*, it hits *you* & shakes *you*. On clay land it shakes the ground & shakes you thro' the ground. [...]
>
> Shells falling on a church: these make a huge '*corump*' sound, followed by a noise like crockery falling off a tray—as the roof tiles fall off.
>
> (Ludwig 73, emphases Ford's)

Ford's description of these two letters as 'notes' confirm the fact that he is here striving to enrich his theorisation of literary impressionism. Ford appears indeed to write here a study in noise and in auditory impressionism, documenting the various sounds of the war and storing these 'notes' for future writing. The parts of *Parade's End* that occur on the front seem to have been directly inspired from such attention to noise. In *No More Parades*, as in the letter to Conrad, Ford mixes onomatopoeic neologisms with a focus on the physical effect on the senses. The novel's first paragraph, among many other instances, is relevant:

> An immense tea-tray, august, its voice filling the black circle of the horizon, thundered to the ground. Numerous pieces of sheet-iron said, 'Pack. Pack. Pack.' In a minute the clay floor of the hut shook, the drums of ears were pressed inwards, solid noise showered about the universe, enormous echoes pushed these men—to the right, to the left, or down towards the tables, and crackling like that of flames among vast underwood became the settled condition of the night.
>
> (Ford 1925, 9–10)

Ford's expressive description of the sounds of war offers a remarkable consistency from the nonfiction he wrote in service to his later fictional work. He often resorts to a personification of the noise of bombs that makes them appear harmless. In 'Epilogue', 'a shell drop [...] into the church desultorily' (56); this is echoed in *No More Parades*, where 'a few desultory, pleasurable "pop-op-ops" sound[...] from far overhead to the left' (Ford 2011c, 23), and in *A Man Could Stand Up*—: 'This shell appeared heavier and to be more than usually tired. Desultory' (Ford 2011b, 132). The fact that techniques developed in the prose written at the front are taken up in a strikingly similar manner in *Parade's End* reveals that in the midst of the sensations of war, and despite shell-shock, 'numbness' and a feeling of writerly helplessness, Ford did pursue his work of experimentation in matters of mimesis and representation.

Impressionist Resilience and Reinvention in 'Pon... ti... pri... ith'

In 'Pon... ti... pri... ith', an essay written in magnificent French, published in *La Revue des Idées* in November 1918[6] and translated by Saunders in *War Prose*, Ford revisited the memory loss he incurred after being 'blown into the air' by a shell in September 1916. As in 'A Day of Battle', and despite this piece being intended for propaganda, the focus is on finding the means for a verbal expression of war memories and to conjure up a vivid scene for the reader. This essay bears marked similarities with 'Arms and the Mind', which was written two years earlier. Both texts use the paradigm of smoke and cloud to depict the numbness and blurriness of certain memories: the 'shadows of violet smoke' and 'blackish clouds'[7] in 'Pon... ti... pri... ith' (*WP* 31) echo the 'immense cloud of smoke' and the 'hurrying black cloud' on which closes 'Arms and the Mind' (*WP* 41). The two essays also share a fascination for visuality and revolve around the elaboration of a vision. 'Pon... ti... pri... ith' thus opens on 'here is the most coloured picture, the most moving vision of the whole war' (*WP* 30); 'Arms and the Mind' ends on a similar depiction: 'Yes, I have just one War Picture in my mind' (*WP* 41). In both cases, these visions are framed and captured as colourful and minute 'pictures': in 'Pon... ti... pri... ith', Ford evokes 'the most coloured picture', 'clear and light, blue and vermilion, in spite of all the shadows of violet smoke, like those touching illuminations, which represent towns, calvaries and people, such as you can see in the book of hours of Mary Queen of Scots at Rimini' (*WP* 31); where in 'Arms and the Mind', reading place names on a map generates 'extraordinarily coloured and exact pictures behind my eyeballs—little pictures having all the brilliant minuteness that medieval illuminations had' (*WP* 37). In a letter to Joseph Conrad in the autumn of 1916, Ford also described France through the lens of visual and textile arts: '[T]his is France of tapestries—immense avenues along the road, all blue in the September twilight & the pleasant air that gives one feelings of bienaise'[8] (Ludwig 75).

At even closer range, the echoes between the two essays also occur at a syntactic and stylistic level. Let us compare two passages: first, from 'Arms of the Mind':

> I could make you see the court of Henry VIII; the underground at Gower Street; palaces in Cuba; the coronation—anything I had seen, and still better, anything I hadn't seen. [...] Today, when I look at a mere coarse map

of the Line, simply to read 'Ploegsteert' or 'Armentières' seems to bring up extraordinarily coloured and exact pictures behind my eyeballs—little pictures having all the brilliant minuteness that medieval illuminations had—of towers, and roofs, and belts of trees and sunlight; or, for the matter of that, of men, burst into mere showers of blood and dissolving into muddy ooze; or of aeroplanes and shells against the translucent blue.—But, as for putting them—into words! No: the mind stops dead, and something in the brain stops and shuts down.

(*WP* 36–7)

And now from 'Pon… ti… pri… ith':

> I could perfectly well tell you what I did, what I said, thought and accomplished on the 6th July 1891, a quarter of a century ago; or even in September 1892, when I visited the town of Albert to write an account of its art-nouveau church… Art nouveau! and I remember very well what I wrote about it. But as for what happened to us between the 6th and the ? July 1916—to we others of the Welch Regiment—it only comes back to me as some fragments, confused, comic or even pathetic, as in a cubist picture…
>
> (*WP* 32)

The same rhythm and opposition can be found between the beginning of each paragraph, with 'I could perfectly well tell you' and 'I could make you see' followed by enumerations, and their final clauses, which share the same syntax: 'But, as for putting them—into words' and 'But as for what happened to us'. Even though the second essay is a translation from French by Max Saunders, Ford's original French text follows a similar syntax and movement. Both paragraphs end on the stylistic representation of fragmentation and confusion. A similar structure can also be found in 'Epilogue':

> If, before the War, one had any function it was that of historian. […] One could approach with composure the Lex Allemannica, the Feudal System, problems of Aerial Flight, the price of wheat or the relations of the Sexes. But now, it seems to me, we have no method of approach to any of these problems.
>
> (*WP* 59)

Here again, the first sentence starts with the modal 'could' and is rebuffed by another sentence starting with 'but'. Another stylistic echo can be traced between 'Arms and the Mind' and 'War and the Mind'. The phrase 'No: the mind stops dead' (*WP* 37) finds its counterpart in 'No: the mind connected nothing from the maps' (*WP* 43). Such correspondences between the various pieces written from the front suggest that in the very process of lamenting the representational aporia of his extreme experience, Ford was assiduously testing out aesthetic effects in an attempt to express it against all odds. This can be related to similar echoes between the various pieces that form Mary Borden's *The Forbidden Zone*: in both cases, these correspondences confirm the aesthetic self-consciousness of the authors.

Additionally, 'Pon… ti… pri… ith' summons the cubist and futurist avant-gardes to liken the vignette that stands at the heart of the piece to 'one of those Futurist or cubist pictures which we had discussed throughout July 1914' (*WP* 31). He grows even more specific when actually depicting the scene:

> It only comes back to me as some fragments, […], as in a cubist picture…
> In a corner of this picture is the menu of a sort of restaurant Duval, in Cardiff; 'sweetbread à la financière, fourpence'; and the left eye of a crying woman; and part of Newport station and the large nose of a Colonel; and then, of Waterloo station—the livid light, the canopy, high and banal; and the mothers, and the wives and girlfriends of the Welch officers; and the little brown Tommies, heavily engrossed; and their wives who were carrying pale babies and the tin badges of their husbands. And all laughing and crying and jostling each other… and the alabaster hands shaking behind the 'photographic representative' of the Northcliffe papers, who has his head hidden under his black velvet hood, and who exhorts us to assume imbecile smiles… Clouds, shadows, pale faces, spirals of violet smoke, out of which loomed the iron columns supporting the station roof—enormous and as it were deathly…
> And then this cubist picture effaced itself and gave way to a small canvas, as who should say Pre-Raphaelite […]'.
>
> (*WP* 32)

This description, with its juxtaposition of fragmented and heterogeneous images, is Fordian impressionism and 'double vision' at its finest; strikingly enough, though, what Ford describes here twice as a 'cubist picture' matches in fact far better the principles of futurism, with the gaze's movement from one fragment to the other, the 'spirals of violet smoke', and the coexistence of manifold scenes and moods that may bring to mind Umberto Boccioni's principle of simultaneity. This is corroborated by Ford's second 'On Impressionism' article, of which the previous description is strongly redolent:

> You will observe […] that you will have produced something that is very like a Futurist picture—not a Cubist picture, but one of those canvasses that show you in one corner a pair of stays, in another a bit of the foyer of a music hall, in another a fragment of early morning landscape, and in the middle a pair of eyes, the whole bearing the title of 'A Night Out'.
>
> (Ford 1914a, 175)

The similarities between 'Pon… ti… pri… ith' and 'On Impressionism' are essential on a number of counts. Firstly, they emphasise the materiality of the 'picture[s]' described, through the mention of the 'canvas' and of a 'corner' in both. These can also be related to the vignettes or 'little pictures' of the war likened to medieval illuminations in both 'Pon… ti… pri… ith' and 'Arms and the Mind'. In each case, the limits of the pictures—their frame—is inferred, and point to the limitations of the vision, but also to its constructedness. The French word used in the opening sentence of 'Pon… ti… pri… ith' is 'tableau', which points more explicitly than 'picture' towards the materiality of the artefact. In both 'Pon… ti… pri… ith' and 'Arms and the Mind', Ford is fully aware that each of these sights of war, through the necessary limiting effect of his vision and the inevitable mediation of his perspective, has shifted from the actual past experience: they have become confined and static pictures, and as such, irretrievably limit the initial, real situations that they depict.

Secondly—and in relation to this first remark—, in both instances, Ford is intent on interpreting these vignettes through specific aesthetic lenses, testing out various aesthetic movements against the vision of his mind's eye. Ford here interweaves a variety of influences, from medieval illuminated pictures all the way to futurism, in a manner akin to his own literary and critical writing, where past influences are not dismissed for the sake of 'mak[ing] it new'. Cubism and futurism, nonetheless, are markedly favoured to represent the visual experience of the war. In her monograph devoted to vision and visuality in Ford's writing, Laura Colombino analyses the influence of painting, from Pre-Raphaelite art to cubism and futurism, on the strong visuality of Ford's descriptions in his writing. Whilst Ford's war essays are not addressed, much of what Colombino notes of visuality in *Parade's End* is relevant to the way in which Ford described the war when watching and writing of it directly behind the line. To Colombino, and in a departure from Ford's pre-war writing, classical forms are only a minor influence in *Parade's End*, as opposed to avant-garde aesthetics:

> The retrieval of classical themes and forms is certainly not the most prominent visual aspect of the tetralogy. If Ford resorts to it now and then, it is only to show, by way of contrast, the fragmentation and tragic loss of meaning which characterised the experience at the front.
>
> (Colombino 146)

In 'Arms and the Mind' and 'Pon… ti… pri… ith', Ford uses traditional modes of visual representation only to highlight their evanescent and fragmented character in his mind's view: they emerge sporadically, amidst a chaotic, incomplete and fragmented landscape.

Furthermore, Ford's interweaving of various aesthetic movements confirms the constructedness of the vignettes here presented. Both aspects suggest that the war can only be apprehended through the mediation of art. Yet this shift from real experience to the artefact is not shown as inducing a lack or a distortion from the initial experience. The aesthetic filters superimposed onto the scenes appear as requisites that allow Ford to generate the right impression within the reader. This is but confirmed in the final section of 'Pon… ti… pri…

ith', where just after grimly reflecting that most of his joyous companions were to die six days later in Mametz wood, Ford records his reverent emotion at being shown Flaubert's house on his way to the front—which points to another fundamental influence in Ford's novelistic writing. This unexpected sight works as an uncanny presence of past literary influences on Ford's mind at war; it confirms that Ford never stopped thinking about literature and experiencing the war from the perspective of storytelling and literary representation. Ford then fantasises on seeing the ghost of Flaubert looking at them from within the house. Where the word 'fantôme' could have been used in the original French version, Ford has opted instead for 'revenant', i.e. a dead who 'comes back' to haunt the living; this choice is even more potent: it emphasises the motif of spectrality, of the reverberation of the past onto the present, and here specifically, of the superimposition of literary influences onto the war context. Literature and the arts thus crop up as persistent reminders of Ford's passionately literary turn of mind; they inhabit—or indeed, haunt—the text and inevitably shape Ford's experience of the war: not just as he records it, but as he lived it. In return, Ford's war experience and literary experiments from the front are reverberated over and over in his post-war work. A double spectrality is at work in Ford's war prose: one, from the past onto the present of the war, where art impresses itself onto the war; another, from the present of the war onto the future, through the pervasive influence of Ford's style at war upon his later writing. This double vectorisation brings to mind Walter Benjamin's Angel of History, whose gaze is fixed on the past yet who is 'propelled' towards 'the future to which his back is turned' (Benjamin 249). Saunders considers that 'Pon... ti... pri... ith' is 'a combination of impressionism and hallucinatory collage that would become the stylistic principle of his post-war writing' (*WP* 30). Although focusing on representational aporia, 'Pon... ti... pri... ith' and 'Arms and the Mind' evince aesthetic experimentation and recurrent motifs that anticipate his most masterful later prose.

Indeed, the fact that these essays, both written during the war yet within a two-year interval, share so many common features, reveals that these aspects were at the heart of Ford's concerns when experimenting with ways of making the war tangible and vivid to the reader. They also herald recurring paradigms in Ford's post-war writing. The conversion of visual memories into illuminated pictures reminiscent of older times brings to mind Tietjens's recurrent hallucinations: his vision of 'a woman in an eighteenth-century dress looking into a drawer in his bureau' and, more generally, the fact that

> [h]is eyes, when they were tired, had that trick of reproducing images on their retinas with that extreme clearness, images sometimes of things he thought of, sometimes of things merely at the back of the mind.
> (Ford 2011c, 19)

Likewise, the motif of the cloud recurs throughout the *Parade's End* novels, particularly in *No More Parades*, where Tietjens sees his worried men like a cloud of dust that would approach and overwhelm a landscape: every one with preposterous troubles and anxieties, even if they did not overwhelm you personally with them... Brown dust...

(Ford 2011c, 43)

Even more specifically, the vision of dark clouds from which faces would emerge is present in both the 1916 and the 1918 essays: 'a darkness out of which shine—like swiftly obscured fragments of pallid moons—white faces' (*WP* 42) in 'Arms and the Mind' and 'Clouds, shadows, pale faces' in 'Pon... ti... pri... ith' (*WP* 32). This network of motifs, reverberating from one piece to the other despite an interval of several years, suggests that Ford was in fact able to build paradigms that would structure his vision and his aesthetic rendering of his war experience not only from the immediacy of the front but also almost a decade later, in his masterful tetralogy.

Conclusion: Towards *Parade's End*

Despite the promising richness of his war prose, the transition towards post-war novelistic writing was a fraught path for Ford, due to shell-shock, manifold personal troubles and his feeling increasingly out of place in England in the early post-war years. In his overview of Ford's war writing in the *Routledge Research Companion to Ford Madox Ford*, Frayn states,

Ford's struggles to write in the immediate post-war years attest to his alienation. They would ultimately lead to the composition of his great post-war series [...], but Ford needed to leave England first.

(Frayn 2019, 185)

At the beginning of 'Arms and the Mind', Ford remarks that the great war narratives tend to be written by authors who did not experience the fight first-hand:

[T]he great books of the psychology of war (such as Stephen Crane's *Red Badge of Courage* or even the *Débâcle* of Zola) [were] written by civilians who had never heard a shot fired or drilled a squad. [...] It was not Hector of Troy—it wasn't even Helen!—who wrote the *Iliad*: it wasn't Lear who wrote *Lear*.

(*WP* 37)

Ford nevertheless tempers this statement: 'Lookers on see most of the Game: but it is carrying the reverse to the queer extreme to say that one of the players should carry away, mentally, nothing of the Game at all' (37). His predicament, by his own admission, is not wholly hopeless.

Ford's difficulty in finding his voice again as a novelist after the war is paired with his impossibility to write of his war experience in the first person. Saunders points out that unlike other authors who had experience of the front and wrote of it in the decades that followed, Ford never used the first-person narrative to tell of his experience, even though he did write several autobiographical works:

> Curiously, what he didn't write was the kind of first-person testimony that became one of the central First World War genres: something comparable to *Goodbye to All That*, *Memoirs of an Infantry Officer*, *Undertones of War*. Indeed, the war falls silently between his two major autobiographical books, *Return to Yesterday* and *It Was the Nightingale*. The first ends with the outbreak of war; the second begins with Ford's demobilisation. He did write the fascinating book of war reminiscences, *No Enemy*, but it is strangely oblique and fictionalised.
>
> (*WP* 13–4)

The opening of *No Enemy* is particularly telling in this respect, as the narratorial instance is multi-layered: 'The writer's friend Gringoire, originally a poet and Gallophile, went to the war' (Ford 2002, 7). Hawkes comments on the elusiveness of the narrative stance:

> With typically Fordian ambiguity, the text introduces its two main figures: Gringoire and the anonymous 'writer', who subsequently dubs himself the 'Compiler' and who ostensibly narrates what follows. In the opening line it is not yet clear that 'the writer' necessarily refers to the individual narrating; like his 'friend' he could simply be a character within the tale.
>
> (Hawkes 107)

The instability of the narrative stance, slipping from one persona in the first person to another in the third person, evidences that *No Enemy* was to some extent a necessary step for Ford to mature into the author of *Parade's End*. The link connecting Ford's war prose and *Parade's End* is indeed the unclassifiable *No Enemy*; delineating the arc leading from Ford's war essays to his later writing through *No Enemy* would fill another chapter, which I regret could not be achieved within the confines of this volume, yet opens promising avenues in Fordian research.

The existence of *Parade's End* demonstrates that Ford was able to come to terms, albeit through a long and tortuous process, with the aesthetic numbness caused by the war. The process leading to this immense war narrative was indubitably initiated on the front. Ford's dedicatory letter to *No More Parades*, the second volume of *Parade's End*, offers us an interesting insight into the slow gestation of the tetralogy. Ford here asserts that the idea for the novels originated as he was on the Ypres Salient:

> Casting about, then, for a medium through which to view this spectacle, I thought of a man […] with whom I had been very intimate and with whom […] I had at one time discussed most things under the sun. He was the English Tory.

> Even then—It must have been in September, 1916, when I was in a region called the Salient, and I remember the very spot where the idea came to me—I said to myself: How would all this look in the eyes of X....—already dead, along with all English Tories? [...]
> To this determination—to use my friend's eyes as a medium—I am adhering in this series of books.
>
> (Ford 2011c, 4–5)

The germination of *Parade's End* thus coincides with the writing of 'A Day of Battle', composed on the Salient in September 1916, as well as with Ford's remarkable letters to Conrad that were discussed earlier. Saunders argues that in 'A Day of Battle', Ford

> was already beginning to think through the central problems of *Parade's End*: how is it possible to *see* such a vast panorama as a world war? From what vantage point can the novelist gain a perspective? What hill can he stand up on? How can he avoid being 'always too close or too remote'?
>
> (*WP* 17)

'A Day of Battle' constituted a turning point in Ford's representational impasse: confronting his predicament as a writer allowed him to update his impressionist mode of representation, through fragmentation and defamiliarisation. This development in fact heightened literary impressionism: it strengthened the validity of its methods against the test of war; it furthermore enriched it with the ethical dimension of making the impression of the war present and vivid in the civilians' minds and of paying tribute to the individual over the collective. Aesthetic innovation and inspiration appear to stem directly from Ford's stance as a writer-combatant. Ford's contribution to modernism, as well as the specificity of this contribution within the landscape of the British avant-garde, are inseparable from his involvement in the war.

Notes

1 Besides Saunders's critical biography, see Brasme 2020.
2 For a detailed account of Ford's engagement in the war, see Saunders 1996a, 479–94 and 1996b, 1–60.
3 For reasons of clarity and ease, *War Prose* is referred to as WP in page references throughout this chapter; whenever possible, page references to this collection have been favoured over those of original publications (although these are documented in the bibliography), as *War Prose* is the most widely available and likely source for the current reader.
4 English translation (mine): 'I am presenting these considerations in the form of a letter, my dear... I would have liked to write rather a neat, balanced, thoughtful essay. But I find it impossible to chisel prose these days. "What do you want"—as our Tommies would say—"it is war!" I have spent twenty-five years looking for cadences, hunting for assonances, with a relentless rage, like that of good father Flaubert. But today I only write letters—long, diffuse, banal'.

5 'm'ont remonté le moral': have raised my spirits.
6 My warm thanks go to Max Saunders, who sent me a copy of the original article in French, which is untraceable online.
7 Translation Max Saunders. Original: 'ténèbres de fumée violette' (233) and 'nuages noirâtres' (234).
8 Sic. 'Bien-aise': well-being, comfort.

Bibliography

Primary Sources

Ford, Ford Madox. 'On Impressionism: 1'. *Poetry and Drama* 2 (June 1914a): 167–75.

———. 'On Impressionism: 2'. *Poetry and Drama* 2 (December 1914b): 323–34.

———. 'Literary Portraits—XLVIII. M. Charles-Louis Philippe and "Le Père Perdrix"'. *Outlook* 34 (8 August 1914c): 174–5. Republished in *War Prose* 207–8.

———. 'Literary Portraits—XLIX. A Causerie'. *Outlook* 34 (15 August 1914d): 206–7. Republished in *War Prose* 208.

———. 'Literary Portraits—LI. The Face of Janus'. *Outlook* 34 (29 August 1914e): 70–1. Republished in *War Prose* 208–9.

———. 'Literary Portraits—LIII. The Muse of War'. *Outlook* 34 (12 September 1914f): 334–5. Republished in *War Prose* 209–10.

———. 'Literary Portraits—LXIX. Annus Mirabilis'. *Outlook* 35 (2 January 1915a): 14–5. Republished in *War Prose* 210–1.

———. 'From China to Peru'. *Outlook* 35 (19 June 1915b): 800–1.

———. *Between St. Dennis and St. George: A Sketch of Three Civilisations*. London: Hodder and Stoughton, 1915c.

———. *When Blood Is Their Argument: An Analysis of Prussian Culture*. London: Hodder and Stoughton, 1915d.

———. 'A Day of Battle': 'Arms and the Mind' and 'War and the Mind' (1916a). Republished in *War Prose* 36–48.

———. 'Epilogue' (1916b). Republished in *War Prose* 52–63.

———. Preface. In *Their Lives*. Edited by Violet Hunt. London: Stanley Paul & Co., 1916c. Republished in *War Prose* 189–90.

———. 'Trois Jours de Permission'. *Nation* 19 (30 September 1916d): 817–8. Republished in *War Prose* 49–51.

———. *On Heaven and Poems Written on Active Service*. London: The Bodley Head, 1918a.

———. 'Pon... ti... pri... ith'. *La Revue des Idées* 233–8. Genève: Société générale d'imprimerie, November 1918b. Translated by Max Saunders and published in *War Prose* 30–5.

———. *Joseph Conrad: A Personal Remembrance*. London: Duckworth, 1924.

———. 'Preparedness'. *New York Herald Tribune Books* 29595 (6 November 1927). Published in *War Prose* 69–74.

———. *Letters by Ford Madox Ford*. Edited by Richard M. Ludwig. Princeton: Princeton University Press, 1965.

———. *The Presence of Ford Madox Ford a Memorial Volume of Essays, Poems and Memoirs*. Edited by Sondra Stang. Philadelphia: University of Pennsylvania, 1981.

———. *The Good Soldier*. New York and London: Norton, 1995. First published in 1915.

———. *No Enemy*. Edited by Paul Skinner. Manchester: Carcanet, 2002. First published in 1929.

———. *It Was the Nightingale*. Edited by John Coyle. Manchester: Carcanet, 2007. First published in 1934.
———. *Some Do Not ...*. Edited by Max Saunders. Manchester: Carcanet, 2010. First published in 1924.
———. *Last Post*. Edited by Paul Skinner. Manchester: Carcanet, 2011a. First published in 1928.
———. *A Man Could Stand Up—*. Edited by Sara Haslam. Manchester: Carcanet, 2011b. First published in 1926.
———. *No More Parades*. Edited by Joseph Wiesenfarth. Manchester: Carcanet, 2011c. First published in 1925.
———. *The Correspondence of Ford Madox Ford and Stella Bowen*. Edited by Sondra Stang, and Karen Cochran. Bloomington: Indiana University Press, 1992.
———. *Selected Poems*. Edited by Max Saunders. Manchester: Carcanet, 1997.
———. *War Prose*. Edited by Max Saunders. Manchester: Carcanet, 1999.
Sassoon, Siegfried. *Diaries, 1915–1918*. Edited by Rupert Hart-Davis. London: Faber and Faber, 1983.
Sinclair, May. 'Chauffeurs at the Front'. *The New Statesman* 3, no. 90 (26 December 1914): 295–7.
Wordsworth, Jonathan, and Samuel Taylor Coleridge. *Lyrical Ballads*. Oxford: Oxford World's Classics, 2013.

Secondary Sources

Adorno, Theodor W. *Problems of Moral Philosophy*. Stanford: Stanford University Press, 2001.
Berrahou, Zineb. 'La Grande Guerre de Ford Madox Ford: de l'histoire à la fiction'. PhD thesis Université Paul-Valéry Montpellier 3, 2016, https://www.theses.fr/2016MON30057.
Blanchot, Maurice. *L'Écriture du désastre*. Paris: Gallimard, 1980.
Bradbury, Malcolm. 'Introduction'. In Ford Madox Ford, *Parade's End*. London: Everyman's Library, 1992.
Brasme, Isabelle. 'Towards an Ethics of Alterity: The Shattered Mirror of Identity in Ford Madox Ford's *Parade's End*'. In *Ethics of Alterity, Confrontation and Responsibility in 19th- to 21st-century British Literature*. Edited by Jean-Michel Ganteau, and Christine Reynier, 97–106. Montpellier: Presses Universitaires de la Méditerranée, 2013.
———. 'Ford Madox Ford et le traumatisme de la Grande Guerre: vers une réappropriation de l'écriture'. In *Les Artistes et la guerre*. Edited by Isabelle Brasme, 60–70. Paris: Houdiard, 2017.
———, ed. *Homo Duplex: Ford Madox Ford's Experience and Aesthetics of Alterity*. Montpellier: Presses Universitaires de La Méditerranée, 2020.
Butler, Judith. *Giving an Account of Oneself*. New York: Fordham University Press, 2005.
Chantler, Ashley, and Rob Hawkes, eds. *War and the Mind: Ford Madox Ford, Parade's End, and Psychology*. Edinburgh: Edinburgh University Press, 2014.
Colombino, Laura. *Ford Madox Ford: Vision, Visuality and Writing*. Bern: Peter Lang, 2008.
Cook, Cornelia. 'Constructions and Reconstructions: *No Enemy*'. In *Ford Madox Ford's Modernity*. Edited by Robert Hampson, and Max Saunders, 191–205. Amsterdam: Rodopi, 2003.
Das, Santanu. *Touch and Intimacy in First World War Literature*. Cambridge: Cambridge University Press, 2005.

Frayn, Andrew. '"This Battle Was not Over": *Parade's End* as a Transitional Text in the Development of "Disenchanted" First World War Literature'. In *Ford Madox Ford: Literary Networks and Cultural Transformations*. Edited by Andrzej Gasiorek, and Daniel Moore, 201–16. Amsterdam: Rodopi, 2008.

———. *Writing Disenchantment: British First World War Prose, 1914–30*. Manchester: Manchester University Press, 2014.

———. 'Ford and the First World War'. In *The Routledge Research Companion to Ford Madox Ford*. Edited By Sara Haslam, Laura Colombino, and Seamus O'Malley, 179–92. London: Routledge, 2019.

———. '"It was in that way that we used to talk, in July, 1914, of Armageddon": Wartime in Ford Madox Ford's *Parade's End* Tetralogy'. In *Literature and Modern Time*. Edited by Trish Ferguson, 25–49. Basingstoke: Palgrave Macmillan, 2020.

Haslam, Sara, Laura Colombino, and Seamus O'Malley, eds. *The Routledge Research Companion to Ford Madox Ford*. London: Routledge, 2019.

Hawkes, Rob. *Ford Madox Ford and the Misfit Moderns: Edwardian Fiction and the First World War*. Basingstoke: Palgrave Macmillan, 2012.

Hynes, Michael. 'Three Dedicatory Letters to *Parade's End*'. *Modern Fiction Studies* 16, no. 4 (Winter 1970–71): 515–528.

———. 'The Genre of *No Enemy*'. *Antaeus* 56 (Spring 1986): 125–42.

———. *A War Imagined. The First World War and English Culture*. London: The Bodley Head, 1990.

Larabee, Mark Douglas. *Front Lines of Modernism Remapping the Great War in British Fiction*. New York: Palgrave Macmillan, 2011.

Levinas, Emmanuel. *Ethics and Infinity: Conversations with Philippe Nemo*. Translated by Richard A. Cohen. Pittsburgh: Duquesne UP, 1985.

———. *Totality and Infinity: An Essay on Exteriority*. Translated by Alphonso Lingis. Dordrecht: Kluwer Academic, 1991.

———. *Alterity & Transcendence*. Translated by Michael B. Smith. New York: Columbia University Press, 1999.

Lodge, David. *The Modes of Modern Writing: Metaphor, Metonymy, and the Typology of Modern Literature*. London: Bloomsbury Academic, 2015.

Longenbach, James. 'Ford Madox Ford: The Novelist as Historian'. *The Princeton University Library Chronicle* 45, no. 2 (1984): 150–66, https://doi.org/10.2307/26402210.

Munton, Alan. 'The Insane Subject: Ford and Wyndham Lewis in the War and Post-War'. In *Ford Madox Ford: Literary Networks and Cultural Transformations*. Edited by Andrzej Gasiorek, and Daniel Moore, 105–30. Amsterdam: Rodopi, 2008.

Ross, Stephen, ed. *Modernism and Theory: A Critical Debate*. London and New York: Routledge, 2009.

———. 'Modernist Ethics, Critique, and Utopia'. In *Ethics of Alterity, Confrontation and Responsibility in 19th- to 21st-Century British Literature*. Edited by Jean-Michel Ganteau, and Christine Reynier, 49–63. Montpellier: Presse Universitaires de la Méditerranée, 2013.

Rummel, Andrea. 'Personal Landscape: Ford Madox Ford, War, and the Mind'. In *History, Memory and Nostalgia in Literature and Culture*. Edited by Regina Rudaitytė, 54–64. Newcastle upon Tyne, UK: Cambridge Scholars Publishing, 2018.

Saunders, Max. *Ford Madox Ford: A Dual Life. Volume 1: The World before the War*. Oxford: Oxford University Press, 1996a.

———. *Ford Madox Ford: A Dual Life. Volume 2: The After-War World*. Oxford: Oxford University Press, 1996b.

———. Introduction to *War Prose*. Edited by Max Saunders, 1–20. Manchester: Carcanet, 1999.

Scarry, Elaine. *The Body in Pain*. Oxford: Oxford University Press, 1985.

Sorum, Eve. 'Empathy, Trauma, and the Space of War in *Parade's End*'. In *War and the Mind: Ford Madox Ford, Parade's End, and Psychology*. Edited by Ashley Chantler, and Rob Hawkes, 50–62. Edinburgh: Edinburgh University Press, 2014.

Steffens, Karolyn. 'Impressionism and Psychoanalytic Trauma Theory'. *War and the Mind: Ford Madox Ford, Parade's End, and Psychology*. Edited by Ashley Chantler, and Rob Hawkes, 35–49. Edinburgh: Edinburgh University Press, 2014.

2 'The Fantastic Dislocation of War'
May Sinclair's Aporetic War Chronicle[1]

Introduction

Contending that the First World War bore a considerable effect on May Sinclair's life, philosophy and writing may appear an astonishing claim since Sinclair was born in 1863 and was therefore 51 when the war broke out. Not only does her date of birth suggest that her cultural and intellectual formation was firmly positioned in the Victorian era and that her literary career and aesthetic choices would have been solidly established by 1914, but her age also implies that Sinclair, as a middle-aged woman, could claim no possible first-hand role on the front. Yet on 28 February 1915, Sinclair confided to fellow novelist Arthur Adcock the extent to which her experience of the war in the autumn of 1914 changed her: 'I feel as if I had never lived, with any intensity, before I went out to [the war] in the autumn' (qtd in Raitt 2000, 148). In her biography of the author, Suzanne Raitt corroborates Sinclair's sentiment:

> In her fiction and non-fiction the war figures both as a climactic and mystical experience of personal autonomy, and as a crucial development of the modern world from which she was prematurely and unjustly excluded.
> (Raitt 2000, 148)

Sinclair's experience of the First World War was nevertheless fraught with ambivalence and paradoxes, and so is the text that resulted most immediately from this experience, *A Journal of Impressions in Belgium*. The present chapter thus centres on Sinclair's account of her brief experience in invaded Belgium during the siege and fall of Antwerp, with a view to determine its impact on her sense of herself and the consequences on her writing.

When the war broke out, Sinclair was a well-known, prolific and respected novelist; this position was in fact used as a selling point in the frontispiece of the first edition by Macmillan, which presents Sinclair as 'Author of "The Three Sisters", "The Return of the Prodigal", etc.'. As Raitt emphasises, 'In 1914 she was an independently wealthy woman whose money gave her a sense of power and who was determined not to be sidelined' (Raitt 1997, 71). Her fame and success, granting her financial security, is precisely what allowed her to

DOI: 10.4324/9781003270812-3

circumvent the 'red tape' that Sinclair addressed in the eponymous short story published in November 1914 and to join the Ambulance Corps set up by Hector Munro, one of the directors of the Medico-Psychological Clinic, which arrived in Belgium in late September 1914. Raitt hypothesises that the reason for Sinclair being accepted into the Corps despite her lack of qualifications must have been her significant financial contribution to the expedition. Sinclair was to be treasurer, secretary and reporter for the Corps, with a view to raising funds from her articles in the press, as she relates at the beginning of the *Journal*:

> They've called me the Secretary and Reporter, which sounds very fine, and I am to keep the accounts (Heaven help them!) and write the Commandant's reports, and toss off articles for the daily papers, to make a little money for the Corps.[2]
>
> (4)

Yet by the end of the 18 days that she spent in Belgium, Sinclair had performed none of those tasks satisfactorily, to her own acute embarrassment. On the nineteenth day of her stay, she was sent back to England, on the ostensible purpose of raising more funds for the Corps, which was in financial straits ('the funds remaining in the leather purse-belt were hardly enough to keep the Ambulance going for another week' [272]), but she was never allowed to go back to invaded Belgium. *A Journal of Impressions* was composed in the next few months, as Sinclair was still reeling from the burning humiliation and regret that this rebuff occasioned. The basis for the *Journal* was the 'Day-Book of Dr Hector Munro's Motor Ambulance Corps' that Sinclair kept while in Belgium, but as is made clear by Sinclair herself, the notes she took *in medias res* were amended and augmented once she was back in Britain. The *Journal* was completed in July; three segments appeared in an earlier and slightly different form in the *English Review* in May, June and July 1915; and the volume as a whole was published in September 1915, making it one of the very first women's accounts of the war to be published. The fact that it was published both by Hutchinson in London and Macmillan in New York, in the autumn of 1915, attests to the initial interest in Sinclair's account of her experience.

While the main primary source for this chapter is *A Journal of Impressions*, it has been complemented by its manuscript and typescript versions, as well as by the 'Day-Book of Dr Hector Munro's Motor Ambulance Corps'. In the absence of a currently circulating edition of *A Journal of Impressions*, the edition used in this chapter is the 1915 American edition by Macmillan.[3]

Sinclair's *A Journal of Impressions* has been respected by several major authors and critics as an important document of the war seen through a woman's gaze. Contemporary writer Rebecca West praised the vividness of Sinclair's depiction: '[B]y her mysterious subterranean methods she makes one ache for Belgium' (West 305–6). At the other end of the 20th century, Samuel Hynes also saluted Sinclair's *Journal* as 'brilliant, moving, and convincing' (Hynes 1990,

94), and as one of the few that rendered 'the reality of a woman's war' (95). Most importantly, Hynes considered that the book 'deserves to be included among the truth-telling narratives of the war, of which all the others were written by soldiers' (95). Hynes's exclusion of all other women's narratives from this canon is all the more striking, as Sinclair's text, as we shall realise, makes no claim for accuracy. Conversely, some of the contemporary press reviews regretted the *Journal*'s overly—and overtly—personal note.[4] In the same vein, Claire Tylee has more recently disparaged *A Journal of Impressions* as appearing 'self-indulgen[t], narcissistic and myopic' to the modern reader, although she acknowledges the genuineness of feeling that permeates Sinclair's account (Tylee 30). The reason for such contrasted views can be explained by the deep-seated contradictory character of Sinclair's text, which will be at the core of the present study.

Since the 1990s, criticism addressing the *Journal* has mostly centred either on the issues of female presence and representation in the context of war or on the relationship between the text and Sinclair's interests in contemporary thinking on psychology and philosophy, particularly idealism. Both angles have brought useful insight into the text, shedding light on topics that were indeed crucial for Sinclair and that informed all of her fictional and nonfictional work. Much of the critical work addressing *A Journal of Impressions* has highlighted Sinclair's precarious and uncomfortable position as a middle-aged woman devoid of any nurse training, yet determined to go to the front and be useful in some manner or other. Sara Prieto thus notes that Sinclair was 'among the few civilian women who entered the war zone without being involved in nursing duties' (Prieto 173). Sinclair's predicament is thus tied to her gender, as is made repeatedly clear by Sinclair herself in the *Journal*. In her chapter 'Contagious Ecstasy' from *Women's Fiction and the Great War*, Raitt thus remarks:

> Women like May Sinclair [...] struggled to make a place for themselves in a world that was preoccupied with the vulnerability of young men, rather than of older women. Her war journals reveal in painful and awkward detail the shame of a middle-aged woman who sees in middle age her last chance at life. [...] [F]emininity is repeatedly experienced and represented as shame at times of social and cultural crisis.
>
> (Raitt 1997, 65–6)

Laurel Forster likewise argues,

> Finding a mode of expression or appropriate tone which could encompass a sense of being protected by the masculine war effort as well as describing the authority of female war work, which also adhered to conventions of propaganda, masculine gallantry and the new feminism proved a challenge to many a fine female writer.
>
> (Forster 231)

Addressing this discomfort, Geneviève Brassard contends that Sinclair's *Journal* is an act of defiance against the gendered roles of the war that excluded middle-aged women: her narrative, she argues,

> express[es] a subtle but subversive resistance to society's expectations for unmarried women of a certain age, namely that they would support the troops at home in traditionally feminine occupations. By travelling to the front as chronicler and philanthropist, Sinclair prove[s] that this war is also the business of women.
>
> (Brassard 3)

The other dual area predominantly addressed by scholarship concerns psychology and philosophy. Raitt's 'Contagious Ecstasy' astutely delineates what she terms the 'perversity' of women's consciousness of the war that was pinpointed by Sinclair: '[T]he association of humiliation with megalomania, and the vicarious sexualized enjoyment of masculine aggression' (Raitt 1997, 67). In his essay 'Clouds and Power: May Sinclair's War' (2014), Luke Thurston engages in a detailed psychoanalytical reading of the *Journal*, in which he also addresses the paradigm of the 'vortex' that is at the core of Sinclair's most notable war novel, *The Tree of Heaven* (1917a), and which he demonstrates is at work in Sinclair's 'libidinal investment in the war as a ritual performance of authenticity' (Thurston 19). In 'La Guerre et le dialogue discursif' ('War and Discursive Dialogue', 2017), Leslie de Bont uses her expertise on Sinclair's philosophical and psychological writing to elucidate Sinclair's handling of the war experience and foregrounds the way in which Sinclair's various areas of interest and knowledge dialogue in the *Journal*:

> The war allows Sinclair to bring modes of discourse (fiction, poetry, philosophical and psychoanalytical essays, critical articles, diaries, etc.) into dialogue, in the sense defined by Bakhtin, to combine them within the same text, in order to produce a work that can truly account for the unprecedented character of the First World War.[5]
>
> (de Bont 2017, 43–4)

Research on *A Journal of Impressions* is also indebted to Christine Battersby for elucidating Sinclair's philosophical influences. Because this chapter concentrates on Sinclair's aesthetic choices, I have opted not to mention at length the philosophical underpinnings of her war account; yet they stand as an indispensable background to the current study. Christine Battersby delivered an enlightening talk on the influence of Schopenhauer on Sinclair's *Journal* during the conference *Networking May Sinclair* organised by Leslie de Bont, Florence Marie and myself in June 2021. At the time of writing this chapter, she is also finishing a chapter that includes an investigation of Schopenhauer's influence on Sinclair, to be published in *The Palgrave Handbook of German Idealism and Feminist Philosophy*, 'Schopenhauer's Metaphysics and Ethics: Mapping Influences and Congruities with Feminist Philosophers'.

Building from these perspectives, this chapter examines the textual detail of *A Journal of Impressions* to consider and assert its productive contradictions. Sinclair's *Journal* exposes itself as unidentifiable, both as a literary object and a testament of the First World War. This intricate and unstable text makes for an arduous and baffling reading experience, which creates in the reader an inkling of Sinclair's own deeply uncomfortable stance in Belgium at war. The one consistent element of this account, it can be argued, is its ambivalence. The narrative's unremitting negativity, where Sinclair's *hubris, hamartia* and ultimate eviction from the stage of war are heralded in the dedicatory poem in a manner reminiscent of the prologue of a Greek tragedy, is however undercut by irony and humour. I posit that the mode that best encapsulates Sinclair's chronicle of her experience is the carnivalesque. Despite its deep unconventionality, the *Journal* successfully captures the unofficial 'high comedy of disaster' (159) inherent in many scenes of war, while rendering obliquely the sense of chaos and horror that the war produced. Despite the generally accepted view of Sinclair's status as marginal and fragile on the avant-garde scene, her account succeeds not as a war journal, but as a fascinating exercise in literary impressionism and modernist experimentation.

A War Journal?

Generic Instability

It may come as no surprise that where literary testimonies of the First World War are concerned, Sinclair's war journal has been seldom studied outside the field of specific criticism on Sinclair. Both its form and content go against the grain of conventional war writing, especially that published during the war. *A Journal of Impressions* is indeed a narrative of deconstruction(s). The title, to start with, breaks any expectation of a conventional war journal, which may repel the prospective reader in search of a truthful, first-hand account of the war. The indeterminacy of the first word, the indefinite 'a', suggests that this book is to be read as but one negligible account among countless others; this is sustained by the word 'impressions', which introduces the paradigms of subjectivity and unreliability, and does nothing to alleviate the reader's perplexity. Any expected mention of the war is replaced by the mere presence of a geographical place—Belgium. Taken out of context, the volume may easily be confused for a travelling diary, which may contribute even further to the reader's confusion. The one definite word of the title, 'journal', soon turns out to be misleading. Sinclair's text indeed defies the codes of the personal journal. Where the diary is traditionally used as a tool towards self-discovery and construction, as is the case for Sassoon's war diaries, Sinclair's 'journal' appears to be constantly bent on denigrating its own author and on invalidating her aims, aspirations and identity. Even the text's claim as a journal is mitigated by the writing process, as is made transparent as early as the introduction by the author herself, who comments on and justifies the gap between the time when events unfolded and the time when she actually wrote about them:

> I was always behindhand with my Journal—a week behind with the first day of the seventeen, four months behind with the last.
>
> This was inevitable. For in the last week of the Siege of Antwerp, when the wounded were being brought into Ghent by hundreds, and when the fighting came closer and closer to the city, and at the end, when the Germans were driving you from Ghent to Bruges, and from Bruges to Ostend and from Ostend to Dunkirk, you could not sit down to write your impressions, even if you were cold-blooded enough to want to. It was as much as you could do to scribble the merest note of what happened in your Day-Book.
>
> ('Introduction', n.p., par. 2–3)

This passage also introduces an important distinction between two texts. Sinclair's immediate account of her time in Belgium was recorded in her 'Day-Book', in a quick, often telegraphic style. This daybook is ostensibly that of the Ambulance Corps: Sinclair has entitled it rather solemnly 'Day-Book of Dr Hector Munro's Motor Ambulance Corps', yet it centres unequivocally on Sinclair's experience. The *Journal of Impressions* was composed more leisurely, at an interval that went from a few days to several months from the days that it chronicles, and was therefore written partly in Belgium and partly in England. Its title and introduction displace the focus from documenting the Ambulance Corps' activities to recording Sinclair's personal response to her experience in Belgium at war. Sinclair's daybook and her journal are thus two clearly different texts. On 6 October—which as we shall realise shortly, turned out to be really the seventh—Sinclair notes in her daybook that she has started writing the *Journal*: 'Wrote Journal up to 26th Sept.' ('Day-Book' MS 9). This is also noted in the *Journal*: 'Wrote "Journal of Impressions" from September 25th to September 26th, 11 A.M.', to which Sinclair adds, 'It's slow work' (141). A footnote in the entry for 10 October likewise establishes that this entry was written in March, 1915: 'I record these details (March 11th, 1915)' (206). Whilst such notes generate a transparency in the writing process, they also destabilise the genre of the *Journal*. The criteria that are established when examining Sassoon's diaries in the next chapter are certainly not met in Sinclair's text. Where Sassoon's diary entries were consistently written on the same day as the events that they recorded, the *Journal* was written at an increasing temporal distance from the days that it chronicles. Sinclair even stresses the inevitable memory loss that these gaps occasion: in the entry for 4 October, where Sinclair mentions having 'no vivid recollection' of passing through besieged Antwerp, a footnote specifies, 'At the time of writing—February 19th, 1915. My Day-Book gives no record of anything but the hospitals we visited' (125). This lack is all the more salient as this visit to Antwerp stands out in the *Journal* as one of the most eventful days from Sinclair's time in Belgium—one that the reader certainly expects her to document in minute detail, given that the yearning for such action is expressed time and again at the beginning of the *Journal*.

A Pervasive Negativity

One of the most arresting traits of the *Journal* is indeed its relentless negativity. The word 'nothing' occurs no less than 94 times in this relatively short tome; negative turns equally abound. The dedication that inaugurates the volume begins with a negation: 'I do not call you comrades' ('Dedication', n. p., l. 1). Likewise, the introduction that follows opens on the stark statement, 'This is a "Journal of Impressions", and nothing more' ('Introduction', n. p., l. 1–2). These 'impressions' are further belittled as being at times 'insubstantial to the last degree' ('Introduction', n. p. par. 2). The introduction is framed with a self-deprecatory, negative description of what it is *not*, paired with positive references to other works that *do* recount the story of the field ambulances:

> For the Solid Facts and the Great Events [the readers] must go to such books as Mr. E. A. Powell's 'Fighting in Flanders', or Mr. Frank Fox's 'The Agony of Belgium', or Dr. H. S. Souttar's 'A Surgeon in Belgium', or 'A Woman's Experiences in the Great War', by Louise Mack.
> ('Introduction', n. p. par. 1)

An echo to this self-critical preamble can be found in the article that Sinclair wrote for *The New Statesman* in December 1914, in which she was asked to talk about the drivers of Munro's Ambulance Corps, but concludes with, 'After all, you cannot "write about the chauffeurs"' (Sinclair 1914a, 296). This article is briefly discussed and set in relation with Ford's writing in the previous chapter.

Opening a piece of war writing with expressions of representational frustration is a trope common to other war narratives, such as Borden's *The Forbidden Zone*, and as examined in the previous chapter, representational aporia informs much of Ford's essays on war. Yet there is a crucial difference where Sinclair's text is concerned. The first and foremost reason for the negativity of Sinclair's war narrative is not her inability to represent what she sees, but her failure to actually witness the war first-hand. The most recurrent theme of the *Journal* is Sinclair's despair at feeling that she is left out of action and missing it all—and 'if you miss it you will have missed reality itself' (69). As she complained to Ezra Pound, her time in Belgium was above all one of 'boredom': 'it is very boring for the Secretary who sees nothing—nothing at all, & does nothing but sit snug in the Flandria Palace' (qtd in Raitt 2000, 155 and Thurston, 21). Among the countless instances of missed opportunities that occur in the text, we may look at Sinclair's long-awaited excursion to Antwerp on 4 October. The episode is but a series of setbacks for both Sinclair and the reader, starting with the date of the entry, which is missing in the daybook's manuscript, with 'Sunday' added on in red ink at a later date (probably as Sinclair was writing the *Journal*). In a footnote to the date inscribed in the *Journal*, Sinclair confesses to being 'puzzled about this date':

> It stands in my ambulance Day-Book as Saturday, 3rd, with a note that the British came into Ghent on their way to Antwerp on the evening of that day. Now I believe there were no British in Antwerp before the evening of Sunday, the 4th […]. I was ill with fever the day after the run into Antwerp, and got behindhand with my Day-Book. So it seems safest to assume that I made a wrong entry and that we went into Antwerp on Sunday […]. Similarly the events that the Day-Book attributes to Monday must have belonged to Tuesday. And if Tuesday's events were really Wednesday's, that clears up a painful doubt I had as to Wednesday, which came into my Day-Book as an empty extra which I couldn't account for in any way. There I was with a day left over and nothing to put into it. And yet Wednesday, the 7th, was the first day of the real siege of Antwerp. On Thursday, the 8th, I started clear.
>
> (114–5)

No less than five consecutive days are thus dated erroneously in the daybook, which creates confusion not only for the reader but for Sinclair herself, as the daybook is her main source of information for the *Journal*. The aim of keeping a daybook—especially for the secretary of an Ambulance Corps who was expressly entrusted with this task, and whose legitimacy in Belgium was conditional on such work—is to retain a faithful record of events, complete with accurate dates. Here this very aim turns out to be defeated. This failure is all the more salient as it concerns one of the rare entries in Sinclair's *Journal* where something is actually going on.

Such an inauspicious beginning only confirms the endlessly anticlimactic mode that prevails in this entry. Going to Antwerp, where the main events were taking place at the time, should have been sensed as momentous by Sinclair, as this was her chance at last of getting closer to the centre of action: Sinclair had hitherto been left behind as she was neither a nurse nor an ambulance driver. It does appear initially that Sinclair attempts to mark the significance of the occasion as she muses, 'I shall see the siege of Antwerp and hear the guns that were brought up from Namur'. The narration of the excursion starts with the portentous mention of 'a vision, heavenly, but impalpable, aerial, indistinct, of the Greatest Possible Danger' (115), laden with lofty adjectives and capitalised words. Yet, although she was anticipating exaltation when waiting hopelessly for such action in the previous pages of the *Journal*, Sinclair ends up being curiously apathetic when she does set out: '[T]he odd thing is that there is no excitement at all'. As in Borden's 'Moonlight', where 'the other world was a dream' and where 'there is […] nothing left in the world but War' (Borden 57–8), Sinclair senses that the war is now the norm: '[T]he really incredible things are the things that existed and happened before the War' (115). As a result, her job as a war reporter no longer appears as thrilling: 'I have been a War Correspondent all my life—*blasée* with battles' (116). Such a statement is astonishing since Sinclair has until then never been close to action. Yet this stance itself is in turn undermined by Sinclair's actual experience—or lack thereof—of the war: the landscape is beautiful and serene, as is also underlined in the daybook's manuscript: 'Absolutely peaceful country as far as St Nicholas' ('Day-Book' MS 6), the choice of adjective being particularly ironic. When Sinclair anticipates bombardment and danger, the incongruous 'peaceful' appears again, this time in the *Journal*: 'Every minute you look for the flight of the shells across the grey […]. But the grey is utterly peaceful' (123). The final let-down occurs then, the inverted climax in this long series of disillusions, through a conversation between an outraged Sinclair and a flippant Munro:

> And at last you turn in a righteous indignation and say: 'Where is the bombardment?'
> The bombardment is at the outer forts.
> And where are the forts, then? (You see no forts.)
> The outer forts? Oh, the outer forts are thirty kilometres away.
> No. Not there. To your right.
> And you, who thought you would have died rather than see the siege of Antwerp, are dumb with disgust. Your heart swells with a holy and incorruptible resentment of the sheer levity of the Commandant.
> A pretty thing—to bring a War Correspondent out to see a bombardment when there isn't any bombardment, or when all there ever was is a hundred—well then, *thirty* kilometres away.
>
> (123–4)

This seemingly trifling exchange is packed with undermining devices, to the point that these few lines may appear as epitomising the *Journal*'s strategy of demystification. Sinclair's outrage, highlighted by the quotation marks that frame her first question, is defused by the absence of direct speech markers in the dialogue that follows, an absence that creates confusion and compels the reader to pause in order to assess who is talking. This confusion is deepened by the fact that the expected use of the first person is replaced by second-person narrative where Sinclair refers to herself: '(you see no forts)', the parentheses acting as a further distancing device. This process of misdirection diverts our focus from Sinclair's ire and generates in the reader a disorientation that echoes that felt by Sinclair, who is unable to read the landscape: 'No. Not there. To your right'. In the same vein, Sinclair's professed 'righteous indignation' is undercut by the use of hyperbole, as it turns into 'disgust' and 'holy and incorruptible resentment', too excessive to be taken at face value, especially as it is directly followed by the trivial 'a pretty thing' and the explicit correction of yet another hyperbole: 'a hundred—well then, *thirty* kilometres away', with the use of italics further distancing the author's perspective from the voice here rendered. Sinclair in the *Journal* may often be construed as an *alter ego* of Catherine Morland in Jane Austen's *Northanger Abbey*, undergoing a similar series of disappointments from her initial unreasonable expectations when starting a journey away from the habits of home; this passage in particular offers a striking parallelism with the miscarried excursion to Blaize Castle that takes place in chapter

XI, volume I of *Northanger Abbey*. Hector Munro may be likened to John Thorpe, taking the unknowing and naive Sinclair along in his car under false pretences—at least from Sinclair's perspective. In both cases, the fiasco is signalled and emphasised by miscommunication and a dysfunctional conversation. There is, however, a significant difference between Austen's Quixotic character and the protagonist of the *Journal*: where Catherine Morland is just a fictional character in a third-person narrative, treated derisively yet affectionately by an external narrator within an openly comedic structure, Sinclair is talking about her own self, in the sombre and very much *non* fictive context of Europe at war. Her self-professed naivety is set in stark contrast with the events actually unfolding around her, and Sinclair's stance towards herself is judgemental and merciless. The entire narrative is fraught with an undercurrent of self-criticism on the part of Sinclair for her reckless and self-centred behaviour.

Textual Sabotage

The *Journal* indeed reveals two contrasting voices which are both Sinclair's: one that belongs to Sinclair as she experiences the events recounted; the other that belongs to her as she writes up the *Journal*, at a growing temporal distance from her time in Belgium, and that encroaches on the narrative through a recurrent process of narrative metalepsis as defined by Gérard Genette: 'any intrusion by the extradiegetic narrator or narratee into the diegetic universe [...] or the inverse' (Genette 1980, 234–5). Two particular devices allow this second voice to surface, and at best question, but most often openly disparage the first voice. The first device is the presence of question marks between brackets: '[?]', with a typographical distinctiveness. No less than 15 are scattered across the text as beacons of Sinclair's constant self-doubt. These can be found in the *Journal's* manuscript, and have been deliberately left intact in the final publication. The second device, which is much more antagonistic, is the relentless use of footnotes to rectify the text. We have already noted the long, puzzled footnote highlighting the inaccuracies in the dates of the daybook from 3 to 7 October. This is but one of Sinclair's gentler comments: most of the 38 footnotes offer wry corrections to the text. Thus, to the statement 'he looks as if he meant it', is appended this footnote: 'He didn't. People never do mean these things' (107). More tersely, when Sinclair mentions the flow of refugees: 'all the streams seem to flow into Ghent and to meet in the Palais des Fêtes', the footnote corrects: 'This is all wrong. The main stream went as straight as it could for the seacoast—Holland or Ostend' (120). When Sinclair the war correspondent excitedly joins fellow reporters in an endeavour to locate the Belgian batteries on 7 October, Sinclair the narrator provides a castigating footnote: 'I can't think why we weren't all four of us arrested for spies. We hadn't any business to be looking for the position of the Belgian batteries' (149). The most emblematic correction is perhaps that concerning Sinclair's doubts as to hearing the barking of dogs or the firing of machine guns; here is the main text:

> All night there has been a sound of the firing of machine guns [?]. At first it was like the barking, of all the dogs in Belgium. I thought it *was* the dogs of Belgium, till I discovered a deadly rhythm and precision in the barking.
>
> (174)

Sinclair thus belatedly concludes to having heard the noise of war at last. Yet the footnote comes, again disproving this hoped-for significance:

> I'm inclined to think it may have been the dogs of Belgium, after all. I can't think where the guns could have been. Antwerp had fallen. It might have been the bombardment of Melle, though.

This paragraph, along with its footnote, and their several reversals concerning the origin of the noise—fateful war or trivial dogs—encapsulates the spirit of the *Journal* and its author's constantly hesitant stance, concurrently hoping that she is witnessing and recording 'the real thing' and fearing that she is missing it altogether. Here Sinclair is literally unable to grasp the language of the war, as she cannot make sense of its sounds. Sitting beneath the text, the footnotes are wedges driven by Sinclair into her own narrative, visually and figuratively undermining the text's foundation.

As a result of simultaneously bemoaning her uselessness in the war and sternly contradicting her own account, Sinclair continually belittles her contribution to the Corps as an author. When describing the organisation of the Ambulance Corps, she stresses her duties as diminutive:

> Keeping the Corps' accounts only takes two hours and a half [...]. Writing the Day-Book—perhaps half an hour. The Commandant's correspondence, when he has any, and reporting to the British Red Cross Society, when there is anything to report, another half-hour at the outside; and there you have only three and a half hours employed out of the twenty-four, even if I balanced my accounts every day, and I don't.
>
> (68)

Sinclair's other duty is that of reporter, but the main issue, of course, is lacking any content to write about when one isn't permitted near action:

> True that *The Daily Chronicle* promised to take any articles that I might send them from the front, but I haven't written any. You cannot write articles for *The Daily Chronicle* out of nothing; at least I can't.
>
> (68)

Likewise, a few days later, when Sinclair attempts to make herself useful at the *Palais des Fêtes*, yet is not allowed to due to restrictions, she laments,

> Five days in Ghent and not a thing done; not a line written of those brilliant articles (from the Front) which were to bring in money for the Corps. (87)

Besides the series of negations and the frustration rendered through monosyllables, the alliterative parenthesis '(from the Front)' bears much meaning: the proximity to the front is implied as adding value to any article, yet the parentheses act as a visual barrier, signalling Sinclair's exclusion from action.

Sinclair's situation as a writer grows worse as the days unfold, for the lack of content to write about is compounded by her material limitations: she complains that she has 'a bad pen, never enough paper and hardly any ink, and nothing at all to write about' (88), along a hierarchy that ironically implies a superiority of the material. On 8 October, when Sinclair moves to the Hôtel Cecil opposite the hospital, where she hopes she can be of help, she realises with dismay that her room 'hasn't got a table, or any space where a table could stand', concluding, 'I have never seen a room more inappropriate to a secretary and reporter' (162). Whilst her concerns grow increasingly trivial through the focus on material details, these obstacles affect Sinclair's sense of her worth not just as a would-be help in the war but more essentially, as a writer. The successful author, whose renown has played no small part in her managing to join the Ambulance Corps, is unable to perform the task that most defines her in society. Sinclair looks disconsolately at herself from the outside, mentioning herself in the third person: 'the wretched Secretary and Reporter' (87), and further down, in a phrase that encapsulates Sinclair's stance of frustrated helplessness and remoteness from action: 'Nothing for the wretched Secretary to do but to stand there at the far end of the village, looking up the road to Lokeren' (166). The governing mode of Sinclair's journal is, therefore, one of negativity: since it cannot chronicle the war, its main topic is Sinclair's debacle as a war writer. *A Journal of Impressions* ultimately emerges as the negation of a war journal.

'The High Comedy of Disaster': Sinclair's Carnivalesque Narrative

An Oxymoronic Account

Besides such straightforward negativity, the *Journal* incorporates indirect yet efficient devices and distancing modes to undermine the reader's expectations of a war journal. One such mode is that of the constant gap between expectation and reality—more precisely, between the impressions that were anticipated by Sinclair on embarking for Belgium, and those that she actually experiences. Sinclair's text works as a palimpsest, where her would-be, fantasised narrative of the war is conveyed ironically and superimposed with her more sober account of her experience. Literary *topoi* are thus used derisively, in a deflated context that generates incongruous feelings or situations. All the traditional codes of war writing are inverted: where situations of extreme danger and courage may warrant the recourse to literary tropes such as those of chivalry or heroism, here they are used ironically because they apply to situations where not much danger is present. Thus the despair felt by Sinclair and some of her companions at lacking occupation and at being safe in a country at war is rendered in tragic overtones: those of the Corps left behind from expeditions to fetch wounded soldiers feel 'hopeless gloom' (45) and are 'disgusted with their fate' (36). The ironical tragic mode is made increasingly explicit as the narrative goes on, describing those 'overpowered by this tragedy of being left behind' (46). This whole paragraph teems with the lexical field of grief:

> The eighteen-year-old child is threatening to commit suicide or else go home. She regards the two acts as equivalent. Mr. Riley's gloom is now so awful that he will not speak when he is spoken to. [...] Dr. Haynes's melancholy is even more heart-rending, because it is gentle and unexpressed.
>
> (46–7)

The frequent association of incongruous, almost oxymoronic adjectives with the word 'safety' strengthens the discrepancy between the reality of the situation and the 'impressions' that it creates: Sinclair thus feels that she is left in 'intolerable safety' (88), or in 'ignominious safety' (148). The same process is at work when Sinclair describes the landscape, as noted earlier, with the recurrence of word 'peaceful'.

Conversely, those of the Corps who *are* allowed to go near the front to fetch wounded soldiers are described in a strikingly comedic mode. This expedition is likened to a picnic party, presided over by Dr Bird, who looks like 'an enormous cherub':

> Dr. Bird, the young man with the head of an enormous cherub and the hair of a blond baby, hair that *will* fall in a shining lock on his pink forehead, Dr. Bird has an air of boisterous preparation, as if the ambulance were a picnic party and he was responsible for the champagne.
>
> (30)

When the ambulance comes back from the battlefield, the trivial analogy is sustained, with the group 'impossibly safe' (an ironical counterpoint to the 'intolerable' or 'ignominious safety' of those left behind), 'like children after the party, too excited to give a lucid and coherent tale of what they've done' (44). After the next expedition, Sinclair likewise describes the childish elation of Munro at being under fire:

> His face was radiant, almost ecstatic. He was like a child who has rushed in to tell you how ripping the pantomime was.
> 'We've been *under fire!*'
>
> (49)

Another literary trope that recurs through the narrative as a means to undermine the *Journal*'s *Erwartungshorizon* is the frequent use of the mock-heroic style. The chauffeurs are often described in ironically heroic terms, when their 'tumultuous passions' (26) are directed at what Sinclair senses are trifling matters, in contrast with the danger they do constantly experience when driving to and from the front to fetch the wounded. The chauffeurs indeed obstinately resist their orders to drive women into danger. The paradigm of chivalry is used along two simultaneous yet opposite modes: it is made to sound concurrently sincere through the perspective of the chauffeurs and ironical through that of feminist Sinclair. They demonstrate 'mistimed chivalry' (269) when flatly refusing to drive women in their cars. One of them is likened to an improbable yet inflexible Shakespearean figure, 'standing fixed on the steps of the Hospital, looking like Hamlet, Prince of Denmark, in khaki, and flatly refusing to drive his car into Bruges' (269). The topic of what she termed 'mistimed chivalry', with its implications on the gender divide that she felt were outdated, was so aggravating to Sinclair that she explored this tension between male chivalry and an ironical female perspective at more length through the novelistic form of *Tasker Jevons*, published a year later. This aspect is analysed by Leigh Wilson in her PhD thesis and her paper, '"She in Her "Armour" and He in His Coat of Nerves": May Sinclair and the Re-writing of Chivalry' (2003). The conversation about chivalry between Tasker Jevons and Viola, as Jevons resents Viola's presence in Belgium (Sinclair 1915e, 117–8), is directly in the wake of Sinclair's frustration at the chauffeurs' 'chivalry' in the *Journal*.[6]

The ironical use of literary *topoi* is also in full force during the aforementioned expedition to Antwerp, when Sinclair overhears the name 'Achille' and, unable to override her own literary turn of mind, concludes it must be the name of a hero when it is in fact just a password:

> The soldier is confiding some fearful secret to M. C— about somebody called Achille. M. C— bends very low to catch the name, as if he were trying to intercept and conceal it, and when he *has* caught it he assumes an air of superb mystery and gravity and importance. With one gesture he buries the name of Achille in his breast under his uniform. You know that he would die rather than betray the secret of Achille. You decide that Achille is the heroic bearer of dispatches, and that we have secret orders to pick him up somewhere and convey him in safety to Antwerp. You do not grasp the meaning of this pantomime until the third sentry has approached us, and M. C— has stopped for the third time to whisper 'Ach-ille!' behind the cover of his hand, and the third sentry is instantly appeased.
>
> (117)

Besides the deflation of 'Achille' from a heroic figure descended from the *Iliad* to a mere password, the irony also lies in the discrepancy between the soldiers' self-importance as they are passing along the secret password to one another and the fact that Sinclair has actually heard it all. What little Sinclair can witness of the war certainly does not offer the pump that she had anticipated.

The mode that may best describe Sinclair's endeavour throughout the journal is that of the carnivalesque as defined by Mikhail Bakhtin. As noted in the introduction, Leslie de Bont has remarked on the discursive nature of the *Journal* (2017); this discursive nature logically translates into an endless dynamic of inversion. One of the most striking scenes in this respect occurs rather early on, as the Corps breaks down into inappropriate mirth and farcical behaviour reminiscent of the Saturnalia. The passage is so astonishing and rich in literary references that it bears being quoted at length:

> Suddenly [...] madness came upon our mess. The mess-room was no longer a mess-room in a Military Hospital, but a British school-room. Mrs. Torrence [...] was no longer an Arctic explorer, but the wild-western cowboy of British melodrama. She was the first to go mad. One moment she was seated decorously at the Lieutenant's right hand; the next she was strolling round the tables with an air of innocent abstraction, having armed herself in secret with the little hard round rolls supplied by order of the Commandant. Each little roll became a deadly *obus* in her hand. She turned. Her innocent abstraction was intense as she poised herself to aim.
>
> With a shout of laughter Dr. Bird ducked behind the cover of his table-napkin. [...] He is not a Cathedral, but he suffered bombardment all the same. She got his range with a roll. She landed her shell in the very centre of his waistcoat.
>
> Her madness entered into Dr. Bird. He replied with a spirited fire which fell wide of her and battered the mess-room door. The orderlies retreated for shelter into the vestibule beyond. Jean was the first to penetrate the line of fire. Max followed him.
>
> (82–3)

The staggering inappropriateness of the scene resides in the fact that the company is not merely having fun, but actually playing at war. In a supreme irony, this is in fact the closest that Sinclair ever gets to a battle: and she does not miss her one chance at penning a description that matches the countless descriptions of battle that she would have read in the press of the time, with the mention of all the expected terms, such as '*obus*', 'bombardment', 'range', 'shell' or 'line of fire'. References to theatricality and to comedy become increasingly explicit:

> With the entrance of Prosper Panne the mess-room became a scene at the *Folies Bergères*. There was Mrs. Torrence, *première comédienne*, in the costume of a wild-western cowboy; there was the young Lieutenant himself, looking like a stage-lieutenant in the dark-green uniform of the Belgian Motor Cyclist Corps; and there was Prosper Panne. He began by picking up Mrs. Torrence's brown leather motor glove with its huge gauntlet, and examining it with the deliciously foolish bewilderment of the accomplished clown. After one or two failures, brilliantly improvised, he fixed it firmly on his head. [...] Out of his round, soft, putty-coloured face he made fifteen other

faces in rapid succession, all incomparably absurd. He lit a cigarette and held it between his lower lip and his chin. The effect was of a miraculous transformation of those features, in which his upper lip disappeared altogether, his lower lip took on its functions, while his chin ceased to be a chin and became a lower lip. With this achievement Prosper Panne had his audience in the hollow of his hands. He could do what he liked with it. He did. [...]

Flushed with success, Max rose to his top-notch. Moving slowly towards the open door (centre) with his back to his audience and his head turned towards it over his left shoulder, by some extraordinary dislocation of his hip-joints, he achieved the immemorial salutation of the *Folies Bergères*— the last faint survival of the Old Athenian Comedy.

Up till now Jean had affected to ignore the performance of his colleague. But under this supreme provocation he yielded to the Aristophanic impulse, and—*exit* Max in the approved manner of the *Folies Bergères*.

(83–5)

The description moves from the generic description of a comical scene when Mrs Torrence 'strifes' Dr Bird, to an ever-deepening sustained metaphor, going back all the way to the roots of European theatre with the reference to Athenian comedy and the 'Aristophanic impulse'. Although they may seem to describe an exceptional scene within the *Journal*, these masterful pages probably expose best the comedic potential that permeates the *Journal*.

Laughter at War

While this aspect has been the object of little to no interest in scholarship on the *Journal of Impressions*, comedy is quintessential to the peculiar quality of Sinclair's text. The discordant note that the scene brings to our expectation of a war journal may call to mind Herbert Spencer's definition of laughter in 'Physiology of Laughter':

> [L]aughter naturally results only when consciousness is unawares transferred from great things to small—only when there is what we call a *descending* incongruity.
>
> (Spencer 400, emphasis his)

In investigating the conditions for laughter, Spencer—whose work was of much interest to Sinclair—emphasises a downward dynamic associated with incongruity. Both paradigms have already emerged as fundamental features of the *Journal* in the present study and now appear inseparable from comicality.

The comical mode in the *Journal* also and more specifically seems to borrow from, or at least to largely correspond to, Henri Bergson's analysis of the comic. The mechanisms of comicality as outlined by Bergson in *Laughter* (1900) indeed often come to mind when perusing Sinclair's text. While I wasn't able to establish whether Sinclair commented privately on Bergson's *Laughter*, it is highly probable that she had read it attentively, given her profound interest in Bergson's work. A number of passages in the *Journal* display a comical quality that matches some of the categories outlined by Bergson in *Laughter*. Thus some scenes make their participants—Sinclair included—appear like clowns in a pantomime, as when stretcher bearers refuse to continue carrying a wounded soldier and Sinclair pretends to pick up the stretcher on her own:

> Then, to my horror, the bearers dumped him down on the paving-stones. They said he was much too heavy. [...] [T]he bearers stood stolidly in the middle of the road and mopped their faces and puffed. The situation began to feel as absurd and as terrible as a nightmare.
> So I grabbed one end of the stretcher and said I'd carry it myself. I said I wasn't very strong, and perhaps I couldn't carry it, but anyhow I'd try.
> They picked it up at once then, and went off at a good swinging trot over the paving-stones that jolted my poor Flamand most horribly.
> (170–1)

Several ingredients of the comic as defined by Bergson are here at work: firstly, the emphasis on physical over moral aspects: the bearers 'mopp[ing] their faces and puff[ing]', and Sinclair—who was a small woman, and emphasises her not being 'very strong'—pretending to carry the stretcher on her own. This corresponds to Bergson's 'law' that '*Any incident is comic that calls our attention to the physical in a person, when it is the moral side that is concerned*' (Bergson 50–1; Bergson uses italics to highlight the various 'laws' and 'formulas' of the comic that are interspersed in his text). Secondly, the scene, with Sinclair attempting to play the part of a stretcher bearer, and the latter being turned into mere onlookers, corresponds to the logic of inversion which Bergson asserts is another trigger for laughter: 'Picture to yourself certain characters in a certain situation: if you reverse the situation and invert the roles, you obtain a comic scene' (Bergson 94). Lastly, the immediateness of the bearers' taking up the stretcher again constitutes a mechanical gesture that matches Bergson's famous definition of '[s]omething mechanical encrusted on the living' (Bergson 37). More largely, here, physical gestures take over action, which corresponds to the following formula: '*instead of concentrating our attention on actions, comedy directs it rather to gestures*' (Bergson 145).

Among several similar scenes, one in particular is strongly redolent of the clownesque, yet with an added, darker twist to the perspective:

> It seemed ages before the merry little *infirmier* came back with Russell's clothes. And when he did come he brought socks that were too tight, and went back and brought socks that were too large, and a shirt that was too tight and trousers that were too long. Then he went back, eager as ever, and brought drawers that were too tight, and more trousers that were too short. He brought boots that were too large and boots that were too tight; and he had to be sent back again for slippers. Last of all he brought a shirt which

> made Russell smile and mutter something about being dressed in all the colours of the rainbow; and a black cutaway morning coat, and a variety of hats, all too small for Russell.
>
> (177–8)

Bergson's analysis of comical repetition comes to mind: 'Wherever there is repetition or complete similarity, we always suspect some mechanism at work behind the living' (34), along with the reference to clownish clothing, either too small or too large, and in jarring colours. To today's reader, this scene may even evoke the Beckettian absurd, with shoes that are either too large or too tight, as for Estragon in *Waiting for Godot*. Yet this seemingly light-hearted scene is split into two moments that frame Sinclair's realisation that another wounded is in much poorer condition than was initially diagnosed:

> It struck me that Cameron's head must be smashed in on the right side and that some pressure on his brain was causing paralysis. [...] The Belgian doctor found that Cameron's head *was* smashed in on the right side, and that there was pressure on his brain, causing paralysis in his left arm.
>
> (177)

Laughter thus coexists seamlessly with horror in Sinclair's *Journal*, as she attempts to offer a totalising account of her experience. In *Gay Science*, Nietzsche argues that laughter is one of the conditions for knowledge; in a twist from Spinoza's motto in *Tractatus Politicus*, who recommended: '*non ridere, non lugere, neque detestari, sed intelligere*', i.e. 'not to laugh, not to lament, not to curse, but to understand', Nietzsche considers instead,

> What else is this *intelligere* than the form in which we come to feel the other three at once? One result of the different and mutually opposed desires to laugh, lament, and curse?
>
> (Nietzsche 1974, 261)

Laughter is endowed with a critical and demystifying function in the *Journal* that aims to defuse any grandiloquence and eschew any departure from Sinclair's actual experience, where despair, horror and comicality were constantly intertwined.

Besides its critical function, laughter has an aesthetic dimension that serves to reveal the essential humanity of the *Journal*'s protagonists. Bergson thus states,

> There is something esthetic [sic] about [laughter], since the comic comes into being just when society and the individual, freed from the worry of self-preservation, begin to regard themselves as works of art.
>
> (Bergson 20)

The comical mode is a way for Sinclair to outline her experience; literally, it is used to provide a representational frame to her account that signals the external gaze of the onlooker: that of Sinclair the secretary and reporter looking at others, that of Sinclair the author looking at herself and rewriting the initial 'Day-Book' into the *Journal*, and, inevitably, that of the reader of said *Journal*. The three scenes here explored—the makeshift attack in the mess-room, the pantomime with the stretcher bearers, and the dressing-up of a soldier in clownish attire—all display a strong theatricality. Such theatricality establishes an additional frame in the representation that allows critical distance but also compels us to look at the literariness of such descriptions.

A Dialogic Dynamic

I have digressed from the notion of the carnivalesque to explore more largely the comedic dimension of Sinclair's war account; I now propose to go back and investigate more precisely the dynamic of inversion that is everywhere at work in the *Journal*. It is worth noting that towards the end of the *Journal*, when the hospital is evacuated, and Cameron, the man wounded in the head, is carried away, Sinclair cannot bear to see his bare feet and covers them with her coat: 'It is anguish to see those thin white feet on the stone; I take off my coat and put it under them' (241): yet another sartorial detail, though in a wholly opposite mode from previously, here redolent of the parable of the Good Samaritan. Likewise, the scene in the mess-room emulating a bombardment finds its counterpart in the flippant attitude to the war of various British non-combatants in Sinclair's text. The war correspondent whom Sinclair refers to as 'Mr L.' thus treats the war as a British show:

> On our way, while we were about it, he said, we might as well stop and have a look at the Belgian batteries at work—as if he had said we might as well stop at Olympia and have a look at the Motor Show on our way to Richmond. (148)

Conversely, Ghent's quintessential festive place, the *Palais des Fêtes*—which, significantly, is also likened to the Olympia (53), is turned into a place of disconsolation, as it becomes a refugee centre. The *Palais des Fêtes* is the archetypal carnivalesque *locus* in Sinclair's narrative, not only because its usage is inverted but also because it hosts indiscriminately the highest and the lowest of Ghent's society:

> The rigidly righteous *bourgeoise* lies in the straw breast to breast with the harlot of the village slum, and her innocent daughter back to back with the parish drunkard. Nothing matters. Nothing will ever matter any more. (54)

It is worth noting that this reversal, or here levelling of values, leads to further expressions of absurdity. The words 'absurd' and 'absurdity' recur no less than 19 times in the narrative. The main philosophical source regarding the absurd for Sinclair would have been Schopenhauer, for whom the absurd is a mode of the anti-sublime. Christine Battersby reminds us that 'Schopenhauer had argued that tragedy—above all the other types of poetic art—can best generate the experience of the "sublime", and take man "beyond" the illusions of the phenomenal world' (Battersby 2013, n. p., par. 16). This is confirmed by Schopenhauer's disciple, Nietzsche, who defines art in *The Birth of Tragedy* as a 'saving sorceress', alone able to heal humanity from the absurd:

> She alone knows how to turn these nauseous thoughts about the horror or absurdity of existence into notions with which one can live: these are the sublime [*das Erhabene*] as the artistic taming [*Bändigung*] of the horrible, and the comic [*das Komische*] as the artistic discharge [*Entladung*] of the nausea of absurdity.
> (Nietzsche 2000, 60, qtd in Battersby 2013)

In Sinclair's narrative, the anti-sublime works as an aesthetic means of coming to terms with the feeling of absurdity. Yet tragicality and comicality coexist in a constant dialectics. Sinclair's expression of and strategies of coping with absurdity are inseparable from a refusal of embracing the tragic mode exclusively or without ironical distance. At the micro-textual level, this is rendered through the recurring device of the oxymoron. The following example epitomises the overarching tone of the *Journal*:

> I found all that was left of a Hendon bus, in the charge of two British Red Cross volunteers in khaki and a British tar. The three were smiling in full enjoyment of the high comedy of disaster. [...] The bus was a thing of heroism and gorgeous ruin.
> (159–60)

Battersby underlines the connection between incongruity, a notion explored earlier in this chapter, and the transition from seriousness to laughter:

> In chapter 8 of volume II of *The World as Will and Representation* [...], Schopenhauer claims that which is truly humorous is not in conflict with the sublime, but can be found alongside it. True humour derives, according to Schopenhauer, from 'the sudden apprehension of an incongruity between [...] a concept and the real object thought through it'. [...] He then adds that because 'the opposite of laughter and joking is *seriousness*', and because incongruity is integral to that which is laughable, 'the transition from profound seriousness to laughter is particularly easy', and 'the more capable of complete seriousness a person is, the more heartily can he laugh'.
> (Battersby 2013, par. 20)

The dynamic tension displayed throughout the text between pathos and humour allows Sinclair to concurrently explore the absurdity *and* the sublime inherent in the war in a peripheral manner that perhaps best renders the multifariousness of her experience. This largely explains why *A Journal of Impressions* resists any normative classification as a war journal. The voice that emerges out of these various distancing and discursive devices generates a dissonance from the expected narrative: a counterpoint from the anticipated melodic line, which ends up being mostly absent, yet ever present in Sinclair's and the reader's mind as the expected, normative war narrative. Sinclair's war narrative is inherently dialogic.

Sinclair's Incongruous Geography of the War

Sinclair likewise develops an oxymoronic poetics of space that contributes to articulating her uncomfortable and incongruous experience of a country at war. Laurel Forster has studied Sinclair's relationship to space as a female presence intruding on the warzone and remarks,

> Sinclair's diary is unusual in making the connection between psychical and physical landscapes. She offers neither practicalities nor overview, but she does make detailed links between the war zones she encountered and her emotional responses.
>
> (Forster 233)

Although Forster does not examine the *Journal* in close textual detail, this comment—and Forster's article as a whole—does encompass Sinclair's relationship to space in the *Journal*. One of the most notable features of Sinclair's treatment of space is the recurrent paradigm of sight-seeing, which is also at work—albeit in a different tone—in Borden's and Sassoon's war writing. Sinclair underlines, not without guilt, her initial feeling of being a mere tourist and enjoying the novelty of Belgium. The *Journal*'s title, which as remarked earlier may have been that of a travel diary, partakes of this ambivalent stance. The Ambulance Corps' first few days in Ghent bear 'all the appearance of a disorganised Cook's tourist party' (21), with Sinclair having to remind herself that 'our Daimler is not a touring car but a motor ambulance' (11). Sinclair even provides a grim parody of the Baedeker guides, describing the exact *modus operandi* to experience melancholy when sight-seeing in a country at war:

> [I]f you have never known what melancholy is and would like to know it, I can recommend two courses. Go down the Grand Canal in Venice in the grey spring of the year, in a gondola, all by yourself. Or get mixed up with a field ambulance which is not only doing noble work but running thrilling risks, in neither of which you have a share, or the ghost of a chance of a share; cut yourself off from your comrades, if it is only for a week, and go into a Belgian café in war-time and try to eat *brioches* and drink English tea all by yourself. This is the more successful course. You may see hope beyond the gondola and the Grand Canal. But you will see no hope beyond the *brioche* and the English tea.
>
> (104–5)

The Baedeker is in fact mentioned *verbatim* when Sinclair describes her perambulations in Ghent:

> Walked through the town again—old quarter. Walked and walked and walked, thinking about Antwerp all the time. Through streets of grey-white and lavender-tinted houses, with very fragile balconies. Saw the two Cathedrals and the Town Hall—refugees swarming round it—and the Rab—I can't remember its name: see Baedeker—with its turrets and its moat.
>
> (112–3)

The Baedeker guide, however, is mentioned dismissively here, as this walk takes place on 3 October, and Sinclair's mood has shifted: her deeper concern about the impending fall of Antwerp is superimposed over this sight-seeing activity, which is performed only on the surface. This shift is confirmed a few lines further on as Sinclair describes the attitude of the refugees:

> Why, the very refugees have the look of a rather tired tourist-party, wandering about, seeing Ghent, seeing the Cathedral.
>
> Only they aren't looking at the Cathedral. They are looking straight ahead, across the *Place*, up the street; they do not see or hear the trams swinging down on them, or the tearing, snorting motors; they stroll abstractedly into the line of the motors and stand there; they start and scatter, wild-eyed, with a sudden recrudescence of the terror that has driven them here from their villages in the fields.
>
> (113–4)

Forster has noted this juxtaposition of Belgium as a place of tourism and as a space at war:

> The war-torn Belgium is described as a tourist venue, and the spatial images of war-zone and Flemish landscape are awkwardly juxtaposed. The idea that a country at war might at once encompass touristic landscapes and war-torn villages and battlefields is an arresting juxtaposition and raises questions about privilege and non-combatants. At the very least, Sinclair's first-hand observations of her surroundings refute a totalising image of a country at war.
>
> (Forster 235)

This juxtaposition brings to the fore issues of representation. The stances of Sinclair and the refugees, both 'seeing' the sights of Ghent yet unable to fully take in the view, capture the paradoxical nature of Sinclair's representation of Belgium at war. What is not supposed to matter is nonetheless described, which reveals that it has been noticed after all. The superimposition of two visions, of two states of mind, corresponds to Ford's description of impressionist writing:

> I suppose that Impressionism exists to render those queer effects of real life that are like so many views seen through bright glass—through glass so bright that whilst you perceive through it a landscape or a backyard, you are aware that, on its surface, it reflects a face of a person behind you. For the whole of life is really like that; we are almost always in one place with our minds somewhere quite other.
>
> (Ford 1914a, 174)

As in Ford's description, impressions are layered and superimposed in order to render the complexity and unanticipated ambivalence of the war experience. Sinclair's spatial expression of the war occurs once again in a dialogic mode that goes against the grain of conventional war writing. Forster has highlighted the significance of space in Sinclair's overall representation of the war:

> It is her engagement with the places and spaces of the different war zones which enables her to write a war narrative at such odds with convention. Place becomes a catalyst for stating the truth of her experience.
>
> (Forster 243)

Sinclair's description of the statue of Flora in the hall of the Flandria Palace Hotel—a 600-room building completed only two years before—exemplifies her relation to space as a means to explore and express her experience of the war:

> A colossal Flora stands by the lift at the foot of the big staircase. Unaware that this is no festival of flowers, the poor stupid thing leans forward, smiling, and holds out her garland to the wounded as they are carried past. Nobody takes any notice of her.
>
> (20)

The incongruity of the statue as the glamorous Flandria Palace Hotel is converted into a military hospital, is due to the—apparent—uselessness of art and decoration at a time of war; the result is the statue's invisibility. It is worth noting that this uselessness and incongruity are inseparable from the statue's feminine attributes. The personification of the statue through the feminine pronouns, along with the pathetic fallacy inherent in the phrase 'the poor stupid thing', suggest that Flora may be construed as a projection of Sinclair: useless, incongruous, and invisible, 'feel[ing] like a large and useless parcel which the Commandant had brought with him in sheer absence of mind' (281). Yet the very permanence of Flora's gesture, offering flowers to the unseeing wounded, may appear as a resistance of the arts to the destruction enacted by the war. If Flora is a projection of Sinclair within a space transformed by war, this may also be construed as a comment on Sinclair's seemingly derisory, yet essential role on the scene of Belgium at war as a representative of the persistence and resilience of the arts. Indeed, in spite of its flagrant flaws and inherent negativity, the *Journal of Impressions* nevertheless stands resolutely as a piece of war literature.

Sinclair's Liminal Stance

The figure of Flora, standing in the entrance of the hotel and beckoning from the margin of a space now dedicated to the care of the wounded, also brings to the fore the paradigm of liminality. Claire Drewery has devoted a study to the liminal in the short fiction of four modernist women writers, among whom Sinclair is included. Although it is not concerned with *A Journal of Impressions*, Drewery's analysis is also relevant and enlightening when considering Sinclair's stance in the war. Relying on anthropological studies that first theorised liminality, Drewery defines it as 'a condition encountered whenever boundaries are crossed, whether fictional, cultural, political or psychological' (Drewery 2011, 1). She also highlights the potentiality inherent in liminality in the wake of Victor Turner, who in *From Ritual to Theatre* defines liminality as

> an interval, however brief, of *margin* or *limen*, when the past is momentarily negated, suspended, or abrogated, and the future has not yet begun, an instant of pure potentiality when everything, as it were, trembles in the balance.
>
> (Turner 44)

Such a suspension of time and feeling of 'pure potentiality' is described very early on in Sinclair's *Journal*, as the Ambulance Corps drives from Ostend to Ghent just after arriving in Belgium:

> I am going straight into the horror of war. For all I know it may be anywhere, here, behind this sentry; or there, beyond that line of willows. I don't know. I don't care. I cannot realize it.
>
> (10)

This feeling intensifies as signs of the war appear in the landscape:

> Half-way between Bruges and Ghent an embankment thrown up on each side of the road tells of possible patrols and casual shooting. It is the first visible intimation that the enemy may be anywhere.
>
> A curious excitement comes to you. I suppose it is excitement, though it doesn't feel like it. You have been drunk, very slightly drunk with the speed of the car. But now you are sober. Your heart beats quietly, steadily, but with a little creeping, mounting thrill in the beat. The sensation is distinctly pleasurable. You say to yourself, 'It is coming. Now—or the next minute—perhaps at the end of the road'. […] At the moment you are no

longer an observing, reflecting being; you have ceased to be aware of yourself; you exist only in that quiet, steady thrill that is so unlike any excitement that you have ever known.

(12–13)

The use of the second person here appears inseparable from Sinclair's acute alertness to the shift in her situation. The double deixis, pointing to Sinclair as two distinct referents, is an expression of the liminality of the moment: as Sinclair is passing from relative peace to a country openly at war, the second person signifies a detachment from her past, habitual self, and her sense of alienation from the self that is emerging and experiencing such unprecedented sensations. In anthropological studies, the liminal is inherent in rites of passage. Arnold van Gennep thus defines liminality in *The Rites of Passage* as a 'transition between' (Gennep 15, qtd in Drewery 2). Drawing from van Gennep and Turner, Drewery goes on to specify that the rite of passage is 'a tripartite structure, [...] involv[ing] an individual stripped of status, detached from a fixed point in the social structure and undergoing the transitional, or *limen* phase' (Drewery 2). This description fully applies to Sinclair as she reaches Ghent.

If Sinclair's experience can be construed as a rite of passage, this invites the question: what is Sinclair transitioning towards, and how does this translate into her writing?

From Representational Crisis to an Alternative Mimesis

Towards 'Naked, Shining, Intense Reality'?

As she opens the chapter devoted to the war in her biography of May Sinclair, Suzanne Raitt remarks,

> The outbreak of war in August 1914 radically changed May Sinclair's sense of priorities. [...] [S]he felt that the war had irreparably altered both her own consciousness and the world in which she lived. [...] It quickly came to represent to her—as to so many others—the possibility of a new and more vivid life, one in which the usual conventions were suspended.
>
> (Raitt 2000, 148)

Raitt thus argues that the war stood as a defining and pivotal epoch in Sinclair's life, one that may lead towards a different, higher form of existence. This is confirmed by Leslie de Bont, who draws connections between the *Journal* and Sinclair's *A Defence of Idealism* (1917b):

> For Sinclair, war is first and foremost a rich context, allowing sublimation and the appearance of absolute reality, [...] described in her philosophical essay written in 1917, where she likens the war hero to artists and lovers.[7]
>
> (de Bont 2017, 45)

De Bont then quotes from *A Defence of Idealism*—I am quoting a slightly longer extract than she uses, as the final clause is particularly relevant to the topic at hand:

> Lovers and poets and painters and musicians and mystics and heroes know them: [...] moments when things that we have seen all our lives without truly seeing them, the flowers in the garden, the trees in the field [...] change to us in an instant of time, and show the secret and imperishable life they harbour; moments of danger that are sure and perfect happiness, because then the adorable Reality gives itself to our very sight and touch.
>
> (Sinclair 1917b, 379)

In the same vein, Raitt quotes an unpublished essay that Sinclair wrote during the war:

> [T]here is no doubt that these values were precisely what we were beginning to lose in 'life and literature', along with Religion, that is to say our hold on Reality, before the War. Most of us—with the exception of one or two poets—were ceasing to live with any intensity, to believe with any conviction compatible with comfort, and to feel with any strength and sincerity. Yet we were all quite sincerely 'out for' reality without recognising it when we saw it and without any suspicion of its spiritual nature.
>
> And Reality—naked, shining, intense Reality—more and not less of it, is, I believe, what we are going to get after the War.
>
> (qtd in Raitt 1997, 68 and 2000, 150)

One may be tempted to be contaminated by Sinclair's excitement here—the phrase 'contagious ecstasy' (157), one of the most-quoted of the *Journal* (see in particular Raitt 1997), may also apply to the reader—and to infer that Sinclair did find this superior, capitalised 'Reality' in Belgium. However, in an article that challenges conventional scholarship on war literature, Luke Thurston tempers this enthusiasm by underscoring the constructed character of Sinclair's lyrical assertion against the backdrop of the exaltation that prevailed in the early days of the war. Sinclair's declaration, Thurston argues, is a 'fantasy', one that is explored and developed further in the *Journal*:

> The *Journal* is fascinating [...] in reworking the reality of what happened, with all the quixotic frustrations of its intensely self-conscious protagonist, to produce the basis for a complex fantasy, to be developed in Sinclair's subsequent work, that centers on an imaginary 'vortex' sweeping together art, sex, and war. This fantasy [...] can shed light on both the moment of early modernism and the critical response to it.
>
> (Thurston 21)

Thurston goes so far as to suggest that Sinclair is herself swept into the 'unclean moral vortex' that she denounces in *The Tree of Heaven*. As the first part of this chapter has demonstrated, and as Thurston also makes clear, it is doubtful whether Sinclair often or ever fully experienced this 'naked, shining, intense Reality' in Belgium. What does emerge in the *Journal*, however, is the *representation* of a peripheral approach to this 'Reality' and of the feelings—or 'impressions'—that this approach generates, which is where Sinclair's account succeeds.

The Fruitful Mediacy of Writing

For all its display of indefiniteness and negativity, *A Journal of Impressions* is in truth an elaborate account, where every effect is carefully calibrated. As highlighted earlier, Sinclair makes no mystery of the fact she writes up each entry of the *Journal* some time after the quick notes jotted down in the daybook, and at a distance from the events she recounts: this deliberate and overt delay has important consequences on the nature of her war chronicle, as it makes its constructedness visible. The manuscript for the *Journal* is indeed replete with strikethroughs and add-ons that evidence a thorough and elaborate process of rewriting (see Figure 2.1).

To this layer of rewriting is added another, when Sinclair moves on to the typescript: this is in turn heavily amended, with the names altered and many additions or removals. A number of footnotes, for instance, which were commented upon earlier in this chapter as offering corrections on the initial account, are added at this later stage, either in the manuscript or in the typescript (see Figure 2.2).

Yet in either case, since Sinclair wrote most entries a few weeks or even months after the events, these footnotes are artificial: she could easily have amended the text directly. Sinclair's deliberate use of footnotes is one of the many stylistic effects that she employs to foreground the impression of uncertainty and instability, and to generate it in turn in the reader, whose initial reading of the main text is disproved by the footnotes. These footnotes, as remarked earlier, operate as an effective metaleptic tool that enhances Sinclair's process of self-humiliation, but they are also a salient token of Sinclair's wish for a metamorphic and dynamic text. Rebecca Bowler has also demonstrated the further degree of fabrication of the *Journal* as opposed to earlier versions of the same entries, delineating the differences between the *Journal* and the three extracts published in the *English Review* a few months before the *Journal* was completed (Bowler 2016, 180–3).

Not only does Sinclair openly inform the reader about the temporal distance of the *Journal* versus the 'Day-Book', as noted earlier, but she contends that this in no way discredits the authenticity of her account, considering that the notes from the daybook are sufficient mementoes to conjure up and 'write out' impressions later:

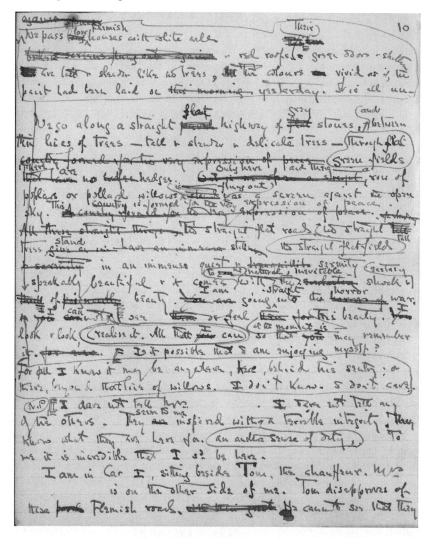

Figure 2.1 Page 10 of May Sinclair's manuscript for *A Journal of Impressions*. May Sinclair papers, Ms. Coll. 184, Kislak Center for Special Collections, Rare Books and Manuscripts, University of Pennsylvania

But when you had made fast each day with its note, your impressions were safe, far safer than if you had tried to record them in their flux as they came. However far behind I might be with my Journal, it was *kept*. It is not written 'up', or round and about the original notes in my Day-Book, it is simply written *out*.

The key word, of course, is that also present at the heart of the title: 'impressions'; around this word revolves indeed what is at stake and what I now want to

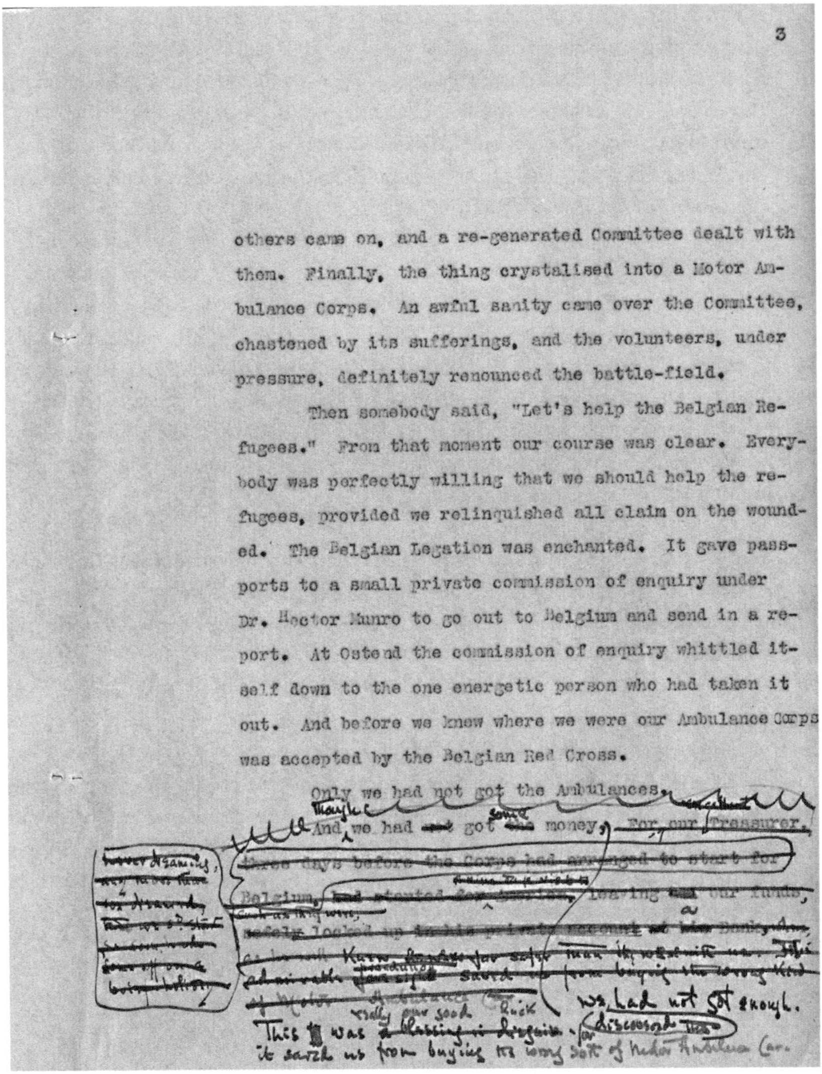

3

others came on, and a re-generated Committee dealt with them. Finally, the thing crystalised into a Motor Ambulance Corps. An awful sanity came over the Committee, chastened by its sufferings, and the volunteers, under pressure, definitely renounced the battle-field.

Then somebody said, "Let's help the Belgian Refugees." From that moment our course was clear. Everybody was perfectly willing that we should help the refugees, provided we relinquished all claim on the wounded. The Belgian Legation was enchanted. It gave passports to a small private commission of enquiry under Dr. Hector Munro to go out to Belgium and send in a report. At Ostend the commission of enquiry whittled itself down to the one energetic person who had taken it out. And before we knew where we were our Ambulance Corps was accepted by the Belgian Red Cross.

Only we had not got the Ambulances.

Though we had got some money, we had not got enough.

This was ... It saved us from buying the wrong sort of Motor Ambulance Car.

Figure 2.2 Page 3 of May Sinclair's typescript for *A Journal of Impressions*. May Sinclair papers, Ms. Coll. 184, Kislak Center for Special Collections, Rare Books and Manuscripts, University of Pennsylvania

demonstrate is successful in Sinclair's account. Thurston has commented on Sinclair's sense that entries written at a distance from the day were paradoxically closer to her actual experience than an account written on the same day would have been:

> Contrasting the 'flux' of her daily experiences in the warzone with the later rewriting of her scribbled notes as a coherent text, she notes the hygienic

effect of this deferred recollection. Each of the days in Belgium, she writes, 'had its own unique incorruptible memory, and the slight lapse of time, so far from dulling or blurring that memory, crystallized it and made it sharp and clean' […]. Whereas the real of the experience is figured as amorphous, ungraspable, non-inscribable—figured, that is as surplus matter—the process of writing, like the photographic development of a negative, returns the mnemic image to clarity and legibility.

(Thurston 23)

As Rebecca Bowler states in her study on literary impressionism, Sinclair shared with Ford Madox Ford the belief that 'temporal distance is, ironically, necessary to the effect of immediacy in recording impressions' (Bowler 2016, 9). Bowler also analyses the effect that the additions in the *Journal* generate in comparison with the earlier entries published in the *English Review*, asserting that they contribute to strengthening the account's participating in literary impressionism: the augmented passages, she argues, give

a truer and more rounded impression than the original. […] Sinclair is doing here what Ford says that impressionism *should* do: give 'a sense of two, of three, of as many as you will, places, persons, emotions, all going on simultaneously in the emotions of the writer'.

(Bowler 2016, 181)

Everything, therefore, points to Sinclair's *Journal* as a work of literary impressionism, as it had been explored and practiced by Ford for about a decade by the time Sinclair wrote the *Journal*, and as he famously theorised in June and December 1914 in Harold Monro's short-lived journal, *Poetry and Drama*. In her analysis of the *Journal of Impressions* on the May Sinclair Society website, Charlotte Jones underlines the similarities between Sinclair's and Ford's impressionism:

Sinclair's introduction echoes even more closely Ford's preface to his 1911 impressionistic, semi-autobiographical reminiscence, *Ancient Lights*:
This book, in short, is full of inaccuracies as to facts, but its accuracy as to impressions is absolute […] I don't really deal in facts, I have for facts a most profound contempt.

Bowler's monograph on literary impressionism likewise establishes precise connections between Ford's and Sinclair's versions of impressionism, bringing their writing together in the final chapter of her monograph.

An important aspect of literary impressionism resides in the meticulous structuration of representation, through the device theorised by Ford as *progression d'effet*, and defined in *Joseph Conrad: A Personal Remembrance*:

In writing a novel we agreed that every word set on paper—*every* word set on paper—must carry the story forward and that, as the story progressed, the story must be carried forward faster and faster and with more and more intensity. That is called *progression d'effet*, words for which there is no English equivalent.

(Ford 1989, 225)

Through *progression d'effet*, Sinclair's text is endowed with a striking circularity, where tropes, words or situations occurring towards the beginning of the journal are mirrored towards the end, which intensifies their emotive charge. Thus the insistence on the 'intolerable safety' (89) of staying behind, away from danger, in the first few entries of the journal, is mirrored in a chiasmic structure when the hospital is evacuated from Ghent: 'Your sense of safety grows intolerable' (248). Likewise, the 'ghostly roses [...] growing on a ghostly tree' (58) in the garden of the *Palais des Fêtes* at Ghent are echoed by the 'enchantment' (253, 254) and 'supernatural detachment' (256) of the garden that Sinclair visits at Ecloo, when the Corps is hosted by friends of Commandant Munro. The Belgian nurses welcoming the Corps on their arrival at the Flandria Palace Hotel are repeatedly described as 'angelic' (17, 18, 19, 36); they find their counterpoint in an English nurse with 'the tact of a heavenly angel' (272) as the party has arrived in Ostend after fleeing Ghent on 12 October. The emotional intensity of such echoes is paired with the poignancy that tinges the last few pages of the narrative, whose unhappy ending the reader knows from the very first pages of the *Journal*: it seems Sinclair is also reconsidering and taking leave of the most enduring impressions that she has experienced during her time in Belgium.

All of this demonstrates the constructedness of the *Journal*, which makes it a far cry from a *bona fide* war diary: the very use of impressionist techniques thus seems to paradoxically defeat the apparent purpose of authenticity. Bowler compellingly brings to light the disingenuousness of Sinclair's pretence of authenticity in the *Journal*, as well as the limitations of the claims of writing faithfully from memory, through a joint analysis of *The Good Soldier* and Sinclair's *Journal* in which Sinclair as narrator is made to appear as staggeringly akin to Dowell. Bowler for instance analyses the way in which the voice of Sinclair the narrator writing in 1915 destabilises and undermines the attempts to recreate the impressions of Sinclair the secretary. The passage that Bowler comments on, describing Sinclair's first thrill when approaching the war, was quoted earlier in this chapter (12–3 of the *Journal*). Bowler starts by delineating the devices through which this passage aims at impressionism, through the switch to the present tense and the second-person singular. However, she remarks,

This passage is [...] a good example of Sinclair's attempt to render the impression as it was received, with no interference from subsequent reflection. She does not manage it: the Sinclair-narrator who is experiencing, in the present tense, a pleasurable apprehension of danger, is cut across by the Sinclair who has thought about the experience later [...].

(Bowler 2016, 179)

The 'you' pronoun indeed shifts in this paragraph: it moves from Sinclair the secretary in September 1914, depicting her own sensations—'a curious excitement comes to you'—, to Sinclair the narrator in 1915, pausing, distancing herself from the scene, scrutinising her earlier self and correcting the initial representation: 'not that you imagine anything at the moment'. Once again, the metaleptic intrusion of Sinclair's later voice, writing a few months after the fact, undermines the effects of her earlier voice, attempting to recount her impressions. The pervasive use of the second person heralds the writing of *Mary Olivier* (1919)[8] where second- and third-person narratives keep alternating, one of the text's most striking narratological devices. The systematic use of 'you' in *Mary Olivier* confirms that Sinclair was evidently fully alert to the power inherent in the double deixis, and further sustains the claim that the complexity of the narrative voice in the *Journal* was carefully designed.[9]

Yet an ultimate riddle persists. Although the text keeps undermining itself, both in its ability to recount events which were, after all, mostly experienced peripherally, and in its ability to render impressions, it also emerges as a carefully wrought piece. Is not this apparent failure, then, part and parcel of Sinclair's agenda: does it not participate in a specifically Sinclairian poetics, one that is made of reticence, suppression, but also of intense expressivity?

A Poetics of Reticence

Let us delve a little deeper into Sinclair's use of the technique of *progression d'effet*. The most memorable phrase that recurs through the text is undeniably the French sentence *'c'est triste, n'est-ce pas?'*. When it is first introduced, by a 'dear little Belgian lady' showing Sinclair around the Palais des Fêtes where four thousand refugees are being sheltered, it is linked to one of many expressions of Sinclair's inability to not only render, but to even feel impressions:

> 'Et ces quatre petits enfants qui ont perdu leur père et leur mère. C'est triste, n'est-ce pas, Mademoiselle?'
> And you say, 'Oui, Mademoiselle. C'est bien triste'.
> But you don't mean it. You don't feel it. You don't know whether it is *'triste'* or not. You are not sure that *'triste'* is the word for it. There are no words for it, because there are no ideas for it. It is a sorrow that transcends all sorrow that you have ever known. You have a sort of idea that perhaps, if you can ever feel again, this sight will be worse to remember than it is to see. You can't believe what you see; you are stunned, stupefied, as if you yourself had been crushed and numbed in the same catastrophe.
>
> (56)

Whilst negating the possibility of finding *le mot juste* to represent the experience underway, this passage triggers one of the text's most expressive phrases that recurs hauntingly through the narrative via the technique of *progression d'effet* and is singularised by the italics and the use of French: '*c'est triste*'. This sentence, explicitly emptied of 'mean[ing]' and 'feel[ing]' in its first occurrence, gains in expressiveness through repetition: '*triste*' occurs 12 times in the *Journal* at moments of great yet apparently detached poignancy, and each incidence is increasingly endowed with the cumulated emotive charge of the previous occurrences. The use of French and of the italics may seem to convey detachment; then again, it may also signal the impossibility of finding a proper mode of expression in one's habitual language, and the need for a foreign language to convey the unfamiliarity of the sensation. Jean-Jacques Lecercle has analysed the use of foreign words in modernist texts in a manner that wholly resonates with Sinclair's narrative:

> The function of the foreign word is subversive in an entirely positive sense: it de-familiarises, de-nationalises, de-reifies and dis-enchants the language in which it appears. […] Such critical and subversive function has its positive aspect: it opens up language to the construction of thought, it opens up language to its future by forcing it to go back to its past […].
> (Lecercle 22)

Sinclair was fascinated by spectrality: this italicised phrase, an endless echo to the 'dear little Belgian lady''s remark, likewise haunts the text, relentlessly imposing its unfamiliarity. In an inverted process from Freud's *Unheimlich*, where the familiar seems strange when recurring unexpectedly, here the alien is made to become familiar through its repetition, whilst retaining all of its foreignness. This may be related to Borden's opposing the civilian world as an intolerably abnormal 'other world' and war as the only conceivable locus (Borden 57). Therefore, even as she states the impossibility to convey impressions as they are not even articulated in her own mind, Sinclair introduces one of the most effective impressionist devices in the entire *Journal*.

In a similarly paradoxical dynamic, one of the rare passages where Sinclair does succeed in adumbrating the impact of the war onto her mind is brought about by preterition:

> I don't want to describe that ward, or the effect of those rows upon rows of beds, those rows upon rows of bound and bandaged bodies, the intensity of physical anguish suggested by sheer force of multiplication, by the diminishing perspective of the beds, by the clear light and nakedness of the great hall that sets these repeated units of torture in a world apart, a world of insufferable space and agonizing time, ruled by some inhuman mathematics and given over to pure transcendent pain. A sufficiently large ward full of wounded really does leave an impression very like that. But the one true thing about this impression is its transcendence. It is utterly removed from and unlike anything that you have experienced before. From the moment that the doors have closed behind you, you are in another world, and under its strange impact you are given new senses and a new soul. If there is

horror here you are not aware of it as horror. Before these multiplied forms of anguish what you feel—if there be anything of *you* left to feel—is not pity, because it is so near to adoration.

(40–1)

This passage is crucial in Sinclair's narrative, as it depicts her first contact with wounded soldiers. The paralipsis that opens the paragraph encapsulates the tension between Sinclair's sense of inadequacy as a witness and the obstinate persistence of literary representation. Sinclair does signify her refusal to 'describe [...] the effect' of the scene, i.e. to render impressions. Yet the account is one of the most evocative within the *Journal*, rich with enumeration, double repetitions ('rows upon rows' occurs twice), triple alliterations ('bound and bandaged bodies'), nouns almost systematically paired with adjectives, parallelisms that intensify the enumerative effect ('a world of insufferable space and agonizing time'). What is at stake here is a representational shift: while Sinclair voices a crisis of representation, she simultaneously signals *towards* a different form of mimesis—one that is founded on a liminal position ('the doors have closed behind you'), poised between ordinary life and 'transcendence'. Transcendence is merely approached: the journey towards an alternative mimesis is still in progress; but in a process akin to anamorphosis, the *tableau* here painted, containing both the description and its disruption, gestures towards a different form of experience, not just sensorial and emotive, but spiritual.

The peripheral approach to this new form of impression is also expressed through a poetics of suppression. Sinclair's manuscript is thus occasionally scored with dotted lines, which work as a visual fragmentation of the text and are peculiarly expressive. One such instance occurs when Sinclair recounts the death of a wounded soldier and deplores the incessant and intolerable flow of inane words on the part of a 'little Englishman' who is also part of the scene:

> Hanging on to the hood and swaying with the rush of the car, [the little eager Englishman] talked continually. He talked from the moment we left Melle to the moment when we landed him at his street in Ghent; explaining over and over again the qualifications that justified him in attaching himself to ambulances. He had lived fourteen years in Ghent. He could speak French and Flemish.
>
> I longed for the eager little Englishman to stop. I longed for his street to come and swallow him up. He had lived in Ghent fourteen years. He could speak Flemish and French. I felt that I couldn't bear it if he went on a minute longer. I wanted to think. The dying man lay close behind me, very straight and stiff; his poor feet stuck out close under my hand.
>
> But I couldn't think. The little eager Englishman went on swaying and talking.
>
> He had lived fourteen years in Ghent.
>
> He could speak French and Flemish.

> . . . .
> The dying man was still alive when he was lifted out of the ambulance. He died that evening.
> . . . .
>
> (191–2)

The Englishman's pointless logorrhoea—perhaps a projection of what Sinclair fears she may be doing in the *Journal?*—is opposed to the silence of 'the dying man', and to Sinclair's suppressed emotion. Sinclair's dotted lines interrupt the flow of the text to effectively stop any vain attempt at expression—or indeed any parasitical speech that may desecrate the significance of the moment. Death and the intolerable are indeed often marked by blanks in the pages, by the isolation of short sentences as single paragraphs and by these striking dots, a visual mark of linguistic dismemberment that may bring to mind later texts traditionally labelled as 'postmodern'.

Sinclair's account of the fall of Antwerp is marked by a similar reticence of expression, and is again detached from the rest of the text by a dotted line:

> . . . .
> Antwerp is said to have fallen.
> Antwerp is said to be holding its own well.
> All evening the watching Taube has been hanging over Ghent.
> Mrs. Torrence and Janet have gone back with the ambulance to Melle.
>
> (216)

These four lines stand out in the narrative like a poem reminiscent of a haiku, with an effect of alternate rhymes. The anaphora of 'Antwerp', foregrounding the contradiction between the first two lines, is reverberated in the footnote attached to the second line, which settles the contradiction: 'Antwerp had surrendered on Friday, the 9th'. The sentences increase gradually, in a manner that may infer mounting emotion. Yet the emotive charge that these stylistic devices might carry is undermined by the matter-of-fact account and strict adherence to information. This poem is echoed in a condensed form a few pages later, when the fall of Antwerp is confirmed:

> . . . .
> Antwerp has fallen.
> Taube over Ghent in the night.
>
> (223)

Although Sinclair altogether abandons the pretence of rendering her impressions in such extreme moments, these passages are perhaps those where emotion is most palpable, and most effectively generated in the reader. Sinclair's rhetoric of suppression, where traces of emotions are to be found between the lines, in the blanks perforations of the page, is where she best manages her project of an impressionist account of the war. Considering Adorno's analysis of the fragment as a form of resistance to totalisation, Catherine Bernard highlights the tension inherent in the fragment, between failure and hope:

> In this obstinate insurrection against totality, the fragment, the detail, the ruin tell us with peculiar urgency the melancholic bankruptcy of art and its capacity to let the multiple and the heterogeneous seep through: 'the fragment is that part of the totality of the work that opposed totality' (Adorno 2002, 45). The fragmentation of form thus bears a twofold significance, as it is both symptomatic of a world in ruins and carries a dynamic subversive charge. Working both as an anticipatory metaphor for the dystopian failure of totality and as the image of a possible utopian takeover through the very heterogeneity that undermines the system, the fragment is a paradoxical sign.[10]
>
> (Bernard 2005, 33)

Beyond their impressionist technique, and despite their radically differing experiences of the war, fragmentation brings Ford and Sinclair together in their resistance to a consensual, conventional and totalising narrative of the war.

Conclusion

A Journal of Impressions operates as a series of disappointments, for Sinclair as for her readers. Yet once the gap between 'reality' and Sinclair's narrative is established by the author and once the limits of representation are accepted by the reader, the text remains as an irreducible aesthetic object: a precarious literary experiment in impressionist narrative. Written as a therapeutic outlet to come to terms with the trauma and humiliation of her time in Belgium, Sinclair's account begs to be read above all as a work of literature, one that leaves the reader endlessly puzzled, yet which allowed Sinclair to experiment with representation and reflect on the rendering of 'Reality', to a degree that she had never reached before. Beyond—and because of—its manifest flaws, *A Journal of Impressions* resists as an 'authentic artwork', one that matches Adorno's reflection on the relation between art and life:

> Life has been perpetuated through culture, along with the idea of a decent life; its echo resounds in authentic artworks. Affirmation does not bestow a halo on the status quo; in sympathy with what exists, it defends itself against death, the telos of all domination. Doubting this comes only at the price of believing that death itself is hope.
>
> (Adorno 2002, 252)

Sinclair's liminal experience in the Munro Ambulance Corps, at the threshold of a war that remained tantalisingly remote, brought her face to face with herself, as an individual anchored in the limitations of her age, upbringing and gender, but also as a writer. It may appear that the war did serve as a catalyst for Sinclair to move towards a heightened self-consciousness about form. Leslie de Bont thus considers that Sinclair's experimenting with literary impressionism in the *Journal* was further developed in her later novels, albeit in a distinctly Sinclairian manner:

> Quite significantly, this work on impressionism, already contained in the journal's title, is further developed in the final novels; or rather, it is adapted, as Sinclair always does, and confronted to the neo-idealist frames from which she conducts her own dialogist experiments.[11]
>
> (de Bont 2017, 48)

De Bont here touches upon an essential aspect of Sinclair's writing: the dialogic conversation that she establishes throughout her work between the various influences exerted upon Sinclair by her passionate interest in contemporary ideas and aesthetics. This dialogism also explains the *Journal*'s constant instability, suspended between the urge to witness and the sense of its impossibility, between intense emotion and the deflation of pathos, between the absurd and the transcendent. All coexist in an incessant vibration that endlessly revives the precariousness of the text. In this unresolved tension resides the true Sinclairian voice. Adorno's reflection on the dynamic contradiction between the engagement and autonomy of art helps us understand the status of Sinclair's odd war chronicle. Despite her urge *and* her ostensible failure to write the war, Sinclair produces a work of literature that expresses the persistence of humanity even when confronted to its limits: as Sinclair states stalwartly, '[T]his record has at least the value of a "human document"' ('Introduction', n. p.). Sinclair in her *Journal* is ultimately less interested—and certainly less successful—in recording the war than humanity, with its weaknesses, its lacks, its fractures, all brought forward through the uprooting condition of being at war.

Notes

1 I am immensely grateful to Rebecca Bowler for generously sharing the material she photographed from the Sinclair archives, particularly Sinclair's manuscript and typescript of the *Journal of Impressions*, as well as the manuscript of the 'Day-Book' that Sinclair kept for the Munro Ambulance Corps during her time in Belgium.
2 Where no other reference is given, the page numbers refer to Macmillan's 1915 edition of *A Journal of Impressions*.
3 This edition is also available online, both on the Gutenberg and archive.org websites.
4 For a detailed account of the contemporary reception of the *Journal*, see Raitt 2000, 163–4.
5 My translation. Original text: 'la guerre va permettre à Sinclair de faire dialoguer les modes de discours (fiction, poésie, essais philosophies et psychanalytiques, articles critiques, journaux intimes etc.), comme le définit Bakhtine, de les combiner au sein d'un même texte, afin de produire une œuvre qui puisse vraiment rendre compte du caractère inédit de la Première Guerre mondiale'.

6 My warm thanks go to Leslie de Bont for drawing my attention to this link between the *Journal* and *Tasker Jevons* and for steering me towards Wilson's research.
7 My translation. Original text: 'Chez Sinclair, la guerre est d'abord un contexte riche, permettant la sublimation et l'apparition de la réalité absolue, décrites ici dans son essai philosophique de 1917, où elle apparente le héros de guerre aux artistes et aux amants'.
8 This parallel was also suggested to me by Leslie de Bont.
9 While I have lacked the space to address this more precisely here, Sandrine Sorlin's monograph The Stylistics of 'You': Second-Person Pronoun and Its Pragmatic Effects provides a detailed and illuminating analysis of the effects of the use of second-person pronoun that has much contributed to my becoming more attuned to the power of double deixis in war narratives.
10 My translation. Original text: 'Dans cette insurrection obstinée contre la totalité, le fragment, le détail, la ruine nous disent avec une urgence particulière la faillite mélancolique de l'art et sa capacité à laisser sourdre le multiple, l'hétérogène : "the fragment is that part of the totality of the work that opposed totality" (Adorno 1997, 45). La fragmentation de la forme fait ainsi doublement signe puisqu'elle est tout à la fois symptomatique d'un univers en ruines et porteuse d'une charge subversive dynamique. Tout à la fois métaphore par anticipation de la faillite dystopique de la totalité et image d'une possible relève utopique par cette hétérogénéité même qui malmène le système, le fragment est un signe paradoxal'.
11 My translation. Original text: 'De manière tout à fait significative, ce travail sur l'impression, déjà contenu dans le titre du journal, sera développé plus avant dans les derniers romans; ou plutôt, il sera adapté, comme Sinclair le fait toujours, et confronté aux cadres néo-idéalistes à partir desquels elle mène ses propres expériences dialogistes'.

Bibliography

Primary Sources

Austen, Jane. *Northanger Abbey*. Oxford: Oxford World's Classics, 2008. First published 1817.

Bergson, Henri. *Laughter: An Essay on the Meaning of the Comic*. Translated by Cloudesley Brereton and Fred Rothwell. New York: Macmillan, 1911.

———. *Le Rire: Essai sur la signification du comique*. Paris: Garnier Flammarion, 2013. First published 1900.

Borden, Mary. *The Forbidden Zone*. London: Heinemann, 1929. https://archive.org/details/forbiddenzone00bord/.

Ford, Ford Madox. 'On Impressionism: 1'. *Poetry and Drama* 2 (June 1914a): 167–75.

———. 'On Impressionism: 2'. *Poetry and Drama* 2 (December 1914b): 323–34.

———. *Joseph Conrad: A Personal Remembrance*. New York: Ecco Press, 1989. First published 1924.

Nietzsche, Friedrich. *The Gay Science*. Translated by Walter Kaufmann. New York: Vintage, 1974. First published as *Die Fröhliche Wissenschaft* 1882.

———. The Birth of Tragedy. In *Basic Writings of Nietzsche*. Translated by Walter Kaufmann. New York: Vintage, 2000. First published as *Die Geburt der Tragödie* 1872.

Sinclair, May. 'Chauffeurs at the Front'. *The New Statesman* 3, no. 90 (26 December 1914a): 295–7, https://archive.org/details/sim_new-statesman_1914-12-26_3_90/.

———. 'Day-Book of Dr Hector Munro's Motor Ambulance Corps' (unpublished manuscript, 1914b). Manuscript. May Sinclair Papers, Kislak Center for Special Collections, Rare Book and Manuscript Library, University of Pennsylvania.

———. 'A Journal of Impressions' (unpublished manuscript, 1915a). Manuscript. May Sinclair Papers, Kislak Center for Special Collections, Rare Book and Manuscript Library, University of Pennsylvania.
———. 'A Journal of Impressions' (unpublished manuscript, 1915b). Annotated typescript. May Sinclair Papers, Kislak Center for Special Collections, Rare Book and Manuscript Library, University of Pennsylvania.
———. 'From a Journal'. *The English Review* 20 (May, June, July 1915c): 168–83, 303–14, 468–76, https://archive.org/details/sim_english-review-uk_1915-05_20; https://archive.org/details/sim_english-review-uk_1915-06_20/; https://archive.org/details/sim_english-review-uk_1915-07_20/.
———. *A Journal of Impressions in Belgium*. New York: Macmillan, 1915d, https://archive.org/details/journalofimpress00sinciala/; https://gutenberg.org/ebooks/31332.
———. *Tasker Jevons: The Real Story*. London: Hutchinson, 1915e, https://archive.org/details/taskerjevonsreal00sincuoft.
———. *The Tree of Heaven*. New York: Macmillan, 1917a, https://archive.org/details/treeofheaven00sinc; https://gutenberg.org/ebooks/13883.
———. *A Defence of Idealism: Some Questions and Conclusions*. London and New York: Macmillan, 1917b, https://archive.org/details/defenceofideali00sinc.
———. *Mary Olivier. A Life*. London: Cassel, 1919, https://gutenberg.org/ebooks/9366.
West, Rebecca. 'Miss Sinclair's Genius'. *Daily News* 1915. In *The Young Rebecca: Writings of Rebecca West 1911–17*. Edited by Jane Marcus, 305–6. London: Virago, 1982.

Secondary Sources

Adorno, Theodor. *Aesthetic Theory*. Translated by Robert Hullot-Kentor. London: Continuum, 2002. First published in 1997.
Bakhtin, Mikhail. *Problems of Dostoevsky's Poetics*. Translated by Caryl Emerson, and Wayne C. Booth. Minneapolis: University of Minnesota Press, 1984.
Battersby, Christine. 'Behold the Buffoon': Dada, Nietzsche's *Ecce Homo* and the Sublime'. In *The Art of the Sublime*. Edited by Nigel Llewellyn, and Christine Riding. London: Tate Research Publication, 2013, https://www.tate.org.uk/art/research-publications/the-sublime/christine-battersby-behold-the-buffoon-dada-nietzsches-ecce-homo-and-the-sublime-r1136833.
———. 'With Schopenhauer at the Belgian Front: May Sinclair's War Journal and Related Texts'. Video presentation, *Networking May Sinclair* conference, 24 June 2021, Nantes University, https://mediaserver.univ-nantes.fr/videos/5/.
———. 'Schopenhauer's Metaphysics and Ethics: Mapping Influences and Congruities with Feminist Philosophers'. *The Palgrave Handbook of German Idealism and Feminist Philosophy*. Edited by Susanne Lettow, and Tuija Pulkkinen. Basingstoke: Palgrave Macmillan (n.d.).
Bernard, Catherine. 'L'art de l'aporie: penser l'impensable avec Adorno et Benjamin'. *Études anglaises* 58, no. 1 (2005): 31–41.
Boll, Theophilus. *Miss May Sinclair: Novelist: A Biographical and Critical Introduction*. Cranbury: Associated University Presses, 1973.
de Bont, Leslie. '"I Hate Soldiering": Ford, May Sinclair, and War Heroism'. In *War and the Mind: Ford Madox Ford, Parade's End, and Psychology*. Edited by Rob Hawkes, and Ashley Chantler, 142–58. Edinburgh: Edinburgh University Press, 2015.

———. 'La Guerre et le dialogue discursif : idéalisme et intériorité à l'épreuve de la première guerre mondiale chez May Sinclair'. In *Les Artistes et la guerre*. Edited by Isabelle Brasme, 43–50. Paris: Houdiard, 2017.

———. *Le Modernisme singulier de May Sinclair*. Paris: Presses de la Sorbonne Nouvelle, 2019.

Bowler, Rebecca. *Literary Impressionism Vision and Memory in Dorothy Richardson, Ford Madox Ford, H.D. and May Sinclair*. London and New York: Bloomsbury Academic, 2016.

Brassard, Geneviève. '"War Is the Greatest of Paradoxes": May Sinclair and Edith Wharton at the Front'. *Minerva Journal of Women and War* 2, no. 1 (Spring 2008): 3–21.

Drewery, Claire. *Modernist Short Fiction by Women: The Liminal in Katherine Mansfield, Dorothy Richardson, May Sinclair and Virginia Woolf*. London and New York: Routledge, 2011.

Forster, Laurel. 'Women and War Zones: May Sinclair's Personal Negotiation with the First World War'. In *Inside Out: Women Negotiating, Subverting, Appropriating Public and Private Space*. Edited by Teresa Gómez Reus, and Aránzazu Usandizaga, 229–48. Leiden: Brill, 2008.

Genette, Gérard. *Narrative Discourse: An Essay in Method*. Translated by Jane E. Lewin. Ithaca: Cornell University Press, 1980.

van Gennep, Arnold. *The Rites of Passage*. New York and London: Routledge, 2004. First published in 1960.

Gómez Reus, Teresa. 'Racing to the Front: Auto-mobility and Competing Narratives of Women in the First World War'. In *Women in Transit through Literary Liminal Spaces*. Edited by Teresa Gómez Reus, and Terry Gifford, 107–24. London: Palgrave Macmillan, 2013.

Hynes, Samuel. *A War Imagined: The First World War and English Culture*. London: The Bodley Head, 1990.

Jones, Charlotte. 'May Sinclair's Impressions of War', https://maysinclairsociety.com/may-sinclairs-impressions-of-war/.

Lecercle, Jean-Jacques. 'Autonomy Versus Commitment: Eliot, Adorno, Bakhtin and Foreign Words'. In *Autonomy and Commitment in Twentieth-Century British Literature*. Edited by Jean-Michel Ganteau, and Christine Reynier, 15–30. Montpellier: Presses universitaires de la Méditerranée, 2010.

Phillips, Terry. 'The Self in Conflict: May Sinclair and the Great War'. In *The Literature of the Great War Reconsidered: Beyond Modern Memory*. Edited by Patrick J. Quinn, and Steven Trout, 55–66. Basingstoke: Palgrave, 2001.

Prieto, Sara. '"Without Methods": Three Female Authors Visiting the Western Front'. *First World War Studies* 6, no. 2 (2015): 171–85.

Raitt, Suzanne. '"Contagious Ecstasy": May Sinclair's War Journals'. In *Women's Fiction and the Great War*. Edited by Suzanne Raitt, and Trudi Tate, Oxford: Clarendon Press, 1997.

———. *May Sinclair: A Modern Victorian*. Oxford: Clarendon Press, 2000.

Sorlin, Sandrine. *The Stylistics of 'You': Second-Person Pronoun and Its Pragmatic Effects*. Cambridge: Cambridge University Press, 2022.

Spencer, Herbert. 'On the Physiology of Laughter'. *Macmillan's Magazine* (March 1860): 395–402.

Thurston, Luke. 'Clouds and Power: May Sinclair's War'. *Journal of Modern Literature* 37, no. 3 (2014): 18–35.

Turner, Victor. *From Ritual to Theatre: The Human Seriousness of Play*. New York: PAJ, 1982.
Tylee, Claire. *The Great War and Women's Consciousness: Images of Militarism and Womanhood in Women's Writings 1914–64*. Iowa City: University of Iowa Press, 1990.
Wilson, Leigh. '"It Was as if She Had Said…": May Sinclair and Reading Narratives of Cure'. PhD thesis University of Westminster School of Social Sciences, Humanities and Languages, 2000, https://westminsterresearch.westminster.ac.uk/item/944z3/-it-was-as-if-she-had-said-may-sinclair-and-reading-narratives-of-cure.

———. '"She in Her "Armour" and He in His Coat of Nerves": May Sinclair and the Re-writing of Chivalry'. In *Feminist Forerunners: New Womanism and Feminism in the Early Twentieth Century*. Edited by Ann Heilmann, 179–88. London: UK Pandora, 2003.

3 Writing Oneself at War

Siegfried Sassoon's War Diaries

Introduction

Siegfried Sassoon wrote relentlessly about his experience of the war, in a diversity of formats and at varying degrees of spatial and temporal proximity to—or distance from—the front line. It appears indeed that from the time that he enlisted on 4 August 1914, the very day of Britain's Declaration of War, to the completion of his autobiographical memoirs in 1945, Sassoon's fictional, non-fictional and poetic writing was largely dominated by the war and by his aspiration to articulate his own experience, impressions and opinions as an infantry officer. This has been widely noted by criticism. Robert Hemmings thus states that Sassoon 'was doomed to retrace repeatedly the shadowy ground of his memories' (Hemmings 2007, 284). Likewise, Mark Rawlinson remarks, 'Siegfried Sassoon […] remained captive of [his] war experience: Sassoon's serial re-composition of his war story was a life-long struggle with the legend that overcame the late poets of the war' (Rawlinson 82). With words such as 'doomed', 'captive' or 'struggle', both statements imply that Sassoon's persistent reiteration of his own war experience negatively affected him, both on a personal and psychological level, and as a writer. One of the purposes of the present chapter is to investigate the validity of this notion by delineating the impact of the war on Sassoon's inspiration and style as an author. Likewise, the notion that 'the legend that overcame the late poets of the war' was cause for struggle is revisited, as it will transpire that Sassoon was building and relishing this 'legend' for—and of—himself even before he started publishing his war poetry.

Sassoon enlisted in the British Army and joined the Sussex yeomanry as soon as the United Kingdom declared war on Germany. He wasn't to reach France until the autumn of 1915, due to illness and to breaking his arm in a riding accident. Serving in Northern France and the Somme as part of the 1st Battalion of the Royal Welch Fusiliers, Sassoon started engaging in—sometimes uncalled-for and disruptive—acts of bravery after the death of his friend David Thomas in March 1916. These reckless actions earned him the nickname of 'Mad Jack' among his men but also inspired them with confidence (Egremont 104). After single-handedly capturing a German trench with hand grenades in broad daylight, he also rescued several soldiers under heavy fire, for which he was awarded

DOI: 10.4324/9781003270812-4

the Military Cross in July 1916. Sassoon was wounded twice in action: he was shot in the shoulder during the Battle of Arras, in April 1917, and shot in the head in July 1918, after which he spent the remaining few months of the war in England. In the interval between receiving these two wounds, and as he was convalescing in London from his shoulder injury, Sassoon often met and corresponded with Lady Ottoline Morrell's circle of pacifist friends, among whom Bertrand Russell and Lady Ottoline spoke the most eloquently against the war. Their influence, along with his own disillusionment with the conduct of the war, caused him to issue his famous 'Soldier's Declaration' against the continuation of the war in June 1917. He was eventually persuaded by his friend Robert Graves to avoid court-martial by pleading shell shock and was sent to Craiglockhart War Hospital in Edinburgh, where he was treated by Dr W. H. R. Rivers, an encounter that was to mark him profoundly. Sassoon then went back to France, not because he had regained any trust in the government's handling of the war, but out of a strong feeling of duty towards 'his men'; he was sent to Palestine for a brief few weeks in the early spring of 1918 and eventually came back to the Western Front in May 1918.

Sassoon turned to poetry writing from a very young age and published his first collection at his own expense in 1906, on his 20th birthday (Egremont, 33). His early work was strongly redolent of 19th-century poetry, bearing the influence of poets such as Wordsworth, Swinburne, Tennyson and Rossetti; his poems immediately preceding the war were composed under the auspices of Georgian poetry, which Sassoon greatly admired. Before 1914, however, success was elusive, and Sassoon felt little confidence in his accomplishment as a poet, writing to Edward Marsh—the editor of the *Georgian Poetry* anthologies—in October 1913, that he didn't believe he would 'ever publish any poems', as he felt that what poetry he had written the previous summer was 'utterly hopeless' (qtd in Egremont, 57).

Sassoon's poetic inspiration and ensuing acknowledgement were ignited by the war, and his posterity as a major literary figure of the early 20th century has largely been due to the poetry that he wrote during the conflict. Since 1917, with the publication of his collection *The Old Huntsman*, Sassoon has indeed been celebrated and canonised as one of the most prominent of the war poets. His semi-autobiographical fictional trilogy, which will be most often referred to here as the *Sherston Memoirs*, has also been the object of critical attention, albeit to a much lesser extent than his poetry; the middle volume of the trilogy, the *Memoirs of an Infantry Officer*, which deals with the war, has been deemed of particular interest by scholarship (Moeyes 1997, Bowen 2005, Hemmings 2007, 2008, Giovanelli 2020, Ricketts 2020, to name but a few). Surprisingly little attention, however, has been paid to the diaries that Sassoon wrote whilst on active duty on the Western Front and briefly in Palestine. These diaries have been used largely for their documentary value, both by Sassoon's biographers—among whom Jean Moorcroft Wilson (2014), Max Egremont (2005) and John Stuart Roberts (1999)—and by Sassoon as biographer of his own self, in the fictionalised *Sherston Memoirs* as in his official autobiography. They have not, however, been examined as a work of literature. Paul Moeyes's monograph on Sassoon, *Scorched Glory*, is the most comprehensive critical study of Sassoon's writing as it examines at length not only his poetry, but his prose; yet while it focuses on his poetry, the Sherston trilogy, and his three autobiographies, it does not consider Sassoon's diaries from the angle of criticism, stating that 'the subject of this book is Sassoon's literary work', as opposed to his biographical writing (Moeyes x). The diaries are only quoted insofar as they provide insight into Sassoon's state of mind and development as a poet.

In her volume on the war poets, Sarah Montin asserts that to this day, the poetry of the First World War persists in the United Kingdom as a locus of textual commemoration, in which the war poets 'contribute nowadays to the construction of a national mythology' (Montin 2018, 18).[1] Montin remarks that in France, war literature was mostly celebrated through prose narratives, whereas war poetry was largely overlooked; conversely, in the United Kingdom, the war poets endure as paramount figures in the celebration and commemoration of the First World War (Montin 2018, 16–7). This may explain why Sassoon's *Memoirs of an Infantry Officer*—and to a much greater extent his war diaries—garnered much less attention than his poetry, and why his posterity as a writer is due largely to his canonisation as a war poet. This chapter examines however to what extent Sassoon's war notebooks, beyond their documentary quality, function as a literary workshop within which Sassoon developed—and indeed jotted down—the poetry that earned him his stance as a prominent war poet. To go even further, I argue that the diaries stand as a work of literature in their own right, and that their worth as a literary object leaves no room to doubt. This chapter demonstrates that Sassoon's diaries deserve to be read in their own right, not merely for the direct account that they provide of an officer's experience of the front but also for the poetic intensity that many entries vibrate with. Close textual analysis will demonstrate that many of the entries in Sassoon's diaries, written from the spatial and temporal immediacy of the war, can be considered as equal in literary value to his war poems; it may be argued that some indeed rival, or surpass, his later fictionalised and biographical memoirs.

This chapter is based on a close reading of the diaries that Sassoon kept from his arrival to France, in November 1915, to Armistice Day, on 11 November 1918.[2] The edition and publication in 1983 of these diaries by Sassoon's literary executor Rupert Hart-Davis, has been tremendously useful, and whenever possible, references to the diary entries are made to this edition. Hart-Davis's edition has been advantageously complemented by the perusal of the manuscript diaries that were digitised and have been made freely available online since 2014 by the Cambridge Digital Library. These high-quality photographs of every single page of Sassoon's notebooks have proved invaluable, especially at a time when the COVID-19 pandemic made travel impossible. They offer a renewed insight into Sassoon's writing, allowing us to assess the variations in handwriting, as well as to visualise effects of juxtaposition of prose and poetic accounts of the same experience that do not appear systematically in Hart-Davis's edition. The materiality of the notebooks—as much as it can be appreciated through a screen—has often proved illuminating, bringing an additional layer to the analysis of Sassoon's writing.

The main focus of this chapter is to define Sassoon's war diaries as a genre and literary object. Sassoon's journal entries are strikingly protean in their style, in a way that reflects the fluidity of Sassoon's intents as he kept his diary. Philippe Lejeune's work on the diary as distinct from autobiography is helpful to delineate the generic singularity of Sassoon's war journal, which ultimately appears to evade the traditional divide between diary writing and the autobiography. Additionally, these small notebooks that Sassoon filled assiduously while in active service were used as a repository for literary experimentation and can be identified as a writing workshop, a reservoir for Sassoon's future work. Sassoon's war diaries famously paved the way for his semi-autobiographical novels, the *Sherston Memoirs*, as well as for his future memoirs. The diaries nonetheless played a no less crucial role in the genesis of his war poetry, although this has been hardly noted.

Three pages into his preface, biographer Max Egremont presents Sassoon as a 'national myth' (Egremont xi). Egremont concludes the same paragraph with the statement,

> More than anyone, [...] Siegfried Sassoon created this [vision of 'a callous, out-of-touch High Command and the sacrifice of innocents in the apparently unceasing hell of the Western Front'], through his poetry and his prose, turning it into one of the most resonant myths of our times.
>
> (Egremont xi)

From the outset of his biography, Egremont thus asserts Sassoon both as a myth *and* as a myth builder, contributing to creating a vision of the First World War that remains prevalent in today's representations of the war. One of the aims of this chapter is therefore to assess to what extent this myth was built by Sassoon himself, decades before he memorialised himself via both the (slightly) fictional *Sherston Memoirs*, published between 1928 and 1936, and his own autobiographical memoirs, published between 1938 and 1945. A contrastive approach with the diaries he wrote during the war may help realise the difference—or indeed, absence thereof—between immediate records and retrospective memoirs, written at a distance from the war. This invites questions as to the immediacy of representation in Sassoon's war diaries: if Sassoon consistently writes of his own self as a literary figure and a cultural construct, does this not qualify the directness of his account of his war experience? Or is this literary and cultural filter indeed the only possible way for Sassoon to apprehend and articulate his time in active service? Lastly, this mythical dimension leads us to interrogate the peculiar nature of Sassoon's diaries as a mode of expression of the self. It appears that from the very immediacy of the war, Sassoon was already navigating between the diary format, the autobiographical mode and the memoir. This chapter will thus interrogate the singular form of Sassoon's diaries and investigate the ways in which their writer challenges the limits of the genre.

The Generic Fluidity of Sassoon's War Diaries

War diaries are customarily considered to be more candid accounts of the war. In their introduction to *Working in a World of Hurt*, Carol Acton and Claire Potter delineate the differences between diaries, letters and memoirs as various modes on a spectrum of individual articulation of the war experience. Although their volume focuses on narratives written by medical personnel in warzones, this categorisation is valid for any personal account of the war. Diaries, they argue, are 'less mediated than letters and memoirs', as they are not controlled either by an external, official censor, in the case of letters, or by an internalised censorship that is inseparable from the prospect of a public audience, in the case of memoirs: the notion of an 'over-the-shoulder reader' 'may cause individuals to self-censor not only censorable details but also more personal intimacies' (Acton and Potter 2015, 17). Diaries kept behind the front lines may thus appear as privileged documents to gain as unmediated an access as possible to individual experiences of the First World War. Yet the specificity and the protean nature of Sassoon's diaries invite us to reconsider this classification. While they do achieve what is expected of a diary, i.e. record factual details as well as personal experience, this occurs along a whole range of stances and modes of writing of the self.

The Diary as 'Antifiction'

The first few entries of Sassoon's war journals are written in what can be termed a predictable and traditional diary style, aiming at logging precise and unbiased information. Here is the full entry for the first day in the diary, as Sassoon travels from Britain to France:

> Wed. Nov. 17th
> 1.15 Victoria.
> Got to Folkestone pier 6., *Victoria*, sailed about 7 in bright moonlight; for Boulogne. Changed course after an hour and reached Calais 9.30. Last hour rough.
>
> (19)

These initial entries document factual details, with a focus on exact times, place names and an emphasis on numbers, besides the precise hours: 'pier 6', '320 officers', etc.; and on the weather: 'quiet grey weather', 'weather cold and frosty, but dry' (19). Not unlike the weather here described, Sassoon's style as he inaugurates his war journal is 'dry', as a result of the short clauses, the choice of disyllables or monosyllables, the constant use of parataxis, and the elliptical phrasing that erases the first-person subject. These terse, matter-of-fact entries carry a minimal emotive charge, which is perhaps only palpable in the laconic clause: 'did nothing' (19), which may convey a suppressed frustration and subtly account for their own aridity. The blank style here seems to match what Lejeune deems constitutional of a diary: 'The diary is not, originally and fundamentally, a work of literature: it is a practice, and its purpose is its author's life' (Lejeune 2011).[3]

Sassoon's diary entries also match Lejeune's definition of the diary as regards the writing's timeframe: they invariably relate events and feelings that have occurred on the day they are written. Sassoon's notes when he reads back his journal are minimal and remain in the diaries' margins, clearly identified as later comments rather than as forming part of the entry. This conforms with the time constraint that Lejeune ascribes to the diary format:

> When midnight strikes, what I have dated from the day that just passed must no longer be altered. Any later change would make me leave the diary territory and slip into that of autobiography, which grants itself the freedom to recreate the past in light of the present.[4]
>
> (Lejeune 2011)

To Lejeune, the immediacy of diary writing plays an integral part in its authenticity. In this respect, he opposes the diary and autobiography:

> The value of the diary is linked to the authenticity of the *trace*: any later alteration would ruin this value. The diary is the enemy of autobiography. [...] Like watercolour, the diary doesn't fare well with touch-ups.[5]
>
> (Lejeune 2011)

Sassoon himself, reading his diary from a few years' distance, expressed the discrepancy between the truth of his immediate account and that, unreliable, of his own memory:

> This was the truth, as near as I could get it,
> Although that truth is truth to me no longer.
>
> (Sassoon 1921)

Lejeune defines the diary as 'antifiction' because it 'face[s] up to the impossible truth [...], faithfully and without resorting to invention' (Lejeune 2009, 201). To Lejeune, whilst both genres aim at recounting the past, the fundamental difference between autobiography and the diary lies in their 'opposite moods: autobiography lives under the spell of fiction; the diary dotes on truth' (Lejeune 2009, 201).

Keeping an accurate account of his life on the front was indeed one of Sassoon's foremost goals in keeping a war diary. This is palpable through his relentless attention to geographical precision, a consistent feature of his journal. Besides the first two entries already quoted, many entries start with a precise notation of Sassoon's movements: the entry for 30 January 1916 merely documents his battalion leaving Montagne to reach Picquigny to Vaux (37); likewise, on 12 April 1917, he notes that his battalion has reached St Martin-Cojeul, 'about four kilometres north-west of Croisilles, three kilometres south-east of Wancourt' (153). Sassoon also meticulously records his location: the entry for 23

May 1916 opens with '[o]n Crawley Bridge' (64); 8 April 1918 finds him in his bivouac 'on a hill-top near Suffa' (230; Sassoon served in Palestine from late February 1918 to early May 1918). Sassoon often even specifies his exact location as he is writing, going so far as to indicate the milestone on which he is sitting: 'Amiens 29.7k. Péronne 22.9k' (69, 30 May 1916). Retracing the exact itinerary of Sassoon's whereabouts throughout his time at the front a century later would probably prove to be a relatively effortless task. Such precision indeed matches the tone of the detailed, matter-of-fact regimental records of the First World War. The *Regimental Records of the Royal Welch Fusiliers* are especially relevant for Sassoon and will be the object of deeper focus at the end of this chapter. Sassoon also often couples this geographical accuracy with a precise indication of his own perspective: not just where he stands—or sits—but in what direction he is looking: 'Looking west from the support line' (67, 26 May 1916); 'Looking north from the hill behind Morlancourt' (69, 31 May 1916); 'looking down on the courtyard where some officers are playing cricket' (152, 8 April 1917). Sketches sometimes complement the visuality of the written description: the entry for 15 March 1916 is enlivened with a sketch of roofs and a steeple (MS Add.9852/1/5, 36v).[6]

Through the years, and regardless of location or circumstances, Sassoon's diary thus conveys a consistent urge to record his experience and perception with as much accuracy as possible. This is confirmed, if needs be, by a metatextual comment by Sassoon on his own diary writing, as he concludes his entry on 7 June 1916, finding himself dissatisfied with what he has just penned: 'I haven't written down anything which will bring this hour back to me vivid and true. It's the little details that speak out clear' (75).

The Diary as Writing Workshop

One of Sassoon's intents is thus evidently to bear witness as truthfully as possible—a purpose that was prevalent for anyone writing about the war from the front. Another important reason for Sassoon's scrupulous notetaking was his hope to use these observations for later work intended for publication: this developed in the immediate term via his war poetry, 10 years later with the *Memoirs of an Infantry Officer*, and yet a further 10 to 15 years in his own autobiography. In this respect, Sassoon's diaries also perform as a writing laboratory, or as Françoise Simonet-Tenant argues, 'un atelier d'écritures': a 'writing workshop' where accounts of direct experience are juxtaposed with drafts for poetry, reading lists, and—as becomes clear when reading Sassoon's later prose—passages that are sometimes used as many as three or four times in later publications. As such, the diary becomes itself endowed with literary value:

> For a long time, the personal diary was seen as a mere source of historical and biographical information. Gradually, it has come to be reconsidered as an object of critical study in its own right, one that may reach much beyond a simple blind improvising gesture with a limited scope.[7]

This may also help to explain the fluidity of style in Sassoon's journal writing. To Simonet-Tenant, the diary is 'a versatile object, rich with a diversity of writing styles that may occur at very different stages of the genetic process of the work of literature' (Simonet-Tenant 2011).[8] As a result—and this is where Simonet-Tenant's definition of the relationship between fact and fiction in the genre of the diary tempers the more clear-cut opposition suggested by Lejeune— 'the diary has then become an inextricable mixture of reality and fiction'.[9] Some diarists indeed consciously use their journals as reservoirs for their future work. In this case, the diary operates as a pivot between life and writing.

Sassoon's style develops as he writes: the entries keep growing in length and stylistic intensity, and become exercises in prose poetry. The terse style of the first few pages gradually gives way to a growing lyrical expressivity that in turn works as fertile ground for his poetry, which is directly written down in the notebooks that Sassoon uses as diaries. When perusing the manuscripts, one soon notices that prose entries of particularly salient virtuosity are consistently followed with their pendant in poetic form. As an example, the first pages of the year 1916, written on 3 January (MS Add.9852/1/4, 14v-sq)[10] are full of lyrical surges; they clearly inspire the poem 'To Victory', written on the next day and visible a few pages further on in the notebook (MS Add.9852/1/4, 17v).[11] Sassoon describes the sunlight in the Somme Valley as a 'living masterpiece of landscape-painting' (31) and feels as happy as if he were back in the English countryside. The concluding lines are lyrical:

> O the beauty, the glory of what I saw, and see every day—so easily lost, so precious to the blind and the weary; so heavenly to men doomed to die. The ghost of Apollo is on these cornlands—Apollo in Picardy; it was here that he ground the kern and plied the flail, and lived at the farm.
>
> (31–2)

The appeal to transcendence through the word 'heavenly' and the invocation to Apollo hark back to an idealised painterly England, and the use of the vocative 'O' and of decorous phrasing such as 'ground the kern and plied the flail' find a direct pendant in his poem 'To Victory', composed the next day and copied out in the diary (32). Diary writing is here clearly used as a laboratory to try out phrases and images before Sassoon turns to the poetic format. It works as an interface between experience and literature, as the catalyst that allows its author to transform life experience into art.

The development and maturation of Sassoon's poetic voice indeed follows that of his voice as a diarist. This is most palpable when reading Sarah Cole's meticulous analysis of the development and evolution of Sassoon's style as a war poet in the chapter she devoted to Sassoon in *The Cambridge Companion to the Poetry of the First World War* (2013). The complexity and instability of his style and tone as a poet match that of his diary entries. The next part will investigate the example of the pastoral mode as one of the major aesthetic inspirations in Sassoon's writing.

Pastoral Prose

Sassoon's delight in the pastoral style, which was influenced by Georgian poetry and also occurred more broadly in the wake of Romantic poetry, has been examined in a number of critical works. Fussell points out the influence of the pastoral in the *Sherston Memoirs* (2013), while Hemmings (2007) and Montin (2015, 2018) analyse his war poems from the perspective of the pastoral mode. Montin offers a precise analysis of the specific use of pastoral in First World War poetry:

> In war-poetry as in real life, Paul Fussell tells us, the most striking moments of pastoral occur in brief moments 'sandwiched between bouts of violence and terror' (Fussell 2013, 235). The main function of these pastoral interludes is to provide an idealised and often nostalgic refuge from conflict, in the guise of an Arcadian or an Edenic landscape. However, rather than rely on archetypal pastoral images (the bucolic landscapes of Virgil or Bion), the war-poets often counted on direct reminiscences of their own childhood overlaid with more contemporary poetic associations. This shift from the Golden Age, constructed by Classical and Renaissance aesthetics, to 'ideas of "home"' and 'the summer of 1914' (Fussell 235) re-actualized the pastoral mode.
>
> (Montin 2015, 2–3)

This, and more largely the various analyses of Sassoon's fictional and poetic work from the perspective of pastoral writing, also wholly applies to his journal. Indeed, the omnipresence of the pastoral mode in Sassoon's war writing originates in his diaries, through lengthy and exquisite passages of what may be termed pastoral prose. The opening of his entry for 25 January 1916 offers a representative sample of his delight and virtuosity in the exercise of pastoral prose:

> Riding out this morning in sunshine and stillness—the landscape like a bowl of wine, golden; light spreading across the earth, and earth drinking its fill of light; down by Warlus the village shepherd stamps up and down the fallows on his numb feet, with his hood over his head; alone with his flock and his dogs and his two goats, and a hundred busy black rooks, and a few hares popping up and scuttling across the wheat, stopping to listen, and then away again—big sandy ones.
>
> (35)

The entry starts on a powerful musical note, with the rhyming 'riding' and 'morning' followed by the alliterative pair 'sunshine and stillness'. The short nominal clauses conjure up the sense of a theatrical setting, and the view is explicitly defined as a 'landscape'. The accumulation effect conveyed by the numerous semi-colons creates a feeling of profusion of nature. The influence of

19th-century poetry is palpable in the extended metaphor of the light as 'wine', contained by the landscape and absorbed by the earth. The downward and zooming-in movement of the gaze, from the cosmos implied by sunlight to the earth, then to the human figure, then to the animals, with a gradation in size from the cow to the hares, is strongly redolent of the pastoral poetry inherited from Virgil that was very influential in 19th-century poetry, pointing to an ideal macrocosm where the various kingdoms of life coexist harmoniously. A more obvious reference to the pastoral mode is the focus on the shepherd and on his close relationship with the animals he cares for, highlighted by the repetition of the possessive pronoun in 'his flock and his dogs and his two goats'.

Likewise, when Sassoon goes out for a stroll in Bourecq on 5 December 1915, he devotes another long entry to celebrate this humble country village near Béthune, where mining and agriculture mould the landscape (23). The present tense brings the moment closer to the reader. Strikingly, the war is only mentioned passingly and obliquely, as a duty to which Sassoon must return: in these early pages of Sassoon's diary, written before he has approached the front line, the war often hardly appears to shape the landscape at all. Ironically, the most direct hint at war in the previous paragraph is through a military metaphor describing 'a troop of mules', looking in fact quite innocuous. As is typical in these richly detailed passages, the description abounds in aural as well as visual details. A whole pastoral soundscape emerges, where nature and rural life blend organically: 'the homely caw of a rookery', the curé's greeting, the church-bells, the 'clatter' of mules, the song of the thrush. Although notes such as 'the curé' and 'the first I've heard in France' grant this soundscape the specific colour of a French countryside, Sassoon is grasping for details that are reminiscent of English rurality. Throughout the diaries, and as noted earlier, he constantly compares the French countryside with its geologically identical Kentish counterpart, such as in the following remark, describing the villages 'with steeples, as in England. It is a little like parts of East Kent; and the Tickham hills' (24).

Nevertheless, and as in the poetry he wrote during the war, moments of pure pastoral delight soon give way to more nuanced or ironical descriptions, contrasting the apparent serenity of the countryside or the blossoming of flora into new life with the destruction caused by war. The war's timeline is thus simultaneously measured by and contrasted to nature's rhythm: 'long before the orchards break into blossom', he muses, his battalion will have 'marched away, back to no-man's-land, with death in [their] hearts, mocked by the glory of the coloured earth' (25).

Sassoon sometimes offers a sharp paratactic contrast between the violence of war and its pastoral background:

> Fine and warm. Did attack on Le Quesnoy before lunch. Walked through woods beyond Le Fayel after lunch. Beautiful country—[…]like a picture by Wilson Steer—a faint golden light over all, austere, and yet delicate in tone and outline.
>
> (25)

The parallelism suggested by 'before lunch' and 'after lunch' enhance the dichotomy between the attack and the ensuing stroll and celebration of the countryside. The antithetical *topoi* of Arcady and Armageddon are even improbably conflated:

> This country is more like Arcady than anything I ever saw [...]. And we can hear the big guns booming fifty kilometres away, and Armageddon is still going on.
>
> (26)

In the same vein, Sassoon purposely projects an English pastoral scene over the war landscape and soundscape. Such is the case of his musings on the evening of 19 July 1916, during the Battle of the Somme (95–7). This entry conveys the tension inherent in Sassoon's writing, a tension that only increased as the war went on, between the comforting recourse to the pastoral and a growing anti-pastoral mode. The entry starts with a deliberate effort to experience the scene as if it were taking place in England: the sound of artillery is likened to 'someone kicking footballs', the red caps of the Indian cavalry to poppies and the smell to that of Sassoon's favoured pre-war activity: 'I could almost catch the evening smell of autumn that always reminds me of early cub-hunting'. The aim is to find solace in familiarity: 'I'd found comfort for a while in being something like my old solitary self'. Yet the last few lines express a stance that is exactly opposite, since Sassoon blames his companions for muffling the extraordinariness of the war experience as they 'dull' his 'impressions of the vivid scenes', and for 'mak[ing] the strangeness commonplace'. Sassoon here deplores a sort of inverted uncanniness, where the unfamiliar is made familiar; this indicates a wish to sense and express the extreme unfamiliarity of the war as it is. This wish, however, is at odds with what he has himself just been indulging in: projecting the familiar—an English pastoral setting—onto the unfamiliar—the French landscape at war. This inconsistency matches Montin's analysis of the pastoral in war poetry: 'the pastoral's "poetics of self-contradiction" (Haber 1994, 1), its way of "working insistently against itself" (Haber 1994, 1) is also a keystone of the war pastoral' (Montin 2015, 7).

Sassoon also regularly tests the limits of traditional writing, as in his paradoxical entry from 6 December 1915:

> Twice I saw our shadows thrown on to a white wall by a transport-lamp in rear of the column. Once it was a few colossal heads, with lurching shoulders and slung rifles, and again, on a dead white wall, a line of *legs only*, huge legs striding along, as if jeering at our efforts. [...] About 3.30 the sky cleared, and we marched under the triumphant stars, plough and bear and all the rest—immortal diadems for humble soldiers dead and living.
>
> (24)

The style is different from Sassoon's more customary lyrical descriptions: he is no longer attempting to capture the shadow of pastoral England in the French countryside but developing a new aesthetics that may account for the unprecedented spectacle afforded by the war: in this case, the troops' movement at night, where shadows are distorted and the senses are heightened. The unfamiliarity is expressed by the distortion of shapes and proportions due to the light effect of the transport-lamp, which also conveys a dehumanisation of the marching soldiers, rendered in a vision of dismemberment, with '*legs only*' (the emphasis is Sassoon's) being visible. The style here is more akin to vorticism and to the sharp, dehumanising lines of Wyndham Lewis's war paintings. The final sentence, however, displays unexpected pomp, and falls back into a well-known—perhaps even *too* well-known—mode of writing. The metaphor of the constellations as 'immortal diadems', set in antithesis with the 'humble' qualifier and the set collocation 'dead and living', all contribute to a sentimental—one may venture even hackneyed—representation, which stands in startling tension with the preceding description. In his introduction to his monograph devoted to Sassoon's post-war writing, Robert Hemmings pinpoints Sassoon's complex relationship to modernist modes of writing and its connection to his role in the war: 'Sassoon observes that "the wholly authentic soldier poet[s] are both ancient and modern in their technique"' (Hemmings 2008, 1, quoting Sassoon 1945b, 10). Hemmings describes how Sassoon distanced himself from literary modernism in the interwar years: 'Characterising his aesthetics as happily, indeed confrontationally Victorian, Sassoon took a kind of perverse pride in distinguishing himself from the high modernists' (Hemmings 2008, 5–6). Indeed, even though Sassoon may have superimposed a perspective of irony and loss onto a more traditional pastoral mode, his diaries celebrate nature to their very last pages. As Hemmings argues about his poetry,

> Blunden once wrote that 'no poet of twentieth-century England, to be sure, was originally more romantic and floral than young Siegfried Sassoon' ([Blunden] 25). The conventional critical view is that 'the war changed all that' (Fussell 91), but Blunden would not have agreed. The war may have helped to eliminate the limpid floridity of Sassoon's immature pre-war poetry, but it did not alter the 'romantic' approach that characterised much of his war writing and informs his memoirs.
>
> (Hemmings 2007, 269)

This remark also wholly applies to his war diaries. Nevertheless, moments of closeness to combat qualify and inflect Sassoon's tendency to the pastoral mode and to lyricism.

Impersonality in the Face of Extreme Danger

Although entries written in lyrical and highly expressive prose abound as the diaries progress, Sassoon reverts to a more detached tone whenever he is in situations of extreme danger. Such is the case for his entry written on the night of 25 May 1916, when he rescued several soldiers under heavy fire in a failed raid, an action for which Sassoon earned the Military Cross. This momentous entry could not be reproduced here, but deserves to be read and scrutinised in full (65–7), as it recounts Sassoon's first direct contact with action and heavy fire. It is written almost entirely in the present tense, an unusual choice in Sassoon's diaries, and is governed by parataxis, which strongly contributes to Sassoon's attempt to maintain an overall neutrality of tone. The precision in numbers and the detailed account of the company's movements defuses any potential pathos: '[E]veryone is accounted for now; eleven wounded (one died of wounds) and one killed, out of twenty-eight'. Sassoon's short homage to Corporal O'Brien, one of the very few segments written in the preterit, remains firmly positioned on the side of an official tribute, where emotion is stiffly contained. The whole entry displays acute sensory alertness, with an emphasis on sounds due to sight being limited by night-time (for a detailed analysis of the sensory experience of the First World War, see Das 2005). Sassoon thus notes not only the sound of firing and bombing but also the splashes of the men trudging in the mud, the clicking of the guns, the patter of bullets and overturned clods of earth in the puddles, and eventually, the singing of larks at dawn. He is entirely bent on recording his perception—and not his emotions—as faithfully as possible. His care to document his own limited sensory experience, and not a reconstruction of the scene, leads to passages akin to modernist fragmentary writing, aided by the numerous dashes, with flickers of the scene glimpsed amidst the overall darkness:

> There are blinding flashes and explosions, rifle-shots, the scurry of feet, curses and groans, and stumbling figures loom up from below and scramble awkwardly over the parapet—some wounded—black faces and whites of eyes and lips show in the dusk.
>
> (65–6)

The impersonal tone, along with the enumeration of the heterogeneous elements perceived, the blend of aural and visual elements, the dehumanising fragmentation of the soldiers' faces into 'whites of eyes and lips' and the stark contrast with their blackened faces, all combine to create an intense defamiliarising process, which contributes to the sense of emotional detachment from the scene, whilst not sacrificing to its intensity. This may be the closest to 'high modernism' that Sassoon's writing may reach, although as noted earlier, complying with the codes of modernist writing was not part of Sassoon's aesthetic agenda. The stylistic potency of this entry matches Sarah Montin's analysis of war poetry's relationship with high modernism. To Montin, the formalism inherent in high modernism is incompatible with war poetry, which is inevitably anchored in a historical referent: 'War poets, for whom literature works as a mode of consciousness, experience, or even salvation, are humbler in their experimentation, for they obstinately intend to communicate the incommunicable' (Montin 2018, 28).[12] Montin uses Sartre's definition of committed literature to account for war poetry:

War poetry, believing yet in poetry's ability to convey the world, stands on the side of *revelation*[13] (of a truth, of an object, 'tell[ing] the truth about the war' in Sassoon's words [Sassoon 1945, 40]) rather than of the *creative act*, centred on form.[14]

(Montin 2018, 28–9)

This intent to 'reveal' and to 'communicate the incommunicable' is also fully relevant to Sassoon's diary writing.

Sassoon's dispassionate tone is especially striking when he notes how close the snipers are: 'The bloody sods are firing down at me at point-blank range. (I really wondered whether my number was up.)' (66). The unexpected intrusion of the preterit tense, combined with the brackets, adds yet more distance. On the next day, the effect of the raid on Sassoon is incongruously likened to pre-war frivolities: 'This morning I woke up *feeling as if I'd been to a dance!*—awful mouth and head!' (67, emphasis Sassoon's; the exclamation marks are present in the manuscript, though omitted in the 1983 edition).

In a way that will become characteristic when processing a significant experience, Sassoon then rewrites the event in a variety of modes. As a conclusion to the entry relating the raid, a short paragraph, written probably the next day—the ink is a darker shade[15]—displays a brief moment of introspection, combined with the past tense. Yet even then, Sassoon remains detached from the extreme danger that he was just confronted with as he examines, almost clinically, the nature of the emotions that he and his men experienced:

> There was no terror there—only men with nerves taut and courage braced—then confusion and anger and—failure. I think there was more delight than dread in the prospect of the dangers; certainly I saw no sign of either.
>
> (67)

Additionally, on the page preceding the entry just quoted but probably also written a day or so later, Sassoon couches a condensed, more official version of the events. This version is in turn contrasted with the official communiqué from G.H.Q on Friday 26 May, which Sassoon copied down in his diary just below his condensed version:

> 'At Mametz we raided hostile trenches. Our party *entered without difficulty* (!!!) and maintained a spirited bombing fight, and finally withdrew at the end of twenty-five minutes'. (The truth which is (less than) half a truth!!!).[16]
>
> (67, Sassoon's italics and brackets)

The communiqué's inaccuracy justifies Sassoon in his own endeavour to faithfully narrate his experience of the failed raid.[17] Sassoon's compulsion to relate his experience in as detailed and dispassionate a manner as possible corresponds to the discourse of the 'testimony' that Shoshana Felman and Dori Laub describe in their eponymous volume:

> Joining events to language, the narrator as eye-witness is the testimonial *bridge* which, mediating between narrative and history, guarantees their correspondence and adherence to each other. This bridging between narrative and history is possible since the narrator is both an *informal* and *honest* witness [...]. Once endowed with language through the medium of the witness, *history speaks for itself*. All the witness has to do is to *efface himself*, and let the *literality of events* voice its own *self-evidence*.
>
> (Felman and Laub 101)

This ideal of an 'informal and honest witness' is however made fragile by the very use of language: as soon as experience is mediated through words, an inevitable shaping and filtering takes place. The limitation of the testimonial value of Sassoon's diaries will be discussed in more detail towards the close of this chapter.

The direct stylistic links between the diaries and Sassoon's war poetry have been highlighted earlier. Besides the poems that stand next to the prose entries in Sassoon's notebooks and that often seem to emanate from some of these entries, many passages in the diaries can also be found almost *verbatim* in the *Sherston Memoirs*, which were written ten years after the war. Predictably, in *Memoirs of an Infantry Officer*, Sassoon writes at length of the events of 25 May 1916 and shares a plethora of details, many of which are directly borrowed from the diary. The narrative of the events occupies an entire chapter (Sassoon 1930, 22–8). Sherston's version is written in the preterit tense, and the account is complemented by an access into the thought process of Sherston, thus adding affect to the detached diary entry of 1916. This matches the difference pinpointed by Acton and Potter between diaries and memoirs:

> Unlike diaries and letters which tell an immediate story, memoirs are necessarily more reflective, especially as they are often written years after the war, when the experience and the meaning it carries as a whole can be contemplated from a distance. [...] Especially these may show a very conscious awareness of revealing or seeing that had been shut down during the war.
>
> (Acton and Potter 2015, 18)

Nevertheless, the chapter in *Memoirs of an Infantry Officer* closes on an exact quotation of the General Headquarters' Communiqué that Sassoon had copied down in his diary. Where the diary isolates the communiqué between two lines, it is italicised in the *Sherston Memoirs*: both devices share the same purpose of underlining the dissonance between the collective, official account and Sassoon/ Sherston's direct and individual experience of the raid.

Sassoon's Account of the First Day of the Battle of the Somme

This chapter has so far examined entries that tend to display either one or the other mode in Sassoon's way of writing of his war experience: factual, lyrical or suppressedly intense in particularly momentous events. Whilst the metamorphic quality of Sassoon's diary writing is best felt when reading his journal as a whole, a few single entries do manage to encapsulate on their own the complexity and ambivalence of Sassoon's intents when recording his experience of the war. Such is the case of the long report that Sassoon wrote during the fateful opening of the Battle of the Somme, on 1 July 1916. Sassoon's battalion was to be in support of the action, so he did not take direct part in the initial fighting, but he had a good vantage point from which he witnessed the attack, as his battalion was positioned in front of the village of Mametz, one of the major junctions of the offensive. In the *Memoirs of an Infantry Officer*, Sherston deems that his battalion had 'the fortunate role of privileged spectators' (Sassoon 1930, 55). In his journal entry for 1 July 1916, Sassoon strives for visual and aural precision through a painstakingly detailed entry (82–5), writing at short intervals through the day and carefully recording the time: '7.30'; '7.45'; 9.30'; 9.50', etc, demonstrating that he was writing directly as the battle unfolded. This temporal immediacy is allied with an effort to record factual details, which is conveyed—as on 25 May—by the use of the present tense, paratactic sentences and a dispassionate tone. In addition to the apparent factualness of this account, Sassoon's position as onlooker is underscored through the many mentions of visuality: 'I have seen', 'watching the show', 'I saw', 'have another look', 'I can see', 'I am looking at', etc., demonstrating that it isn't only the spectacle that matters in the diary, but its spectator. Sassoon wants to remember his perception and sensations as much as he wants to remember the events of the day. However, this emphasis on his own stance as witness introduces an unavoidable bias to the account. The diary does not simply record the events but recounts Sassoon's individual and necessarily limited perspective on them. This corresponds to the shift in the nature of the gaze during the First World War that has been noted by many critics, among whom Paul Virilio (2009), Samuel Hynes (1990), Jean Gallagher (1998), Santanu Das (2005) and Claire Bowen (2005). Bowen thus states,

> The disaster of the Great War, as understood in Europe, at least, was unmanageable both in its geographical extent and in its effects. [...] for most protagonists, the literal perception of events was necessarily limited. The First World War, by its very size, was a war of fragmentation [...]. [...] The experience of the first World War trench soldier at the Front was physically limited by earth walls and a patch of sky [...]'.
>
> (Bowen 3)

Virilio opens his essay *War and Cinema* on the indissociable link between war and representation—and therefore, on the indispensable presence of spectators to validate the war:

> 'War can never break free from the magical spectacle because its very purpose is to *produce* that spectacle' [...] There is no war, then, without representation [...]. Weapons are tools not just of destruction but also of perception.
>
> (Virilio 2009, 7–8)

However, Virilio then asserts that this oculocentric ideal of the war was made obsolete by the Great War, as D. W. Griffith realised when he was sent to the front to shoot propaganda footage:

> Towards the end of the First World War, when Griffith arrived at the French front to make his propaganda film, the last romantic battle had long since taken place, in 1914 on the Marne. The war had become a static conflict in which the main action was for millions of men to hold fast to their piece of land, camouflaging themselves for months on end [...]. To the naked eye, the vast new battlefield seemed to be composed of nothing.
>
> (Virilio 2009, 19)

Ford Madox Ford was faced with the same scopic issues, as discussed in the first chapter; like him, Sassoon is indeed deeply aware of the limitations of his own perception of the fighting, notwithstanding his privileged position. The numerous mentions of his stance as onlooker, while emphasising what he *can* see, also adumbrate all that he *cannot* witness.

Sassoon's endeavour to record the events as faithfully as possible—albeit with a full awareness of the limitations of his perspective—doesn't preclude moments of poetry, as in the first paragraph of the day's entry:

> The air vibrates with the incessant din—the whole earth shakes and reeks and *throbs*—it is one continuous roar.
>
> (82)

This sentence is composed of a series of strikingly regular iambs: the first clause forms an iambic pentameter, while the second and third clauses are both iambic tetrameters. This poetic regularity is contrasted with an abrupt series of interjections standing out in a single line, which appears much more akin to vorticist poetry:

> Inferno—inferno—bang—smash!

Besides the absence of syntax and the fragmentation conveyed by the dashes, the line moves from a noun to sheer onomatopoeias, with the words themselves growing shorter. Further down, a few factual sentences are followed with a clear cultural reconstruction of the sight before Sassoon as a 'landscape' and of the events as a 'show':

> 7.45 a.m. The artillery barrage is now working to the right of Fricourt and beyond. I have seen the 21st Division advancing on the left of Fricourt; and some Huns apparently surrendering. Our men advancing steadily to the first line. A haze of smoke drifting across the landscape—brilliant sunshine. Some Yorkshires on our left (50th Brigade) watching the show and cheering as if at a football match.
>
> (82)

The entry constantly juxtaposes the violence of the events, conveyed in particular by the recurring mention of the endless deafening noise, with mundane remarks, such as 'had a shave' at 9:30. Later during this same historic morning, Sassoon states dispassionately, 'Just eaten my last orange'. This trivial sentence is directly followed with a strongly visual description of the fighting:

> Just eaten my last orange. I am staring at a sunlit picture of Hell, and still the breeze shakes the yellow weeds, and the poppies glow under Crawley Ridge where some shells fell a few minutes ago. [...] A bayonet glitters.
>
> (83)

These few lines capture the versatility and fluidity of Sassoon's diary writing: the description, while striving for accuracy, simultaneously highlights the paradoxical beauty of the scene, marked with effects of intense light, with the glowing of the poppies, the glitter of the bayonet and this oxymoronic 'sunlit picture of Hell'. As in some of Ford's descriptions, the word 'picture' again adds a cultural layer to the experience and filters the experience through literary references, following a process that is constant in Sassoon's writing.

Predictably, such a significant entry was much used in Sassoon's later prose writing. In *Memoirs of an Infantry Officer*, the narrator even explicitly refers to the notebooks in which he wrote his war diaries, and informs the reader that he will be quoting directly from them: 'A small shiny black notebook contains my pencilled particulars, and nothing will be gained by embroidering them with afterthoughts' (Sassoon 1930, 55). The material depiction of the notebook leaves no doubt as to the actual source for Sherston's narrative. Here is but one among many excerpts that proves quite illuminating as to the way in which Sassoon used his diaries in this semi-fictional autobiographical novel:

> 7.45. The barrage is now working to the right of Fricourt and beyond. I can see the 21st Division advancing about three-quarters of a mile away on the left and a few Germans coming to meet them, apparently surrendering. Our men in small parties (not extended in line) go steadily on to the German front-line. Brilliant sunshine and a haze of smoke drifting along the landscape. Some Yorkshires a little way below on the left, watching the show and cheering as if at a football match. The noise almost as bad as ever.
>
> (Sassoon 1930, 55–6)

The focus of this chapter is Sassoon's immediate writing from the front line, so both texts will not be compared in much detail, but it is worth observing that this is a minimally edited rewriting of the passage quoted earlier from the diary. Other such instances abound in the *Memoirs of an Infantry Officer*: Sassoon's diaries were a material used again and again in later publications, often with minimal corrections.

The Teleological Perspective of Sassoon's Diaries

Consequently, while Lejeune's argument that the diary is a *praxis*, as opposed to an *œuvre*, a work of literature, retains some relevance, it begs to be nuanced in the case of Sassoon's journals. Sassoon was not only writing of his experience, and gazing at the war, but gazing at *himself* as he was experiencing the war. This is made most evident when one examines the question of teleology. The absence of teleology is usually considered one of the main defining traits of diary writing. In Lejeune's phrasing,

> the diarist writes a text whose conclusion he does not master. He progresses blindly towards an unknown end, accepting it only partly depends on him. The diary accepts its own limits, exploring and postponing every day an ending that eludes it'.[18]

(Lejeune 2011)

The absence of a known ending grants the diary an anticlassical form since the traditional *post hoc ergo propter hoc* logic established by Barthes as the basis for traditional linear narration is impossible:

> There is a strong presumption that the mainspring of the narrative activity is to be traced to that very confusion between consecutiveness and consequence, what-comes-*after* being read in a narrative as what-is-*caused-by*. Narrative would then be a systematic application of the logical fallacy denounced by scholasticism under the formula *post hoc, ergo propter hoc*, which may well be the motto of Destiny whose 'language', after all, finds its expression in narrative.[19]

(Barthes 1975, 248)

The context of the war and the high probability of dying at the front explain why this general rule of the diary is undermined in the case of Sassoon. His journal displays a tendency to look ahead and imagine the future, thus vectorising the events and feelings recorded towards an imagined ending, and fabricating a linear development. Sassoon often writes in the mode of the future perfect, envisioning how his participation in the war *will have* gone down in history—putting himself alternatively in the perspective of his dying at the front, or conversely of his surviving and continuing his literary career. In either case, he strives constantly to imbue his diaries with a teleological perspective. On 16 July

1916, he thus conjures up a vectorised narrative of his survival. After reminiscing on his pre-war life in rural England, leisurely filled with cricket matches, he looks ahead:

> I'll never be there again. If I'm lucky and get through alive, there's another sort of life waiting for me. Travels, and adventures, and poetry; and anything but the old groove of cricket and hunting, and dreaming in Weirleigh garden. When war ends I'll be at the crossroads; and I know the path to choose. I must go out into the night alone.
>
> (94)

Sassoon often considers his life in spatial terms—the past taking place in idle, pastoral England, the present being that of the trenches, and the future looming dimly ahead. The last two sentences generate a spatial construct of his life as a journey, using the traditional *topos* of the 'path' and the 'crossroads'. As in countless other entries, Sassoon displays a tendency to write about his own life not on the mode of the diary, but as a traditional narrative where consecutiveness matches consequence. The connection that Barthes establishes between a linear narrative founded on a *post hoc ergo propter hoc* logic and the expression of what he terms 'Destiny' appears particularly apt. Sassoon is bent on bringing to light his own destiny in his personal narrative, in the effort to build a myth out of his experience.

Writing a Myth of Oneself[20]

From his birth and his mother's choice of the Wagnerian 'Siegfried' as his name, notwithstanding the absence of any link to Germany on either side of the family (Sassoon came from a line of Sephardic Jews on his father's side and a long-standing Cheshire farming family on his mother's), Sassoon was predestined and perhaps in no small way conditioned to cast his self as a mythical figure. Ironically, the front line of the Battle of Arras in which Sassoon was to be shot in the shoulder in April 1917 was called 'Siegfried' by the Germans, as reported by his company's regimental records: 'We called It the Hindenburg Line—the Germans, with their love for the myths and sagas of legendary days, called it Siegfried!' (Ward 260). Sassoon himself was fully aware of the opportuneness that his first name provided in his endeavours to represent himself as a mythical character, as is evidenced by his choice of title for the third volume in his autobiography, *Siegfried's Journey* (1945a), which is strongly redolent of Wagner's third opus of *Der Ring Des Nibelungen*, entitled *Siegfried*. More largely, Sassoon grew up in a late-19th-century atmosphere that was suffused with cultural and literary references (see, for instance, Egremont 5–10).

One of the most striking aspects that surfaces from the beginning of Sassoon's war diaries is that even before serving in the war, Sassoon was striving to build a version of his own self not as a mere person, but as a self-conscious persona, or indeed, personage. This propensity was only heightened by the war. One of Sassoon's prevalent worries on the front was to fail to fulfil his destiny as a hero;

after being shot in the shoulder in the Hindenburg Tunnel, on 16 April 1917, he concludes the next day's entry with a note of palpable relief: 'My luck never deserts me; it seems inevitable for me to be cast for the part of "leading hero!"' (156). The theatrical imagery emphasises Sassoon's awareness of his self-identification as a literary character—and even as an archetype, as implied by the quotation marks framing 'leading hero'. This sense of role-playing is recurrent in the diaries, as in the following remark: 'I'm never alone here—never my old self—always acting a part—that of the cheery, reckless sportsman—out for a dip at the Bosches' (94). Although Sassoon was aware of his conforming to a type among his fellow lieutenants, and seems here to deprecate the phenomenon, his whole diary shows him gazing at himself and constructing his identity as an archetype. In *Living Autobiographically: How We Create Identity in Narrative*, Paul Eakin argues that this compulsion to write of ourselves as characters in a narrative is intrinsic to human nature. He thus opens his first chapter by quoting the neurologist Oliver Sacks: 'It might be said that each of us constructs and lives a "narrative", and this narrative *is* us, our identities' (Sacks 1987, 110, quoted in Eakin 2008, 1). To Eakin, shaping our lives into narratives is integral to our self-construction:

> There is a mutually enhancing interplay between what we are and what we say we are. [...] When it comes to our identities, narrative is not merely *about* self, but is rather in some profound way a constituent part *of* self.
>
> (2)

My object is consequently not to pinpoint a discrepancy between what Sassoon might 'really' have been or done and the way he represented it in his diaries—such an attempt has been proved as void since Ricœur's work on memory, history and representation. Rather, this section aims at highlighting the ubiquitous presence of literary and cultural references inherent in Sassoon's shaping of himself as a lieutenant.

One of the prevalent components inherent in Sassoon's self-construction as an archetypal figure is his sense of sacrifice to the nation through his active war service. On 3 December 1915, summoning the memory of his brother who was killed in action in Gallipoli just a month previously, Sassoon reviews his past life and states solemnly:

> I have seen beauty in life, in men and in things; but I can never be a great poet, or a great lover. The last fifteen months have unsealed my eyes. I have lived well and truly since the war began, and have made my sacrifices; now I ask that the price be required of me. I must pay my debt. Hamo went: I must follow him. I will.
>
> (22–3)

The sustained metaphor of the debt owed to the nation adds to the peremptory declarative mode conveyed by the anaphoras of 'I have' and 'I must' and by the shift in modals from 'have' to 'must', and finally 'will'. This ideal of self-sacrifice initiated by the death of his brother is articulated in poetic form a few days later in the short poem 'Brothers' (later renamed 'To My Brother'), written on 18 December (27). The affectedness of the second stanza, with its stereotypical images of the 'laurelled head' and the 'light' of glory, matches the tone of the prose entry with the metaphor of the debt owed and paid to the country. This use of stereotype abounds in Sassoon's journal and early war poetry, as in 'Absolution', written in April 1915 and revised in September of the same year. The religious overtones of the poem are again sustained by an emphasis on light: 'beauty shines', and time is assimilated to 'a golden wing'. Such imagery conforms with the consensual and authorised representation of participation in the First World War as a sacrifice to the nation, in its etymological sense of 'making holy'. In Vincent Sherry's words, 'In the political economy of the war, the figure of the sacrificial offering appears and reappears to consecrate an otherwise uncertain purpose—to make holy, *sacer-facere*' (Sherry 2018, 92).

The sacrificial dimension of Sassoon's experience of the war takes on increasing complexity as the diaries progress. Another prevailing feature in Sassoon's self-identification as a legend is the consciousness of his role as a poet soldier. Sassoon often writes of himself and of his duty in service as a representative of poets on the front. Examining the probability of his dying, he observes on 31 March 1916 that it is not worth being in combat for a poet unless one distinguishes oneself through bravery: 'No good being out here unless one takes the full amount of risks', he comments, adding that his ambition to earn military honour is 'for the sake of poetry and poets, whom I represent' (50). In the same vein, a few days later, Sassoon, considering the strong probability of his being killed, reflects that he would rather die in a manner that demonstrates a poet's bravery, to 'let people see that poets can fight as well as anybody else' (52). Sassoon's major worry if he is killed is indeed to have died before making a mark in the landscape of English poetry. Coolly considering the prospect of his death as he is waiting for his newly published collection *The Old Huntsman* to reach him at the front, he states, 'No sign of my book yet. I do want to see it before I get killed (if death is the dose which April means me to swallow)' (148).

Lastly, Sassoon's construction of himself as a sacrificial figure finds an expression in his care for the soldiers he is accountable for as second lieutenant. This concern may appear at odds with his omnipresent focus on his own experience; this ambivalent tone in the diaries matches the duality of his voice in his war poetry, which Paul Moeyes has noted:

> From the moment he arrived for his first spell in the trenches there is a gradual development of two different strains in his poetry, which usually co-exist without any problems, but which sometimes oddly clash. On the one hand there is Sassoon's personal voice, the voice of the privileged young man who struggles to come to terms with the realities of war. But on the other hand there is the voice of the subaltern, the young officer who develops a sense of responsibility for the men under his command.
>
> (Moeyes 1997, 33)

Sassoon is as vitriolic about his fellow officers as he is sympathetic—albeit often with a note of condescension—towards the soldiers under his command. He often refers to them as 'my men', a phrase that implies a wider concern for humanity. On Tuesday, 3 April 1917, during the Holy Week preceding Easter, he expresses his wish to become a hero in connection with his improving relationship with the battalion he has recently joined: 'The Second R.W.F. are gradually taking me to their bosom. It will be best for me to stay here now and try to become a hero' (148). On the same day, he wrote the poem 'Foot Inspection'. With the mention of the soldiers' 'naked feet' and the officer persona bending on a private's 'blistered toes', the scene evokes the Maundy Thursday ritual of the washing of the feet, commemorating Christ's washing his apostles' feet on the eve of his Passion. The officer persona is consequently identified as a Christlike figure, a sacrificial lamb who gives his life no longer for his nation, but for his men: '[H]e never knows/ How glad I'd be to die, if dying could set him free / From battles'. The Levinassian celebration of the other's face as the locus and expression of their individuality and vulnerability is here translated to the soldiers' feet. Yet words such as 'pity' or 'stoop' betray Sassoon's inescapable sense of superiority. The final line evidences that his foremost concern is not merely of caring for his men, but of sensing their admiration and acknowledgement of his efforts.

Sassoon's self-identification as a martyr for his fellow soldiers became clearer as the war progressed; it crystallised in Sassoon's statement against the war, and later in his decision to go back to the front out of duty for his men. In his statement, 'A Soldier's Declaration', released on 15 June 1917, he thus declares, 'I am a soldier, convinced that I am acting on behalf of soldiers'. Once he goes back into service after his stay at Craiglockhart, his concern is more pronounced: 'I am nothing but what the Brigadier calls "a potential killer of Germans (Huns)". O God, why must I do it? *I'm not*. I am only here to look *after* some men' (261).

Sassoon's sense of himself as martyr, however, was not devoid of some self-questioning and derision. After going to great lengths to make sure his 'men' get their tea after an exhausting train journey, Sassoon mixes his sense of achievement with self-doubt:

> Alone I did it. Without my help they would have had none. And I was proud of myself. It is these little things, done for nameless soldiers, that make the war bearable. So I sit and wonder if I'm really a good chap, or only rather a humbug.
>
> (257)

Likewise, on yet another page where Sassoon expresses his wish to 'set an example', he does wonder at the validity of his urge to conform to a literary ideal, here shaped by the words of the Metaphysical poet Richard Crashaw:

I must go on till I am killed. Is it cussedness (because so many people want me to survive the war)—or is it the old spirit of martyrdom—'ripe men of martyrdom', as Crashaw says?

(162)

The mythical dimension of Sassoon's self-narrative explains to a large extent the specific and unstable format of the diaries that Sassoon wrote during the war. Since he conceived of his life as a novel, and of his own self as a mythical figure, a would-be hero, the traditional, non-teleological nature of the diary is disrupted. An important aspect of this disruption is the inscription of the reader within the diary. On 20 May 1916, Sassoon concludes his entry as follows (emphasis mine):

But let anyone who reads this know that I was four weeks at Flixécourt, and four weeks happy and peaceful—and free, with my books and my work and the heaven of spring surging all round me over the noble country, and lighting the skies with magnificence.

(63)

From within the intimate form of the diary, which is not primarily intended for perusal by a third party, Sassoon conceives of his writing—and consequently, of his representation of himself—in a scopic relationship with an audience. Lejeune's definition of the diary as a *praxis* rather than an *opus* cannot fully account for the particular case of Sassoon's journal because it evades and exceeds the intimate scope of the traditional diary form.

The complexity inherent in Sassoon's war diary interrogates the testimonial quality examined at the beginning of the chapter. Claire Bowen has devoted an article examining the relationship between Sassoon's diaries and the *Memoirs of an Infantry Officer*, where she also compares the journal with its immediate poetic counterparts, as on 22 April 1916:

Both the diary entry and the poem are the product of very short-term memory, the latter noted, apparently, also in real time. The point here, as in Sassoon's later war poems, is to respond to what Shoshana Felman calls a 'crisis of truth' [...] by testimony. [...] By virtue of his position as a witness, Sassoon the narrator is necessarily the provider of truths which are unavailable to the papers and even to the war correspondents and photographers who are only near the Front but not on it and certainly not combatants.

(Bowen 5)

Bowen then quotes the same passage from Felman's *Testimony* that is mentioned earlier in the chapter (Felman and Laub, 1991, 101); she does remark that

having been an eye-witness is no guarantee at all of accuracy. The temporal, spatial and social limitations of the on-site, real-time observer and his/her preoccupations when dealing with the immediate situation preclude any hope of objective, complete reporting and this was particularly true in the fragmented, upside-down world of the trench soldier. [...] The expression of individual experience both feeds and feeds upon the grand narrative of the catastrophic event.

(Bowen 11)

Furthermore, the constant presence of cultural and literary references in Sassoon's mind as lenses through which he views his experience, as analysed earlier, undermines this ideal of 'correspondence and adherence' between history and the testimony. The inevitable filter and reshaping of experience, intrinsic to any mediation through words, is particularly pronounced in the case of Sassoon. Bowen is aware of this when she analyses the entry diary for 26 April 1916 and its corresponding passage in the *Sherston Memoirs*:

What Sassoon—and Sherston—see, and what is of capital importance, is landscape observed through the prism of a Georgian education and practice. [...] Sassoon's 'ordinary' landscape is a received one of disciplined nature, visually that of Constable and of Samuel Palmer—immutable, an expression of harmony, inspiration and echo of the finer feelings and instincts of the human. There is, in Sassoon's work, both in the *Diaries* and the *Memoirs*, a clear inscription of habits of writing and perception taken from a relatively recent English past and what he sees is mediated through a profoundly assimilated literary tradition.

(Bowen 8)

Bowen's article is rich with illuminative remarks and subtle analysis. My main reservation lies in the fact that the difference it establishes between the *Diaries* and the *Sherston Memoirs* is mainly one of perspective: to Bowen, the *Memoirs* are retrospective, which allows the inscription of a linearity, a causality, where the *Diaries* are immediate, with no outlook on the future:

Sassoon's present melts into the immediate past ('yesterday', 'yesterday evening', 'today') and its consequences ('I have', 'they have been'). Sherston's present is more than ten years after the Armistice and the narrative voice shifts between a simple account of the past ('I watched', 'he grinned', 'there were') and the lessons learned in retrospect. 'One has to find things out as one goes along' (Sassoon, 1929, unpaginated) is a thought neither expressed nor implied in the *Diaries* which are remote from such long-term considerations. Such thoughts are an integral part of the *Memoirs* in which the older and wiser Sassoon-Sherston narrates a refocused account of the material of the *Diaries*.

(Bowen 9)

Although this discrepancy between the diaries and the *Sherston Memoirs* is valid to an undeniable extent since the diaries were indeed written at a very short temporal distance from the events they narrate, it is often manifest that Sassoon wrote them with the future—and his hoped-for posterity—in mind, and probably with a view to using his writing as material for future publication. While the recreation of history as myth is more forcefully obvious in the *Sherston Memoirs*, the process of reconstructing history as legend was already well underway in the *Diaries*.

The final part of this chapter will attempt a synthesis of the various modes of representation present in Sassoon's diaries, by looking at an example of particularly rich and layered writing.

An Instance of Intensely Layered Writing: Recounting the Attack on Fontaine-lès-Croisilles (11–17 April 1917)

The most striking entry as regards the layering of various modes of writing—and the consequent layering of temporal perspectives—is probably that recounting Sassoon being under heavy fire and receiving a wound to the shoulder during the attack on Fontaine-lès-Croisilles in the Battle of Arras, on 16 April 1917. This entry describes Sassoon's most direct and brutal experience of combat. Sassoon inaugurated a new notebook to recount the events (MS Add.9852/1/10); the first page, not reproduced in Hart-Davis's edition of the diaries, bears the carefully underlined title 'The Sleepless Days' and was manifestly written after the entries of the next few pages, as it recapitulates the days leading up to the Battle of Arras and Sassoon's wound.[21] Sassoon's handwriting, usually quite neat, becomes increasingly sprawling in the next few pages: probably under the simultaneous strains of haste, intense stress and trauma—not to mention his wound—and of the urge to recount his experience while it was still vivid. As with the account of the first day of the Battle of the Somme, Sassoon's descriptions emphasise the act of seeing, as on 14 April 1917:

> I have seen the most ghastly sights [...]. The dead bodies lying about the trenches and in the open are beyond description [...]. Our shelling of the line [...] has left a number of mangled Germans—they will haunt me till I die. And everywhere one sees the British Tommie in various states of dismemberment—most of them are shot through the head—so not so fearful as the shell-twisted Germans.
>
> (154–5)

Sassoon's urge to bear witness yields a dramatically different result, however, from his usually detailed depictions: the bodies are 'beyond description' and are only mentioned insofar as they leave a lasting imprint on Sassoon's memory: '[T]hey will haunt me till I die' (155). The writing style is different from anything else written in the diaries: whilst it is evidently more forceful than the matter-of-fact entries of army movement or routine billeting, the style is devoid of the lyrical intensity of Sassoon's contemplative entries when he is at some distance from the front. Although Sassoon's diaries have hitherto displayed a rich expressivity, his endeavour to represent the war in all its 'truth' surpasses words when confronted with the abjection of mangled corpses.

Any form of pathos is avoided until the final few words. The full diary entry for 16 April 1917, the day when Sassoon was shot in the shoulder, is worth reading closely (155–6). The governing tone is informative; as with the description of the first day of the Battle of the Somme that was our focus earlier, there is an emphasis on exact numbers. Most arresting is Sassoon's account of his being shot: 'I got a sniper's bullet through the shoulder and was no good for about a quarter of an hour. Luckily it didn't bleed much' (155). Sassoon even prepares to continue bombing the German trench after being shot and has then to walk several kilometres before he is tossed about in a bus for an hour and a half to the Casualty Clearing Station. Pain and shock are mostly suppressed in a strongly contained style, which stands in a remarkable contrast from Sassoon's actual handwriting[22]—as well, of course, as from the lyrical entries that he delights in throughout his diaries. The mention of pain and exhaustion only occurs towards the end, and only after Sassoon has expressed concern for his battalion and relief that no one was killed. The sentence '[w]ritten about 7.30 p.m. with rain pelting on the roof and wind very cold' confirms the immediacy of the recording from the actual events. The phrase 'never mind', opening the last sentence, encapsulates Sassoon's restraint; yet the final few words, quoting his close friend Robert Graves's poem 'Escape', inflect the informational and unemotional quality of the account. Even as Sassoon is huddled at the Casualty Clearing Station, exhausted, in deep pain from being shot in the shoulder and in shock from surviving open fire, he is already rewriting his trajectory through the lens of lyrical verse.

The next day's entry confirms Sassoon's compulsion to immediately rewrite—and relive—his experience in a literary format, as it comprises a list entitled 'Things to remember' (MS Add.9852/1/10, 10v–2v),[23] which are fragments of impressions and sensations felt during the attack. Here is an excerpt from this list:

> Things to remember
> The dull red rainy dawn on Sunday April 15 […].
> During the relief—stumbling along the trench in the dusk, dead men and living lying against the sides of the trench one never knew which were dead and which living. Dead and living were very nearly one, for death was in all our hearts. Kirkby shaking dead German by the shoulder to ask him the way.
> On April 14 the 19th Brigade attacked at 5.30 a.m. I looked across at the hill where a round red sun was coming up. The hill was deeply shadowed and grey-blue, and all the Country was full of shell-flashes and drifting smoke. A battle picture.
> Scene in the Hénin Dressing Station. The two bad cases—abdomen (hopeless) and ankle. The pitiful parson.

The strongly visual details are already reconstructed into cultural objects: 'a battle picture', or a 'scene'. Many items from the list are missing from the 1983 edition of the diaries. One element that is not present adumbrates that Sassoon was evidently writing down these memories with future writing in mind: 'Scene in Chaplin's H.Q. 3.15 to 5.45 am Monday. *Worth a full description*' (MS Add.9852/1/10, 11v; my emphasis). Just a few hours after experiencing direct trauma, Sassoon was already thinking of his experience as a future past, and as material for later writing. The present is automatically sensed as a future past, as a memory to come. Sassoon's narrative of the war is thus multi-layered: even as he is writing a matter-of-fact, unpathetic account *in medias res*, he is thinking of potential later versions, which contributes to explaining the plethora of sensory details. This confirms the singularity of Sassoon's war diaries within the genre of diary writing.

Besides these two entries of 16 and 17 April, Sassoon had two other opportunities of narrating the event, his own involvement and his receiving a wound over the next few days. The attack on Fontaine-lès-Croisilles was recorded by Sassoon himself in the *Regimental Records of the Royal Welch Fusiliers*. This long, detailed account adds yet another layer to Sassoon's narrative of his experience. Here is the introductory paragraph:

> Our 2nd Battalion took over from the 13th Northumberland Fusiliers, in the Hindenburg Line itself. [...] Their role was limited to the supplying of 100 bombers in support of the Cameronians [...]. In the attack of the 16th April 75 of these bombers became engaged. The attack was not a success. At one time some 300 yards had been won, when 2nd Lieutenant Sassoon and Sergeant Baldwin distinguished themselves.
>
> (Ward 280)

The whole of this adventure is then described by none other than Sassoon:

> At 9 p.m. the relief of the 21st Division began. There must have been some hazy moonlight, for I can remember the figures of men propping themselves against the walls of the communication trench; seeing them in some sort of ghastly half-light I wondered whether they were dead or asleep, for the attitudes of some were like death, uncouth and distorted. [...]
>
> The company we were relieving had departed, so there was no one to give me any information. I didn't even know for certain that we were in the front line.
>
> (Ward 280)

Here is an excerpt from the next day's account, still by Sassoon himself:

> When it was dark I went with a cheery little guide to discuss the operation with the Cameronian Company Commander in his front-line dugout. (Was it the front line? I don't know. I only know that I felt very

incompetent and misinformed, and that the officer I talked to seemed full of knowledge and trench topography which meant nothing to my newly arrived mind)'. [...] I returned with the feeling that I hadn't the faintest idea what it was all about or what I should do in the way of organising my command. [...] By the mercy of God I got hold of Ralph Greaves; [...] to him I confided my incompetence, and [...] I sat and ruminated on my chances of extinction the next morning.

(Ward 281–2)

Sassoon opens several sentences with 'I can remember', indicating that this account was written at some temporal distance from the event, though we cannot know the exact interval between the event and its narrative; this phrase also highlights the potential fragility of his account since it is done from a necessarily faulty memory. He also keeps mentioning his inability to fully apprehend the events while he was in action. Surprisingly, this public record is written on a much more personal note than in his personal diary: Sassoon focuses as much on his own sensations as he does on the events. The most striking passage to this effect is probably the record of his feelings after being shot:

After about a quarter of an hour I began to feel active and heroic again, but in a different way—I was now not only a hero but a wounded hero! I can remember talking excitedly to a laconic Stokes mortar officer [...]. My only idea was to collect all our available ammunition and renew the attack [...] It did not occur to me that there was anything else going on the Western Front excepting my own little show. My overstrained nerves had stirred me up to such a pitch of febrile excitement that I felt capable of the most suicidal exploits. [...] Nevertheless I was still boiling over with the offensive, and my activity was only quelled by a written order from the Cameronian Colonel, who told me that we must not advance owing to the attack having failed elsewhere. This caused an anticlimax to my ardours.

(Ward 284–5)

Sassoon is here candidly exhibiting his reflections on his newly gained status as 'not only a hero but a wounded hero'. This exposition of his inner state is not devoid of self-derision: even as he is posturing as an archetype, he is also aware and wishes the reader to be aware, of the pretentiousness and vanity of his stance. It is worth noting that Sassoon heavily pilfered from this record to write the corresponding narrative in the *Memoirs of an Infantry Officer*. In both instances, the temporal distance allows the introduction of affect into a narrative that was originally blank in the initial, immediate account of the event.

The third short-term account of the Hindenburg Tunnel adventure was composed from the hospital on 22 April, as Sassoon was convalescing from his wound: it is a draft of what will become his poem 'The Rear-Guard' in *Counter-Attack* (MS Add.9852/1/10, 15r–16r[24]). This poem conflates Sassoon's most recent experience in the Hindenburg Tunnel with an earlier incident when

Sassoon's company commander, Kirkby, mistook a corpse for a sleeping soldier and asked him the way (Egremont 135). Like the regimental record, this poem is written in an ambivalent mode that is redolent of the grotesque—down to the etymological meaning of the word, *'grottesco'*, which appears relevant to this underground scene. The comedic potential is conveyed by the word 'winked', the potentially clownish attitude of the exploring soldier, 'bump[ing] his helmet' and 'tripping', the heterogeneous enumeration of incongruously trivial objects ('tins, boxes, bottles'), the coarse 'you sod'; this comicality intersects with the abjection of the final description. Here again, when faced most directly with horror, representation becomes peripheral. The horror of the description can only appear like a negative, by showing precisely what this body is not—asleep and alive. Sassoon here simultaneously highlights and derides the impulse to reshape the unbearable into the familiar: in a process akin to an inversion of the uncanny, what initially seems mundane—a lazy soldier—is brutally made horrendous—a decomposing corpse. It is through this anamorphic shift from the familiar to the abject that a glimpse is offered of what remains ultimately unconveyable through words.

Conclusion

Was Sassoon's war journal, then, merely the self-indulgence of 'an egotist', as he stated in his poem 'On Reading My Diary'? His notebooks certainly display a deep interest in himself as he is experiencing the war and subsequently maturing as a writer. However, his diaries coruscate with a wide-ranging multiplicity of intents and significance. They stand as a document of the war lived by a lieutenant and of the evolution of his stance towards the war; they vibrate with Sassoon's passion to remember and bear witness. In a manner that transcends and contains all of these aspects, Sassoon's war diaries can and must ultimately be read as a work of literature in their own right, multi-layered in their rendering of the complex and varied experience of an 'infantry officer' and of a rare intensity in their transmission of war experience. The diaries make us as present as is possible to the multiple sensations of a combatant at war. The abundance of self-portrayal and the richness of the landscape and soundscape surrounding combat do not suppress the representational impasse when faced with the shock and horror of the mass destruction enacted in the First World War. Yet it allows the introduction of affect and gives the reader the closest possible glimpse of what it was to live—and to fear death—at the front.

Notes

1 My translation. Original text: 'participent aujourd'hui à la construction d'une mythologie nationale'.
2 For all extracts from Sassoon's writing in this chapter: copyright Siegfried Sassoon by kind permission of the Estate of George Sassoon. Permission was financed by the Études Montpelliéraines du Monde Anglophone (EMMA), Université Montpellier 3.

126 *Siegfried Sassoon's War Diaries*

3 My translation. Original text: 'le journal n'est pas, à l'origine et fondamentalement, une œuvre: il est une pratique, et sa finalité est la vie de son auteur'.
4 My translation. Original: 'Quand minuit sonne, ce que j'ai daté du jour qui vient de s'écouler ne doit plus être modifié. Tout changement ultérieur (adjonction, suppression, déplacement, substitution) me ferait quitter le territoire du journal pour glisser vers celui de l'autobiographie, qui se donne la liberté de recréer le passé à la lumière du présent'.
5 My translation. Original: 'La valeur du journal est liée à l'authenticité de la trace: une altération ultérieure ruinerait cette valeur. Le journal est l'ennemi de l'autobiographie. […] Le journal, comme l'aquarelle, ne supporte guère la retouche'.
6 The manuscript page can be accessed here: https://cudl.lib.cam.ac.uk/view/MS-ADD-09852-00001-00005/29.
7 My translation. Original text: 'On a longtemps réduit le journal personnel à une simple source de renseignements historiques et biographiques. Peu à peu on en est cependant venu à le considérer comme un objet d'étude à part entière et à concevoir qu'il pouvait aller bien au-delà d'un geste d'improvisation aveugle et sans envergure'.
8 My translation. Original text: 'objet polyvalent, riche de formes d'écritures diverses qui peuvent intervenir à des moments très différents du processus génétique de l'œuvre'.
9 My translation. Original text: 'Le journal est alors devenu un mixte inextricable de réalité et de fiction'.
10 The manuscript pages for 3 January 1916 start here: https://cudl.lib.cam.ac.uk/view/MS-ADD-09852-00001-00004/30.
11 Manuscript page for 'To Victory': https://cudl.lib.cam.ac.uk/view/MS-ADD-09852-00001-00004/36.
12 My translation. Original text: 'Les poètes de guerre, pour qui la littérature a valeur de conscience, d'expérience, voire de salut, se montrent plus humbles dans leurs expérimentations car ils visent obstinément la communication de l'incommunicable'.
13 'I reveal the situation […] to myself and to others in order to change it'. Sartre 37.
14 My translation. Original text : 'La *war poetry*, croyant encore à la capacité de la poésie à transmettre le monde, se place du côté du *dévoilement* (d'une vérité, d'un objet, "dire la vérité sur la guerre" dans les mots de Sassoon) plutôt que de l'*acte créateur*, centré sur la forme.
15 Manuscript page: https://cudl.lib.cam.ac.uk/view/MS-ADD-09852-00001-00006/27.
16 Manuscript page: https://cudl.lib.cam.ac.uk/view/MS-ADD-09852-00001-00006/19.
17 The official citation in July 1916, describing the events for which Sassoon earned the Military Cross, appears closer to his experience: '2nd Lt. Siegfried Lorraine Sassoon, 3rd (attd. 1st) Bn., R. W. Fus. For conspicuous gallantry during a raid on the enemy's trenches. He remained for 1 ½ hours under rifle and bomb fire collecting and bringing in our wounded. Owing to his courage and determination all the killed and wounded were brought in'. *Supplement to the London Gazette* (27 July 1916): 7441.
18 My translation. Original text: 'Le diariste écrit un texte dont il ne maîtrise pas la conclusion. Il avance en aveugle vers une fin inconnue, dont il accepte qu'elle ne dépende qu'en partie de lui. Le journal accepte ses limites, il explore et repousse de jour en jour une fin qui lui échappe'.
19 Original text: 'Tout laisse à penser, en effet, que le ressort de l'activité narrative est la confusion même de la consécution et de la conséquence, ce qui vient *après* étant lu dans le récit comme *causé par*. Le récit serait, dans ce cas, une application systématique de l'erreur logique dénoncée par la scolastique sous la formule *post hoc, ergo propter hoc*, qui pourrait être la devise du Destin, dont le récit n'est en somme que la "langue"' (Barthes 1966, 10).
20 A loose reference to Judith Butler's *Giving an Account of Oneself* (2005).

21 Manuscript page: https://cudl.lib.cam.ac.uk/view/MS-ADD-09852-00001-00010/5.
22 Manuscript page: https://cudl.lib.cam.ac.uk/view/MS-ADD-09852-00001-00010/19.
23 Manuscript page: https://cudl.lib.cam.ac.uk/view/MS-ADD-09852-00001-00010/22.
24 Manuscript page: https://cudl.lib.cam.ac.uk/view/MS-ADD-09852-00001-00010/31.

Bibliography

Primary Sources

Sassoon, Siegfried. *Siegfried Sassoon to E. Marsh*, 23 October 1913. Letter. From Berg Collection at the New York Public Library.
———. 'On Reading My Diary'. *The New Republic* 25, no, 325, (23 February 1921): 368.
———. *Memoirs of a Fox-Hunting Man*. London: Faber and Faber, 1928.
———. *Memoirs of an Infantry Officer*. London: Faber and Faber, 1930.
———. *Sherston's Progress*. London: Faber and Faber, 1936.
———. *The Old Century and Seven More Years*. London: Faber and Faber, 1938.
———. *The Weald of Youth*. London: Faber and Faber, 1942.
———. *Siegfried's Journey, 1916–1920*. London: Faber and Faber, 1945a.
———. 'Introduction'. In *Poems from Italy: Verses Written by Members of the Eighth Army in Sicily and Italy July 1943–March 1944*. Edited by Siegfried Sassoon. London: Harrap, 1945b.
———. *Diaries, 1915–1918*. Edited by Rupert Hart-Davis. London: Faber and Faber, 1983.
———. 'Digitised Collection of Sassoon's War Journals'. *Cambridge Digital Library*, 2014, https://cudl.lib.cam.ac.uk/collections/sassoon/1.

Secondary Sources

Acton, Carol, and Jane Potter. *Working in a World of Hurt: Trauma and Resilience in the Narratives of Medical Personnel in Warzones*. Manchester: Manchester University Press, 2015.
Barthes, Roland. 'Introduction à l'analyse structurale des récits'. *Communications* 8 (1966): 1–27.
———. 'An Introduction to the Structural Analysis of Narrative'. Translated by Lionel Duisit. *New Literary History* 6, no. 2 (1975): 237–72.
Blunden, Edmund. *War Poets: 1914–1918*. London: Longmans, 1958.
Bowen, Claire. 'Sherston and Sassoon in France'. *Études Britanniques Contemporaines* 29 (2005): 1–13.
Bruce, Susan. 'Sherston's Imaginary Friend: Siegfried Sassoon's Autobiographical Prose and the Idea of Photography'. *Biography* 30, no. 2 (2007): 173–93, http://www.jstor.org/stable/23540472.
Butler, Judith. *Giving an Account of Oneself*. New York: Fordham University Press, 2005.
Cole, Sarah. 'Siegfried Sassoon'. In *The Cambridge Companion to the Poetry of the First World War*. Edited by Santanu Das, 94–104. Cambridge: Cambridge University Press, 2013.
Das, Santanu. *Touch and Intimacy in First World War Literature*. Cambridge: Cambridge University Press, 2005.
Eakin, Paul. *Living Autobiographically. How We Create Identity in Narrative*. Ithaca: Cornell University Press, 2008.

Egremont, Max. *Siegfried Sassoon: A Biography*. London: Picador, 2005.
Felman, Shoshana, and Dori Laub. *Testimony: Crises of Witnessing in Literature, Psychoanalysis, and History*. London: Routledge, 1991.
Fussell, Paul. *The Great War and Modern Memory*. Oxford: Oxford University Press, 2013. First published 1975.
Gallagher, Jean. *The World Wars through the Female Gaze*. Carbondale: Southern Illinois University Press, 1998.
Giovanelli, Marcello. 'Construing and Reconstruing the Horrors of the Trench: Siegfried Sassoon, Creativity and Context'. *Journal of Literary Semantics* 48, no. 1 (2019): 85–104.
———. 'Siegfried Sassoon, Autofiction and Style: Retelling the Experience of War'. In *Narrative Retellings: Stylistic Approaches*. Edited by Marina Lambrou, 113–27. London: Bloomsbury Academic, 2020.
Haber, Jane. *Pastoral and the Poetics of Self-Contradiction*. Cambridge: Cambridge University Press, 1994.
Hemmings, Robert. '"The Blameless Physician": Narrative and Pain, Sassoon and Rivers'. *Literature and Medicine* 24, no. 1 (2005): 109–26.
———. 'Landscape as Palimpsest: Wordsworthian Topography in the War Writings of Blunden and Sassoon'. *Papers on Language and Literature* 43, no. 3 (2007): 264–90.
———. *Modern Nostalgia: Siegfried Sassoon, Trauma and the Second World War*. Edinburgh: Edinburgh University Press, 2008.
Higonnet, Margaret, and Patrice Higonnet. 'The Double Helix'. In *Behind the Lines: Gender and the Two World Wars*. Edited by Margaret Higonnet, Jane Jenson, Sonya Michel, and Margaret Collins Weitz, 31–48. New Haven: Yale University Press, 1987.
Higonnet, Margaret. 'Not so Quiet in No-Woman's-Land'. In *Gendering War Talk*. Edited by Miriam Cooke, and Angela Woollacott, 205–26. Princeton: Princeton University Press, 1993.
Hildebidle, John. 'Neither Worthy Nor Capable: The War Memoirs of Graves, Blunden, and Sassoon'. In *Modernism Reconsidered*. Edited by Robert Kiely, 101–21. Harvard: Harvard University Press, 1983.
Hynes, Samuel. *A War Imagined. The First World War and English Culture*. London: Pimlico, 1992.
Lejeune, Philippe. 'Le journal comme "antifiction"'. *Poétique* 149, no. 1 (2007): 3–14.
———. *On Diary*. Translated and Edited by Jeremy Popkin, and Julie Rak. University of Hawai Press, 2009.
———. 'Le journal: genèse d'une pratique'. *Genesis* 32 (2011), http://journals.openedition.org/genesis/310.
Lloyd, Christopher. 'Siegfried Sassoon Diaries 1915–1918'. *The Review of English Studies* 35, no. 138 (1984): 263–64.
Moeyes, Paul. *Siegfried Sassoon, Scorched Glory: A Critical Study*. New York: St. Martin's Press, 1997.
Montin, Sarah. '"Not Flowers for Poets' Tearful Foolings": First World War Poetry, Flowers and the Pastoral Failure'. *War, Literature and the Arts* 27 (2015): 1–14.
———. *Contourner l'abîme: Les poètes-combattants britanniques à l'épreuve de la Grande Guerre*. Paris: Presses Universitaires de Paris Sorbonne, 2018.
Rawlinson, Mark. 'Later Poets of the First World War'. In *The Cambridge Companion to the Poetry of the First World War*. Edited by Santanu Das, 81–93. Cambridge: Cambridge University Press, 2013.

Ricketts, Harry. 'The Great War and Othering the Self: Siegfried Sassoon and Ford Madox Ford'. In *Homo Duplex: Ford Madox Ford's Experience and Aesthetics of Alterity*. Edited by Isabelle Brasme. Montpellier: Presses Universitaires de la Méditerranée, 2020.

Roberts, John Stuart. *Siegfried Sassoon, 1880–1967*. London: Cohen, 1999.

Sacks, Oliver. *The Man Who Mistook His Wife for a Hat*. New York: Harper, 1987.

Sartre, Jean-Paul. *'What Is Literature?' and Other Essays*. Cambridge, Mass: Harvard University Press, 1988.

Simonet-Tenant, Françoise. 'Le journal personnel comme pièce du dossier génétique'. *Genesis* 32 (2011), https://doi.org/10.4000/genesis.425.

Sherry, Vincent. 'Bare Death: The Failing Sacrifice of the First World War'. In *Sacrifice and Modern War Literature: The Battle of Waterloo to the War on Terror*. Edited by Alex Houen, and Jan-Melissa Schramm, 92–112. Oxford: Oxford University Press, 2018.

Tait, Adrian. 'Hardy, Sassoon, and Wessex: The Enduring Appeal of the Immutable'. *The Thomas Hardy Journal* 29 (2013): 140–61.

Virilio, Paul. *War and Cinema: The Logistics of Perception*. Translated by Patrick Camiller. London: Verso, 2009. First published 1989. Original French version 1984.

Ward, C., and H. Dudley. *Regimental Records of the Royal Welch Fusiliers (late the 23rd Foot). Vol. III: 1914–1918* (1928). Uckfield: Naval & Military Press, 2005.

Wilson, Jean Moorcroft. *Siegfried Sassoon*. New York: Duckworth, 2014.

4 From the 'Bleeding Edge' of War
The Singular Voice of Mary Borden[1]

Introduction

Within the landscape of World War One nursing, Mary Borden stands out on multiple counts. When the war broke out, Mary Borden Turner, a Chicago-born millionaire then living in Britain, had published her first two novels, *The Mistress of Kingdoms* (1912) and *Collision* (1913), under the pseudonym of Bridget MacLagan. Written in a relatively traditional narrative style, both had a marked feminist perspective, and the second novel, set in India and inspired by the years Borden had spent in Lahore and Kashmir as the wife of a missionary, dealt with questions of race and colonisation in a strongly satirical tone that anticipated Forster's *A Passage to India*, published in 1924. Both novels received favourable reviews, establishing her as a promising American novelist in Britain. Borden was active on the London literary scene, using the considerable wealth she had inherited from her late father to entertain fellow writers such as E. M. Forster, Ford Madox Ford (then Hueffer), Violet Hunt, who became a friend of Borden's, and Wyndham Lewis, with whom Borden was involved in a brief affair in the summer of 1914. She also actively supported female suffrage and had a brief spell as a suffragette in 1913, when she flung stones at the Treasury Building during a protest and crashed a window, spending five days in prison as a result.

In August 1914, Borden was living in London and was pregnant with her third child; her situation as a soon-to-be mother of three children and the wife of a Scottish missionary did not predestine her to volunteer as a war nurse behind the front lines. Like Sinclair, although for different reasons, no one expected her to disentangle herself from her social role to embark for France on her own; not to mention that she had no nursing qualifications or experience whatsoever. Yet even as she was still pregnant, Borden 'put her name down with the London Committee of the French Red Cross' in late 1914 (Conway 38); in early 1915, as soon as she was well enough to travel, and her daughter not being quite two months old, she set off on her own for France to serve as a nurse. Borden was trained on the spot, in a makeshift hospital set up in the casino at Malo-les-Bains, an improbable setting that will receive further attention later.

DOI: 10.4324/9781003270812-5

The story of Borden's military hospital is itself remarkable. Taking on a nursing role as an American or a British woman was no straightforward task in the early months of the war. As Jane Conway points out in her biography of Mary Borden, 'during the first year of the war political, military and social resistance to women's involvement at the front made it extremely difficult for them to take an active role' (Conway 42). All of the other British women who offered to set up hospital units at the front were turned down by the British authorities and told to 'go home and keep quiet' (Das 187, quoting from Margot Lawrence's biography of Elsie Inglis). This explains why Borden, along many other American and British women, volunteered to nurse French rather than British soldiers. However, the nurses in charge of French soldiers on the Franco-Belgian front were under the command of the *Croix-Rouge française*, and the French nursing officers looked down on their recruits from Britain and Northern America, going so far as to impede their work as carers (Conway 41). Borden eventually decided to circumvent the nursing authorities; in accordance with her strong-willed temperament and her refusal to follow rules when they made poor sense to her mind, she wrote directly to General Joseph Joffre, asking for his permission to found and lead a hospital that would be under the direct authority of the French Army, and not of the Croix-Rouge. Joffre agreed, and Borden was able to found the Hôpital Chirurgical Mobile n°1, which became operational in July 1915. Borden thus single-handedly established and funded the only hospital unit on the Franco-Belgian front that wasn't under the control of the Red Cross. It is worth noting that as in Sinclair's case when she asked to be included in Monro's ambulance corps, Borden's winning argument was ultimately financial: she wasn't, after all, a professional nurse. The hospital was set outside the village of Rousbrugge, near Ypres, only 11 kilometres behind the firing line. In 1916, during the Somme offensive, Borden set up a new hospital at Bray-sur-Somme, l'Hôpital d'Évacuation, 5 kilometres behind the line; with its 2,000 beds, it was the largest military hospital in the French Army (Conway 50).

Borden's field hospital was unique in several other aspects. Intriguingly, when searching the hospital archives for the First World War, no *Hôpital Chirurgical Mobile* n° 2 or 3 can be found: this 'n° 1' has thus come to signify singularity rather than precedence in a series of other such mobile hospitals. Borden's *Hôpital Chirurgical Mobile* remained one of the most independent nursing units of the First World War. With a 5% mortality rate, it also boasted the lowest mortality rate on the entire front, a feat that caused it to be dubbed '*le petit paradis des blessés*' by the *poilus*, to the point that the wounded expressly asked to be sent there (Conway 47). Most relevantly for the topic at hand, there seems to have existed a correlation between the independent status of Borden's unit and the number of testimonies that were written by nurses operating there: in her study *Nurse Writers of the Great War*, Christine Hallett remarks, 'It would appear that those nurses who worked most independently were the ones who were also most likely to write memoirs and war narratives' (Hallett 2016, 16). Ellen La Motte, a professional nurse in Borden's hospital, published her anti-propagandist memoir, *The Backwash of War*, in 1916; La Motte's memoir regularly features among studies on First World War nurses' writing. Maud Mortimer, who also volunteered at the Hôpital Chirurgical Mobile, authored *A Green Tent in Flanders* (1917), which appears to be directly inspired by Borden's hospital, although no names are given. The Canadian Agnes Warner, Borden's head nurse, wrote letters to her family that were published by her mother and sisters, unbeknownst to the author, as *My Beloved Poilus* in 1917 (Hallett 2016, 9). Finally, Borden herself conveyed her experience through fragments of prose and poetry that came to be published in 1929 as *The Forbidden Zone*.[2]

The Forbidden Zone stands as an atypical piece of testimony of the First World War, one that does not fit any pre-determined category. Published in 1929, yet predominantly written during the war, in the temporal and spatial immediacy of the front, it is not a diary, nor a memoir such as Vera Brittain's *Chronicles of Youth* and *Testament of Youth*. Nor is it just a collection of poems akin to those written by the well-known war poets—such as Siegfried Sassoon, Robert Graves, Wilfred Owen or Isaac Rosenberg. It is not a vast semi-fictional, semi-autobiographical narrative of the war either, such as Ford Madox Ford's *Parade's End* tetralogy (1924–28), Graves's *Good-Bye To All That* (1929) or Sassoon's *Memoirs of an Infantry Officer* (1930), all published around the same time as *The Forbidden Zone*. In her preface, Mary Borden refers to her texts as 'sketches and poems', and to the volume as a 'collection of fragments'—adding a few lines further on that they are 'fragments of a great confusion' (Borden, 'The Preface', n. p.). Jasie Stokes has underscored the singularity of Borden's collection, remarking that '*The Forbidden Zone* is […] a combination of at least three genres: lyric essay, short story and poetry' (Stokes 116). Ariela Freedman has also commented on the unclassifiable nature of Borden's war volume, asserting that 'her fictionalized memoir thus offers an original and profound articulation of a war which evaded easy categorization by a writer who did the same' (110). *The Forbidden Zone* is indeed a heterogeneous medley of fragments: some are in prose yet bear a strong poetic quality, such as 'The Captive Balloon'; others are in free verse that reads almost like prose, like 'The Hill'. Most fragments mix landscape, portrait and narrative. One piece, 'In the Operating Room', even reads as a grotesque semi-macabre, semi-farcical theatre sketch. All work as vignettes that offer a disjointed vision of Borden's experience as a war nurse. Max Saunders defines *The Forbidden Zone* as a 'memoir by fragment, by impression' (Saunders 181), which emphasises the text's generic instability. In a letter to her lover, Edward Spears, Borden, mentioning one of the first pieces that she wrote for *The Forbidden Zone* and that was originally published in the *English Review* in 1917, foregrounded the equivocal nature of her work: 'I'm beginning *a sort of poem*' (qtd in Conway 77, emphasis mine). Borden also directly addresses this lack of normativity in her preface to the collection, asserting it as integral to the process of representation of the war and essential to the authenticity of her testimony: 'Any attempt to reduce the[se impressions] to order would require artifice on my part and would falsify them' ('The Preface', n.p.). The final piece of the volume, a poem entitled 'Unidentified', ending on the word 'unknown', acts as a retrospective metapoetic comment on the entire volume.

Despite the popularity of the flurry of war narratives published in the late 1920s and early 1930s, *The Forbidden Zone* was met with mixed reviews, much to Borden's dismay (see Conway 150). The volume was out of print from 1930 to 2008, when it was finally re-edited by Hazel Hutchison for Hesperus Press; this re-edition, however, omits all of the poems, which formed the third section of Borden's original collection. To this day, the volume as a whole is out of print. The poems were published separately by Paul O'Prey at the Dare-Gale Press in 2015, a century after they were written. This explains why this chapter references the original 1929 edition, readily available online, instead of Hutchison's re-edition, notwithstanding the latter's merits. Borden's bold aesthetic choices were the first cause of affront brought forward by critics when *The Forbidden Zone* was first published. As Laurie Kaplan remarks,

> Shocked reviewers found Borden's language too 'graphic', the style too experimental, and the scenes in the hospital in general, and in the operating room in particular, hideously 'dreadful'.
>
> (Kaplan 36)

Borden's writing style thus appeared questionable to the same extent as the subject handled. Kaplan argues that 'as an experimental literary artifact, the book is consciously anti-conventional—as anti-conventional as the author herself' (35). Borden's unconventionality certainly played an important part in the cool reception of her war writing.

This chapter delineates the multifarious modes through which Borden's war prose set itself at odds with existing cultural and aesthetic norms. Borden's resistance to the conventional consideration of war nursing and nurse writing and her refusal of the accepted vignette of the war nurse bear momentous consequences on her aesthetic choices when writing of her war experience. Besides gender issues or questions of traumatic writing, what emerges out of these disjointed sketches is a phenomenology of the radically unfamiliar war experience. This phenomenology is established through a strong pictorial style, a geography of isolation and estrangement, and a peripheral and spectral mode of writing that develops around absence. Finally, this chapter examines the arduous question of representation in Borden's war writing, which I consider is probably one of the major though overlooked reasons for its disregard when it was published. Borden's prose demonstrates a multifaceted and unstable narrative voice, a conspicuous sophistication and a constant navigation between mimetic representation and innovative aesthetics. I argue indeed that besides questions of social and cultural normativity, Borden's war prose challenges the divide between avant-garde and traditional representations.

The question of trauma narratives, and of the manner in which trauma both impedes and shapes accounts of the war by nurses, has been at the heart of much research on writing by World War I nurses (See for instance Higonnet 2002; Hallett 2009; Acton and Potter 2012, 2015; Fell and Hallett 2013). Another major perspective developed on nurse writers of the war has been their challenging of traditional gender divides (cf. Gilbert 1983; Higonnet 1987; Gilbert and Gubar 1989; Tylee 1990; Higonnet 1993; Gallagher 1998; Geiger 2015; Grayzel and Proctor 2017). These various approaches have been invaluable to deepen the understanding of nurse writing. Hazel Hutchison's *The War That Used Up Words: American Writers and the First World War* (2015) is concerned with Mary Borden, among other American authors who wrote during the war. Drawing primarily from the perspective of cultural history, it investigates the impact of the war on the American literary scene and the specificity of the American literary response to the war. The purpose of this chapter is to prolong these discussions on Borden's war writing and delineate a phenomenology of the war that has tended to be eclipsed by questions of trauma and gender representation in recent criticism. The aim is not to oppose the rich criticism that has of late illuminated war writing by nurses, but rather to propose an added, complementary perspective. Examining the phenomenology that emerges from Borden's literary account of the war allows us to focus on the very act of witnessing the war through the senses and on Borden's attempt to recount this sensory experience and recreate a trace of it in the reading experience. The issue negotiated in those texts is also of an ontological nature. What becomes of the subject experiencing the war? What are the tools at their disposal to articulate this experience? And how can the writer generate a hint of this feeling of ontological disruption within the reader?

Writing in Defiance of the Conventional Nurse Figure

The Invisibilisation of the Nursing Gaze

During the First World War, the construction of the nurse figure was marked with a paradoxical tension. The nurses caring for the wounded on the various fronts of the war were idealised as avatars of the Virgin Mary, bent over the soldiers sacrificed to the nation, absorbing and purifying their suffering. One need look no further than the texts of the present study: May Sinclair's description of nurses in *A Journal of Impressions* is almost systematically connected to the word 'angel'. Such imagery, laudatory though it may seem, has contributed to distorting and downplaying the experience of the war by nurses. This has been pointed out in a number of studies on First World War nurses, among which Carol Acton and Jane Potter's joint analysis (Acton and Potter 2015, 36). Because it eschewed the grim reality of the nurses' experience, such idealisation erased their attempts at expressing their individual accounts—and traumatic experience—of the war and of war nursing. The discourse that prevailed in war propaganda and in the general media, with its ready-made, romanticised image of the nurse as immune to the direct experience of combat, subsequently dismissed the nurse as a gazing and witnessing subject in the war. This erasure participated in a more general exclusion of all women from the theatre of war. Jean Gallagher has devoted an illuminating study on the female gaze in the two World Wars. Examining Edith Wharton's satirical short story, 'Writing a War Story', Gallagher investigates the critique of the visual role ascribed to women during the First World War through the contrast between the female protagonist's narrative, ensconced in the 19th-century tradition of war representation, and in effect unread by the soldiers with whom she shares her narrative, and the accompanying illustration, a photograph of herself in a nurse's uniform, that conversely receives much attention and appreciation on the part of the soldiers: 'The soldiers' answer [...] shifts the terms of mimesis from verbal to visual and from the woman as a writing subject [...] to the woman's reproduced image as the object of the male desiring gaze' (Gallagher 15–6). Wharton's short story thus exposes and parodies the iconography of women caregivers in which the woman's position is frozen as an object, and not a subject, of sight.

This limitation of the visual role of women present on the front to mere objects of the male gaze is confirmed by the contemporary reception and posterity of the testimonies written by nurses at the front. Over the course of the war and for most of the 20th century, the nurses' accounts of their experience—through private letters and diaries, as well as through texts intended for publication—held a secondary place in collective memory; narratives of the war produced by carers, especially female, were generally considered as inferior in terms of testimonial value to those produced by the soldiers, who were regarded as the only legitimate actors of the war (see, for instance, Geiger 1–2). Thus the gaze of female actors in the war was ignored: the nurses' ability to see the war was itself made invisible.

The Silenced Voices of War Nurses

Since the nurses' gaze was made invisible, their writing was in turn ignored or even silenced when it did not coincide with the idealised vignette of the war nurse. As Christine Hallett has established in 'Emotional Nursing', successful accounts of war nursing were primarily written by Voluntary Aid Detachment nurses, first because they were often written in a 'classic romantic form', offering 'adventure stories and "page-turners"' (Hallett 2013, 87), but also, Hallett argues, because the figure of the volunteer nurse was 'romantic', as she was considered 'a classic mid-twentieth-century heroine'. More than that, Hallett demonstrates that many of the VADs who wrote of their experience 'wanted to be viewed as romantic heroines' and 'rewrote their war experiences according to the literary and ideological conventions of war memoirs set up by successful male combatant [...] authors' (Hallett 2013, 88). Nurses' narratives that went against the grain of such a romanticised version of war nursing tended to be suppressed during the war. As has been demonstrated by a number of scholars (among whom Tylee 1990; Higonnet 1993; Gallagher 1998; Hallett 2013; Acton 2013; Geiger 2015), direct accounts of the war by non-combatants, especially women, did not sit well with the public in the immediate afterwar, or even in the following decade. Margaret Higonnet thus examines the resistance to female writing on the war experience, both on grounds of 'gendered gentility' or 'propriety' and because experiencing and representing the war was claimed as a male prerogative:

> If she wrote realistically, she could face official censorship for producing demoralizing, unpatriotic texts. A veteran, who had risked and perhaps given his life to the nation, might be justified in holding the leaders of the nation to account for the bloodshed it had exacted. But a woman who had not been called upon to make parallel sacrifices, from this point of view, had no right to criticize the very system that protected her.
>
> (Higonnet 1993, 207)

The widespread disapproval of realistic accounts from non-fighters means that openly blunt testimonies written in the direct immediacy of the war, such as those of La Motte or Borden (though the limits of such directness in the case of Borden's account will be examined and qualified later), are rarities; unsurprisingly, both were silenced during the war on the grounds that they may prove demoralising for soldiers and civilians. Ellen La Motte's unflinching descriptions and uncompromising tone in *The Backwash of War* caused it to be immediately censored by both British and American authorities. Likewise, the publication of *The Forbidden Zone* was by no means a smooth process. In 1917, Borden published three poems and a prose sketch in the prestigious *English Review*, which she included in *The Forbidden Zone*. She submitted the whole manuscript of *The Forbidden Zone* for publication in the same year. The publishers at Collins were ready to buy it, but the military censors requested the deletion of several passages, with the argument that they would damage morale; a French translation of the book was treated likewise by French censorship (Conway 77). Borden, however, refused to edit these passages out of her texts, as she sensed they would impair the integrity of her account (Conway 77). This explains why *The Forbidden Zone* was only published in 1929, with the addition of five pieces that were written after the war, and which will therefore not be scrutinised in the present study.

Before official censorship even took place, women present on the front often suppressed and edited out their accounts of their war experience. In their introduction to *First World War Nursing: New Perspective*, Hallett and Alison Fell delineate the manifold reasons for a nurse's wish to censor her own narrative of the war, 'from a desire to protect her relatives from the sordid truth to a careful attention to what might or might not safely pass the official censor's gaze'. Another reason highlighted by Hallett and Fell is 'deliberate emotional distancing' (Hallett and Fell 2013, 6). In addition to these reasons, the sense of a lack of legitimacy was internalised by female nurses; as has been established by Higonnet, it is inseparable from the question of authenticity: 'Authentic speech, it has often been repeated, could only come from the trenches in the disabused words of a man who had 'seen' combat' (Higonnet 1993, 205). This perceived legitimacy and authenticity of war narratives is conditional not only on the ability to see the war but also on the position, both geographical and cultural, from which this gaze could take place. Talking specifically about Borden and *The Forbidden Zone*, and building from Higonnet's analysis, Acton states,

> Women writers, [...] particularly frontline nurses, are hyperconscious of their presence in *The Fordidden Zone* where their 'seeing' is complicated by their ongoing struggle to establish the legitimacy of their noncombatant perspective as well as by cultural constraint on what and how they see and what they reveal.
>
> (Acton 2004, 57)

These joint questions of legitimacy and authenticity have been an essential topic in scholarship on female war writing (among which Acton 2004, Higonnet 1993 and 2002, Hallett 2009 and 2013).

Writing as an Assertion of the Nurse's Scopic Power

In such a context, the writing that nurses did carry out can be construed as an act of resistance to the pervasive invisibilising and silencing dynamics of state censorship, public opinion and internalised suppression, especially when it challenged the norms established by propaganda in nursing imagery. In his study on the sensorial—particularly haptic—experience of war, Santanu Das, who has devoted a large part of his volume to nurses' accounts, remarkes on the specific potency of nurse narratives, contending that memoir writing is a way for the nurse to assert her experience to herself as well as to the world:

> For the First World War nurse, writing a journal, testament or memoir becomes a ritual in owning experience as much to oneself in the solitude of recollection as to the rest of the world.
>
> (Das 226)

The Forbidden Zone strikes first and foremost by the strong visuality of the texts it is made of. Each piece starts with a minute description of the war environment that is so replete with visual details and colours that it allows a full landscape to emerge. Marcello Giovanelli has recently foregrounded the role of landscape in the emotional impact of Borden's descriptions, as it is the site of a strong connection between language and experience. He quotes from Douthwaite, Virdis and Zurru's introduction to *The Language of Landscapes*:

> The term [landscape] refers firstly to the description of concrete physical worlds, and secondly, but crucially, to the experiences those worlds engender [...] and in particular to the linguistic means employed to describe those physical phenomena and the experiencing of those phenomena.
>
> (Douthwaite *et al.* 2019, 2, qtd in Giovanelli 2022, 3)

'Belgium', the first piece in the collection, opens on nominal sentences that read like stage directions, aiming to establish as direct a visual contact as possible between the reader and the environment described. 'Bombardment' teems with colours, with the gradual increase in sunlight (the scene takes place at sunrise) unfolding as an underground narrative that runs parallel to the actual bombardment, and the light rendered by 'a million silver worlds'; the 'long white beach' set against the 'green water'; the contrast of the 'pale buildings' and 'violet shadows'—which incidentally, may bring to mind the 'shadows of violet smoke' in Ford's 'Pon... ti... pri...ith'. The metaphor of the painted landscape, implied at first, is made explicit in the sentence 'the daylight brightened, painting the surfaces of the buildings with pale rose and primrose' (7).

Along with the painterly quality of Borden's descriptions, words denoting sight abound in the collection. They can refer to the gaze of the plane, ominously 'watching' in 'Bombardment' as the town is shelled and erupts in flames; that of the nurse, watching from a distance; and that of the reader, who as early as the first piece, 'Belgium', is being explicitly shown the landscape of war: 'Come, I'll show you' (2), the persona invites us, using many deictics and involving our senses: 'if you listen you can hear', urging us: 'you see those men?' (2). Hutchison has outlined the multifarious forms that observation takes in *The Forbidden Zone*:

> Observation in this text can mean many things: an uncomprehending survey of the battlefield; a personal engagement with a human drama; an aerial, epic detachment; spying for military purposes; or the intimate and intent process of watching as an element of physical, clinical care.
> (Hutchison 2013, 141)

The 'I' in Borden's pieces exists mainly as a watcher, as a gaze framing the scene. Yet although the persona is often passive and contemplative in *The Forbidden Zone*, her gaze, working as the point of contact between the war and the reader, is powerful. Several pieces in the collection develop a one-sided dialogue between the narrator, often present through the first person, and the reader, directly addressed as 'you'.[3] The very first pronouns of the opening text—and thus of the whole collection—, 'Belgium', are second-person pronouns; and they are associated with verbs of perception: 'you listen', 'you can hear', 'you feel'. Even before the 'I' appears, this addressee points to an implicit addresser, who becomes explicit further down the page: 'Come, I'll show you'. The 'I' exists here as a mere guide to the reader; this ostensive function is implied in all the deictic devices of the text: the enumeration of landscape items, as if pointed to on a picture; the 'here are', 'there's', etc. The relationship between the 'you' and the 'I' is that of a joint gaze that comes together in the first-person plural: 'if we wait we may see him' (3). The scene of war is thus mediated through a relationship between the witness, 'I', and the reader, to the point that the latter is brought into the picture, as an onlooker standing next to the persona. In his stylistic examination of 'Belgium', Giovanelli points out the strategies in

'Belgium' that 'invite closeness or projection into the world of the text and thus facilitate an "embodied perspective"', such as 'the extended use of the second person pronoun "you" and various kinds of spatial, temporal and social deixis' (Giovanelli 8); he is particularly interested in the use of *-ing* forms that abound in 'Belgium', as according to cognitive grammar, they 'impose summary scanning and profile an internal perspective on the event being described' (Giovanelli 12). Borden's testimonial intent is to make the scene present to those absent from the war through distance or time. In this context, the absence of tenses in the initial nominal sentences, followed by the deictic present in the rest of the piece, ensures that the scene is forever present—both in its meaning of here and now—to the reader. The present and presence of the scene are reactivated in each reading. This inaugural piece encapsulates Borden's aim in this collection: to bring the war as close as possible to our minds and senses.

The visuality of Borden's descriptions is complemented by a striking auditory precision, both through description and an intensely musical writing. Nora Lambrecht has devoted a detailed study of 'the art of noise' in *The Forbidden Zone* in her PhD dissertation and in an article, both published in 2017, where she investigates how *The Forbidden Zone*'s 'sonic environment' renders 'the material acoustic ecology of war' (Lambrecht 2017b, 36). Along with a meticulous description of noises, Borden's acoustic representation of the war is achieved through an extremely musical and alliterative prose that recreates—albeit at a considerably and unavoidably dimmed volume—the noises that it depicts. In 'Bombardment', the extended metaphor of the aeroplane as a mosquito minimises its destructive power but also aims to express its sound; it is paired with numerous alliterations in the voiceless dental fricatives /s/ and /θ/, as in the phrases 'superbly poised now in the spotless sky', 'waiting for some strange thing to happen' (7) or 'circled smoothly' (8). Similar phenomena abound in the collection. Lambrecht thus analyses with great acumen the effect of the recurrent word 'mud' in 'Belgium' (Lambrecht 2017a, 19–20).

Borden's evocative landscapes and soundscapes of war thus challenge the widespread consideration of women witnesses as lacking a powerful and legitimate gaze (and ear). The preface to *The Forbidden Zone* identifies the pieces as 'pictures', thus enhancing their visual quality. Moreover, while Borden emphasises these pictures' deficiencies from the actual experience, her declaring that this 'dimmed reality' would be nonetheless 'recognise[d]' by the *poilus* is a strong statement in the previously described context: Acton argues that through her 'Preface', Borden 'claims the legitimacy of what she has seen, and at the same time an equality and kinship with the combatant gaze' (Acton 2004, 57).

Demystifying the Idealised Nurse Figure

Another modality of Borden's resistance to the dictates of state propaganda and public opinion resides in her relentless deactivation of the conventional nurse figure. In her texts, Borden not only writes deliberately outside of the expected vignette of the war nurse, but she writes of herself as a nurse from a detached, outside perspective. Das has foregrounded the internalisation of the idealised nurse figure: 'The fetishisation of nurses as healers, as angels of mercy and compassion—a tool of state propaganda—was internalized by many nurses' (Das 202). More specifically, Acton and Potter stress that the idealisation of nurses 'was not only imposed on nursing as a profession from outside, but also from within the profession itself, and through the nurse-narrator's internalization of such discourses' (Acton and Potter 2015, 36–7). Many nurse memoirs thus contributed to perpetuating and strengthening this construction. Borden's fragments, however, have the opposite aim. The explicit figure of the nurse comes late in the volume: it only first appears in 'The Regiment', the sixth piece in the collection. Significantly, in this first occurrence, it appears in the third person, as a remote and impervious character. Whilst the figure begs to be interpreted as a cameo of Borden, this external treatment sheds doubt as to the coincidence between author and character. 'The Regiment', one of Borden's longest pieces composed from the front, was first published in the *English Review* in October 1917. The variations between the 1929 and the 1917 versions are worth commenting upon: although there are few changes, the most significant ones mostly concern the description of the nurse, which is markedly more negative in the initial version. She arrives 'languidly lying back in a motor'; the 'delicate body' of the 1929 version is originally a 'frail, fraudulent body dressed in the white costume of a nurse', with the charged 'costume' replaced with the neutral 'uniform' in 1929 (34); the nurse is then described as 'a white, beautiful fraud branded with a red cross' (Borden 1917a, 347). The paradigm of deception emphasised by the polyptoton on 'fraud' and the choice of the word 'costume' is sustained by her being initially portrayed as a 'lie' in 1917: 'To the regiment the woman was nothing but a lie, and the regiment was indifferent to her lie' (Borden 1917a, 348), whereas the 1929 version reads, 'To the regiment the woman was a puzzle' (35). In its initial version, the first nurse figure that appears in *The Forbidden Zone* is thus painted in an opprobrious light, highlighting the alienness but also the questionable and precarious status of the nurse in a world of male soldiers and officers. Another change between the 1917 and the 1929 versions is the absence of the first person in the initial text, which does occur once at the beginning of the 1929 version: where the latter reads, 'I saw in their eyes' (23), the former version has, 'One saw in their eyes that they were men' (1917a, 343). The initial wartime narrative is thus entirely extra-diegetic, which distances the account even further.

This process is also at work in the first piece of Part Two, 'The City in the Desert'. Here, the first-person singular is present as an internal witness; yet a nurse is also indirectly described in the third person, in a manner that echoes the description of 'The Regiment': 'The small white figure of a solitary woman is crossing a wide open space. She is slipping in the mud. Her white dress is fluttering' (109–10). The woman is not expressly identified as a nurse for defamiliarising purposes, but the inference is not difficult to make, leading us to recognise her as another cameo of Borden. Yet the first-person persona later confesses to also stumbling in the mud: 'The road was slippery' (111). The troubling recurrence of the 'slip' radical leads the reader to go back and read the first occurrence again, making us wonder whether the 'white figure' may not also be that of the first-person persona. Along a cubist logic, the 'I' is thus simultaneously a bystander, looking at the scene from the outside, and a figure in the picture. This 'slippage' between a potentially authorial first-person narrator and the possible projection of Borden as a third-person character in her own story contributes to generating a distance between the reader and the nurse figure, preventing any form of sympathy or identification on our part. This curious tension between the first and the third persons may be paralleled with the discrepancy that Sinclair establishes in her *Journal of Impressions* between her narrating and narrated selves.

The third appearance of the nurse figure occurs in 'Moonlight'. The nurse persona, here talking in the first person, strikes first by her apparent detachment from the horror of her surroundings and the agonising of her patients, a process that will be investigated in more detail later. This detachment, rendered among other tropes by the recurring phrase 'I don't mind', is explained by the nurse's being metaphorically and ontologically dead. Mentioning a fellow carer, the narrator states, 'She is dead already, just as I am—really dead, past resurrection. Her heart is dead. She killed it. She couldn't bear to feel it jumping in her'. (59) All senses are suppressed, and the nurse has become a machine, in a manner strongly evocative of futurism: 'blind, deaf, dead—she is strong, efficient, [...] a machine inhabited by the ghost of a woman' (59–60). No longer alive, no longer sensing, the nurse is also, as has been commented upon by several critics, no longer a woman, or as Borden states, 'a ghost woman' (61). The feminine, angelic, empathetic vignette of the nurse is methodically deconstructed by Borden. Furthermore, the dehumanised nurse is paralleled with an officer: 'He is blind, deaf, dead, as I am—another machine just as I am' (64). Against the conventional hierarchy of war, Borden establishes the nurse on a par with the officer.

The most direct indictments of the traditional, angelic nurse figure occur in 'Paraphernalia' and in the oft-discussed 'Conspiracy'. In the latter, as Das notes, 'Borden openly attack[s] the very ideology of V.A.D nursing—the men are repaired and remade only to be sent back to the trenches' (Das 202). In 'Paraphernalia', the pronouns shift again: the nurse is now addressed in the second person by an accusatory, disparaging and curt persona. This adds yet another layer to the distancing between Borden and the nurse figure that she writes about: Borden represents herself in her text as split into two personas opposing one another. The nurse here is reified as 'busy among [her] things', as if she were just another piece of 'paraphernalia'; she is denigrated as uselessly busying herself against death, and along a perspective echoing 'The Regiment', she is described as a fake, a mere actress going through the motions of nursing, 'flaunt[ing] [her] perfect movements' (124).

Borden thus subverts the archetype of the nurse as stable, idealised and self-suppressed, both through her writing about the war and through the manner in which she pictures herself and her role in a detached, unsympathetic and unstable manner. Writing of herself from the outside is one of the strategies that Borden uses to write outside the conventions of war writing. This also bears consequences on the nature of her text. The question of self-expression and autobiography has been addressed in each chapter of the present volume; Borden's collection is the least autobiographical of all four sets of texts here studied; this resistance to the conventional form of the war memoir has essential aesthetic consequences, as it allows Borden to emancipate her writing from the imperatives of chronology and of a stable narrative instance that should be consistently authorial. Stokes has commented on this specific aspect of Borden's unconventional account:

> While she wrote *The Forbidden Zone* as a memoir, attempting to maintain and claim a profound truthfulness of her experiences in the war, it is not an expression, nor indeed the creation, of the individual self that is 'Mary Borden'. [...] *The Forbidden Zone* differs from other war memoirs not merely in its form, but also in its lack of a unified subjective voice. [...] [W]e follow the second-person directions of a nameless narrator who evades the subjective 'I' through the wasteland of the Forbidden Zone.
>
> (Stokes 117)

Borden's dissociation from the nurse personas present in her pieces has thus far-reaching consequences from a cultural and ideological point of view, but also as regards the phenomenology of the war that emerges from her collection. Borden's going outside of herself to describe her experience as a nurse is also a means to explore the interstitial and liminal stance of the nurse in this 'forbidden zone', forever on the edge of trench warfare, which has tended to be considered as constituting the core of the First World War; this liminality introduces the essential paradigm of geography.

A Liminal Geography of Care

An Ironical Cartography

The phenomenology of war nursing in *The Forbidden Zone* is consistently apprehended through the lens of geography. The entire volume abounds in spatial and topographical elements. When examining the contents page, we may notice a striking consistency in the titles of the various fragments, which are often concerned with geography. In addition to the titles of the two prose parts—Part One is entitled 'The North', Part Two, 'The Somme'—, many chapter titles are concerned with spaces, such as 'Belgium', 'The Beach', 'The Square', 'The City in the Desert', 'In the Operating Room'. These titles denote points on a map, with a zooming-in effect through the first two sections in prose from larger areas—'the North'—to a country—'Belgium'—to smaller and smaller spots, all the way to the final indoors playlet that is 'In the Operating Room'. Additionally, the first part is concerned with outdoor scenes, with a strong focus on landscapes, often unrelated to the world of the hospital; the perspective shifts with the last piece in Part One (not including the pieces written in 1929),

'Moonlight', in which the nurse experiences the outside world from the confines of the hospital, 'through the open door of the hut' (51). This piece, describing the nurse's liminal stance, suspended between interior and exterior spaces, works aptly as a transitional text towards Part Two, which is concerned with the inside of the hospital. 'Moonlight' acts as a hinge in the volume, shifting the gaze from the outside to the inside. As a result, the first part is more concerned with the war and its effects on the landscape and its inhabitants, while 'Moonlight' and the second part focus on war nursing. Part Two bears indeed the subtitle: 'Hospital Sketches'.

This apparent narrowing of focus, which conveys an impression of increasing geographical precision, comes into tension with the overall title, *The Forbidden Zone*, and more generally with the entire paratext opening the volume. Borden dedicated the collection 'to the Poilus who came *that way* in 1914–1918' (emphasis mine); beyond its indeterminacy, the demonstrative 'that' implies an unbridgeable distance from the reader. Both the title and the dedication hint at an indescribable space, one that cannot be outlined precisely—a space that is not even supposed to exist, as this 'zone' is 'forbidden'. Furthermore, this zone is unstable and constantly redefined geographically, since the field hospitals moved along with the armies, as is underscored by the titles of the first two sections of the volume, which outline the progress of Borden's hospital along the line, following the troops' movement. The book's short preface—its own threshold—is an apt place for Borden to highlight the liminality and variability of the space where her experience of the war took place. Geographical elements again abound in this page:

> I have called the collection of fragments *The Forbidden Zone* because the strip of land immediately behind the zone of fire where I was stationed went by that name in the French Army. We were moved up and down inside it; our hospital unit was shifted from Flanders to the Somme, then to Champagne, and then back again to Belgium, but we never left *La Zone Interdite*.

Geography is here consistently associated with the passive voice where Borden and her unit are concerned: 'where I was stationed'; 'we were moved up and down inside it'; 'our hospital unit was shifted'. The relationship between the spaces of war and their inhabitants is characterised by a lack of agency on the part of the latter and is mediated by an invisible, omnipotent authority.

Later in the preface, Borden uses geographical phrasing to articulate her inability to express her experience accurately: 'I have blurred the bare horror of facts and softened the reality in spite of myself, not because I wished to do so, but because I was incapable of a *nearer approach* to the truth' (emphasis mine). Throughout the collection, there persists a tension between geographical precision and vagueness. As noted earlier, most fragments open on an attempt at mapping out the war experience: the ability to grasp events geographically may appear as a means to give a modicum of control to the experience, or at least to its expression. The collection, moreover, is not just concerned with the effect of war on humanity but also on the land where it takes place. Each piece starts with a minute description of the environment, where the war landscape works not as a mere backdrop against which action may take place, but as a governing force, a character of its own in each narrative or vignette. Geography develops as a prevalent theme within most of the pieces, with a ubiquitous concern for topography and geology. However, whilst there is an evident attempt to firmly anchor the various texts in space, this effort is challenged by a growing murkiness, as in 'The City in the Desert', the piece that inaugurates Part Two: with its two nouns denoting places, its spatial preposition and two definite articles, the title demonstrates an emphasis on topography; however, the very question—'what is this city [...]?'—on which the piece opens, dismisses any hope of precision that the reader may have held (109). Further down, this indeterminacy is made final by the name—or lack thereof—of the place:

> That flimsy gate [...] with H.O.E. 32 on it in big black letters, and a flag flying, and those red crosses painted on the iron roofs of the building. H.O.E. 32 must be the name of the place; but why such a name? What does it mean?
>
> (112)

The initials refer in fact to Hôpital d'Évacuation; they were a common acronym during the war, but the meaning is blurred by the process of distantiation and defamiliarisation. This corresponds to philosopher Marc Augé's definition of the non-place:

> [T]he real non-places of supermodernity [...] have the peculiarity that they are defined partly by the words and texts they offer us [...]. Sometimes these are couched in more or less explicit and codified ideograms [...]. This establishes the traffic conditions of spaces in which individuals are supposed to interact only with texts, whose proponents are not individuals but 'moral entities' or institutions.
>
> (Augé 96)

Borden's forbidden zone offers a strikingly prescient example of what Augé describes as a non-place, which he assimilates to the human condition of supermodernity. Furthermore, such indeterminacy also operates as a metatextual reflection on the text that has a direct impact on the reading experience: via this defamiliarising process, the reader is herself positioned in a non-place, where any hope of stable orientation is defeated. Mark Larabee has reflected on the discrepancy between signified and signifier in the topography of the First World War: 'Like the signifiers of maps and signs, even place names no longer pointed to the realities on the ground' (Larabee 24). The uncertainty and instability thus generated between the physical place and its cartographic version led officers (and soldiers), Larabee argues, to abandon the positivist faith in maps and to go back instead to a subjective appreciation of terrain: 'the "purely" subjective therefore became both the first and last resort in dealing with the compromised objectivity of topographical knowledge' (Larabee 24). Although his assessment concerns the perspectival and epistemological shift in male combatants, Larabee's conclusion on this matter is also relevant to the experience of topography that unfolds in Borden's pieces. The dysfunctional topography that unfolds in *The Forbidden Zone* brings to mind the geographical issues present in the texts of each of the authors examined in this volume.

'Bombardment', the second piece in Borden's collection, works as a deeply ironical piece, one that explores various *topoi* only to deconstruct them as the piece develops and the idyllic landscape described is shattered by bombing. This irony also concerns cartography: the bird's eye view that is presented through the plane's perspective appears at first as the ideal angle from which to establish a clear record of the country underneath. Borden even uses the word 'map', and the description at first is clear-cut, outlining 'the wide plain, the long white beach and the sea' (5), a view made possible by military technology. This map is said to be 'unconscious': an unexpected yet eloquent qualifier, as it points to an absence of subjectivity. This vertical, aerial view corresponds to the shift identified by Paul Virilio in the military observation of terrain and combat during the First World War, when he describes the conflict between the French high command initially privileging 'horizontal, perspectival vision' and Gallieni pleading for the use of aerial reconnaissance in the Battle of the Marne, in order to gain a 'vertical, panoramic vision':

> Eventually Gallieni imposed his 'point of view' on enemy movements [...] [I]t seems at least plausible that the happy outcome [...] depended upon *regulation of points of view*—that is, on a definition of the battle image in which the cavalry's perspective suddenly lost out to the perpendicular vision of the reconnaissance aircraft.
>
> (Virilio 91–2, emphasis his)

Yet this map is destroyed under our eyes, as the plane descends and bombs the town, thus being simultaneously the source of this aerial view and the instrument of destruction of the scene it watches. From motionless and impersonal, as on a map, the town shifts, moves as it erupts in flames and as its inhabitants flee; the seemingly objective view on which the piece opens is replaced with a personification of the town as an organic yet ravaged body:

> The face of the city had begun to show a curious change. Scars appeared on it like the marks of smallpox and as these thickened on its trim surface, it seemed as if it were being attacked by an invisible and gigantic beast, who was tearing and gnawing it with claws and teeth. Gashes appeared in its streets, long wounds with ragged edges. Helpless, spread out to the heavens, it grimaced with mutilated features.
>
> (9)

Borden thus conjures up cartography only to negate it not merely as false and incomplete—the people, seen from too far away, are dehumanised as 'ants' or 'midgets', their suffering proportionately minimised; and the town's destruction is tellingly compared to *small*pox—but also as malicious and brutal: the very source of the overhead view is also the cause for the destruction of the country below. The emergence of the town as a wounded body is a means to re-assert a subjective perspective that might restore a closer but also more considerate approach to reality. This matches Jean Gallagher's examination of Mildred Aldrich's account of the Battle of Marne from the vantage point of her house. In *The World Wars through the Female Gaze*, Jean Gallagher develops an indispensable study of the resistance of the female gaze to the evolution of military observation during the two World Wars. She identifies panoramic view as a fantasy that 'promises the civilian observer the ability to see war from a central, military, and therefore "true" vantage point' (Gallagher 30). Borden deflates all hope for the reader of gaining such a view through the scenes that she creates in *The Forbidden Zone*. Gallagher's analysis may also bring to mind the fantasy of an all-observing gaze that underlies Bentham's Panopticon, as theorised by Michel Foucault in *Discipline and Punish*. The plane that is the main character of 'Bombardment', constantly 'watching' yet merely visible as a 'speck' (5) in the immensity of the sky, matches Foucault's description of the Panopticon, 'a machine that dissociates the seeing-being seen pair': 'an important device', Foucault argues, 'because it automates and de-individualises power' (Foucault 203, my translation). The all-encompassing military gaze of the plane, matching that of the Panopticon, thus emerges as a totalising and totalitarian mode of observation.

This gaze is emphatically not that of Borden, or of any nurse persona standing necessarily below the plane: there is once again a clear dissociation between Borden and the viewpoint from which the scene is narrated. Furthermore, along a vertiginous process, the gaze is split, as the plane is itself described by the narratorial instance as if from even higher up: the narrative stance observes this 'watching' plane, this barely visible 'speck', and precisely describes its movements, 'descend[ing] in low spirals' (6), 'poised in the spotless sky' (7), 'cavort[ing]' and 'whirling' (8). Borden layers and qualifies the plane's all-encompassing observation with a narrative gaze that sits even further above, inviting the reader to distance herself from the plane's detached and cruel perspective—when the town 'grimace[s]' and 'convulse[s]', the plane 'laugh[s]'. Gallagher argues that Aldrich's reticence to look at the site of war along a panoramic perspective constitutes a resistance to the totalising effect of military vision, as well as an acknowledgement that such a vision is illusory due to the multi-layered perspective that is inevitably hers:

> What Aldrich looks at and into is a network of visual and verbal discourse about war that screens her retinal perception of battle as effectively as the smoke over the plain.
>
> (Gallagher 34)

Borden likewise excels in positioning screens between the war and the reader, not as a resistance to showing, but as a means to render the complexity of the war scene and the impossibility to convey it directly, transparently and totally. The persona's gaze is regularly emphasised as a frame to the scenes and landscapes depicted in each scene; it is often itself framed by a window, as in 'The Square', 'The City in the Desert' and 'Moonlight': the window stresses the physical limitation of the gaze and works as a metaphor for the unavoidable filter that the persona impresses upon the scene described. 'The Square' thus starts with the words 'below my window': even though the first person is absent from the rest of the text, and the narrative style of this piece is impersonal, these initial three words imply an internal focaliser and set the text in the singular perspective of a persona's (and possibly behind her, Borden's) gaze. This also corresponds to the difference that Acton has noted between the position of male and female witnesses of the war: whereas 'male writers [...] rarely question the validity of their position as observers of and hence witnesses to war',

> women writers [...], particularly frontline nurses, are hyperconscious of their presence in *The Forbidden Zone* where their 'seeing' is complicated by their ongoing struggle to establish the legitimacy of their noncombatant perspective.
>
> (Acton 2004, 57)

A Derisive Intertextual Geography

Along with these ubiquitous frames, Borden's experience of the war, as Ford's, Sassoon's, Sinclair's and so many others'—and as Fussell has long made evident—is inevitably overlaid and coloured with her own literary and cultural references. Hutchison has delineated the weight of literary influences over Borden's war experience (Hutchison 2013, 142). In *The Forbidden Zone*, as in Sinclair's *Journal* examined previously, these references are often treated as derisive remains of a civilisation that is long gone. Borden's texts thus display a constantly ironised intertext that contributes to acting as a double screen between the persona and the scenes of war—the layer of literary reference being additionally superimposed with that of a distanced perspective on this reference—and further disproves the possibility of an objective and stable vision of the war. 'The City in the Desert' thus ironically invokes the hackneyed style of fairytales, with the phrase 'once on a time' (111; the phrase is even transcribed as 'once upon a time' in Hutchison's edition, 74). The biblical narrative of the Flood is also mentioned in this piece, albeit in a much grimmer version, as the scene described offers no hope for redemption:

> Perhaps there has been a new flood, since Noah [...]. Perhaps a new race of men has been hatched out of the mud, hatched like newts, slugs, larvæ of water beetles. But slugs who know horribly, acutely, that they have only

a moment to live in between flood tides and built this place quickly, a silly shelter against the wrath of God [...].

(112)

Several pieces open on ironical pastoral descriptions. The beginning of 'Bombardment' thus describes a moment of suspended beauty in an open landscape that seems untouched by war:

> The wide sweet heaven was filling with light: the perfect dome of night was changing into day. A million silver worlds dissolved from above the earth: the sun was about to rise in stillness: no wind stirred.
>
> (Borden 5)

The alliterations, the marked cadences—the second clause is a perfect iambic hexameter— and the hyperbole of 'a million silver worlds' contribute to making these introductory sentences strongly redolent of Georgian poetry. Several pieces share openings written in a similar style, such as 'The Regiment' and 'The Beach', with echoes from 'Bombardment' in the mention of 'heavens' in the former and 'heavenly' in the latter. However, in each of these pieces, the homage to pastoral poetry is short-lived and quickly debunked by the context in which the landscape unfolds. Borden's reinterpretation of the pastoral mode is utterly opposite to Sassoon's. The ethereal scene on which 'Bombardment' opens is about to be shattered by bombing; the 'summer world' and the 'smiling country' described at length in the first few pages of 'The Regiment' are made to appear derisory when the regiment of exhausted, jaded old men does enter the scene; in 'The Beach', the setting is initially articulated through the inner voice of a young female civilian:

> The beach is perfect, the sun is perfect, the sea is perfect. How pretty the little waves are, curling up the beach. And the sea is a perfectly heavenly blue. It is odd to think of how old the beach is and how old the sea is, and how much older that old, old fellow, the fiery sun.
>
> (42)

This description is instantaneously discredited by the childlike phrasing that belies an excess of naivety, through the simplistic, repetitive sentences, the polyptoton of 'perfect' and the circular phrasing, stalling over the same elements—'beach', 'sun', 'sea', 'perfect', 'old'. This perspective is pitted against the bitter viewpoint of her companion, who has come back from the war with his left foot cut off and his mind irretrievably traumatised. In a manner typical of Borden's writing—as will be examined in greater detail later—the final paragraph operates as a grim echo to the opening one:

> How perfect the beach is. The sea is a perfectly heavenly blue. Behind the windows of the casino [...] men lie in narrow beds. They lie in queer postures with their greenish faces turned up.
>
> (50)

This oblique intertextual mode is a means for Borden to confront and resist conventional styles of description, but also to defeat any expectation of a stable description of spaces. Whenever a panoramic perspective is attempted, the usual codes are defused through defamiliarisation and the ironical use of traditional tropes. Borden thus does not refuse to observe, or to show what she sees, but she resists the vision imposed by military discourse or by propaganda. Like Aldrich, she opts for a 'dialogic' representation:

> The narrative structure of *Hilltop* reflects not the centralized seeing subject of panoramas, but rather a dialogic subject, constituted by the textual gestures of pointing back and forth across the space of correspondence.
>
> (Gallagher 40)

This resistance to a fluid, linear narrative, along with its consequences on the observer (and narrator) as subject, is valid beyond the gender divide that is Gallagher's focus. It maintains an ethical resistance to the totalising vision imposed by propaganda, focusing instead on the individual experience of the narrating witness, but also refusing to erase the singularity of the wounded soldier who is witnessed. This echoes Ford's ethical resistance to the totalising force of war propaganda as demonstrated in the first chapter.

One of Borden's favoured strategies to defuse any hope at a stable and centralised description is to resort to a mode opposite to that of totalisation, through negativity.

Deconstructed Spaces

Many pieces in *The Forbidden Zone* may read like a guidebook, albeit one that quickly takes on an ironical tone, as it is built on a logic of negativity, pointing to what is *not* there instead of what is. This bears a remarkable resemblance to Sinclair's self-derisive guidebook style in some parts of *A Journal of Impressions*, as addressed in the second chapter, and confirms Larabee's argument on the manner in which the deconstructed experience of space in the First World War rendered obsolete the positivism that presided over the Baedeker guide (Larabee 78). The first few paragraphs of the first piece, 'Belgium', read indeed like an inverted Baedeker guide and set the tone for the whole collection:

> On our right? That's the road to Ypres. The less said about that road the better: no one goes down it for choice—it's British now. Ahead of us, then? No, you can't get out that way. No, there's no frontier, just a bleeding edge, trenches. That's where the enemy took his last bite, fastened his iron teeth, and stuffed to bursting, stopped devouring Belgium, left this strip, these useless fields, these crumpled dwellings.
>
> Cities? None. Towns? No whole ones.
>
> (1–2)

The reticence conveyed by the phrase '[t]he less said about that road the better' underscores the representational aporia already brought forward in Borden's preface. The description of the front line as 'a bleeding edge' epitomises Borden's topography of war. Firstly, it reveals that she can only access—and therefore only render—the periphery of the war; secondly, this 'edge' implies a void, a chasm, and portrays the persona and, consequently, the reader, as standing on the brink—not of nothingness, but of the unwatchable, the uninhabitable, the unsayable: that which Borden can only write *around*. It may also be intended by the nurse as a comparison of the trenches with an amputated limb. Borden's geography of lack is most obviously conveyed by the accumulation of forms of negation: yet surprisingly, these negations lead to a more loquacious few lines, where nouns are systematically paired with adjectives, thus implying a greater precision: 'bleeding edge', 'last bite', 'iron teeth', 'useless fields', 'crumpled dwelling'. In a process somewhat akin to Blanchot's poetics of negativity, it seems that naming absence frees up speech. The extended metaphor of the enemy as a metallic beast—the influence of futurism is palpable, and will be addressed later—sounds almost lyrical. The combined devices of asyndeton and accumulation generate a sentence that keeps growing, feeding on itself, in a manner akin to that of the enemy feeding off Belgium. Representation, nonetheless, is once again at a loss in the next sentence: 'Cities? None. Towns? No whole ones'. The desertion of syntax, the use of monosyllables and the negations are echoed by the use of a minimal variety of sounds, where the initial /i/ sounds are quickly engulfed by a long series of deep /o/ sounds.

The aporia inherent in the direct articulation of the war experience has been much discussed in terms of an inability to confront trauma. From a phenomenological perspective, this negative mode of representation also works as a powerful way for Borden to recreate in the reader a hint of the feeling of standing helplessly outside of the events, a feeling that was—paradoxically—at the core of the nursing experience for Borden. For the carers, the violence of the war was witnessed not at first hand, through the direct impact of shells and weapons, but secondarily, and often through what was *lacking* in the landscapes or in the bodies that were brought to them: through the absence of sight, of limbs, of faces, as is constantly portrayed in *The Forbidden Zone*. Borden's descriptions are thus constantly marked with negativity. The soldiers under her care are no longer whole, no longer men, but a sum of what has been damaged in them; they are depicted through their lacks, as in one of the most oft-quoted passages of *The Forbidden Zone*:

> There are no men here, so why should I be a woman? There are heads and knees and mangled testicles. There are chests with holes as big as your fist, and pulpy thighs, shapeless; and stumps where legs once were fastened. There are eyes—eyes of sick dogs, sick cats, blind eyes, eyes of delirium; and mouths that cannot articulate; and parts of faces—the nose gone, or the jaw.
>
> (60)

Likewise, in the piece 'In the Operating Room', the patients are merely identified through the location of their wounds: 'There's a lung just come in', a nurse thus informs the surgeons (128), and she continues: 'There's a knee for you [...], and three elbows' (129). This deconstructive representational mode also bears repercussions on the nature of the characters inhabiting Borden's *Forbidden Zone*. In their introduction to *The Wounded Hero in Contemporary Fiction*, Susana Onega and Jean-Michel Ganteau demonstrate the shift in the contemporary hero's identity from the humanist vision of the hero as invincible to that of a hero defined by their very limits:

> Self-definition by espousing the wound and/or exposing the scar may provide evidence of a paradigm shift from the older vision of the subject as sovereign and autonomous [...] to a more dependent one. [...] Miles away from the humanist conception of the hero or heroine as invincible and autonomous, many a protagonist of contemporary fiction seem to be characterised by capacities strictly delineated by the extent of their incapacities.
>
> (Onega and Ganteau 11–2)

Although Onega and Ganteau's volume focuses on contemporary literature, texts such as Borden's reveal that the origins of the shift they describe can be traced in the First World War. Onega and Ganteau's illuminating demonstration of the fundamental shift in the hero paradigm is remarkably apt for Borden's depiction of the wounded under her charge. Furthermore, this shift in the apprehension of the wounded soldier as hero through his very limits and 'incapacities' has direct reverberations on the status of the nurse narrator as heroine: just as this new hero is in direct opposition with the Enlightenment ideal, likewise the first-person narrator whose gaze frames the scenes rejects the traditional status of heroine assigned to nurses by First-World-War propaganda.

Borden's poetics of negativity generates a potent spectrality throughout her collection. The rhetoric of loss and indirection produces in turn a hazy experience in the reader: one that may be felt as frustrating, and perhaps contributed to the difficult rise of interest in this text, but one that was intrinsic, albeit in a vastly more intense and violent form, to the phenomenology of the war for the non-combatant carers. The title and overall space of Borden's book, this 'Forbidden Zone', encompasses the nurse's experience of the space of war: Stokes aptly assimilates it to Judith Butler's concept of the 'zone of uninhabitability':

> Historically, the category of woman has inhabited a kind of forbidden zone, what Judith Butler calls the 'zone of uninhabitability', which is designated as abject and 'populated by those who do not enjoy the status of the subject [...]' (Butler 3). [...] Borden's memoir eludes the universal (male heteronormative) human subject with which she cannot fully identify and instead it becomes a kind of autobiography of the abject.
>
> (Stokes 117–8)

The Forbidden Zone is a space that the nurse is not allowed to exist in as subject, and consequently to witness, or to write about. The title also works both as metaphor and metonymy for the text: a text where the closest the reader may hope to reach the war experience lies in the blank of the page, in the apparent neutrality of the gaze, in the persona split between an 'I' and a 'her', in the seeming unfeelingness of tone.

The frontispiece illustration of the original volume, a print by Percy Delf Smith, who arrived at the Somme in October 1916 to serve with the Royal Marine Artillery, is in keeping with the negativity of the spaces depicted by Borden.[4] Operating as a prefatory landscape to Borden's 'Forbidden Zone', it shows what remains of a burnt tree, splitting the page vertically, standing over a landscape ravaged by war. The caption beneath reads, 'The zone at Thiepval, near the Somme, in 1916'—where 'near' can be construed as a preemptive comment on the peripherality of the spaces of care within the landscape of the First World War. The print is entitled *Solitude*; save for the dead, black, vertical tree, the whitish, levelled landscape appears empty. This matches Virilio's consideration of the 'aesthetics of disappearance' in the photographs of sites of the Second World War, as is underscored by Eamonn Carrabine in 'Traces of Violence': 'Some of the most unsettling and moving images of conflict are those where the photographer has arrived only to find a place where something used to be: the evidence only of an absence' (Carrabine 639). The expressive force of *The Forbidden Zone* resides in 'the rest that can never be written' ('Preface', n. p.), which can only be approached peripherally in the course of the collection. As Acton asserts, '[T]he shared experience is defined through an unseen text only available to the reader as an absence' (Acton 2004, 58).

Interstitial Spaces

The spaces in which Borden's sketches take place are transitional: they are often beaches, that work as interfaces between the earth and the sea, such as in 'Bombardment', or 'The Beach'; as noted earlier, there are also many windows through which the focaliser gazes out at the war, as an outsider, as in 'The Square', 'The City in the Desert' and 'Moonlight'. The field hospital itself is an interface, designed to process soldiers from their wounded state back to combat, to more specialised hospital units further away from the front, or to their graves. This dimension is foregrounded at the end of the preface: 'I have dared to dedicate these pages to the poilus who *passed through* our hands during the war' (emphasis mine). The evacuation hospital is akin to a purgatory, where soldiers are brought from hell to the '*le petit paradis*', where they are either granted the relief of death—'the Angel, the peacemaker, the healer' (54), or are sent back to hell. Borden's '*petit paradis des blessés*' is a sham: as is made clear in 'Conspiracy', its goal is to heal soldiers only to send them back to the front line: 'It is arranged that men should be broken and that they should be mended. [...] And we send our men to the war again and again, just as long as they will stand it; just until they are dead' (117).

Jasie Stokes astutely proposes a correspondence between the space's negativity and its transitional quality, drawing from Marc Augé's definition of non-place (Augé 94). The concept of non-place has been mentioned earlier in relation to the abstruseness of the 'H.O.E.' acronym, but it is also and more importantly marked with 'transit and movement', which Stokes demonstrates is relevant to the space of the Forbidden Zone:

> The Forbidden Zone is a non-anthropological and non-historical space, characterised by its temporary function during the war as a space of transit and movement, a constantly fluctuating landscape of roads and mobile hospitals.
>
> (Stokes 118–9)

The transitional quality of the space is reverberated in the position of the nurse persona who inhabits this Forbidden Zone. Each text delivers a vignette exploring the interstitial stance of the nurse, suspended between the civilian world and the army, the sound and the wounded, the living and the dead, the men and the women, without truly belonging to either group. Ariela Freedman has outlined this liminality, stating that in depicting the nurse and the wounded soldier 'rather than the civilian woman and the active combatant', Borden stands 'in a sequestered zone between the home front and the front line, as well as between traditionally gendered roles' (Freedman 121). This interstitial stance is particularly manifest in 'The Regiment', where the lone figure of the nurse is poised between the separate groups formed by the regiment, the officers and the townspeople. The reader is made to enter into the collective minds of the soldiers and the townspeople through the stream of consciousness technique, and the narrative enacts a mute—albeit arduous—dialogue between the various groups taking part in the scene. I am again quoting from the original story Borden published in the *English Review*:

> The town shuddered, but there was sympathy between the regiment and the town.
>
> The town said to the regiment:
>
> 'You are strangers, but we know you; you come from the war. You are welcome'.
>
> The regiment said to the town:
> 'We have left our homes. You are kind, but we cannot stay here'.
>
> (Borden 1917a, 346)

In contrast, when the nurse enters the scene, she stands as an individual, whilst all the other protagonists are depicted collectively as unified groups, endowed with a collective mind; and she cannot initiate a dialogue with either the town, or the regiment:

> Her shadowed eyes said to the regiment:
>
> 'I came to the war to care for your wounds'.
>
> But the regiment said:
>
> 'You are lying!' […]
>
> To the regiment the woman was nothing but a lie, and the regiment was indifferent to her lie.
>
> To the town she was a strange thing, as fantastic as a white peacock.
> (Borden 1917a, 347–8)

The nurse is an abnormality, an intruder among the characters of the war, just as the area where she works, this Forbidden Zone, is an a-topia within the landscape of war. Where the dialogue between town and regiment enacts an acknowledgement of the other group's alterity, and thus of their humanity, the nurse is animalised and objectified as 'a lie', 'a strange thing' and 'a white peacock'. Stokes has explored the abjection of the nurse from the perspective of other categories of humanity: the carers, she argues, were 'marked as a kind of forbidden zone', and therefore 'bereft of their status as subjects' (Stokes 121).

Suspended between the various communities generated by the war—the civilians, the soldiers, the officers—who have found the means to dialogue, the nurse stands alone, estranged from others as from herself.

Writing Alienation

An Experience of Estrangement

The most striking tone that prevails in Borden's collection is that of detachment. Borden's collection is replete with devices of defamiliarisation. Besides their distancing effect, these defamiliarising devices trigger a process of *différance* as theorised by Jacques Derrida: they generate a cognitive distance that causes a delay in our recognition of what is being described. Things and places are often anthropomorphised: the sustained metaphor of the shelled town as a ravaged face has already been noted in 'Bombardment'. In 'The Regiment', the country is 'smiling' (21), whereas the town is 'low-browed' and 'moody' (22); in 'The Square', the 'machines of war', i.e. the various cars used for military purposes, are described at length along a process of personification. The text starts with a nod to futurism, through the motors that stand 'panting and snorting' (13). The exact same phrase, applied to ambulances and lorries, can be found in 'Moonlight'

(63); the *in absentia* metaphor of the horse is strongly reminiscent of Marinetti's description in the manifest published in *Le Figaro* in February 1909, where the cars are 'snorting machines' whose 'chest' he 'caresses'.[5] However, this initial hint at futurism shifts to an anti-futuristic tableau, depicting the degeneracy of futuristic ideals in the third paragraph:

> The limousines and the touring cars and the motor lorries are all debauched; they have a depraved look; their springs sag, their wheels waver; their bodies lean to one side. [...] The great motor lorries crouch [...] crouch in the square ashamed, deformed, very weary.
>
> (14)

The personification ultimately works along a dynamic opposite to that of futuristic ideals.

Conversely, human beings are consistently animalised or reified: the nurse is a 'machine' in 'Moonlight' (59–60); the inhabitants of the shelled town in 'Bombardment' are reduced to a variety of insects: 'ants', 'midgets', 'beetles', 'vermin' and a 'human hive' (8). In 'Moonlight', the agonising patient is repeatedly assimilated to a 'wounded cat' and further reified as 'a thing that is mewing' later on. People are consistently minimised as 'little [...] women' (13, 15) or 'little men' (17), and even assimilated to toys: the officers 'salute each other stiffly like wooden toys' (14) and the sentinels are put away in a box, like tin soldiers (17–8).

Borden also repeatedly favours the adoption of a child's perspective and idiosyncrasies of speech to generate a dynamic of defamiliarisation. Playing on the polysemy of 'balloon' as a toy versus an engine of war, 'The Captive Balloon' thus entirely appears as written from the perspective of an uncomprehending child, which reinforces the abnormality and strangeness of the scene. The sentences are simplistic and marked by parataxis. The present tense matches the cognitive frame of a young child, living in an eternal present. The phrase 'they say', implying an adult's authority, also implicitly points to the nonsensical yet inescapable decisions made by higher authorities. The description seems to be disconnected from reality, and is more akin to the fictional universe of children's literature: 'They say that a man lives in the balloon' echoes the nursery rhyme 'there was a man lived in the moon', a hypothesis sustained by the rhyme of 'balloon' and 'moon', or possibly *The Wonderful Fairies of the Sun* by American poet Ernest Vincent Wright in 1896:

> There's a very common notion, which was long ago begun,
> That a man lives in the Moon.

The whole form of the text sounds like a nursery rhyme, with the phrase 'the captive balloon' recurring like a burden, and the phrase 'an oyster in the sky' framing the text in a manner reminiscent of traditional ballads. The phrase 'They are beautiful, proud and adventurous' echoes chivalric children's literature with its ternary rhythm, culminating on the three-syllable Latin word; it sounds like a sentence learned by rote and merely parroted by the childlike voice. The first two paragraphs of the next piece, 'The Square', likewise operate along a minimising strategy that distances and downplays the context through a childlike perspective. The strong tendency to polysyndeta, reinforced by the absence of serial commas, seems to imitate a description made by a young child: 'and the touring cars and the motor lorries and the ambulances'; 'a great noise and a great smell and a great dust' (13); 'the limousines and the touring cars and the motor lorries' (14). The 'uniforms with silver hair and gold braid' or the 'flourish of capes' are reminiscent of the description of fairy-tale heroes. The comparison of officers to 'wooden toys', noted earlier, participates in this childlike perspective.

As in Sinclair's narrative, Borden's text is replete with oxymorons and carnivalesque inversions that foreground the distance between civilian life and the world of war. 'War had that day the aspect of a country fair', the narrator remarks in 'The Regiment' (22), a simile that brings to mind Sinclair's likening Munro's first ambulance expeditions to a picnic party. In 'The Square', the seemingly innocuous officers who have just been compared to 'wooden toys' meet in fact to 'hold murderous conferences and make plans of massacre' (14). On arriving in France in early 1915, Borden was trained in a makeshift hospital set up in the casino at Malo-les-Bains and was struck by this incongruous backdrop for the suffering and death of soldiers. She highlighted this oxymoronic situation in 'The Beach', through the voice of a wounded soldier:

> They've a gala night in our casino whenever there's a battle. Funny sort of place. [...] You never saw such a crowd. They all rush there from the front, you know—the way they do from the racecourse—though, to be sure, it is not quite the real thing—not a really smart crowd. [...] Gamblers, of course, down and outs, wrecks—all gone to pieces, parts of 'em missing, you know, tops of their heads gone, or one of their legs. When they take their places at the tables, the croupiers—that is to say, the doctors—look them over. Come closer, I'll whisper it. Some of them have no face.
>
> (Borden 46)

The speaker, an amputee, addresses his lover, whose loveliness, wholeness and immunity from the trauma of combat and trench life he cannot help resenting. The sustained metaphor exploiting the incongruity of the casino's transformation into a hospital is deftly managed, with a gradation in the simile: the description first deploys *double entendre* through the words 'gala night', 'funny', 'motors', 'rush', 'crowd', that may make the addressee momentarily wonder whether the scene described is not really that of a casino night. The pivotal shift towards a more explicit—and gruesome—meaning is initiated by the word 'front' and is made complete when the phrase 'wrecks—all gone to pieces—' is no longer figurative, but to be taken at face value: 'parts of 'em missing'. The reversal is made complete through the affected correction: 'the croupiers—that is to say, the doctors', and the final horror of the phrase 'some of them have no faces'. This shift from the lexical field of gambling and frivolousness to that of the war hospital and the horrifically wounded soldiers reinforces the abjection of the scene described; this defamiliarising process serves as a tool to exert violence onto the audience and the reader, relentlessly addressed in the text through the phrases 'you should watch', 'you never saw', 'you know', 'of course' and, most of all, the final 'come closer'. The matter-of-fact tone of the wounded soldier aims at forcing his audience—and indirectly the reader—to face the cognitive gap between his own jaded experience of the mangled bodies of the war and her—our—shock at the description.

Nursing from the Edge of Oneself

The question of the dissociation between Borden, the narrator and the nurse persona, has been addressed earlier in terms of Borden's resistance to the conventions of memoir writing and to the vignette of the nurse figure. It is also an expression of the extreme unfamiliarity of the experience of war nursing; its consequences on narrative and aesthetics reach wider than the issues of cultural representation and autobiographical writing. The 'I' as a unified subject has deserted the Forbidden Zone. In the few instances where the first person is present, it exists as a mere interface between the reader and the scene of war, as if the I was herself that Forbidden Zone, that impossible space of transition between the civilian world and the world of war. 'In the Operating Room', the last prose piece written from the immediacy of the front, is composed as a playlet. The desertion of the first-person subject has reached its peak: the narrative stance is obliterated by the choice of the theatrical genre. The perspective is utterly exterior, and the nurse, just one character among others, is mostly silent, as opposed to the surgeons and patients. In 'Blind', a piece written later for inclusion in the 1929 edition, the narrator, for a moment clearly authorial, muses,

> I think that woman, myself, must have been in a trance, or under some horrid spell. Her feet are lumps of fire, her face is clammy, her apron is splashed with blood [...]. She does not seem to notice the wounds or the blood'.

(151)

The reason why I am making this exception in including a passage from a piece that was not written from the front is, first, that it matches the metaleptic shift that is enacted in Sinclair's narrative as her narrating self, writing from England, comments on her narrated self, witnessing Belgium at war. Secondly, the dissociation between 'that woman' and 'myself' reveals that even as she was living through her nursing duties, Borden was noting details for future writing in a remote part of her mind that she could not consciously register at the time. Acton and Potter have relevantly considered this passage from the perspective of trauma studies: 'Psychological survival and the ability to behave professionally, [Borden] implies, are only possible in this state of detachment in which she can stand outside herself' (Acton and Potter 2015, 44–5). Besides this analysis, the narratorial consequences of the phrase 'she does not seem to notice the wounds or the blood' are potent: the preterition device reveals the phenomenon of dissociation between the persona in the immediacy of the moment, acting—or rather, in Barthesian terms, being *acted*—as a nurse, whose consciousness is numbed, on the one hand, and of Borden as prospective author of *The Forbidden Zone*, who does 'notice' and actively compiles these details in her writer's mind. This dissociation also allows Borden to reappropriate the moment as a sensible, perceiving subject, which was impossible in the immediacy of the nursing task—and even 'forbidden', as it would have prevented her from carrying out her nursing duties.

In the phenomenology of war established in *The Forbidden Zone*, the extreme unfamiliarity of the war experience, its exceptional character, becomes the accepted norm, as a condition for the survival of the subject. Conversely, in this world cut off from the rest of the world, the familiar and trivial situations of life outside the war become abnormal and are sensed as intolerable: they jeopardise the integrity of the system developed on the front line and in the Forbidden Zone and, thus, threaten to reactivate within the subject the awareness of an alternate form of life, outside of war, that would make her current experience unbearable by contrast. This inversion between the familiar and the extraordinary is made particularly clear in the piece entitled 'Moonlight', where the nurse persona muses on the whole of life experience as being contained in war:

> The other world was a dream. Beyond the gauze curtains of the tender night there is War, and nothing else but War. Hounds of war, growling, howling; bulls of war, bellowing, snorting; war eagles, shrieking and screaming; war fiends banging at the gates of Heaven, howling at the open gates of hell. There is War on the earth—nothing but War, War let loose on the world, War—nothing left in the whole world but War—War, world without end, amen.
>
> (57–8)

This passage is strongly redolent of *The Book of Revelation*, where four animals guard the throne of God:

> And around the throne, on each side of the throne, are four living creatures, full of eyes in front and behind: the first living creature like a lion, the second living creature like an ox, the third living creature with the face of a man, and the fourth living creature like an eagle in flight. And the four living creatures, each of them with six wings, are full of eyes all around and within, and day and night they never cease to say, 'Holy, holy, holy, is the Lord God Almighty, who was and is and is to come!'
>
> (*Revelation* 4:6–8, English Standard Version)

It is probable that this apocalyptic vision was more or less consciously influenced by Mary Borden's mother, who was a member of a fundamentalist church and whose uppermost concern throughout her adult life was the issue of salvation, of the original sin and of the Final Judgement. Borden's testimony of the war here takes on definite accents of sacrality, in keeping with Max Saunders's analysis. Reading *The Forbidden Zone* along the concept of testimony theorised by Shoshana Felman (1991), Saunders argues:

> War writing [...] moves between [...] two rhetorical poles: on the one hand, documentary realism that seeks to represent the facts; to bear witness; to give testimony. But, on the other hand, this is always already bound up with sacralization. As Felman argues, a testimonial attitude comes from feeling the event is in excess; that it is a mystery.
>
> (Saunders 188)

Borden's text takes on an incantatory quality, through the hammering recurrence of the word 'War', which replaces the iteration of 'holy' in *The Book of Revelation* and is capitalised in a manner that assimilates it to a biblical or mythological power. The quick shift from the past to the present tenses, along with the accumulation of nominal phrases paired with present participles, excludes temporality from the description. The present tense thus gains a gnomic quality—no longer pointing at a specific situation in space and time but describing an immutable state. The incantatory character of the paragraph is reinforced by its strong musicality, through the recurrence of /w/ sounds, creating reverberations of the initial consonant of 'war' in other words—'world', 'growling', 'howling', 'bellowing', 'without'. The onomatopoeic power of the numerous verbs denoting sounds—'growling, howling', 'bellowing, snorting', 'shrieking and screaming', 'banging'—creates an aural association of the word 'war' with the apocalyptic sounds of the animals mentioned. The concluding 'amen' reinforces the finality of the tirade. It seems that war is literally the 'ultimate word of the world', if we are to adopt a grim inversion of Bakhtin's aphorism (Bakhtin 166). Yet the unusual tone, with its grandiloquence, may appear forced, and points to an ironical, detached undercurrent; and the persona remains in a liminal position: standing silent and motionless behind 'the gauze curtains' of the night (57), she watches and listens to the war from the edge.

From Abject to Reject

The most radical locus of estrangement in *The Forbidden Zone* is that of the wounded body and the corpse. Julia Kristeva's and Elaine Scarry's works on horror and pain provide useful insights into the absolute barrier and incommunicability generated by suffering. Scarry's *The Body in Pain* opens on a geographical metaphor to convey the 'unsharability' of physical pain:

> When one hears about another person's physical pain, the events happening within the interior of that person's body may seem to have the remote

character of some deep subterranean fact, belonging to an invisible geography that […] has no reality because it has not yet manifested itself on the visible surface of the earth.

(Scarry 3)

It may therefore be no surprise that the wounded body first appears metaphorically, through the ravaged landscape, in Borden's text: through the 'bleeding edge' of the country in 'Belgium', 'where the enemy took its last bite' (1–2); or the town in 'Bombardment', who turns from a body 'asleep, […] pillowed on the secure shore' (6), to 'wounded earth' (7), and finally shows a 'convulsed face', 'attacked by an invisible and gigantic beast' (9). The collective bodies of the country or town herald the ravaged bodies of soldiers in the following pieces; being remote from physical bodies, they also anticipate the absolute alienness of suffering. Due to its exceptional character, 'physical pain', Scarry argues, 'does not simply resist language but actively destroys it' (4). In this perspective, pain normally operates as an unbridgeable divide between wounded and carers: it constitutes the limits of representation. In *Powers of Horror*, Julia Kristeva likewise defines abjection as a radical opposition to the subject, a menace that threatens to encroach upon its boundaries and jeopardises meaning: 'What is *abject* […], the jettisoned object, is radically excluded and draws me toward the place where meaning collapses' (Kristeva 1982, 2). Considering the abjection of the corpse, Kristeva argues: 'Refuse and corpses *show me* what I permanently thrust aside in order to live. […] The corpse […] is a border that has encroached upon everything' (3). The liminality intrinsic to the Forbidden Zone and its inhabitants—carers and wounded alike—thus ultimately generates abjection as it threatens the limits between subject and non-subject. The core of abjection in Borden's text is enacted in this continuous and irresolvable tension between 'showing' and the threat of 'meaning collaps[ing]'. Borden's pieces have us stare directly at limbs forgotten on tables and pushed aside or even thrown on the floor to make cocoa, or at bits of brain coming off of bandages and chucked in a basin—quite literally, refuse, which Kristeva puts on a par with corpses; they have us inhale 'that dank smell of a rotting swap, the smell of gas gangrene', and listen to 'the little whimpering voice of a man who is going to die in an hour or two' (51).

Yet to the nurse persona in 'Moonlight', these smells, these sounds, are the only ones that are tolerable: 'I don't mind', she repeats, describing her 'routine'. Most significantly, the voice of the agonising soldier is the one signifier that she comprehends: 'That little sound I understand' (52), asserting in even stronger terms later, '[h]e tells the truth to me. He tells me what I know to be true' (56). Borden in her letters talked of her own resistance to the wounded as abject: 'I am becoming obsessed again by the obscenity of the war', she confided to her lover Louis Spears.

> The wounded that have come in today are beyond all descriptions […]—I am on night duty tonight—you will say I ought not to do it—but the morale is not all that it might be and I want to be an example to the women that weep and wail'.
>
> (9 August 1917, qtd in Conway 76)

I propose that what is at stake in Borden's text can be related to Irving Goh's theorisation of the *reject* in his eponymous volume addressing Jean-Luc Nancy's question, 'who comes after the subject?' (Irving 1). Considering the work of authors who write '*against* a whole outlook or world order, very much dominated by materialism and violence', Jean-Michel Ganteau and Susana Onega have foregrounded the 'positive, constructive force' of the reject, quoting from Goh that 'the *reject* is not always passive' but that it 'can actively express a force of rejection in retaliation to the external forces acting against it' (Goh 7, emphasis his, qtd in Ganteau and Onega 4). In the Forbidden Zone, the nurse and the wounded soldier are both abject, but in *The Forbidden Zone*, Borden reverses this abjection into a constructive force, both ethically and aesthetically. This corresponds to Goh's analysis of the 'auto-reject':

> The *auto-reject* [...] is always able to think (itself) anew constantly and to be always open to what arrives to thought and to itself, which arrives not only from the future but also from the past. Auto-rejection involves creative regeneration, therefore, and not [...] self-annihilation.
>
> (Goh 7)

Beyond ideological, moral and aesthetic norms and conventions, there unfolds in Borden's text a resistance that reaches far deeper than culture and ideology: a resistance to the metaphysical limitations between subject and abject, where the subject, on the brink of disappearing—the nurse in 'Moonlight' is 'dead', a 'ghost'—retrieves and preserves on the page the integrity of the wounded and dying soldiers as subjects. That untenable, intrinsically liminal position, which Borden invites us to share in, is where the power of Borden's representation resides, despite—and I argue, because of—its manifold struggles.

Conclusion: Modernism and Mimesis

Just as the Forbidden Zone is an interstitial space, *The Forbidden Zone* likewise navigates an uncomfortable zone between the sayable and the unsayable: from the periphery of horror, it aims at sharing the experience with the reader, without effacing the extreme precariousness of such representation. Borden's representation is itself essentially liminal and invites us to reassess the divide between traditional mimesis and modernist technique. Reflecting on the representation of bodies at war in contemporary arts and literature, Catherine Bernard states of Chapman's *Great Deeds Against the Dead*,

> By a disturbing paradox, the scene is both realistic and a simulacrum [...]. Representation is replaced by a logic of presentation, or ostension, which literalises the horror of war.[6]
>
> (Bernard 107)

As Ganteau and Onega, Bernard focuses on contemporary aesthetics; yet I contend once more that this process of ostension, along with its many challenges, is at work in *The Forbidden Zone*. Borden's text transcends the representational divide between traditional mimesis and modernism; it may even adumbrate later forms of representation. The manifold phenomena of dissociation, of a split persona writing of herself from the outside, all point to the decentring of the subject that is fundamental to modernist aesthetics; they are indeed rendered, as has been noted, by fragmentation, the constant slippage between first-person and third-person narratives, and the various distancing devices studied in this chapter. Comparing Borden's war account to those published in the same year by Remarque, Graves and Manning, Das asserts, 'Borden does not suffer by comparison: here at last is a highly conscious literary modernist' (220). Kaplan likewise argues that the generic fluidity of *The Forbidden Zone*, which she relates to Helen Zenna Smith's *Not So Quiet.... Stepdaughters of War* published in 1930, contributes to the text's modernist aesthetics: 'In transforming women's war diaries and memoirs into hybridized memoir fictions', Kaplan argues, 'Smith and Borden develop a modernist interpretation of the chaos of war reality' (Kaplan 37). Borden was fascinated with the avant-garde authors of pre-war London: besides her close ties to the Hueffers and to Wyndham Lewis mentioned in the introduction to this chapter, she appears in Gertrude Stein's *Autobiography of Alice B Toklas* as a fervent admirer of Stein herself: 'She was very enthusiastic about the work of Gertrude Stein and travelled with what she had of it and volumes of Flaubert to and from the front' (Stein 185). That works by both Stein and Flaubert were brought to the front as probable sources of inspiration is in keeping with the complex aesthetic nexus that emerges in *The Forbidden Zone*.

Borden's collection displays indeed a constant tension between a dynamic of fragmentation, loss and chaos, and an overarching voice that endeavours to tie all the fragments together and grants—or feigns to grant—each of them an internal unity, in a manner that strongly evokes the principles of what was to be canonised as 'high modernism'. Besides the geographical unity remarked earlier between the titles of the various parts and several pieces, many texts thus echo one another: 'Bombardment', 'The Regiment' and 'The Beach' open on similarly ironical Arcadian settings. Some leitmotivs recur through the collection that tie the pieces together: the 'glittering' and 'laughi[ng]' aeroplane of 'Bombardment' can be found again in 'The Regiment' as 'a fearless, capricious, gay glittering creature of pleasure' (21); motors are 'panting and snorting' in both 'The Square' and 'Moonlight'; in many pieces, there develops a polyptoton on 'heaven'. The opening of the first piece in Part Two, 'The City in the Desert', echoes some features of the first piece in Part One, 'Belgium', with the omnipresence of mud, the accumulation of questions and a one-sided dialogue between the first-person narrator and a second-person addressee. Both pieces conclude on the phrase 'come away'. These common points are but a few examples that point to the sophistication and structuredness of the volume as a whole. Besides this overarching structural energy, each piece is painstakingly organised, or to quote Borden, 'It is all carefully arranged' (117). Most texts are punctuated by the repetition of the same formulas. 'Sentinels' is even structured by a trio of repetitions that succeed one another, unfolding like the movements of a concerto: 'it is always the same', 'sometimes' and the fateful 'they will be destroyed'. Most pieces develop in a ballad-like manner, where one of the initial sentences is repeated as the piece concludes; yet the final occurrence is grimly coloured by what has come between. Thus 'The Beach' opens and closes on the remark 'the sea is a perfect heavenly blue', but between its two occurrences, the wounded soldier's perspective as well as the casino and its bleak inhabitants have appeared. In 'The City in the Desert', the sentence 'the place is [...] new and still and desolate' likewise occurs in the second and the last paragraphs, but the second occurrence is inflected by the presence of the stretcher bearers carrying the wounded to the hospital. The initial vision is thus deflated through the alternative viewpoint that developes between the first and the last paragraphs. This broken circularity emphasises the shift in perspective brought about by the witnessing of wounded or dead men in the environment of the Hôpital d'Évacuation. This may be related to the circularity and *progression d'effet* at work in Sinclair's war narrative: in both cases, the fact that the text is framed with the same words or tropes intensifies their emotive charge.

Yet while they point to a powerful structural agency on the part of Borden, these repetitions also signal the exhaustion of language. The musicality of Borden's text is simultaneously the token of a language petering out, stuttering on the same words before ending abruptly. Most of the writing, furthermore, is characterised with monosyllables and short, paratactic sentences: language seems to be wearing itself out. Several pieces end on expressions that signal the failure of language: 'come away' ('Belgium'), 'nothing' (Bombardment), 'empty' ('Sentinels'), 'take them away' ('Paraphernalia').

Ann-Marie Einhaus considers that Borden's writing in *The Forbidden Zone* expresses 'an attempt and a failure to employ new, innovative techniques to the desired effect of communicating personal impressions' (Einhaus 302). To her, Borden's failure resides in her attempts to combine mimetic and modernist approaches. I contend that Borden's combination of modernist and mimetic modes of representing the war is in itself expressive of the inextricable aporia of representing the abject. Borden's writing eschews neither the act of showing nor its inescapable challenges. While I disagree with Einhaus's sense that Borden's text is a failure in witnessing, I concur with her argument that Borden's text, as that of other writers addressed in this volume, evidences the fraught relationship between war representation and modernism. Although modernist modes of representation can be considered as anti-mimetic, and therefore as obstructing the witnessing duty felt by writers at war, they are here—as in Ford's war prose—used towards an updated mimesis. Borden's apparent failure conveys the contradictory energies that inform her pieces, in which she strives to approach as closely as possible the core of her war experience whilst retaining the essence of her helplessness in reproducing the phenomenology of the war. Catherine Bernard's reflection on the representation of the disfigured First World War soldier in Pat Barker's *Toby's Room* is here relevant:

> The geometry of this now improbable body [...] escapes anatomy. The text struggles to have us visualise the forces exerted on it; yet it is in this anatomical resistance that the physics of bodies at war is heard and understood.[7]
>
> (Bernard 109–10)

This resistance of representation is not only unavoidable: it also captures the essence of the mangled body at war. Furthermore, Borden's refusal to smooth out the asperities of her representation of war is of a profoundly ethical significance. Bernard's evaluation of what is at stake in Henry Tonks's pastel drawings of the *gueules cassées* is enlightening:

> The ethics that emerges, in the flesh bruised yet worthy of being observed and caressed by the pastel, is of course reminiscent of that defined by Emmanuel Levinas in *Humanism of the Other* (1972) when he speaks of the face of the other which 'imposes itself on me without my being able to cease to be responsible for his misery' (49). [...] An empirical counter-knowledge imposes itself in the painter's gesture, contravening the gendered norms of identity and therefore enacting a critical work.[8]
>
> (Bernard 111)

At odds with the masculine ideal of the powerful and invulnerable soldier at war, with the corresponding saccharine vignette of the nurse as a holy virgin mother and with all norms of representation, Borden acts ultimately as a vector of history, aiming to make present to us the uninhabitability of her stance, the unutterable extraordinariness of the soldier's suffering, and the unique connection between both, through care. In Das's words, '[I]n some obscure way that goes beyond literary affect, our bodies are touched' (Das 228). Borden's voice, tenuous though it may appear through the constantly unstable narrative frame, is the connecting point between the *poilu* and us, the readers.

Notes

1 Some of the analyses present in this chapter were initially published in an article written for *Miranda*, 'A Nurse in the Great War: The Exceptional Voice of Mary Borden'. *Miranda* [Online], 23: 2021.
2 Although I have made every effort to find the copyright holders for Borden's work, I have not been able to trace them. I would ask the rights holders to please contact me if they find issue with the quotations from Borden's *The Forbidden Zone* in this study.
3 While I have lacked the space to address this more precisely here, Sandrine Sorlin's monograph The Stylistics of 'You': Second-Person Pronoun and Its Pragmatic Effects provides a detailed and illuminative analysis of the effects of the use of second-person pronoun.
4 The illustration can be accessed here: https://archive.org/details/forbiddenzone00bord/page/n7/mode/1up.
5 The original French text has a lexicon that is more directly specific to horses: 'Nous nous approchâmes des trois machines renâclantes pour flatter leur poitrail'.

6 My translation. Original text: 'Par un troublant paradoxe, la scène est tout à la fois réaliste et simulacre [...]. À la représentation se substitue une logique de présentation, ou d'ostension qui littéralise l'horreur de la guerre'.
7 My translation. Original text: 'La géométrie de ce corps désormais improbable [...] échappe à l'anatomie. Le texte peine à nous faire visualiser les forces qui s'exercent sur lui et pourtant c'est dans cette résistance anatomique que s'entend, que se comprend la physique des corps en guerre'.
8 My translation. Original text: 'L'éthique qui se devine, dans la chair meurtrie et pourtant digne d'être observée et caressée par le pastel, n'est pas sans rappeler bien sûr celle que définit Emmanuel Lévinas dans *Humanisme de l'autre homme* (1972) quand il parle du visage d'autrui qui "s'impose à moi sans que je puisse cesser d'être responsable de sa misère" (49). [...] [C]'est un contre-savoir empirique qui s'impose dans le geste du peintre, contrevenant aux normes genrées de l'identité et faisant ainsi œuvre critique'.

Bibliography

Primary Sources

Borden, Mary. *The Mistress of Kingdoms; or Smoking Flax*. London: Duckworth, 1912.
———. *Collision*. London: Duckworth, 1913.
———. 'The Regiment'. *The English Review* 25, no. 4 (October 1917a): 341–51, https://archive.org/details/sim_english-review-uk_1917-10_25.
———. 'Unidentified'. *The English Review* 25, no. 5 (December 1917b): 482–6, https://archive.org/details/sim_english-review-uk_1917-12_25.
———. 'Where Is Jehovah?'; 'The Song of the Mud'; 'The Hill'. *The English Review* 25, no. 2 (August 1917c): 97–9; 100–1; 101–2, https://archive.org/details/2englishreview25londuoft.
———. *The Forbidden Zone*. London: Heinemann, 1929, https://archive.org/details/forbiddenzone00bord/.
———. *The Forbidden Zone*. Edited by Hazel Hutchison. London: Hesperus Press, 2008.
———. *Poems of War and Peace*. Edited by Paul O'Prey. Brighton: Dare-Gale Press, 2015.
La Motte, Ellen. *The Backwash of War*. New York and London: G.P. Putnam's Sons, 1916, https://archive.org/details/backwashofwar00lamoiala.
Marinetti, Filippo Tommaso. 'Manifeste du Futurisme'. *Le Figaro*, 20 February 1909.
Mortimer, Maud. *A Green Tent in Flanders*. New York: Doubleday, Page & Co, 1917, https://archive.org/details/greententinfland00mortrich.
Stein, Gertruge. *Autobiography of Alice B Toklas*. London: Penguin Classics, 2001. First published 1933.
Warner, Agnes. *My Beloved Poilus*. St. John, N.B: Barnes, 1917, https://archive.org/details/mybelovedpoilus00warngoog.
Wright, Ernest Vincent. *The Wonderful Fairies of the Sun*. Boston: Roberts Brothers, 1896, https://en.wikisource.org/wiki/The_Wonderful_Fairies_of_the_Sun.

Secondary Sources

Acton, Carol. 'Diverting the Gaze: The Unseen Text in Women's War Writing', *College Literature* 31, no. 2 (Spring 2004), *Literature Online*: 53–79.

Acton, Carol, and Jane Potter. '"These Frightful Sights Would Work Havoc with One's Brain": Subjective Experience, Trauma, and Resilience in First World War Writings by Medical Personnel'. *Literature and Medicine* 30, no. 1 (Spring 2012): 61–85.

———, and Jane Potter 'Negotiating Injury and Masculinity in First World War Nurses' Writing'. In *First World War Nursing: New Perspectives*. Edited by Alison Fell, and Christine Hallett, 123–38. London: Routledge, 2013.

———. *Working in a World of Hurt: Trauma and Resilience in the Narratives of Medical Personnel in Warzones*. Manchester: Manchester University Press, 2015.

———. '"Their Wounds Gape at Me": First World War Nursing Accounts and the Politics of Injury'. In *Living War, Thinking Peace (1914–1924): Women's Experiences, Feminist Thought, and International Relations*. Edited Bruna Bianchi, and Geraldine Ludbrook, 44–63. Newcastle upon Tyne: Cambridge Scholar Publishing, 2016.

Andrews, Maggie, Alison Fell, Lucy Noakes, and June Purvis. 'Representing, Remembering and Rewriting Women's Histories of the First World War', *Women's History Review* 27, no. 4 (2018): 511–5.

Augé, Marc. *Non-Places: Introduction to an Anthropology of Supermodernity*. Translated by John Howe. London: Verso, 1995. Original French version 1992.

Bakhtin, Mikhail. *Problems of Dostoevsky's Poetics*. Translated by Caryl Emerson, and Wayne C. Booth. Minneapolis: University of Minnesota Press, 1984.

Barthes, Roland. 'Introduction à l'analyse structurale des récits'. *Communications* 8 (1966): 1–27.

———. 'An Introduction to the Structural Analysis of Narrative'. Translated by Lionel Duisit. *New Literary History* 6, no. 2 (1975): 237–72. Original French version 1966.

Bernard, Catherine. *Matière à réflexion. Du corps politique dans la littérature et les arts visuels britanniques contemporains*. Paris: Presses de l'Université Paris-Sorbonne, 2018.

Blanchot, Maurice. *L'Écriture du désastre*. Paris: Gallimard, 1980.

Butler, Judith. *Bodies that Matter. On the Discursive Limits of 'Sex'*. London: Routledge, 1993.

Carrabine, Eamonn. 'Traces of Violence: Representing the Atrocities of War'. *Criminology & Criminal Justice* 18, no. 5 (November 2018): 631–46, https://doi.org/10.1177/1748895818789448.

Conway, Jane. *Mary Borden: A Woman of Two Wars*. London: Munday Books, 2010.

Das, Santanu. *Touch and Intimacy in First World War Literature*. Cambridge: Cambridge University Press, 2005.

Derrida, Jacques. *L'Écriture et la différence*. Paris: Seuil, 1967.

Douthwaite, John, Daniela Francesca Virdis, and Elisabetta Zurru, eds. *The Language of Landscapes*. Amsterdam: John Benjamins, 2019.

Einhaus, Ann-Marie. 'Modernism, Truth, and the Canon of First World War Literature'. *Modernist Cultures* 6, no. 2 (2011): 296–314.

Fell, Alison, and Christine Hallett, eds. *First World War Nursing: New Perspectives*. London: Routledge, 2013.

Fell, Alison. 'Remembering First World War Nursing: Other Fronts, Other Spaces'. *Journal of War & Culture Studies* 11, no. 4 (2018): 269–72.

Felman, Shoshana, and Dori Laub. *Testimony: Crises of Witnessing in Literature, Psychoanalysis, and History*. London: Routledge, 1991.

Foucault, Michel. *Surveiller et punir: naissance de la prison*. Paris: Gallimard, 1975.

Freedman, Ariela. 'Mary Borden's *Forbidden Zone*: Women's Writing from No-Man's-Land'. *Modernism/Modernity* 9, no. 1 (2002): 109–24.

Fussell, Paul. *The Great War and Modern Memory*. Oxford: Oxford University Press, 2013. First published 1975.

Gallagher, Jean. *The World Wars through the Female Gaze*. Carbondale: Southern Illinois University Press, 1998.

Geiger, Maria. 'No Trench Required: Validating the Voices of Female Poets of WWI'. *War, Literature and The Arts* 27 (2015): 1–13.

Gilbert, Sandra. 'Soldier's Heart: Literary Men, Literary Women, and the Great War'. *Signs* 8, no. 3 (1983): 422–50.

Gilbert, Sandra, and Susan Gubar. *No Man's Land: The War of Words*. New Haven: Yale University Press, 1989.

Giovanelli, Marcello. 'Cognitive Grammar and Readers' Perceived Sense of Closeness: A Study of Responses to Mary Borden's "Belgium."' *Language and Literature* (June 2022), https://doi.org/10.1177/09639470221105930.

Goh, Irving. *The Reject: Community, Politics, and Religion After the Subject*. New York: Fordham University Press, 2014.

Grayzel, Susan R., and Tammy Proctor, eds. *Gender and the Great War*. Oxford: Oxford University Press, 2017.

Gromada, Jennifer. '"I Have Something Vital to Do Here": The Modernist Mode in the Writings of Mary Borden'. PhD thesis Drew University, 2019.

Hallett, Christine E., *Containing Trauma: Nursing Work in the First World War*. Manchester: Manchester University Press, 2009.

——— '"Emotional Nursing": Involvement, Engagement, and Detachment in the Writings of First World War Nurses and VADs'. In *First World War Nursing: New Perspectives*. Edited by Alison Fell, and Christine Hallett, 87–102. New York: Routledge, 2013.

——— *Nurse Writers of the Great War*. Manchester: Manchester University Press, 2016.

Hammerstein, Katharina von, Kosta, Barbara, and Shoults, Julie, eds. *Women Writing War. From German Colonialism through World War I*. Berlin: De Gruyter, 2018.

Higonnet, Margaret, and Patrice Higonnet. 'The Double Helix'. In *Behind the Lines: Gender and the Two World Wars*. Edited by Margaret Higonnet, Jane Jenson, Sonya Michel, and Margaret Collins Weitz, 31–48. New Haven: Yale University Press, 1987.

Higonnet, Margaret. 'Not so Quiet in No-Woman's-Land'. In *Gendering War Talk*. Edited by Miriam Cooke, and Angela Woollacott, 205–26. Princeton: Princeton University Press, 1993.

———. 'Cassandra's Question: Do Women Write War Novels?' In *Borderwork: Feminist Engagements with Comparative Literature*. Edited by Margaret Higonnet, 144–61. Ithaca: Cornell University Press, 1994.

———. 'Another Record, a Different War'. *Women's Studies Quarterly* 23, no. 3–4 (1995): 85–96.

———, ed. *Nurses at the Front: Writing the Wounds of the Great War*. Boston: Northeastern University Press, 2001.

———. 'Authenticity and Art in Trauma Narratives of World War I'. *Modernism/Modernity* 9, no. 1 (2002): 91–107.

Hutchison, Hazel. 'The Theater of Pain. Observing Mary Borden in *The Forbidden Zone*'. In *First World War Nursing: New Perspectives*. Edited by Alison Fell, and Christine Hallett, 139–55. New York: Routledge, 2013.

———. *The War That Used Up Words: American Writers and the First World War*. New York: Yale University Press, 2015.

———. 'Very Chicago: Mary Borden and the Art of Fiction'. *Midwestern Miscellany: Journal of the Society for the Study of Midwestern Literature* (2016), https://aura.abdn.ac.uk/handle/2164/6174.

Kaplan, Laurie. 'Deformities of the Great War: The Narratives of Mary Borden and Helen Zenna Smith'. *Women and Language* 27, no. 2 (2004): 35–43.

Kelly, Alice. *Commemorative Modernisms: Women Writers, Death and the First World War*. Edinburgh: Edinburgh University Press, 2020.

Kristeva, Julia. *Powers of Horror*. Translated by Leon Roudiez. New York: Columbia University Press, 1982. Original French version 1980.

Lambrecht, Nora, '"But If You Listen You Can Hear": War Experience, Modernist Noise, and the Soundscape of *The Forbidden Zone*'. *Modernism/Modernity* 2, no. 1 (8 March 2017a), https://doi.org/10.26597/mod.0005.

———. 'The Art of Noise: Literature and Disturbance 1900–1940', PhD thesis Johns Hopkins University, 2017b, https://jscholarship.library.jhu.edu/handle/1774.2/58670.

Larabee, Mark Douglas. *Front Lines of Modernism. Remapping the Great War in British Fiction*. New York: Palgrave Macmillan, 2011.

Lawrence, Margot. *Shadow of Swords: A Biography of Elsie Inglis*. London: Michael Joseph, 1971.

Marcus, Jane, 'Corpus/Corps/Corpse: Writing the Body in/at War'. In *Not so Quiet ... Stepdaughters of War*. Edited by Helen Zenna Smith, New York: The Feminist Press, 1989.

Onega, Susana, and Jean-Michel Ganteau, eds. *The Wounded Hero in Contemporary Fiction: A Paradoxical Quest*. London: Routledge, 2018.

Raitt, Suzanne, and Trudi Tate. *Women's Fiction and the Great War*. Oxford: Clarendon Press, 1997.

Saunders, Max. 'War Literature, Bearing Witness, and the Problem of Sacralization: Trauma and Desire in the Writing of Mary Borden and Others'. In *Memories and Representations of War: The Case of World War I and World War II*. Edited by Elena Lamberti, and Vita Fortunati, 177–92. Amsterdam: Brill, 2009.

Scarry, Elaine. *The Body in Pain*. Oxford: Oxford University Press, 1985.

Smith, Angela. *Women's Writing of the First World War*. Manchester: Manchester UP, 2000.

———. *The Second Battlefield: Women, Modernism and the First World War*. Manchester: Manchester University Press, 2001.

Sorlin, Sandrine. *The Stylistics of 'You': Second-Person Pronoun and Its Pragmatic Effects*. Cambridge: Cambridge University Press, 2022.

Stokes, Jasie. 'Fragments of a Great Confusion: Abjection, Subjectivity, and the Body in Mary Borden's *the Forbidden Zone*'. In *Corporeality and Culture: Bodies in Movement*. Edited by Karin Sellberg, Lena Wånggren, and Kamillea Aghtan, 115–26. Oxford: Routledge, 2015.

Tylee, Claire. *The Great War and Women's Consciousness: Images of Militarism and Womanhood in Women's Writings 1914–64*. Iowa City: University of Iowa Press, 1990.

Virilio, Paul. *War and Cinema: The Logistics of Perception*. Translated by Patrick Camiller. London: Verso, 2009. First published 1989. Original French version 1984.

Epilogue

Flora stands as an incongruous figure in the Flandria Hotel of Sinclair's journal; Borden's Arcadian landscapes are tinged with sarcasm; Sassoon's pastoral descriptions become more disabused as the war goes on; Ford's illuminated vignettes only stand in contrast to what he *cannot* describe of the war.

Yet in these apparently anecdotal notes persists what connects all four authors: the quest for the faltering power of human creation in spite of the most horrific of experiences, amidst the apparent destruction of Western civilisation. This quest does not necessarily point towards an epiphanic resolution; it remains tentative, uncertain and self-derisive. Yet this very hesitation, these lacks, the unspeakable around which these oblique descriptions are written, do allow the reader to fathom the extremity of the war experience. Beyond the First World War, all these texts speak of humanity: that of their writers and that, more crucially, of the people they witnessed—soldiers, chauffeurs, carers, refugees, civilians, who endure in their accounts. If the present volume has incited you to read these pages anew, my work here is done.

Index

Page numbers followed by n indicate notes.

19th century 4–5, 55, 97, 104–5, 107, 115, 135; *see also* romanticism

abject 9, 11, 122, 125, 151, 154, 157, 159–61, 163
absence, *see* lack
absurd 70–4, 91
accuracy 30, 41, 43–4, 57, 62, 84, 100–2, 106, 109–10, 113, 119, 122, 124; *see also* precision
acronyms 27, 144, 153
Adorno, T. 9, 32, 37, 90–1
aesthetic experimentation 2–4, 9–11, 19, 39, 44, 46–7, 59, 90–1, 98–9, 102–3, 108, 133, 163
affect 8, 10, 21, 27, 29–30, 32, 39, 57, 67, 72, 75, 80, 84–9, 91, 100, 108–10, 124–5, 134, 137–8, 150, 163–4
alliteration 66, 88, 104, 139, 148, 159
alterity 8–9, 30–9, 64, 118, 153–4, 164; *see also* ethics
ambivalence 3, 10, 49, 55, 59, 75, 77, 111, 125; *see also* paradox
animalisation, *see* dehumanisation
anthropomorphising, *see* personification
anticipation 7, 29, 47, 59, 62–3, 66, 90, 100, 109, 114–5, 117, 120, 158; of future writing 7, 10, 42, 99, 103, 120–1, 123, 157
anticlimax 62–3, 124
aporia of representation 4, 9–11, 20, 23–5, 31, 38, 39, 44, 47, 50, 61, 86–91, 125, 147, 150, 163
artillery, *see* bombing
Augé, M. 144, 153, 166
Austen, J. 63–4

authenticity 27, 58, 81, 85, 90, 101, 107, 116, 132, 136, 137; *see also* truthfulness
autobiography 5, 10–1, 19, 49, 96–102, 113, 116, 132, 142, 151, 157; *see also* memoir

ballad 30, 155, 163
Baedeker guides 75–6, 149; *see also* tourism
Bakhtin, M. 10, 58–9, 66–9, 156, 159
Barthes, R. 114–5, 158
Battersby, C. 58, 74
Belgium 2, 7, 10, 19, 37, 56, 59, 65, 75–6, 78, 143, 149, 150, 157; Antwerp 2, 55, 60–2, 65, 68, 76, 89; Ghent 60, 62, 64, 66, 73, 75–6, 78–9, 85, 88–9; Ypres 5, 18, 21, 26, 37, 49, 131, 149
Benjamin, W. 7, 47
Bergson, H. 70–2
Bernard, C. 90, 161, 163–4
Biblical references 118, 147, 158–9
Boccioni, U. 45
Body 32, 87, 121, 125, 140, 145–6, 150, 157, 159–61, 164
bombing 6, 10, 18, 23, 33, 40–4, 63, 65, 69, 73, 106, 108–9, 113, 121–3, 126, 138, 145–6, 148, 154–5, 160
de Bont, L. 58, 69, 79–80, 91, 92n6, 92n8
Borden, Mary 1–2, 4–11, 21, 45, 61–2, 75, 87, 130–64, 169; 'The Beach' 142, 148, 152, 156–7, 162–3; 'Belgium' 138–9, 142–3, 149–50, 160, 162–3; 'Blind' 157; 'Bombardment' 138–9, 145–6, 148, 152, 154, 155, 160, 162, 163; 'The Captive Balloon' 132,

Index

155–6; 'The City in the Desert' 140–2, 144–5, 147, 152, 162–3; 'Conspiracy' 141, 152; *Collision* 130; *The Forbidden Zone* 130–64; 'The Hill' 132; *The Mistress of Kingdoms* 130; 'In the Operating Room' 132, 142, 151, 157; 'Moonlight' 62, 141, 143, 147, 152, 154–5, 158–62; 'Paraphernalia' 141, 163; 'The Regiment' 140–1, 148, 153–4, 156, 162; 'The Square' 142, 147, 152, 154–6, 162
Bowen, C. 111, 119–21
Bowen, S. 25
Bowler, R. 81, 84–5
Butler, J. 37, 126, 151

care 11, 117, 141, 150–1, 152, 154–5, 157; *see also* alterity; ethics
carnivalesque 10, 59, 66–75, 156
cartography, *see* maps
censorship 100, 136–7
chivalry 67–8
circularity 85, 148, 163; *see also* structuredness
cloud, smoke, shadow, paradigms of 20, 39–40, 43, 45, 47–8, 106–7, 113, 122, 138, 146
clownish situations 69, 71–3, 125
cognitive limits 6, 21–2, 26, 35, 154, 155, 157
coherence, *see* consistency
colours 38, 43–6, 72, 105, 113, 117, 122, 137–9, 148, 163
comedy 10, 59, 64, 66, 68–74, 125
commemoration 12, 98–9, 118; *see also* remembrance
communication 4, 30, 33, 64, 108–9, 163
confusion 6, 11, 22, 41, 44, 61–4, 109, 132, 140; of the reader 59, 62–3, 90
connection, *see* contact
Conrad, Joseph 16, 21, 26, 29, 31, 41–3, 50, 84
consistency 36, 42–5, 60, 84–5, 99, 101–3, 143, 155, 162–3
constructedness 10–1, 46, 80–1, 85–6, 99,112, 115–7, 121, 123, 140, 162–3
contact 4, 9, 11, 12, 19, 28, 35, 88, 108, 118, 138, 143, 161, 164
contradiction 27, 40, 57, 65, 89, 91, 106, 128, 163; *see also* ambivalence
convention 5, 10, 11, 32, 57, 59, 75, 90, 107, 133–5, 137, 139, 161; opposition to, *see* unconventionality

cubism 4, 7, 44–6, 141
cultural and literary influences 4–7, 46–7, 55, 66–70, 91, 99, 104, 112–3, 115–6, 118, 120, 123, 137, 147, 159

danger 62–3, 66–8, 80, 85, 107–10
Das, Santanu 6, 8, 13, 22, 108, 11, 131, 137, 140–1, 162, 164
death 7–9, 11, 24, 29, 31–5, 40, 47, 88–90, 96, 105, 108, 116–8, 121–3, 125, 141, 152–3, 156, 159–1, 163
deconstruction, *see* negativity
defamiliarisation 23, 50, 87, 107–8, 125, 140, 144, 149, 154–7; *see also* unfamiliar
dehumanisation 23–4, 31, 35, 39, 107–8, 141, 146–7, 154–7; *see also* objectification
deixis 8, 79, 86, 138–9, 143, 147, 149, 161, 163
delay 59–62, 65, 81, 83–4, 86, 154
delight, *see* pleasure
detachment 19, 24, 39, 79, 85–7, 89, 107–11, 113, 136, 138–9, 140–1, 146, 154, 156, 158–9
detail, *see* accuracy, precision
dialogism 58, 73–5, 77, 91, 148; *see also* carnivalesque
diary 5, 8, 10, 59–62, 66, 75, 85, 99–103, 113–6, 119, 123–5, 137
disorientation, *see* confusion
disruption, *see* undermining devices
dissociation 7, 11, 64–5, 141–2, 146, 152, 157–8, 162, 168
distance 20–2, 34–5, 50, 60, 64, 66, 81, 90, 138–40, 160
Distantiation 4–5, 63, 66, 73–5, 109, 136, 141, 143–7, 154, 156, 162
double deixis 63, 79, 85–6, 138–9, 141–2; *see also* pronouns
Drewery, C. 78–9
duty, sense of 5, 16, 20, 29–31, 38–9, 97, 105, 117–8, 160, 163

Egremont, M. 2, 96–7, 99, 115, 125
emotion, *see* affect
enemy 38–9, 78, 126, 149–50, 160
English Review 56, 81, 84, 132, 136, 153
enumeration 44, 88, 108, 125, 138
Erwartungshorizon 59–60, 66, 68–70, 75, 139, 149
estrangement 48, 79, 87, 133, 140, 153–5, 159–60

172 Index

ethics 8–11, 16, 19–20, 24–5, 29–39, 50, 64, 118, 149, 153–4, 161, 164
exactness, *see* accuracy
excitement 7, 41, 62, 64, 67, 78–80, 86, 124
exhaustion 25, 35, 47, 103, 118, 122, 155, 148; of language 163
expressivity 5, 10, 29–30, 39, 45, 87–9, 103, 122, 152

factualness 2, 22, 27, 39, 84, 89, 100–3, 111–2, 121–3, 143, 157, 159
failure of representation, *see* aporia
Felman, S. and Laub, D. 8, 110, 119, 159
feminism 57, 68, 130, 141
fiction 17, 19, 23–5, 27–9, 37, 39, 42, 47, 49, 55, 57, 96–101, 103–4, 113, 155, 162; *see also* novel
Flaubert, G. 24, 47, 162
Ford, F. M; *see also* Hueffer 1–11, 16–54, 61, 77, 84, 85, 90, 112–3, 130, 132, 138, 147, 149, 163; 'A Day of Battle' 9, 18, 21–3, 26–7, 31–3, 38–41, 43, 50; *see also* 'Arms and the Mind' and 'War and the Mind'; A Man Could Stand Up— 30–1, 43, 50; *see also Parade's End*; *Ancient Lights* 84; 'Arms and the Mind' 21–3, 26–7, 31–3, 35–6, 39–40, 43–4, 46–8; *see also* 'A Day of Battle'; *Between Saint Dennis and Saint George* 18, 29; 'Epilogue' 9, 22, 33–8, 42, 44; 'From China to Peru' 30; *It Was the Nightingale* 28, 40, 49; 'Just People' 24–5, 37–8; *Joseph Conrad: A Personal Remembrance* 84; 'Literary Portraits—XLVIII. M. Charles-Louis Philippe and "Le Père Perdrix"' 28; 'Literary Portraits—XLIX. A Causerie' 30; 'Literary Portraits—LI. The Face of Janus' 29–30; 'Literary Portraits—LIII. The Muse of War' 20, 40; *No Enemy* 11, 24, 36, 49; 'On Impressionism' 17–9, 21, 45–6, 77, 84; *Parade's End* 2, 3, 9, 11, 17, 26, 28–31, 35, 38, 40, 42–3, 46–50, 132; *No More Parades* 38, 40, 42–3, 47–8; and dedicatory letter to 30, 49–50; *see also Parade's End*; 'Pon… ti… pri… ith' 9, 43–8, 138; 'Pink Flannel' 19, 23; 'Preparedness' 35; *The Good Soldier* 2, 16–8, 85; *True Love and a G.C.M* 23–4; 'War and the Mind' 22–3, 33, 38–9, 44; *see also* 'A Day of Battle'

Forster, E. M. 1, 130
fragmentation 2, 10–1, 17, 23, 27, 33, 40, 44–6, 48, 50, 72, 88–90, 108, 11–2, 120, 122, 132, 141, 146, 152, 162–3
framing devices 4, 6–7, 23, 33, 43, 46, 72–3, 138–9, 146–8, 151–2, 159
Frayn, A. 3, 18, 48
French language, use of 24, 29, 34, 43–4, 46–7, 86–8, 105, 143, 164
Freud, *see* uncanny
Fussell, P. 1, 4, 6, 22, 104, 107, 147
future perfect 7, 47, 99, 114–5, 120–1, 123, 157; *see also* anticipation
futurism 4, 45–6, 141, 150, 154–5

Gallagher, J. 3–4, 6, 11, 134–5, 146, 149
gaze 6–7, 11, 33, 45, 47, 56, 105, 111, 136–9, 143, 151–2; female 134–9, 146–7; male 135
gender 3–4, 6, 36, 55–8, 68, 75, 77, 91, 130–1, 133–41, 146–55, 164
genre 5, 10–1, 19, 45, 53, 59–60, 99–107, 122–3, 132, 157, 162
geography 7, 11, 23, 27, 43, 75–8, 101–2, 111, 133, 136, 142–2, 159–60, 162; *see also* maps
Georgian poetry 97, 104, 120, 148
ghost, *see* spectrality
Graves, R. 2, 97, 122, 132, 162
Griffith, D. W. 112
grotesque 125, 132

Hallett, C. 3, 131–3, 135–7
happiness 7, 19, 47, 74–5, 103–5, 109, 119, 122
haunting, *see* spectrality
Hemmings, R. 2, 96–7, 104, 107
hero, heroine, heroism 67–8, 74, 79–80, 115–9, 124, 135, 151, 156
Higonnet, M. 3, 133–7
history 7–8, 16–7, 21, 26, 40, 44, 47, 108, 110, 114, 119, 121, 153
horror 7, 10, 16, 30, 32, 59, 72, 74, 78, 88, 125, 141, 143, 157–61
Hueffer, Ford Madox, *see* Ford, Ford Madox
humanity 6, 9, 18, 20, 23–5, 28, 30–2, 35–6, 38–9, 72, 74, 91, 118, 120, 144, 151, 154–5, 169
humiliation 56, 58, 81, 90
Hunt, V. 19, 130
Hynes, S. 4, 17–8, 21, 23, 40, 56–7, 111

Index

idealisation 103–5, 116, 118, 134–5, 139–41, 145, 151, 164
immediacy 2–3, 5–6, 12, 17, 22, 24, 37, 40, 46, 48, 55, 60, 84, 98–9, 101–3, 110–1, 108, 111, 114, 119, 121–5, 132, 135, 136, 143, 147, 150, 158, 160
immensity 6, 19, 21–2, 29–30, 34–5, 38–40, 42–3, 49–50, 112, 146
impasse, *see* aporia
impressionism, *see* literary impressionism
inaccuracy 57, 62, 64, 84, 109, 143–4
incommunicability 4, 16, 26–7, 29–31, 39, 44–5, 61, 67, 86–90, 108–9, 121, 143, 152, 160, 163
incongruous 63, 66–7, 70, 74–5, 77, 109, 125, 156, 169
indeterminacy 27, 33, 37, 43, 59, 81, 143–4
individuality, *see* singularity
instability 11, 23, 49, 59–60, 81, 85, 103, 119, 132–3, 142–4, 147–9, 158, 164
intertextuality 6, 24, 47, 66–72, 104–5, 113, 115, 118, 120, 147–50, 155, 162
invisibilisation 33, 77, 134–7, 160–1
irony 4, 7, 10–1, 49, 63, 66–9, 74, 107, 142–9, 159, 162

James, H. 4
journal, *see* diary
journalism 2, 9–10, 12, 18, 20–1, 30, 33, 35, 56, 61–2, 64–6, 81, 132, 136, 153
joy, *see* pleasure

Kristeva, J. 159–60

La Motte, Ellen 131, 136
landscape 7, 10, 12, 22–3, 27, 45–6, 48, 50, 62–3, 67, 75–8, 103–6, 112–3, 120, 125, 132, 137–9, 142–5, 148, 150, 152–4, 160, 169; *see also* painting
Larabee, M. 4–7, 22, 41, 144–5, 149
lack 11, 25, 28, 32, 46, 60, 62, 65–7, 75, 91, 112, 114, 133, 136, 139, 142–5, 150, 152, 169
laughter 10, 59, 69–74, 146, 162
legend, *see* myth
legitimacy 62, 135–9, 147
Levinas, E. 9, 32, 34, 36–7, 118, 164
Lewis, W. 1, 107, 130, 162
light 40, 43–6, 77, 87, 100, 103–5, 107, 113, 117, 119, 123, 138, 148, 162
liminality 10–1, 78–9, 88, 90, 142–3, 153–4, 159–61

limitation of perception 6–7, 22, 35–6, 46, 102, 108, 111–2, 119, 135, 147; of representation 66, 85, 90–1, 106, 110, 114, 160
literary impressionism 4, 9–11, 17–8, 20–1, 24, 26–7, 34, 38–47, 50, 59, 77, 84–7, 90–1
literary trope, *see topos*
lyricism 2, 30, 80, 103, 106–7, 111, 121–2, 132, 150

manuscript 56, 61, 64, 81–3, 88, 98, 103, 109
maps, mapping 7, 11, 22–3, 41, 43–4, 142–6; *see also* geography
Marinetti, F. T. 155
Marsh, E. 97
Masterman, C. 18, 25, 28, 41
Masterman, L. 25, 29, 41
materiality 12, 31–2, 35, 42, 45–6, 66, 84, 98, 113, 144; *see also* physicality
matter, *see* materiality
mediation 8, 46, 49–50, 100, 110, 119–20, 138; *see also* framing devices; screened perception
memoir 2, 5, 8, 10, 96–100, 102, 107, 120–1, 131–2, 135, 137, 140, 142, 157, 162; *see also* autobiography
memory 19, 25, 30–1, 43–4, 47, 60, 84–6, 96, 101, 104–5–6, 111, 115–6, 119, 121–5; *see also* remembrance
mental block 22–3, 26–7, 44, 89
Merleau-Ponty, M. 8
metalepsis x, 7, 64, 81, 86, 157
metaphor 23, 35–6, 70, 90, 105, 107, 116–7, 138–9, 141, 147, 150, 153, 154–6, 160
metatextuality 40, 102, 132, 144
mimesis 4–5, 11, 43, 79, 88, 133, 135, 161–3
modernism 4–5, 7, 9–10, 16, 39, 44–6, 50, 59, 80, 107–8, 133, 141, 154–5, 161–3
morality 9, 20, 28, 32, 35, 37, 81, 161
Mortimer, Maud 132
mot juste 42, 86
mud 44, 108, 139–40, 147, 162
multi-layered writing 7, 49, 77, 81, 99, 113, 121–5, 141, 146–7; *see also* palimpsest
Munro, Hector 2, 56, 63–4, 67, 85; Hector Munro's Motor Ambulance Corps 2, 10, 56, 60–1, 65–7, 69, 75, 85, 90, 131

musicality 39, 104–5, 139, 155–6, 159, 163; *see also* alliteration; sounds
myth 1, 4, 10, 27, 96, 98–9, 103–4, 115–21, 159

narrative technique 3, 5, 7, 11, 17, 20, 23, 49, 59, 63–5, 85–6, 113–6, 119–21, 130, 138, 140–2, 146–7, 149, 153, 157–8, 162–4
negativity 10, 17, 59, 61–4, 66, 78, 86, 125, 141, 145–6, 149–53; *see also* lack
noise, *see* sounds
non-place 11, 144, 153
nurses 3, 6, 11–2, 85, 130–65; abjection 151–2, 159–61; idealisation 11, 85, 134–6, 140–1, 164; internalised idealisation 140; romanticisation 134–5; interstitial or outside stance 142–3, 150, 152–4, 159; invisibilisation 134–7; objectification 141, 155; self-censorship; seen as lacking legitimacy or 'frauds' 135–7, 140–1, 147; self-alienation 139–42, 157–8, 162; silencing 135–7; scopic power 137–9; writing 131–2, 134–7

objectification 35, 135, 141, 154–5, 160; *see also* dehumanisation
observation 6, 22, 27, 31, 41, 50, 76, 79, 102, 111–2, 119, 120, 138, 145–7, 149
opposition 5, 7, 16, 21, 107
Outlook 20, 30
oxymoron 66–7, 74–5, 113, 156

pain 122, 159–60
painting 8, 21, 39–40, 43–7, 88, 103–7, 112–3, 120, 122, 125, 133, 137–8, 141–2, 145, 152, 155, 164, 169
palimpsest 7, 66; *see also* multi-layered writing
panorama 26, 50, 145–6, 149; *see also* observation
paradox 6–11, 16, 19, 32, 34, 38–41, 55, 76, 83, 85, 87, 90, 106, 113, 134, 150, 161; *see also* ambivalence
paralipsis, *see* preterition
parataxis 39, 100, 105, 108, 111, 155, 163
pastoral (and anti-pastoral) 4, 6, 103–7, 148, 162, 169
pathos (and lack thereof) 10, 39, 59, 74, 91, 108, 122–3, 141
patient 11, 141, 151, 155, 157; *see also* wounded

peripheral mode of representation 11, 23, 74, 81, 88, 125, 133
periphery 10–1, 142–3, 150, 152, 159–61; *see also* liminality
personification 42, 77, 145, 154–5
phenomenology 7–8, 11, 22, 133–4, 137, 142, 150–1, 163
physicality 42, 70–1, 75, 87, 111, 137–8, 144, 147, 159–60, 164; *see also* materiality
picture, *see* painting
pleasure 31, 43, 74–5, 78, 85, 104–5, 109, 122, 162; *see also* happiness
poetry 10, 20–1, 29, 30, 89, 96–9, 102–10, 117–9, 122, 124–5, 148, 155
Poetry and Drama 17, 21, 84
post-war writing 9, 11, 16, 19–20, 40, 47–50, 69, 86, 97–8, 107
posterity 29, 97–8, 121
precision 7, 27, 33–4, 39, 60, 100–2, 105, 108–9, 111, 123, 137, 139, 143, 150, 157–8; *see also* accuracy
preterition 87–8, 158
progression d'effet 84–7
pronouns 5, 33–4, 39, 138–9, 141, 162; first-person 5, 39, 49, 63, 100, 138, 140–1, 147, 151, 157; second-person 5, 63, 79, 85–6, 138, 142; third-person 5, 33, 49, 64, 66, 86, 140–1, 147, 162
propaganda 9, 18, 20, 30, 32, 43, 57, 112, 134, 137, 139, 140, 149, 151
psychology 9, 18, 20, 26, 40, 57–8, 75, 78, 96, 158; *see also* trauma
punctuation 27, 63–4, 88–9, 104, 108–9, 112, 116, 156, 162

Raitt, S. 55–8, 61, 79–80, 91
reader 4, 10, 27, 43, 46–7, 57, 59, 60–3, 66, 72–3, 75, 80–1, 85, 59–90, 100–2, 105, 113, 119, 124, 134–5, 139, 141, 143–4, 146–7, 151–3, 155, 161, 164, 169
reality 4, 6, 10, 24, 32, 37, 46, 57, 61, 65–6, 74, 77, 78–81, 84, 90, 103–4, 117, 119, 134, 139, 143, 146, 155, 160, 162
refugees 64, 73, 76, 86, 169
reject 11, 159–61
Remarque, Erich Maria 2, 162
remembrance 29, 31, 33, 116, 122–5
remoteness, *see* distance

repetition 18, 27, 40, 57, 61, 67, 72–5, 85–8, 96, 105, 113, 139, 141, 148, 155, 159–60, 162–3
representation 3–11, 17, 19–20, 22, 24–6, 32, 37–40, 42–7, 50, 57, 59, 61, 72–3, 76–81, 84, 88, 90, 99, 107, 111–2, 116–7, 119, 121–2, 125, 132–6, 139, 149–51, 157, 160–4; *see also* aporia
resistance: aesthetic, to tradition 74–5, 77, 137, 142, 149, 157; cultural, to conventions 5, 11, 41, 58, 68, 131, 133, 135–7, 139, 142, 157; ethical 9, 32, 35, 37, 90, 161, 164; psychological 26, 161
restraint, *see* reticence
reticence 22, 86–90, 100, 111, 122, 136–7, 150; *see also* silence
retrospection 5, 7, 96, 99, 120, 132; *see also* memory; remembrance
romanticism 5, 30, 97, 104, 107; *see also* 19th century
Ross, S. 9, 39

sacralisation 62, 117–8, 134, 158–9, 164
sacrifice 33, 99, 116–8, 134, 136
Sassoon, S. 1–2, 5–6, 8, 10–1, 19, 21, 29, 59–60, 75, 96–125, 132, 147–8, 169; autobiographical memoirs 96, 98–9, 102, 107, 115; 'A Soldier's Declaration' 97, 118; *Counter-Attack* 124; *The Old Huntsman* 29, 97, 117; *Memoirs of an Infantry Officer* 2, 10, 49, 96–9, 102, 104, 107, 110–1, 113–4, 119–21, 124; 'On Reading My Diary' 125; 'The Rear-Guard' 124; 'To Victory' 103
Saunders, M. 2, 10, 16–9, 24, 27, 33, 39–41, 43, 44, 47–50, 132, 159
scale, *see* immensity
Scarry, E. 32, 159–60
Schopenhauer, Arthur 58, 73–4
scopic dimension, *see* visuality
screened perception 4, 6, 99, 113, 146–7; *see also* framing devices; mediation
self-criticism 10, 59, 61, 64–5, 73, 118, 124–5, 140–1
sensoriality 6–8, 10–1, 22, 26, 39, 41–3, 65, 78, 80, 86, 105–8, 111–2, 121–2, 124–5, 134, 137–9, 141, 150, 156, 159–60, 164
Sinclair, M. 1–2, 4–6, 8, 10–1, 33, 41, 55–91, 130–1, 134, 141, 147, 149, 156–7, 163, 169; 'Day-Book of Dr Hector Munro's Motor Ambulance Corps' 56, 60, 62–3, 65, 73, 81–2; *A Journal of Impressions* 2, 10–1, 55–91, 134, 141, 147, 149; *Mary Olivier. A Life* 86; *Tasker Jevons* 68; *The Tree of Heaven* 58, 81
shell shock 18, 25, 27, 43, 48, 97
sight-seeing, *see* tourism
silence 3, 19–20, 27, 36, 88–90, 135–7, 157, 159; *see also* reticence
singularity 6, 9, 32–9, 41, 50, 110–1, 118, 120, 147, 149, 153
Smith, H. Z. 162
Smith, P. D. 152
Somme 5, 16, 18, 21, 25–6, 34, 37, 96, 103, 106, 111–4, 121–2, 131, 142–3, 152
sophistication, *see* constructedness
sounds 6, 10–1, 22, 41–3, 65, 105–6, 108, 111, 113, 125, 139, 150, 156, 159
space 11, 22, 41, 66, 75–8, 115, 139, 140, 142–4, 149, 151–3, 157, 159, 161; *see also* non-place; uninhabitability; liminality
spectacle 6–7, 69–70, 73, 107, 111–3, 119, 124, 140–1, 157; *see also* theatricality
spectrality 28, 47, 85–7, 103, 121, 133, 141, 151, 161
Spencer, H. 70
Stein, Gertrude 162
Stokes, J. 132, 142, 151, 153–4
structuredness 43–5, 48, 84–5, 161–3
subject 4, 8–9, 27, 134–5, 141, 149, 151, 154, 157, 160–2
subjectivity 8, 59, 142, 145–7
subversion 10, 58–9, 87, 90, 141
suppression, *see* reticence
syntax 39, 43–4, 100, 104–5, 108, 111–2, 150, 155, 163

temporality 7, 17, 39, 46, 60, 64, 78–9, 81, 84–5, 87, 105, 108–11, 115, 120–1, 123–4, 139, 155, 159, 161
tenses 7, 85, 139; future 7, 47, 115; present 7, 47, 85, 105, 108, 111, 115, 139, 155, 159; preterit 108–10, 159
testimony, *see* witnessing
theatricality 69–73, 104, 111, 113, 116, 118, 124, 132, 153, 157; *see also* spectacle
topography 7, 22, 124, 142, 144–5, 150; *see also* mapping

topos 4, 11, 61, 66–8, 104, 106–7, 115–7, 124, 141, 147, 149
totalisation 9, 20, 35–7, 72, 76, 90, 146, 149
touch 8, 22, 164
tourism 75–6, 155–6; *see also* Baedeker guides
tradition 3–5, 7, 10–1, 23, 46, 58–9, 66, 89, 100, 106–7, 114–5, 119, 120, 130, 133–5, 141, 149, 153, 155, 161–2
tragedy 59, 67, 74
transition 48, 74, 49, 103, 143, 152–3, 157
trauma 2–3, 8, 10, 24, 26–7, 32, 39, 59, 90, 121, 123, 133–4, 148, 150, 156, 158; *see also* shell shock
triviality 63, 65–8, 113, 125, 158, 169
trope, *see topos*
truthfulness 18, 27, 57, 59, 77, 84, 87, 101–2, 109, 119, 122, 142–3, 160; *see also* authenticity

uncanny 47, 87, 106, 125
unconventionality 1, 5, 10–1, 18, 32, 59, 62, 75, 77, 79, 87, 90, 132–42, 149, 151, 161, 164; *see also* resistance
undermining devices 6–7, 10, 26, 59, 62–6, 68, 85–6, 89–90, 114, 120
unfamiliarity 5, 87, 106–7, 133, 157–8; *see also* defamiliarisation
uninhabitability 11, 150–1, 164
unreliability 5, 59, 101
unsayable, *see* incommunicability

vagueness, *see* indeterminacy
vastness, *see* immensity
violence 23, 26, 32, 37, 104, 113, 121, 125, 146, 150–2, 157, 161
Virilio, P. 6–7, 111–2, 145, 152
visuality 3, 6, 11, 20–3, 25–7, 33, 36, 39–43, 45–8, 62, 65–6, 77, 88–9, 98, 102–3, 105, 107–8, 111, 113–4, 120, 123, 135, 138–9, 145–7, 149, 151, 163–4; *see also* gaze; picture
vorticism 4, 58, 80–1, 107, 112
vulnerability 8, 11, 33, 36, 57, 118, 164

war poetry 2, 10, 96–9, 102–4, 106–10, 117, 119
Warner, Agnes 132
Wharton, Edith 7, 134–5
windows, *see* framing devices
witnessing 2–3, 5–6, 8–10, 16–7, 22, 24, 30, 61, 65, 88, 91, 102, 110–2, 119–21, 125, 131–2, 134–6, 138–40, 147, 149–50, 152, 157, 149, 159, 163, 169
women 3, 6, 33, 55–8, 68, 71, 78, 131, 134–7, 139–41, 147, 150–1, 153–4; *see also* gaze; gender; nurse
Wordsworth, William 30, 97
worry 29, 33–4, 37–8, 47, 66, 72, 76, 115, 117–8
wound 8, 97, 115–6, 121–4, 145–6, 150–1, 158
wounded 9–11, 18, 31–2, 60, 67, 69, 71–3, 77–8, 87–8, 97, 108, 121–2, 124, 131, 149, 152–7, 159–61, 163–4; *see also* patient
Wright, E. V. 155